BREATHING WATER

TANYA BIRD

For Rachel.
The best dance teacher a girl could ask for.

CHAPTER 1

*E*lla resented the chair with its tall back and cold leather. She wanted to stand, to *stretch*, to glimpse herself in a wall-length mirror. But there were no mirrors at Bass Fuel, only clear glass and an expensive view of glistening black water far below.

This was not a dance studio. It was an office.

And this was not an audition but an interview.

She pushed her toes into the plush carpet, but her feet didn't bend in the kitten-heeled shoes. She was tempted to kick them off; she couldn't walk properly in them, anyway. Adding to her discomfort were suit pants that itched and a blazer that felt a lot like a straitjacket. She craved tights and a wire-free bra.

Ella crossed her legs, then uncrossed them, knocking her handbag sideways as she did so. When she bent to straighten it, the office door opened behind her.

'Sorry to keep you waiting' came a familiar voice.

Ella rose and turned to face Barry Taylor, Communications Manager at Bass Fuel—and the man who owed her father a favour. Yes, that was how far off course she had veered: from the stage to job handouts.

1

Barry extended a hand, and she remembered to smile as she took it. 'I haven't been waiting long.'

He gestured for her to sit again. 'How's your father?'

'Well, thank you.'

He walked around the enormous desk that spanned the length of the office. It seemed to take forever for him to reach his chair.

'Let me refresh my memory,' he said, picking her résumé out of a stack of papers and running his eyes over it. 'You completed your master's in dance at Melbourne University, then did a short stint with Melbourne Ballet.'

The "short" part stung. It wasn't *that* short. 'Prior to that, I completed several marketing and communications units as part of my arts degree.'

He glanced up. 'Yes, your father mentioned that.'

'He always insisted I have a backup plan.' She just never thought she would need it.

Barry dropped the résumé onto the desk in front of him. 'Let's be open here. Your father is a partner at LMDC, on the board here at Bass Fuel, and a friend. He's always spoken highly of you, and I suspect the apple didn't fall far from the tree as far as work ethic.' His chair hissed as he leaned back in it. 'Did he tell you this is an entry-level job?'

'Yes.'

He nodded. 'You'll likely spend most of your time either at the printer or fetching coffees from next door.'

Ella reminded herself to appear enthusiastic. 'I thought I passed a coffee shop downstairs.'

'You did, but the coffee next door is much better.' He gave her a conspiratorial smile.

'Next door for coffee. Noted.'

He studied her for a moment. 'I'm sorry the dancing didn't work out. Your dad said you were very good and that you really enjoyed it.'

Enjoyed it? Dance ran through her in place of blood.

'Some bodies just aren't made for that much ballet.' She managed to smile when she said it, but the words stuck in her throat.

'Well, you can still do it for fun, so that's something.'

It *was* something.

He leaned forwards in his chair. 'You know what they say. You can take the girl out of the dance…'

'But you can't take the dance out of the girl?' She hated herself.

He waved a finger at her, smiling. 'That's the one.'

'With regards to the role,' she said, desperate to move on, 'I'm a fast learner. You can just hand me a user manual for the photocopier and I'll have it memorised by the next day.'

He chuckled at that. 'Yes, I heard you're very bright. People around here usually just press buttons and eventually call IT to fix what they broke.' He pushed her résumé away and looked directly at her. 'Outside of important coffee duties, you'll also filter calls, sort emails, schedule meetings—that sort of thing. I'll give you access to my diary.'

She nodded. 'You can just let me know which program you use—'

'And you'll read the manual?'

At least he had a sense of humour—sort of. 'I'll likely be able to figure that one out.'

He rose from his chair and extended a hand to her. 'Let's give you a shot.'

THE ELEVATOR DOORS opened beside Little Bean in the foyer. Ella walked into the mostly abandoned cafe and ordered a latte. Then she headed next door, where the sign read 'B for Brazil'. She looked around at the full tables before joining the short line to order another latte. The lady behind the counter eyed the coffee in her hand as she took the money. It wasn't enough for Ella to be told the coffee was better there, she needed to understand *why*.

'Won't be long,' the woman said.

Ella thanked her and stepped back from the counter— and straight onto someone's foot. A hand caught her elbow at the same time she looked over her shoulder, gaze travelling up until it met cool grey eyes. She immediately stepped to the side, and his hand fell away.

'Sorry,' she said.

He looked down at his boots. 'They're steel-cap, and you weigh nothing.'

'That makes me feel slightly better about my sharp heel landing on your toes.' She realised at that moment that she had slopped coffee over her hand. He also noticed and reached past her, grabbing a handful of serviettes off the counter.

'Was that hot?' he asked. The lady behind the register was waiting to take his order, so he gestured for the person behind him to go ahead.

'No,' Ella said. 'Though it should've been.'

He took the cup from her as he handed her the serviettes. While she cleaned herself up, he read the label aloud. 'Little Bean. Yeah, their coffee's rarely hot.' His eyes met hers again. 'You're brave coming in here carrying that thing. This is a very loyal crowd.'

'Latte for Ella?' the barista called behind her.

She swung around to collect it and thanked the woman. When she turned back, she found the man still watching her through a dark mess of curly hair. It covered one side of his face, reaching past his jaw. She should've felt uncomfortable beneath that penetrating gaze, but something about his manner put her at ease.

'Two cup kind of morning?' he asked, handing her back the cold coffee.

She glimpsed a high-visibility vest poking from his pocket. 'Research. Though I suspect I already know the winner.'

'I'll save you the pain and disappointment of having to drink from the first cup. This place makes the best coffee in Docklands.'

Ella's eyes travelled back up to his unshaven face and tanned skin, a stark contrast to her own, which she fiercely protected from the sun. It was a lifelong habit. Tan lines weren't tolerated in the dancing world.

She was staring.

Had he asked her a question?

His mouth spread into a smile then, revealing pearly teeth and dimples. She focused on them a fraction too long.

'Why do I feel like you're sizing me up for a street fight?' he asked.

Her gaze dropped to his boots, which were covered in a layer of dust, likely something toxic. She tried not to breathe it in. 'How do you suppose that would end for me?'

He laughed, the sound making her look up again.

'I don't know. You look fit enough to take me.'

His response made her smile—inwardly, at least. 'I hope I didn't… scuff your boot.'

He looked down at the shoe, where the lip of the sole was starting to come away. 'It'll polish out.'

'Well, thanks for the coffee tip.' She stepped around him, breathing in the salty air blowing through the door.

'Ella,' he said.

Her feet stilled. He had remembered her name from when the barista had called it. She looked over her shoulder, hoping like crazy he wouldn't ruin the moment with a slimy remark. 'Yeah?'

His gaze travelled down to her legs, and she held her breath as he brushed a finger down his nose.

'You've got coffee on your pants.'

She looked down, and sure enough, there was a brown drizzle of coffee the length of her thigh. She dabbed at it with the serviettes in her hand, knowing it wouldn't help one bit. 'Oh. Thanks.' Meeting his gaze a final time, she forced a smile before fleeing the cafe.

As she rushed along the footpath, trying to put as much space between her and that embarrassing encounter as possible, she sipped from the first cup. Her face screwed up and her throat closed in protest. She tossed it into a bin as she passed by, then tried the second one. It was like liquid velvet on her throat, the aroma filling her senses and the taste making her eyes sink closed for a moment. She didn't normally drink coffee, not because she didn't enjoy it but because it was on the long list of pleasures she had denied herself over the years. She decided that she would drink the entire cup. Savour it, treat herself. But as she strode along Collins Street towards the station, she spotted another bin.

Just walk past it.

She could finally use the drink holder in her car for something other than water and cleansing juices. But her feet had other ideas, stopping directly in front of the bin. Her eyes narrowed on a discarded cigarette butt still smoking in the dispenser on top. It was a timely reminder that there were far worse habits than coffee.

Keep walking.

Ella took another sip and held it in her mouth for as long as possible. Then, with a resigned sigh, she leaned away from the rising smoke as she tossed the almost full cup of godly liquid into the bin.

The dancer inside applauded.

CHAPTER 2

*W*hen Dax exited the cafe, he found Miller leaning against the streetlamp with his arms crossed, squinting into the morning sun. Dax handed his brother one of the coffees.

'Who was that?' Miller asked.

Dax quirked an eyebrow in question.

Miller pushed his still wet hair off his face and laughed. 'Don't play clueless prick with me. The girl you were chatting up at the counter.'

'I wasn't chatting her up. She stood on my foot, then spilt coffee over herself. I just handed her some serviettes to clean herself up.'

'She looked about sixteen.'

'So you're calling me a pervert.'

Miller laughed. 'It's just not like you to flirt with their kind. It's unsettling.'

'What? It's unsettling when I'm *nice* to people?'

A pair of policemen walked by, eyes shifting to Dax as they passed. He nodded a greeting, and they returned the gesture.

'Time to go,' Miller said, 'before one of them recognises you.'

'Funny,' Dax replied, falling into step with him. 'You know they can't arrest me for buying coffee, right?'

Miller glanced sideways at him. 'I'm sure they'd find another reason if they knew who you were.'

Dax didn't exactly have the best record with local police, or more specifically, the water police. They had finally managed to strip him of his marine licence a year back.

They couldn't stop him from swimming though.

The pair wandered back towards their worksite farther down Collins Street, Coburn Construction's latest project. The company was responsible for many of the waterfront buildings in the area. Architecture by the water was their brand.

'What time did you swim this morning?' Miller asked, eyes ahead.

'Early.'

A low chuckle came from Miller. 'Still avoiding Frankie, then?'

'Yep.' Dax glanced sideways at the sushi restaurant as they passed by. The smell was nauseating.

Miller stopped out front of the site, nodding in the other direction. 'Not sure your plan worked long-term.'

Dax looked past him to where Frankie now approached. He drew a tired breath.

'Do you guys ever work?' she called to them in that liquid voice of hers. She was wearing a pencil skirt with a silk shirt tucked into it, a lace bra visible beneath it.

'Coffee break,' Dax said, raising his cup as evidence.

'What are you doing on-site?' Miller asked her.

Frankie held up a stack of payslips, which she handed to him, pushing her long blonde hair to one side as she eyed Dax. He looked right back at her, unblinking. It'd been months since their relationship ended. She wasn't his mate—and he was done apologising for it.

He'd given the relationship a go because both sets of parents had wanted the match to happen. Of course, it helped that she was a stunner. No male with working eyesight could deny that. Leggy as hell with that pinched little waist of hers. But the attraction had worn thin eventually, and he couldn't fake feelings that weren't there. The night of the breakup, Frankie had gone for a swim and not returned for two weeks. It wasn't uncommon for ondines to take to the sea for long spells, but her parents had verbally torn him to shreds and not spoken a word to him since.

'Didn't see you in the water this morning,' Frankie said.

That was very intentional on his part. 'I went early.'

She looked to Miller for confirmation, and he nodded. He would've gone along with whatever Dax had said.

'Well, thanks for these,' Miller said, holding up the slips. 'We should get back to work.'

Frankie touched a finger to the corner of her freshly painted mouth. 'I guess I'll see you both tonight, unless Dax decides to swim later.'

She knew his game.

Dax looked away. 'Depends what time I finish up here.'

Miller shuffled his feet as he looked away. They had all known each other since birth, and choosing a side within a pod was like dividing children during a divorce.

Frankie left with her head high and hips swinging. There wasn't a pair of eyes on-site that didn't follow her: young, old, ondine, human. Even the seagulls seemed to fall silent.

'Well, that wasn't any less awkward than yesterday,' Miller said.

'There was eye contact when she spoke *at* me. That's progress.'

Miller clapped him on the shoulder, and coffee spilled out over Dax's hand. He was immediately reminded of the girl at the cafe, all blue eyes and honey hair falling softly down one shoulder.

Ella.

It was unlike him to remember a woman's name.

'You should get up there, boss,' Dax said. 'These projects don't manage themselves.'

'And you should be helping me with that by now.'

Dax shook his head. 'Someone's got to do the real work.'

He flicked coffee onto Miller, who responded by tossing his now empty cup at his brother. Dax caught it, but the lid popped off, and the remaining froth at the bottom went over him. He swore and shook his other hand.

'Language,' Miller said. 'You're supposed to be an example to the other workers.'

Dax threw the cup back at his brother, but Miller ducked, and it hit a passing labourer.

'Sorry,' Dax said with an apologetic wave. He shook his head at his brother. 'I have to work with him.'

Miller laughed as he walked away.

Dax went to collect the cup and wandered over to the bin. He glanced off down the footpath, not in the direction Frankie had gone but in the direction he'd just come from. Ella's direction, the most doe-eyed little human he'd ever had the privilege of being trampled by. She was attractive as hell as far as her kind went, and it had felt too good to flirt a little, to have a moment.

'Get to work already,' Miller shouted from the scissor lift.

Dax looked up and resisted the urge to give him the finger, saluting him instead. With a final glance down the footpath, he went to fetch his tools.

CHAPTER 3

*E*lla stood in the foyer of the LMDC building, lip clamped between her teeth, watching the glass doors open and close. Her father, Michael Lewis, stood a few feet in front of her.

'It's not what you achieve,' he said, 'it's what you overcome.'

And here come the inspirational quotes.

Ella was trying to hide her first-day nerves from him. 'Who said that?'

'Carlton Fisk.' His eyes creased at the corners. 'This is just the next thing. Who knows what doors will open next?'

She knew none of them would be studio doors. 'It just feels very final.'

He nodded, pretending he understood. 'I wish the dancing had worked out, but it's time for new dreams now.'

'At a fuel company.'

'A very progressive fuel company. Did you read the sustainability report I gave you?'

'Yes. Beautifully crafted words.' She smiled. 'I should go. Don't want to be late.'

He appeared encouraged by that, his eyes lighting up at her words. 'That's my girl. "The best way to predict the future is to create it."'

'Edison?'

'Lincoln.'

She adjusted her handbag on her shoulder. The leather straps would take a few weeks to soften. 'I'll meet you back here after work?'

'We could have lunch if you like. I can make time.'

And he meant it. Her father had always prioritised her despite the demands of his job. He had never missed a concert, performance, or audition. If an audience was permitted, he was there, despite having no genuine appreciation for the arts. He was a man of logic, and ballet was an expression of the heart.

'I'm meeting Lucy,' she said.

He let out a defeated breath, knowing he couldn't compete with her. Ella might have been an only child, but she was not without a sister in life.

'Come here,' Michael said, gesturing her closer. She went to him, and he draped an arm around her shoulders, suddenly looking serious. 'This is just the first necessary step.'

Her eyebrows came together. 'Who said that?'

'I said that.' He kissed her forehead. 'Just be the star we both know you are, and the world will fall into line.'

Ella moved back, extending one leg and sliding it behind the other. She bent, floating her arms into a dancer's curtsy. Passers-by cast curious looks in her direction, but she was immune to judgement. She had built a life around it.

Her father bowed his head in response. 'Always the ballerina.'

'Love you,' she said, turning.

'The future depends on what you do today,' he called to her back.

She waved without looking at him. 'Gandhi. Got it.'

ONE, two, three, four, five, six, seven, jeté. One, two, three, four, five, six, seven, jeté.

Ella's inability to simply walk down a street was a constant source of amusement to those who knew her and highly alarming to strangers, who tended to give her a wide berth. They assumed she was drunk or crazy. She was wearing flats that morning, her heels tucked in her handbag, ready for a sneaky change in the foyer.

One, two, three, four, five, six, seven, jeté.

The sound of construction up ahead broke through her concentration. She squinted in the direction of the site before focusing hard on the footpath, counting aloud to compete with the chorus of tools and machinery.

'One, two, three, four, five, six—'

Ella was pulled to a stop before she could finish the count. Her eyes snapped to the large hand wrapping her arm, then up to the face it belonged to. She relaxed as she recognised the man she had trodden on in the cafe post-interview. 'Oh.'

His grip on her relaxed. 'Ella.'

He remembered her name.

Glancing over his shoulder, he nodded at the driver of the truck backing out behind him, lights flashing and reverse alert deafening all in a twenty-kilometre radius. That was when Ella noticed the STOP sign in the man's hand. She had almost walked straight into the path of the truck.

The man released her arm and took a small step back.

She could feel the disapproving stares of the other pedestrians on her.

'How did you not hear the beeping?' he shouted over the noise.

Of course, now it was all she could hear. 'Sorry. I was distracted.' She tried to bring volume to her own voice, but it barely carried through the dusty air.

Those silvery eyes held amusement. 'Were you jumping over the cracks?'

'No.' She could see why he would think that. She looked past him to the lorry, which had finally reached the road.

'I heard you counting.'

Her eyes met his once more. 'And?'

He swung the sign to SLOW. 'Just curious how high you can go.'

She noted his teasing expression as the other pedestrians walked by. 'I start to get confused past twenty.'

He laughed, a deep sound that drowned out the noise of construction for a moment. That seemed like a good time to politely disengage, but when she went to move, he swung the sign to STOP again. 'How old are you?'

She looked past him and couldn't see anything coming. 'That's… a very rude question to ask a stranger.'

He grinned at that. 'You're not a stranger. We met last week.'

She searched his eyes. 'You never told me your name, so you're still a stranger to me.'

'Dax Coburn. And it's only rude to ask a person's age if they're at an age where they might want to hit pause.'

She frowned up at him. 'Who says I'm not at that age?'

'You're definitely not at that age.'

Still he didn't turn the sign. She looked up at the shell of a building. 'You work here?' She winced at her own question.

'No, I was just passing by and saw the sign. Thought it looked like fun.'

Her gaze fell to his half smirk. 'I guess that explains why you're doing such a bad job, then. You're supposed to let people pass when the road is clear.'

'That so?'

She realised her tone bordered on flirtatious, something she was not experienced at. Historically, the only time she'd paid attention to men was when she was partnered with them in a dance. 'Perhaps you should give the lollipop man his sign back.'

Deep laughter erupted from Dax, and her gaze fell to his dimpled cheeks. He took a moment to catch his breath.

'In construction, those people are called traffic controllers.'

'Oh.' She felt her cheeks heat.

He watched her a moment. 'You heading to work?' She nodded, and when she didn't say anything, he added, 'Are you going to tell me where that is, or should I guess?'

She wondered if she was brave enough to walk past while the sign read STOP. Who was she kidding? She was no rule breaker. 'Bass Fuel. The building with the bad coffee.'

All the light seemed to leave his eyes. She tried to read his expression. *Is that disappointment?*

'Bass Fuel? You work at *Bass Fuel*?'

Definitely disappointment. 'It's my first day there.'

He shifted his weight and spun the sign to SLOW. 'Well, good luck. You better get going if you want coffee,' he said. 'The queue will be out the door at this time of the morning.'

'I don't actually drink coffee.' The second she said it, she wished she could snatch the words back. 'Very often,' she added for clarification.

His expression didn't change. 'You drink it… sometimes?'

'I like it, I've just avoided it in the past.'

'Because you're too young to drink it?'

She caught the glint in his eyes. 'I'm twenty-three.' People always assumed she was younger due to her size.

He didn't look convinced. 'Why do you refrain from drinking it if you like it?'

'Boring reasons. Health reasons.'

His eyebrows drew together. 'Are you sick or something?'

'No, I just… I needed to be physically well, so I watched my diet for a while.' She paused. 'Years, actually.'

'Physically well?'

'Strong.'

His gaze swept over her.

She should've walked off. She was free to, after all. 'Old habits and all that.'

He nodded, but she could tell he was no clearer on the subject.

'Well, have fun'—she gestured to his sign—'controlling the traffic.' She took one step, but Dax spun the sign around again. She breathed out and looked up at him. 'What are you doing?'

He pointed behind him to where another truck was pulling in. 'Sorry, you missed your chance.'

She waited, eyes focused on the truck.

'What's a nice girl like you doing at a place like Bass Fuel?' Dax asked.

Apparently he was a big fan of small talk.

'I'm the new communications assistant.'

'You work with Barry?'

She was surprised he knew who Barry was. 'Yeah. I'm going to be the one fetching his coffee.'

Some of that light returned to his eyes. 'Guess that explains last week's coffee research.'

'You were right, by the way. The first one was bad.'

'I warned you not to drink it.'

A smile grew on her face. 'You expect me to trust the opinion of a stranger?'

He tilted his head. 'They still teaching stranger danger in schools?'

She adjusted her handbag on her shoulder. 'Oh, skilled at holding signs *and* funny.'

He glanced behind him at the truck, which was now a safe distance away, then spun the sign to SLOW as he faced her again. 'Are you right to cross without an adult?'

It was her turn to laugh—she couldn't hold it in. 'I think I'll manage.' She stepped past him, head shaking.

'Keep your eyes up this time,' he called after her, 'and wait for the green man when you reach the crossing.'

She pressed her lips together as she glanced back at him. 'You better focus on your job, lollipop man. People's lives are at stake.' She faced forwards again before letting the smile spread.

Dax's deep laughter followed her a few more paces before being drowned out by the sound of a drill.

CHAPTER 4

*T*he cool October air hit Ella's face as she stepped out of her office building. She followed the path down to the small section of lawn by the water, where enormous sculptures of shells rose from the ground. She spotted Lucy standing with an empty stroller, Caleb running circles around her. The toddler was first to see her, stopping dead in his tracks before bursting into a run.

'Ellaaaaa!'

Ella laughed quietly and dropped her handbag on the ground so she could catch him. 'Oh my goodness. How have you gotten heavier since yesterday? Stop growing.'

Lucy wandered over to join them. 'He never stops eating, that's how.'

Caleb wriggled in Ella's arms. 'We're having lunch with you!'

Lucy winced. 'You don't have to shout in her face. She can hear you, love.' She kissed Ella's cheek. 'So, how's it going?'

'Fine. I spent most of the morning with Steve from IT learning how to log in to various programs.'

'Ooh, Steve from IT. I'm getting a hot nerd vibe.'

Ella screwed up her nose. 'He's middle-aged, balding, and gave up on exercise some years back.'

Lucy made a face. 'Ew. He won't do, then.'

'Won't do for what, exactly?'

Lucy took Caleb from her and tried to wrestle him into the stroller, but his screams of protest quickly changed her mind. 'Your office fling.'

'Oh. Office flings always end well.'

'You know, any fling would do at this point. You're too old to be playing the virgin.'

'I'm not a virgin.'

Lucy straightened with a resigned sigh, catching Caleb's hand before he had a chance to run off. 'Are we really counting Peter?'

'Why would we *not* count Peter? We were together for two years.'

Lucy made a face that suggested Ella should know the answer. 'Because it's *Peter.*' She glanced down to make sure Caleb wasn't listening before adding, 'Peter, who used to tear up during the act, because it was just so beautiful.'

She regretted telling Lucy that, but she'd wanted to know if it was normal. Not normal, as it turned out. 'Well, he's a performer, and why it bothered you, I have no idea.'

'And you stayed with the guy for *two years.*'

Ella rolled her eyes. 'Well, lucky for you, he dumped me after being named principal dancer.'

'You mean lucky for *you*. But for the record, it wasn't fun seeing you broken-hearted, pretending you were fine.'

'I am fine—now. Just annoying that he's a principal dancer and I'm stuck here fetching coffees,' Ella said, looking off in the direction of the water. It shimmered black beneath the overcast sky.

'If I'd known we were having a pity party, I'd have brought wine,' Lucy said.

'I don't think returning drunk from lunch on my first day is a smart move.'

Lucy groaned. 'No office fling. No booze at work. What sort of job is this? You're supposed to be living the life I can't.'

They began walking towards the shops.

'What do you feel like?' Ella asked.

'Coffee,' Lucy replied. 'I need to stay awake on the drive home.'

Ella cast a concerned look at her. 'What age are kids supposed to sleep through the night?'

'I'll let you know when I get there.'

An accidental pregnancy at age twenty had turned Lucy's life upside down. The girls had danced together since they were six, shared the same talent, the same dream, only to meet entirely different roadblocks at the end of it all.

'I thought you were one coffee a day, mornings only,' Ella said.

Lucy gave her a tired look. 'I'm a single mother with a toddler who's dropped his nap and moves at one speed the entire day. I'm a two-cup girl now. Sometimes three. Yesterday four. Don't judge.'

Caleb was between them, holding both their hands while Lucy pushed the stroller with the other.

'There's a good coffee place next to my work,' Ella said. 'It's Brazilian.'

'I'll drink beans from any country right now.'

They arrived at B for Brazil, welcomed by the scent of coffee, bread, and cinnamon. Lucy picked Caleb up so he could better see the food in the display cabinet. He began rattling off requests.

Ella looked around from face to face. As much as she didn't want to admit it, she was looking for *him*.

Dax Coburn.

Construction worker, funny man, and the reason she had struggled to concentrate properly that morning. But he wasn't there.

Lucy placed Caleb back down on the ground. 'Okay. He wants the focaccia with everything taken out except the cheese, and he wants all the green bits scraped off the top of the bread.'

'You mean the herbs?'

'Yep.'

'So… a cheese sandwich?'

'Uh-huh.'

Ella narrowed her eyes on the focaccia as they took a step towards the counter. 'You know, I don't even think it has cheese in it.'

'Welcome to my life.'

Ella suppressed a smile and met Caleb's big brown eyes. 'I'm sure they have plain bread and will make a special sandwich just for you.'

'I just want cheese,' he sang.

After a short wait for their food, they began the walk back to the lawn by the water. Caleb wanted Ella to carry him, so she scooped him up with exaggerated exertion.

'Is that all you're having?' Lucy asked, glancing at the smoothie in her hand.

Ella moved Caleb to her other hip. 'Coconut milk, almonds, chia seeds, fruit, leafy greens. It's a complete meal.'

'It's a dancer meal,' Lucy replied. 'You can eat like a regular human now, you know.' She sipped at her coffee and let out a contented sigh.

Ella stopped still when she spotted Dax approaching with a group of workers. It wasn't just her feet that stopped but her heart, lungs—even her ability to blink.

'What's the matter?' Lucy asked, stopping also.

Dax broke off from his conversation when he saw her,

mouth turning up in a now familiar smile. Ella must've been gripping her smoothie a fraction too tightly, because the lid popped off, sending a spray of liquid in all directions. Of course, Dax witnessed the whole thing.

He said something to the person beside him before walking over to her. Ella tried to set Caleb down, but his legs tightened around her middle. Before Lucy had a chance to help, Dax reached her.

'Smoothie research?' he asked, taking the drink from her. He secured the lid and handed it back.

'Must've been loose,' she lied, feeling Lucy's assessing eyes on her.

Dax turned his attention to the boy in her arms. 'Who's this?'

'That would be my little monster, Caleb,' Lucy said. 'And you are?' She looked between them as she waited for an answer.

Ella swallowed. 'This is Dax, a local lollipop man.'

Lucy looked understandably confused. 'Like a crossing man? Are there schools at Docklands?'

'No,' Dax said.

'He works in construction,' Ella offered by way of explanation.

'Coburn Construction. My family's business,' Dax said, eyes never leaving Ella.

That was news to her.

'I stopped this one from being run over by a truck this morning,' Dax went on. 'She was jumping cracks and practising her counting. Made it all the way to seven unassisted.'

Lucy looked between them, and Ella knew exactly what she was thinking.

'Ah,' Lucy said. 'She was practising her jetés.'

Ella felt her cheeks heat.

'What's a jeté?' Dax asked.

'It's a ballet thing,' Lucy answered. 'So, construction, huh? Did you have to do an apprenticeship or something?'

Ella knew Lucy was just being nosy, but the question came across as patronising.

'I studied engineering at uni, but I can pretty much help out with any aspects of the business.' His gaze returned to Ella. 'I can even hold a sign.'

'You're an engineer?' Ella asked, unable to keep the surprise out of her voice. 'You never mentioned that.'

He shrugged. 'You never asked.'

She watched as he brought a finger to his mouth, tasting the residue of her drink.

'What is that?' he asked.

Before she knew what she was doing, she held it out to him. 'It's a Green Parrot.'

He took it from her, maintaining eye contact as he drank, nodding appreciatively. 'It's not as bad as the colour suggests.'

Ella knew Lucy would give her a lot of flak the second they were alone.

'Ella's a virgin,' Caleb said, his voice much too loud.

Whatever heat had pooled in Ella's cheeks drained from her face along with all colour. 'No I'm not.' The words came out with nervous laughter.

Lucy immediately took Caleb from her, as if that could somehow erase what he'd just said. 'He misinterpreted something we said earlier.'

Dax glanced down at his feet. 'It's fine. I know how kids can be.'

Lucy cleared her throat. 'She's really not. She's very experienced.'

Ella's eyes closed as she willed the ground to split apart and swallow her.

Realising her mistake, Lucy added, 'Not *very* experienced, just the appropriate amount.'

23

'Dax' came a male voice. 'You eating or what?'

Ella opened her eyes and looked in the direction of his friends standing ten metres away, staring at them. None of them appeared particularly friendly. The blonde woman with them stood with her arms crossed. Her bright green eyes held enough heat to make Ella look away.

'Enjoy your Green Parrot,' Dax said. He nodded once at Lucy and winked at Caleb.

Ella stepped past him, walking fast in the opposite direction. The stroller clattered closely behind her.

'I'm so sorry,' Lucy whisper-shouted.

Ella kept her eyes ahead until she reached the lawn. 'The *"appropriate amount"*? What exactly is that amount?'

'I could tell you liked him, and I panicked.'

Ella bent to ensure the grass was dry before sinking down onto it. 'Like him? I barely know him.'

Lucy sat opposite her, placing Caleb between them. 'Stay,' she warned, pre-empting his escape. She handed him the paper bag containing the cheese sandwich, then looked over the top of him at Ella. 'You were *flirting*.'

'No I wasn't.'

'Imagine my surprise. I've known you since you were six and had no idea you even knew how.'

Ella took a sip of her drink, trying not to think about the fact that Dax's lips had covered that straw just moments ago. 'I think it's wishful thinking on your part.'

'You refuse to share drinks with anyone, yet you handed yours to him without any commentary about germs. The man could have chlamydia for all you know.'

'What's chlamydia?' Caleb asked, cheeks bulging.

Lucy screwed her nose up. 'A sore tummy.'

Ella shook her head. 'You can't catch chlamydia from sharing a drink.' Then she second-guessed herself. 'Can you?'

Lucy shrugged as she pulled her salad out of the paper

bag, popped the lid open, and stretched her legs out in front of her. 'He's so far from what I imagined you would go for. All messy hair and callused hands—and that melanoma tan.'

Ella tutted. 'Nasty girl.' Though she couldn't deny that he was a very different breed of man to Peter. He was no dancer.

'He might not know what a jeté is, but I bet he could lift you with one hand,' Lucy said, eyes shining. She too was still a ballerina at heart.

The image popped into Ella's head. One enormous hand spanning the width of her ribcage as she stretched above him.

'Remember the pas de deux you did with Peter in *Sleeping Beauty*?' Lucy asked, pulling Ella from her fantasy.

'What about it?'

'Remember how he *really* struggled to lift you.'

'I was at my heaviest then.'

Lucy laughed that pretty laugh of hers. 'At your *heaviest*? Even at your heaviest, you're half my weight.'

'Slight exaggeration.'

They both watched as Caleb ate his sandwich cheese first. Lucy began to hum a tune, the song from the pas de deux—the number Ella had danced with Peter.

'Oh God,' Ella said. 'Please don't.'

Lucy rose, kicked her shoes off, and began dancing on the grass.

Ella looked cautiously up at her, unable to hold back the smile when she imitated some of Peter's trademark facial expressions. When Lucy extended a hand, Ella shook her head.

'Absolutely not.'

Lucy didn't move.

Letting out a resigned sigh, Ella got to her feet and kicked off her heels. 'Are we really doing this here?'

Lucy spun around in response, overplaying the male lead. She danced a circle around Caleb, who grinned up at her. Ella groaned before joining the routine, throwing in a few pliés. Lucy did a grand jeté as she got more carried away. Ella laughed, turning in front of her with her arms extended overhead. Their moves were caricature, the balls of their feet now grass-stained, but it was convincing enough to stop passers-by, happy to watch their insanity for a moment.

'Ready for the lift?' Lucy asked, stepping one foot back in preparation.

Ella laughed. 'No.'

'Do it,' Lucy said. 'I'm actually stronger than Peter.'

Ella shook her head and stepped up to her friend, pushing off one leg to aid the lift. It wasn't very high, but Ella extended her arms and legs into a pose for the sake of the exercise. Lucy turned in a circle before placing her gracefully back on the ground.

A few people applauded. Lucy took Ella's hand and bowed, gesturing for Ella to curtsy, and then their tiny audience had dispersed.

'We've still got it,' Lucy said, flopping onto the grass. 'Remember when dancing used to be fun?'

'Barely.' Ella picked up her drink. 'I tend to remember other things, like the day my knee popped out.'

'Ah, the big H.'

Ella looked at her. 'It's hypermobility, not cancer.'

Lucy shoved a forkful of salad into her mouth. 'It was a tough decision but the right one. You would've spent more time in surgery than on stage.'

A group passing by made them both look up. It was Dax and his friends. He glanced in her direction, raising his own smoothie in a cheers from afar. He'd actually bought one.

Ella raised hers in response. Then her eyes met with the

glaring blonde from earlier, and she immediately lowered her drink.

'That boy might be hot as hell, but his friends need to work on their social etiquette,' Lucy whispered. 'Bet the girl staring daggers at you is his ex.'

Ella didn't look in their direction again. 'Or maybe his girlfriend.'

'If it is, then she's got every right to glare. If my boyfriend was looking at another woman the way that guy is looking at you, I'd be pissed too.'

Ella glanced at her watch. 'I should head back up.' She leaned over and pressed her lips to Caleb's hair. 'Be good for your mum.'

'Where are you going?' Caleb asked.

'Work.'

'Dancing?'

Ella's heart missed a beat. 'No. Not dancing.' Photo-copying and coffee runs.

Caleb returned his attention to his food.

'Will I see you at Pilates tonight?' Lucy asked.

'Hopefully.' Ella got to her feet and glanced in the direction of the water, where Dax had settled to eat. The group had removed their shoes and socks and were dangling their feet in the water as if it were forty degrees outside instead of nineteen. Dax glanced in her direction, as if sensing her prying eyes. She immediately looked away. 'I'll see you later,' she said, ignoring Lucy's knowing grin.

'Unless you get a better offer?'

Ella didn't bother with a reply.

CHAPTER 5

*S*ubmersion in seawater was an act of spirituality for his kind. It was an exorcism of fatigue, a lifting of the soul, a replenishing of body and mind. In that moment, he was an addict and the water his opioid. It was also a matter of survival. Without seawater, an ondine would weaken, and eventually their body would begin to shut down. That was why they swam morning and night, why they lingered by the water in their lunch breaks, why Coburn Construction had an aquarium the size of a boat inside their head office.

With his feet in the water, Dax's gaze drifted to the lawn, where Ella had sat moments earlier. As he stared after her, a spray of water hit him, pulling his attention back to the group. He looked around for the culprit and found Hurley grinning. Dax flicked two fingers in the air and a film of water came off the sea, hitting his target directly in the face. There was a collective snigger. He checked his surroundings, ensuring no one outside of their group had seen him.

Dax picked up his smoothie, and Frankie's eyes narrowed on it.

'What the hell are you drinking?' she asked.

Dax set it down and picked up his sandwich. 'A Green Parrot.'

Miller frowned. 'A what?'

'It's a smoothie. It's actually pretty good.'

Dax glanced over to where Greta sat with her daughter on her lap, laying food out for her husband, Adrian. She liked to come in at lunchtime and feed him, and Hurley liked to sit with them so he could pinch their food.

'Seems Dax's new tiny human friend has made quite the impression,' Frankie said. 'He's drinking vegetables.'

Dax ignored her.

'Was it that cafe girl?' Miller asked, keeping his tone casual in front of Frankie.

'Yeah. She works close by.'

Miller watched him chew. 'I guess you're bound to run into each other, then.'

Dax cast a tired glance in Miller's direction as he reached for his sandwich.

'You know you can't go there, right?' Frankie said, opening her salad. 'Ondine and human flings are only useful as warnings to our children.'

Dax took a bite. 'Careful. You sound jealous.'

Frankie combed ringed fingers through her golden hair, pushing it to one side as she set her eyes on him. 'Jealous of a human? You've got to be joking. She's a little young for you anyway.'

Miller nodded in agreement.

'She's twenty-three,' Dax said.

Miller looked up at that. 'You asked her age?'

Frankie rolled her eyes. 'She's lying. Trying to get you to drop your pants, and then she'll go crying to the cops when you break her heart.'

Greta covered Ariel's ears with her hands. 'Ah, can we keep it clean, please?'

'Good idea,' Miller said. 'Eat, dip, and then it's back to work.'

Not only was Miller the project manager, he had also stepped up as peacekeeper since their parents had moved to King Island in Tasmania.

'I'm going to head back now,' Frankie said, closing her barely touched salad and pulling her feet from the water. She stuffed them into heels without bothering to dry them. 'I have so much work to get through.'

She had taken over the finances after Dax's mother had stepped down to focus on raising cattle and growing apples. Coburn Construction employed a large number of ondines from the local pod. Outside of construction, there were also doctors, dentists, podiatrists, and others in the healthcare sector. All it took was one X-ray in the wrong hands, or a simple eye screening by the wrong optometrist, and tongues would be wagging all over the city. Throw in a few tech nerds with the ability to hack into records if necessary and they were able to live relatively undetected on land—unless they caught the attention of police.

'I'll walk with you,' Hurley said, brushing his feet off and reaching for his boots.

Frankie didn't object.

Dax caught her hand as she rose. 'You're going to leave over the mention of a woman?' He exhaled. 'Put your feet back in the water.'

She tugged her arm free, her other hand going over the spot where he'd touched her. 'I'm not yours to boss around now. Anyway, I'm not jealous, if that's what you're getting at. I'm protecting the pod.' She glanced in the direction of the others. 'I'll see you guys later.'

That was probably true. The pod looked out for one another in that way. But he also knew a small part of her still believed them to be mates.

He watched Frankie walk away as he took another bite

of his sandwich and swallowed as best he could with a dry, guilty throat.

'You know she's right,' Miller said. 'Humans are never a good idea for us.'

Dax sipped at his drink, coaxing the bread down. 'Stop getting ahead of yourself.'

'Only if you admit you're attracted to the little human.' A smile played on his lips.

'She's not little, she's just… petite.'

'And weirdly protective.'

'And we're done.' Dax reached for his boots and looked over to where Greta, Adrian, and Ariel were playing the adorable family. It was what Frankie had once imagined for the two of them.

'It's not like you to pay that much attention to women,' Miller said. 'Of course we're going to notice and give you shit. Just remember to admire from afar.'

Dax normally had a decent game face around his pod, but apparently he'd forgotten it the moment he'd spotted Ella. His gaze drifted in the direction of the lawn, where her friend was trying to wrestle her son into a stroller. Ella was likely back in the office fetching coffee for Barry while he dreamed up new ways to destroy oceans. A little harsh perhaps, but Flathead Rig was proving to be problematic with its ongoing oil leaks. The problem with slow leaks was that they didn't raise enough flags to prompt real action. It fell upon the pod to bring attention to it. That was how Dax had built a reputation as a greenie troublemaker.

Of all the places she could've worked.

Miller shoved the last bite of his roll into his mouth and collected his rubbish before standing.

'We going?' Adrian asked.

Dax nodded and looked around for rubbish they may

have missed. It wasn't unusual for them to collect other people's on the walk to the bin.

Feet were dried, pants rolled down, boots back on feet. It would get them through the afternoon, sustain them through work until they could swim. While they had evolved over thousands of years, they were still sea creatures at their core.

'Dolphins of the land,' his father liked to joke.

As they passed the Bass Fuel building, Dax looked up, prompting Miller to clear his throat. Dax's eyes snapped forwards. He made sure he didn't look up again. Yet the farther they got from the building, the more aware he became of an invisible pull drawing him back to her.

CHAPTER 6

*E*lla didn't dance as she made her way through Docklands the following morning, but she reminded herself to breathe as she approached the construction site where Dax worked. She hugged herself against the cold air, listening to the hum of running motors and pounding of tools as she passed by. Another traffic controller stood where Dax had been the day before. The sign in his hand read SLOW. Her gaze went up as she continued past, searching for Dax amid the noise. What was she expecting? That he would be perched on a steel frame waving to her as she passed? He had likely forgotten all about her by now.

'Ella.'

She really liked how her name sounded from his mouth, the purity of his tone, the deepness of his voice that passed over her like a warm breeze. She reprimanded herself for giving it too much thought. A few simple conversations with a stranger and she was behaving like the teenage girls she had rolled her eyes at through secondary school. She even found herself glancing over her

33

shoulder, exactly as they had done when passing the lockers of their latest crushes.

He wasn't there, or didn't notice her, or didn't care if he had.

This was not one of the many fairy tales she had danced in. She wasn't Sleeping Beauty—and he was no besotted prince. Dax was the type of man who drove a ute with a bad smell, old takeaway packets littering the floor, and car seats coated in the same dust that had covered his boots the first time they met. He probably talked about sports with the same enthusiasm she spoke of the theatre, openly discussed his sex life at work, and urinated behind the pub when the queue was too long inside.

Ella looked for him again when she passed B for Brazil, but he wasn't there either. She shook him from her head as she entered the foyer of her building.

'Hold the door,' she heard Barry call out as she stepped inside the lift.

She extended an arm and waited for him to join her. 'Morning.'

'You came back,' he said, punching the button on the wall with a finger. 'Didn't scare you off yesterday?'

'I'm tougher than I look.'

Barry chuckled. 'That's what your father said too. I'm going to need coffee. I've got a bit on today.' He glanced sideways at her. 'Ever written a press release before?'

She adjusted her handbag on her shoulder. 'When I was at uni.'

'Not since then?'

She shook her head. 'But I'm sure there are refreshers online. I could draft it for you.'

'I suppose if you're done reading the photocopier manual...' His eyes shone at her.

'Dropped it back to Steve before I left last night.'

That was actually true.

'I saw you taking notes yesterday when he was at your computer,' Barry said. 'Bet he loves you.'

She smiled at the ground, thinking about Lucy's suggestion of an office fling with the man.

The doors opened on the seventh floor, and a Bass Fuel sign screamed a welcome at them from above the reception desk. Susan, the pretty face of the company, smiled a greeting from her prime position. She was in her late twenties, always looked like she'd had her make-up professionally done for work, and somehow survived all day in heels so high Ella's feet ached just looking at them.

'Morning,' she sang as Barry passed the desk.

He nodded in her direction.

The moment he was out of sight, she called to Ella, who turned and wandered back to the front desk. Ella waited to be reprimanded for leaving a glass in the wrong place, or not refilling the paper in the copier, or something trivial she hadn't known to do. Instead, Susan leaned forwards with a conspiratorial smile.

'I saw you talking to one of the Coburn brothers yesterday at the cafe.'

Ella tried to hide her surprise at the mention of him. 'Dax?'

One word. She was tempted to repeat it.

'*Yes*, Dax.' Susan waited. 'And?'

'And...' She had no idea what she was supposed to follow his name with.

'Did he talk to you, or did you talk to him?'

'Ah, both? Why do you ask?'

Susan leaned back a little. 'His group has a reputation for snubbing girls outside of their circle. We think they're part of some sort of exclusive gang—maybe even a cult.'

'Oh.' A cult seemed a stretch, but Susan didn't sound too upset by the idea. 'I don't really know him. I've just run into him a few times.'

'Well, he told you his name.'

Ella suppressed a smile. 'Why would he not tell me his name?'

Susan shrugged and settled back in her chair. 'They're just... very private. We go to the same bar as them almost every Friday, and they're the only guys in the place who don't hit on us. I mean, they're construction workers, for God's sake. They should count themselves lucky if we let them buy us a drink.'

It was amusing to Ella that Susan assumed she was every man's type. 'Did you know Dax studied engineering at uni?' Why she felt the need to talk him up to Susan, who obviously wasn't put off by his job, she had no idea.

'He *told* you that?'

'Yeah. Why? Is he lying?'

Susan put her hands up. 'How would I know? Like I said, he doesn't talk to anyone outside of his group. They're all the same, even the girls.'

Ella's bottom lip disappeared between her teeth. 'Is he... dating any of them?'

'He used to be *very* cosy with the blonde. She was always hanging off him. Then it stopped. Suddenly they were seated on opposite sides of the table looking everywhere but at each other. But she'll still stare daggers at you if you try and speak to him—to any of them.'

At least it wasn't just Ella.

Susan swivelled gently in her chair, crossing her feet at the ankles. 'Let me know if you make any progress with that one.'

'Oh, I won't be making any progress,' Ella said, stepping back from the desk. She didn't have the mental space to date.

'We should get lunch together later,' Susan said, focusing on her computer.

She suspected Susan was looking for an *in* to the

Coburn brothers, and Ella wasn't keen on being a pawn in those types of games. 'I'll likely eat at my desk, but I can grab something for you if you like?'

Susan's gaze flicked to her. 'Thanks, but I try to leave this desk when I can.'

~

ELLA POKED her head into Barry's office at lunchtime. 'I'm going to get food. Do you want something?'

'A sandwich from next door would be great. Surprise me.'

'Sure.'

'And put it on the account, and your lunch too. Technically you're working through your break, and you're part of the Bass family now.'

It was a kind thing for him to say, and yet she wanted to refute it. She'd been a member of the Melbourne Ballet family once. They'd stood by her through every injury, then the surgery. Even then they were prepared to keep her on. That was why she left. They deserved someone dependable who wouldn't fall apart after a long rehearsal.

'Thank you.'

The line was to the door at the cafe, but that wasn't why she hesitated to join it. Dax and his... gang? Cult? Whatever they were, they were standing at the back of the line. Ella's nerves might've sent her fleeing if she hadn't needed to get a sandwich for Barry.

Dax looked in her direction, and her hands went clammy as his cool eyes landed on her. They remained on her as she walked towards him.

'Hey,' he said, straightening.

His friends looked in her direction. Not one smile among them. At least the blonde wasn't there.

'Hi.' Ella was relieved when someone cut in front of her,

creating a buffer between her and Dax. The nerves were ridiculous. She had performed in front of large crowds for years, been judged by her peers and mentors most of her life. Experience had taught her that nerves were a terrible waste of energy.

Instead of turning back to his friends, Dax stepped out of the line and went to stand next to her. Concerned looks from his friends followed him, but he seemed oblivious to their disapproval.

'I looked it up,' Dax said. 'The jeté thing.'

She stared into those thunderous eyes of his. 'You googled jeté?'

'It's a jump where the dancer springs from one foot to the other, extending the leg outwards. Seems that part matters.'

'It does.' Why did it please her so much that he'd gone home and done that?

They watched each other for a moment.

'So, you're a dancer,' he said.

'Used to be.' She cleared her throat. 'You don't have to keep me company. I'm sure your friends would rather you wait with them.'

Dax looked over to where they were speaking among themselves. 'Someone has to stop you from spilling drinks on yourself.'

'That part comes *after* waiting in line.'

He chuckled softly. The sound warmed her insides.

'Probably won't get a Green Parrot,' he said. 'I got teased yesterday.'

'Sorry. That's on me.'

'No, it's on me. I should know better,' he said, taking a step forwards. 'What are you getting?'

'I thought I might try a salad.' She normally despised small talk, but with him she was greedy for any kind of exchange.

38

He glanced in the direction of the display window. 'Do they just call it a salad here?'

She hadn't had a chance to look at the menu written on the chalkboard behind the counter. 'Probably not. What do you normally get?'

'The Smiling Assassin.'

Her eyebrows lifted. 'And what's that?'

'A lamb souvlaki, as far as I can tell. Often wonder what hummus has to do with assassination.'

She couldn't stop from smiling. 'Well, there's the slaughter of the lamb, but I'm wondering why souvlakis are on the menu at a Brazilian cafe. I thought they were from Greece.'

'I think it's just their coffee that's Brazilian.'

Ella looked to the jar sitting on the counter. 'But they sell brigadeiros.'

He followed her gaze. 'What are those?'

'Brazil's answer to the chocolate truffle.'

He seemed impressed by her knowing that. 'You a foodie or something?'

The way he said it made it clear he was not. 'No. I read it on the jar yesterday when I was ordering.'

His mouth spread into a wide smile, the kind she couldn't look away from.

'Are they good?' he asked.

'I've never had one.' She only ate sweets at celebrations or if someone had gone to the effort of making something for her.

He continued to eye them. 'Should we try one, then?'

'All right.' And just like that, her rule changed. It was just one tiny chocolate ball, after all.

They moved forwards in the line as his group stepped to the side to wait for their food.

'Are you meeting your friend for lunch?' Dax asked.

Ella was aware of the others watching them again.

'Lucy? No. She just wanted to meet me for my first day in case it didn't go well.'

'Did it go well?'

She nodded. 'It was fine.'

'Fine?' He studied her. 'Fine's a bit underwhelming.'

'Is it?'

'It's a very polite word.'

'Well, I'm a very polite person.'

He regarded her a moment. 'Barry Taylor's been at Bass Fuel a long time. How is he to work for?'

She peered up at him. 'Good.'

'Fine and good. You're not selling this new job of yours very well.'

His bare arm brushed hers, and she flinched.

'Sorry,' he said.

'It's fine.' She ran her hand over the spot his arm had touched. 'How do you know Barry?'

'He's famous round these parts for making Flathead Rig seem like a good idea. Master of spin.'

She picked up on something in his tone that she couldn't place. 'You don't think the rig is a good idea?'

He leaned on one foot, eyes on the display cabinet. 'I don't think drilling for oil underwater is good for anyone, but that particular rig's a ticking time bomb.'

Before Ella could ask what he meant by that, the man in front moved aside.

'You go ahead,' Dax said.

Ella had forgotten to read the menu, so she pointed to the pre-made salad in the display cabinet. 'One of those to take away, please.'

The lady behind the counter pushed up on her toes to see where she was pointing. 'The Mean Bean Funky Chicken?'

Dax grinned at the ground, and Ella struggled to contain her own smile.

'That's the one. And I'll take that sandwich at the front too.' Ella glanced at Dax as the woman grabbed one of the pre-packed containers stacked behind the salad bowl. He was holding back laughter. 'Stop,' she whispered. 'She'll think we're laughing at her.'

'I've been eating here for two months,' he whispered back, 'and that's the most ridiculous name yet.'

Ella paid the lady and thanked her twice to compensate for their rudeness. As she went to leave, she remembered the brigadeiros. 'Oh, I forgot about the—'

'I got it,' Dax said, pre-empting what she was about to say. He ordered a souvlaki, a bottle of water, and two of the fudge balls, which looked even unhealthier close up. When Ella offered him money, he shook his head. 'My treat.'

'Dax, you coming?' one of his friends called from the door.

'I'll meet you there,' he said.

The guy's eyes landed on Ella before he followed after the others.

'Is that your brother?' Ella asked.

Dax nodded. 'Is it that obvious?'

'You have the same eyes.' She looked him over. 'And jaw, height, nose. Disproportionally large calves.' She was relaxing around him.

He laughed as he stepped up to collect his food. 'Is that right?'

'You're definitely a bit friendlier,' she added as they headed for the door.

'Miller's just cautious with strangers.'

'I heard you're all a bit like that.' The words slipped out before she could stop them.

Dax looked down at her. 'Yeah? Where'd you hear that? Is Barry talking shit about us?'

She slowed as they stepped out onto the footpath. 'Why would Barry talk shit about you?'

He stopped and looked off in the direction of his group. 'Who else do we have in common?'

'No one. We have nothing in common.'

His gaze shifted back to her.

'People,' she corrected, realising what she said. 'We have no people in common. No mutual friends.'

He nodded slowly. 'Right.'

'Susan, our receptionist. She might've mentioned a few things about you and your friends this morning.'

'I don't know any Susans.'

Ella shrugged. 'She seems to know you.'

A smug smile grew on his face. 'So you were talking about me with someone at your work?'

Her cheeks heated. 'She saw us chatting yesterday and asked how I knew you.'

'And what did you tell her?'

'The truth. I barely know you.' His eyes were so intense she had to look away. 'She gave the impression that you're a complicated bunch.'

'And what did you say to that?'

'I told her I avoid complicated.' She immediately regretted saying that. It sounded like she was turning down an offer he hadn't even made.

Dax studied her with an unreadable expression. 'Fair enough. We have that in common.' He held out the paper bag containing the two brigadeiros. 'Should we do this?'

'Let's do it.' She was still trying to figure out what a normal life looked like. The last thing she needed was a guy messing up her neat existence. It was sound logic. So why did her stomach suddenly feel heavy?

Balancing the food on one arm, she dipped her hand into the bag, inspected the ball, and took a small bite. Dax tipped the other one straight into his mouth, eating the whole thing at once.

'Oh my God,' she said. 'It's possibly the best thing I've ever eaten.'

He nodded. 'Comes close for me.'

She popped the rest into her mouth, then covered it with her hand. 'What beats this?'

'A brownie I once had. Straight from the oven, all gooey in the middle.'

Ella couldn't remember the last time she ate a brownie. 'Did you bake it?'

'No, my girlfriend at the time.'

She swallowed, but the sprinkles stuck in her throat, making her cough.

Dax narrowed his eyes at her. 'You okay?'

She nodded, her face heating. 'By chance, was that your ex with you yesterday?'

'Why do you ask?' He took the lid off his water and held it out to her. When she hesitated, he said, 'It's only fair. I drank from your drink yesterday.'

She took it, sipped, and handed it back. He drank from it next, which took the intimacy of the gesture up a level. 'I don't think she's over you, so if you're holding out hope, it's there.'

'I'm not holding out hope.' He sounded firm on that. 'Frankie and I weren't a good fit.'

Frankie.

Of course she had a cool name.

Ella licked her lips, tasting chocolate. 'Why's that?' It was none of her business, but she wanted to hear his answer.

His expression turned serious. 'Just didn't feel right. When you know, you know.'

She looked down at the food, finding his gaze too pene-trating. 'I should get this sandwich up to Barry.'

'Is he too important to buy his own lunch?' There was a hint of agitation in his voice.

'I offered.' She lifted her gaze to meet his. 'Thanks for the brigadeiro.'

His eyes softened. 'Anytime.'

She nodded towards the bay. 'Enjoy the water.'

'And you enjoy your uncomplicated life.'

She knew he meant it as a joke, but an empty feeling swirled in her stomach in place of hunger. 'I feel awkward now because I said that. I'm sure all your friends are great.'

'They are, some of the time.' He glanced in their direction. 'I never asked your last name.'

She laughed awkwardly. 'Why do you want to know my last name?'

He shook his head. 'Kids these days. So suspicious.'

She pressed her lips together to stop from smiling. 'We're doing that again?'

'I'm having trouble believing you're twenty-three. Miller's convinced you're a teenager.'

With an exaggerated sigh, she reached into her bag and pulled out her wallet, opening it with her teeth. She held the plastic window with her driver's licence level with his face.

Dax studied it a moment. 'That's a terrible photo of you, Miss Lewis born April 2, 1995.'

She laughed and closed the wallet. 'It's a driver's licence photo. It's supposed to be bad.' She noted his teasing expression. 'Let's see yours, then.'

He held the empty paper bag between his teeth as he pulled his wallet from his back pocket and slid his licence from the card section. It was a typical man's wallet, containing only a credit card, licence, and cash. Nothing like hers, which was exploding with receipts, loyalty cards, and expired coupons.

Ella narrowed her eyes on the card. 'Oh.'

'*Oh?*'

Another sigh. 'Yours is actually really flattering, Mr Coburn born May 20, 1993.'

'You think?'

'You look quite sophisticated with your hair tied back.'

He watched her as he slid the card back into his wallet. 'How do I look normally?'

Perfect. But she couldn't say that. 'Fine.'

He laughed, and she let the sound wash over her. Then he was backing away, and she was wishing he wouldn't leave.

'I'll see you around, Miss Lewis of legal age.'

She lifted a hand in a wave as he walked backwards a few paces. When he finally turned, she felt the moment their eye contact broke, felt the loss of him. She realised she'd been holding her breath and exhaled heavily. Her gaze fell to his frayed black T-shirt, then moved down his paint-splattered shorts and bronzed legs. He was definitely one of the few rare men who could make steel-cap boots look good.

Dax glanced over his shoulder, stopping when he saw her still standing there gaping like a complete idiot. She thought about looking away, pretending she was watching something else, but somehow she knew he would see straight through the act. Instead, she waved again. His hand went up in response; then he faced forwards again and didn't look back.

CHAPTER 7

*D*ax dropped his keys and wallet on the kitchen bench of the townhouse he shared with Miller. His brother was likely at the head office, one place Dax tried to avoid because of Frankie. He preferred to deal with her via email when it came to work matters, though he hoped that would change with time.

Heading upstairs to his bedroom, he peeled off his work clothes and threw on some board shorts. His energy was low, and the only fix was the sea. It beckoned him with a silent command.

After locking up the house, he crossed Beaconsfield Parade to the beach. The sand was cool on his bare feet, the clouds making it impossible for the sun to heat anything. He released a breath when his feet hit the water; then he continued out until it was deep enough for him to dive in. His energy sang as the water swallowed him. He felt it grow with each stroke and kick of his feet.

Dax didn't have to worry about lifeguards at that part of the beach. At that time of year, he didn't even have to worry about people in the water.

He surfaced and looked around. It was always safer to surface before heading farther out; if he was being watched, spectators would likely panic if he went under and never came back up. He swam above water until he neared Princes Pier, and then he sank down to explore. Fish darted off in all directions, mistaking him for a predator. He ran his fingers along the sea floor, leaving a rising cloud of sand in his wake. Overhead, he could hear the occasional boat passing.

Dax preferred to swim alone, to decide the route and dictate speed. Usually fast, covering around ten kilometres in less than thirty minutes. Speed was a great way to clear the mind, and he really needed to clear his head of a certain woman whose eyes fooled him into thinking he was in the water.

Miss Ella Lewis.

Drinker of green smoothies, performer of jetés, and the only person who could make his pulse quicken by saying 'brigadeiro'.

Ella.

Tiny human Ella with her heart-shaped face and pink lips. He couldn't help but watch them when she spoke. She was a natural beauty, and that was saying something given he had grown up with ondines, known for their alluring traits.

Before he knew what he was doing, he found himself back at Docklands. The quality of water deteriorated the closer he got. Less visibility, more rubbish. Docklands was a dangerous place to swim with its tall buildings. Just about every office and apartment had a view of the water. He was careful not to go too close to the surface, as daylight saving meant it was still light at six o'clock.

He thought about going to Williamstown, because he'd noticed on Ella's driver's licence that she lived there.

Maybe she walked the beach after work. He could picture her barefoot in the shallows, shoes swinging in her hand. He knew she would look gorgeous painted by a setting sun.

Movement atop the nearby wall made him stop. He drifted a moment, eyes narrowing on a woman standing on the stone edge dividing concrete and sea. It wasn't unusual for people to walk along the edge. It wasn't dangerous, just unfortunate if they did lose balance. What held him in place was a sense of familiarity.

He swam closer to get a better look.

It was Ella.

Even in the fading light, with all that water and distance separating them, he knew it was her. Slowly, he edged closer under the cover of black water and watched as she slipped her handbag off her shoulder, then removed her shoes.

What the hell are you up to?

For a moment he thought she was going to jump, but that didn't make sense. He stilled, watching, trying to read her body language, to predict her next move. If she jumped, he wasn't allowed to go to her. There were rules, and he'd been warned many times to stop breaking them.

Pressing her palm to her forehead, Ella drew a large breath that made her entire body swell, then checked her surroundings.

Fuck the rules.

If she jumped, he would go to her. There were plenty of people still in the area, but very few were down by the water at that time of day. Everyone was going home, earbuds in as they rushed to tram stops, carparks, or local restaurants to meet up with friends.

But Ella didn't jump.

She extended one arm to the side, the other in front of her, then rose onto the balls of her feet like a... ballerina.

On the next breath, she turned with a slight hop as she spun around on the ball of one foot.

A smile spread on Dax's face as he watched her. When she told him she was a dancer, this wasn't what he'd pictured. This was proper dancing. This was a beautiful, graceful ballerina, like the kind he'd seen in movies. He couldn't tell you which movie, maybe something Frankie had made him suffer through.

Ella Lewis was a dancer—and a really good one.

He swam closer to get a better view, Ella turning all the while. She stopped after maybe twenty turns, chest rising and falling and something resembling pride on her face. Her mouth turned up in a smile, but it was gone a moment later. Her legs folded, and she slumped down onto the wall, palms slapping the brick. Her head hung like dead weight, her chin almost touching her chest, and her eyes closed.

ELLA PRESSED her fingertips into the cold brick, hoping it would ease the heaviness in her chest. Twenty pain-free fouettés. But there was no audience, no one around to witness the small accomplishment.

Rising to her feet once more, she did a relevé followed by a grand jeté, then finished with four pirouettes and a curtsy, all while balanced on the edge of a wall. She could almost imagine the applause.

Her eyes sank shut as the memory of her last performance came to mind. *Don Quixote.* She had played the role of Altisodora, a young woman in the court of the Duchess who pretended to be in love with Quixote. She had made it halfway through the season before a labral tear, then had rejoined two weeks before the end of the season only to end up in surgery for her knee.

That was the beginning of the end.

Lifting her arms, she prepared to go again. *Swan Lake* contained thirty-two fouettés, so she would do thirty-three.

Just as she was about to begin, a shadow in the water snagged her vision. Lowering her arms, she looked out at the murky water. For a second, she thought she saw a body, but the light was poor and the water dark, and the harder she looked, the more she doubted herself. She went to step back but misjudged the distance, and her foot slipped off the ledge. She was experienced at falling, and she landed on the concrete without so much as a twinge. Thankfully there was no one around to see it.

That's enough dancing on walls for one evening.

Ella bent to fetch her shoes and thought she heard a splash in the water. Straightening, she stepped up to the edge and peered over it. She sucked in a breath when she met two storm cloud eyes below the water's surface. Intense, familiar. Dark hair swirled around a striking bearded face. Then it vanished, swallowed by the inky water. She knew she was losing her mind, because the face looked like Dax.

Wide-eyed, Ella returned to the ledge, kneeling on it this time. She gripped the edge with both hands as she leaned over the water, searching.

Nothing.

Was she really that far gone with her childish crush that she was now seeing him in the water?

'Ella, what are you doing?'

She jumped at the sound of her father's voice so violently that her hands slipped off the edge and she fell forwards. She tried to grab hold of something but soon figured out gravity was against her in that moment. Holding her breath, she braced for the cold shock of the sea. Dax's face flashed beneath the surface once more, reminding her just how fragile the mind could be under stress. As her knees slid off the edge, she was yanked back in the other direction by her shirt. All the air left her lungs with the jolt of the action.

'What the hell are you doing?' her father shouted, dragging her back over the stone edge. His eyes went from the discarded shoes to her jacket as he steadied her on her feet.

She was trembling. 'Sorry, I… I was dancing.'

'*Dancing*?'

'I was challenging my balance,' she said quickly, trying to reassure him. 'Then I saw something…'

'What?' Michael looked in the direction of the water. 'What are you talking about?'

She swallowed. 'A fish.' She winced at the lie. That was what happened when she panicked.

Her gaze shifted to the water farther out. She could feel something out there, feel *him*. Or maybe she was having a moment, like the ones she'd had after her mother died.

She spotted him then, around twenty feet away, eyes above the water.

Dax.

She blinked in case she was seeing things, expecting him to disappear, but he didn't. He watched her through locks of slick hair, eyebrows drawn together in a sharp line.

She held her breath. No one swam in that water. It was for boats and resilient fish. It was there for people to look down on from their fancy offices above. Plus, it was October. You needed a wetsuit to enter southern waters at that time of year.

'Are you okay?' her father asked.

Ella tore her gaze from the water. 'Yes, fine.' It was the word Dax hated.

'Why would you go near the water by yourself?' His grip on her tightened.

'I'm sorry.' She tucked her hair behind her ear. 'But you know I can swim, right?'

'I know that.' He drew a breath and finally let go of her. 'But do you really want to swim in *that* water?'

She breathed out a laugh. 'That was never the plan.'

'I scared you.'

'You did.'

His expression softened. 'Sorry. You know how I am around water.'

He didn't need to apologise or explain. The fear was shared.

Ella went to fetch her shoes, then bent to collect the contents of her bag, which she'd kicked. When she rose, her father dropped her jacket onto her shoulders.

'Let's get you home,' he said.

They were both quiet for most of the trip. It wasn't until they reached Williamstown that he finally asked, 'How was work?'

Ella was staring out the window, convinced she'd lost her mind. The last time she'd hallucinated like that was after her mother passed. The problem had resolved itself with time—and the help of a very expensive child psychologist. 'I drafted a media release today.'

Michael turned the heater down a few degrees. 'Second day and killing it. Good for you.' He sounded proud.

Ella turned to face him. 'Do you know much about Flathead Rig?'

Her father frowned. 'I know the rig makes them a lot of money. Why do you ask?'

She turned back to the window. 'The release I put together today was shutting down rumours of ongoing oil leaks. You know anything about that?'

'You should know by now that I don't buy into rumours.' He glanced sideways at her. 'Want to get a meal at the Yacht Club?'

She shook her head. 'I'm going for a run.'

'With Lucy?'

'Maybe.'

He sighed. 'You can't go by yourself.'

'Then yes, with Lucy.'

One side of his mouth lifted. 'I'll check with her later.'

'I know you will.'

They pulled up out front of the weathered house sitting between two newly renovated ones.

'We really need to paint,' Michael said with a sigh.

Ella smiled. 'You say that every time we pull up.'

'It's relevant every time we pull up.' He turned to look at her. 'Don't run by yourself.' He paused. 'And do me a favour—no more dancing near water.'

She didn't move. '"The cure is always saltwater. Sweat, tears, or the sea." Mum used to say that, remember?'

Michael took a moment before responding. 'She stole it from Isak Dinesen.'

Ella suppressed a smile. 'Thanks for the ride.'

'Any time.'

She exited the car and walked up to the old screen door, forcing her key into a rusted lock. The door whined as it opened, alerting her neighbours—and her neighbours' neighbours—to the fact that she was home. She held it open with her hip while she threw her shoulder into the heavy wooden door behind it. With a final wave to her father, she flicked on the lights and dropped her keys onto the small table before walking to the studio and leaning in the doorway.

She kept replaying the scenes from the water in her mind, trying to decipher what was real. Perhaps the loss of her career had taken more of a toll than she realised. Or maybe Dax really had been there in the bay.

That raised other questions, like why on earth was he there? Of all the places he could swim. Had he followed her? She shook her head. *No.* He must have already been in the water. It likely had nothing to do with her at all. He had been dangling his feet in those waters for weeks.

Pulling her phone from her bag, she dialled Lucy's number. 'Hey, feel like going for a run?'

CHAPTER 8

*D*ax was exhausted when he arrived on-site the next morning. He had barely slept, lying awake angry at himself for not swimming away when he'd had the chance. That was recognition on her face. Now he had three choices: deny it was him, lie about why he was in the water, or avoid her for the rest of his life.

People swam in the bays around Melbourne. Okay, not that bay, but since when did he follow the crowds? She would ask why he was there and would never believe it was a coincidence—and it wasn't. He'd been drawn there. It was as if she'd been waiting for him. Yes, he should've left, but he couldn't bring himself to regret it completely. It felt like his first true glimpse of her.

Miss Ella Lewis was full of surprises.

Then she'd slipped, and he'd had three choices once again: flee and hope Barry Taylor's little PR stooge could swim, rescue her and reveal himself in the process, or move water and lift her to safety. He'd fought off rather determined great white sharks before. What was one tiny dancer?

But someone had gotten to her first, someone she knew

judging by the way they interacted. He was too old to be her boyfriend—her father, perhaps. Or maybe she dated older guys. Dax tried to picture Ella with a sugar daddy, but the image made his skin prickle and caused the bottle of water next to his tool belt to fall over. He watched it roll, then looked around to ensure no one had seen. A loss of control like that was not a good thing. No other woman had ever had that effect on him, where the mere thought of her being taken advantage of by some slimy old fool made his energy surge. He swore under his breath as he reached for the bottle.

'Dax,' one of the carpenters called to him. 'There's a girl on-site looking for you.'

Dax glanced past him, immediately alert. 'She tell you her name?'

The man shook his head. 'Want me to ask?'

It had to be Ella. 'It's fine. I'll go. Where is she?'

'Waiting near the lift. She said it was important.'

Dax's feet were moving then. He found her standing beneath a steel frame, waving a hand in front of her face as she recoiled from the nearby hammer drill—not wearing a helmet. Irritation pulsed through Dax as he continued towards her. All it took was one stray beam swinging in the wrong direction and she would be a goner.

Her hand went down when she saw him approach, back straightening and expression cautious. He removed the hard hat from his head and put it on hers when he reached her. Ella seemed to bend under the weight of it.

'What are you doing?' she asked, reaching for it.

He held it in place. 'What are *you* doing? You can't be on a construction site without the right gear.' He gestured for her to start walking.

She held on to the hat, which was miles too big, then, reading his expression, began walking. He followed closely behind, practically leaning over her in case something should fall from above. They didn't stop until they were standing on the strip of dirt that ran between the site and the next building. Ella removed the helmet and held it out to him, smoothing her ponytail down with her spare hand.

'Can you just wear it while you're here?' His tone was more abrupt than he'd meant it to be. That was what the thought of her getting hurt did to him. 'Please,' he added.

'It's dirty.'

He frowned down at her. 'So is blood if a stray brick hits you.'

She reluctantly put it back on her head. 'You going to give me your boots too?' Her tone wasn't playful but smart.

'Want to tell me what you're doing here?'

She looked around as she gathered her words. 'I need to ask you something, and I need you to be honest with me.'

He crossed his arms, waiting. He was used to lying about what he was, could do it in his sleep. Easiest and quickest way through was to deny he was there, have her think she imagined the entire thing, and get her off-site before he had a chance to feel guilty.

She cleared her throat. 'I was down at the water last night, after work. And I'—she glanced away—'I thought I saw you.'

'Okay.'

'And I'm pretty sure you saw me.'

'*After* work?' He feigned confusion while guilt pounded his gut.

Her hands opened and closed at her sides. 'It was around six.'

He shook his head. 'I finished up here just after four.'

She searched his eyes. 'You weren't... swimming around six?'

'At *Docklands*? You can't swim in the bay, nor would you want to. It's only suitable for boats.'

Her gaze dropped to her feet. 'Oh. I must have... never

mind.' She took a step back from him. 'I really thought I saw you.'

He hated that she was doubting herself. 'What were you doing down at the water at that time?'

She lifted her eyes to him. 'Thinking.' She attempted a smile. 'And hallucinating, apparently. You really weren't in the water?'

'Doing what?'

She hesitated. 'Watching me.' Her eyes sank shut. 'It sounds crazy when I say it aloud, but I saw your face, so clearly, and you hang out there most days.'

'So?'

'So it's… strange.'

The lies weren't flowing as easily as they normally did. He shifted his weight onto one foot and regarded her for the longest time. 'Are you okay? You seem stressed out.'

She took another step back from him. 'Maybe it was your brother or one of your friends.'

'Now my friends were in the water?'

Her face fell, and she removed the helmet from her head and held it out for him to take. 'The only other explanation is that I'm seeing things, and that's not okay. That hasn't happened since my mother passed. I don't know what it means.'

His insides fell. 'Wait. What?'

'I should go.' When he didn't take the helmet, she placed it on the ground between them.

'But we're not done talking.'

She shook her head. 'No, we're done. Either I'm crazy or you're a liar. Both mean I should walk away.' She laughed once. 'If I'm seeing things—and I have a history of it—you should stay away. And if you like to watch women from the water, then I should definitely stay away.'

It was the first time in his life he'd felt compelled to tell someone the truth. That was a dangerous place to be in.

'I have to get to work,' Ella said, turning. 'Sorry I came on-site. It won't happen again.'

'Ella—'

She held up a hand in a wave. 'It's fine. I asked, you answered. We're good.'

Dax ran a hand down his face. 'You're not crazy.'

She stilled, then turned. 'So you were in the water?'

He didn't reply. He *couldn't* reply. There were rules, rules that protected the entire pod. When he didn't respond, she turned, head shaking.

'Can you just wait a second?' he called after her.

She didn't stop this time. 'I have to go to work.'

He linked his hands atop his head as he watched her navigate the potholes.

Shit.

~

ELLA KNOCKED on Barry's door and waited for him to wave her in. He was speaking on the phone when she entered.

'VEPA aren't worried, so why are you?' Barry said, taking the coffee from Ella. 'I spoke to the safety officer at the rig this morning. I'll let you know when there's something to report. Righto. Bye.' He exhaled loudly as he placed the phone down. 'If any more journos call, I'm in a meeting.'

She placed a pile of phone messages on his desk, most of them journalists. 'I'll just leave these here.'

He picked one off the top of the pile, then dropped it on the table. 'Someone's been whispering in their ears again. Smallest amount of oil in the water, and next thing we have VEPA and WorkSafe up our arses along with every paper in Melbourne in our business.'

Ella didn't know much about oil rigs, but she knew the purpose of the press release she'd drafted the day prior.

'Why are they calling today if you provided all the information to them yesterday?'

'Someone's stirring the pot. Local greenies, no doubt.' He turned his chair to face her. 'Anyway, nothing for you to worry about. You did a great job with the press release yesterday. I barely had to change a thing. I know it's early days, but I think you have a bright future for you here at Bass Fuel.'

That comment should've pleased her, but it had the opposite effect. 'Do you want me to type up your feedback for the creative agency this afternoon?'

'That's this afternoon?'

'Four o'clock.'

He rubbed his forehead. 'I haven't even looked over the concepts. Probably won't get near it before lunch.'

'I can't guess your opinion on them, but I can take a look and tell you whether they followed the brief.'

He regarded her over the rim of his coffee cup, then nodded. 'All right. Have a look, maybe give me *your* opinion on them. We'll go over everything at three.'

She nodded. 'Done.'

When Ella returned to her small desk outside Barry's office, she noticed a drink and a paper bag in front of her keyboard. She looked around before sitting and tentatively opening the bag. Her breath caught when a brigadeiro rolled along the bottom of it. She picked up the smoothie, which had "Green Parrot" scrawled across the cup.

'Are you two seeing each other now or what?' Susan said, appearing above Ella's monitor.

Ella gasped and dropped the bag. She hadn't even heard Susan approach. 'No.' They were the opposite of seeing each other as of that morning. 'Did Dax drop these off?'

Susan straightened the front of her shirt. 'You were in with Barry, so he asked me to just leave them on your

60

desk.' She pointed. 'He wrote a message on the bottom of the bag for you.'

Ella picked it up and raised it above her head.

MEET me on the lawn at one.
Dax

'SO YOU'RE NOT SEEING HIM?' Susan asked, confused. 'Because this is all a bit cute for friends.'

Ella shook her head. 'No.'

'Are you going to meet him?'

Ella stared at the open bag, the sugary ball a symbol of her temptation. Picking it up, she dropped it into the bin under the desk.

'Ouch,' Susan said. 'I guess that's a no, then.'

Ella looked up at her. 'I have a lot on today.'

Susan gave her a knowing look. 'But you have to eat eventually.' With that, she wandered back to the reception desk.

The gesture felt like confirmation to Ella that it'd been him in the water. If he hadn't been there, he'd have labelled her crazy and given her a wide berth, not sent her notes and chocolate balls. Perhaps he wanted a chance to explain. In which case she would have to decide if she wanted to give him that chance. She supposed it was a way to end things on a good note.

She caught that thought. End what exactly? They weren't dating. There hadn't even been any mention of it. Good thing too, because he was turning out to be exactly the kind of complication she had vowed to avoid in this new chapter of her life.

Dax Coburn was trouble.

At one o'clock, Ella tapped her finger on the mouse,

eyes on the paper bag in the bin. She had relented and drank the smoothie, but only because she hadn't eaten that morning and would likely skip lunch. When the clock ticked over to one minute past one, Ella wondered how long he would wait for her to show up. She had planned to go, then changed her mind, changed it back, and then chickened out five minutes to one.

Letting out a resigned breath, she snatched up her handbag and made her way downstairs, thankful that Susan was too busy at reception to say anything as she passed by the desk.

Outside, the sun was shining, fooling those still indoors into believing it was warm.

It was not.

Ella pulled her blazer tighter around her as she headed down to the grassed area. She had already decided that if Dax was with his friends, she would turn around and leave. But he was alone, leaning against one of the shell sculptures, looking out at the water while everyone around him looked down at their phones. That visual ate away at her resolve. He was wearing a blue T-shirt with a hole in the sleeve while everyone else wore suits. She liked that he was oblivious to how much he stood out, or that he didn't care.

He looked in her direction as she approached, and the hard lines of his face softened a little.

'Hey,' he said.

She stopped some distance from him. 'Hi.'

'Have you eaten?'

'I had a smoothie earlier.' She attempted a smile, but it fell flat thanks to nerves. 'You?'

'I'm good.' He let out a long noisy breath and pushed himself up to a stand. 'Listen, I couldn't have you thinking you're crazy. You're not crazy.'

She never looked away from him. 'If we're going to have this conversation, I need to know you'll be honest.'

'I'll be as honest as I can be.'

Ella stared up at him. 'What does that mean?'

'It means I'll answer you honestly if I can, and if I can't, I'll tell you so.'

She was immediately wary. 'Were you in the water last night?'

'Yes.'

She swallowed. 'Why?'

'I swim every night—and every morning.'

She was only standing three feet away, but it suddenly felt like a mile. He took a step forwards, as if reading her mind.

'You swim every day?' she asked.

'Yes.'

She thought on that a moment. 'Why didn't you just say that this morning?'

He looked around, brushing a finger down his nose. 'Because I knew you'd ask me why I was there, and I don't really have a good answer for that. I was swimming by, and I spotted you.'

She squinted up at him. 'You were "swimming by"? From where? Going where?'

'I live in Port Melbourne, by the water.'

Her eyes widened. 'Are you telling me you swam from Port Melbourne?'

'Yes.'

Silence.

'Are you a long-distance swimmer or something?'

'I suppose so.'

She searched his eyes, needing more. 'You either are or you aren't.'

'I swim long distances. I don't do it competitively or anything.'

Her mind was swirling. 'You do it for fun? Fitness?'

'Sure.'

'Which one?'

'Both.'

She took a long breath. 'So you were just swimming by and saw me?'

His hand went into his back pocket. 'I didn't know what you were doing, if you were okay, so I stuck around.' He paused. 'Then you started to dance.'

She wanted to cover her face, even though she'd expected him to say that.

He watched her for a long moment. 'You didn't tell me you could dance like that.'

'Well, you didn't tell me you were in the water watching, so…'

He smirked at the ground. 'Yeah, sorry about that.'

'And then I almost fell in.'

'I would've been there in a second if you had.' He looked around. 'Was that your dad?'

She noted the change in his expression. 'Yeah. We carpool.' She saw his shoulders relax. 'Do your friends swim too?'

He shook his head. 'I won't bring them into this conversation.'

She drew a breath and looked out at the water, which seemed less threatening in daylight. 'So what am I supposed to do with the snippets of information you're feeding me right now?'

'Just know your mind is fine. I'm the crazy one who was in the water, watching you. I honestly couldn't look away.' He shifted his feet. 'Can I ask what happened to your mum?'

'Accident.'

'That's all you're going to tell me?'

She tilted her head. 'Are you going to lecture me about holding back details?'

He laughed softly. 'That's fair.'

They were silent a while.

'So that's it?' she finally asked. 'That's the end of the exchange?'

'I'm part of a community that protects its privacy. There are rules.'

'Like what happens in swim club stays in swim club?'

His eyes lightened a shade. 'Something like that.'

'I'd like to think you're the only one mad enough to swim in that water.'

He pushed hair back from his face. 'And I'd like to think you're the only person who would dance barefoot on a ledge, but best not to jump to conclusions.'

She turned her head to hide her smile. 'Sometimes I need to prove to myself that I was once good enough.'

'Do you have to prove it on a ledge?'

She shrugged.

'How serious a dancer were you?'

'Melbourne Ballet serious.'

He frowned and glanced in the direction of her building. 'And what? You gave it up for *Barry*?'

She felt that familiar disappointment close in on her. 'I didn't want to give it up.'

He watched her closely. 'Did they cut you or something?'

She shook her head. 'I kept getting injured. I did everything right, everything to get stronger and better. I trained smarter, ate cleaner than any other dancer, but it was never enough.' She paused, wondering how much to tell him. He seemed to be waiting for her to continue. 'The doctors call it hypermobility. I wonder whether they just needed to give it a title in the end. How else could they explain the injuries?'

Dax looked down. 'Sorry. That can't have been easy.'

She waved off the pity. 'I started classes at three, so twenty years is a pretty good run.'

'Well, if it's any consolation, you looked perfect last night.'

Ella pushed down the emotion rising inside. 'Sometimes I tell myself it's temporary, because the alternative is… a lot.'

'I won't pretend to understand.'

His eyes were so soft when she met them again. 'I'm no wiser as to whether you're a long-distance swimmer or part of a cult that worships satanic gods of the sea, and yet I stand here saying things I don't say in front of anyone.'

'Must the gods I worship be satanic?'

'It would explain the secrecy.'

He nodded. 'And is the worshipping of satanic gods a deal-breaker for you?'

She pretended to think on it. 'Regular above-board sea gods are preferable.'

One corner of his mouth lifted. 'Good to know.'

They began walking back up the lawn towards the path, their arms occasionally bumping. She didn't move away.

'So I'm just supposed to hope this cult of yours isn't dangerous, then?' she asked.

'You're safe with me.' His expression turned serious. 'I promise you that.'

She shouldn't have believed him, had no reason to. So why did she?

'I'm sorry about this morning,' he said when they stopped in front of her building. 'I couldn't concentrate on work after you left.'

She realised that the smell of the ocean wasn't carried on the breeze but on him. It was the smell of summer holidays spent at the beach. The smell of her youth before her mother's death changed everything. She fought the urge to tip forwards against his chest and inhale.

'What are we doing?' she asked out of the blue.

'We're talking.'

'Because we're suddenly friends now?'

His throat bobbed. 'Sure. Why not?'

'We don't work on paper.'

He lifted one shoulder. 'So don't put us on paper.' He started backing away. 'Thanks for meeting me.'

'Thanks for kind of clearing things up but not really.'

'And thanks for the private dance last night.' He said it so loud that passers-by looked in her direction.

She bit back a smile despite herself and shook her head. 'Unkind, Mr Coburn.'

The last thing she saw was his devilish grin as he turned away.

CHAPTER 9

*T*he following week, Ella sat on the lawn outside of her building having lunch with Lucy and Caleb. Her eyes kept drifting to the coffee shop.

'Are you waiting for someone?' Lucy asked, her tone mischievous.

The girls had wandered up to the Sushi Tower for food. Ella had failed to mention it was next door to the site where Dax worked and had been relentlessly teased since.

'No,' Ella replied, focusing on her food again. 'Just appreciating this spring weather.'

Lucy glanced up at the overcast sky, which threatened rain. 'I think you're waiting for your stalker.'

Ella shook her head. 'He's not a stalker.'

'He was in the water *watching* you. What would you call it?'

She thought a moment. Mutual fascination? Ella knew Lucy was right, but something was preventing her from severing ties. 'Let's go with an eerie coincidence.'

Lucy took a large bite and chewed, eyes never leaving Ella. 'He was naked.'

'He was bare chested.'

'You don't think it's weird that he wasn't wearing a wetsuit this time of year?'

'The whole thing was weird.'

Lucy was silent a moment. 'I can't believe he caught you dancing. He was probably so confused. Did you explain what type of dancer you are?'

'He knows I'm not a stripper, if that's what you're getting at.'

Caleb lowered his milkshake and looked up at Ella. 'What's a stripper?'

Ella cast an apologetic look at Lucy. 'A type of dancer.'

'A dancer paid better than most ballet dancers,' Lucy added. 'You know, if things don't work out at Bass Fuel, it's not a bad backup plan.'

Ella tilted her head. 'You joke, but don't think it didn't cross my mind when I was desperate and living on hand-outs from Dad.'

Lucy laughed, then fell quiet, staring off to the side. 'Well, look who it is.'

Ella looked over to where Dax and his friends were strolling along the grass towards the water. Frankie was with the group, eyes narrowed at her. They held a clear warning.

When Dax looked in Ella's direction, her heart beat a little harder in her chest. One corner of his mouth lifted as he raised a hand in a wave. Ella's went up in response. It had been that way for the last week, polite greetings and brief conversations. Every interaction was a tiny high, sustaining Ella until the next one. She would never admit it to Lucy, but he was filling her thoughts more and more with each passing day.

Dax didn't stop, continuing on down to the pier, where they would dangle their feet in the water like it was the middle of summer. She watched them strip off their shoes and socks, chatting and laughing like a bunch of high school kids.

'Do you remember the classical mythology unit we did in our second year at uni?'

Ella tore her eyes from Dax. 'Barely. Why?'

'Yeah you do. I wrote that essay proving the existence of mermaids, remember?'

Reaching for her water, Ella removed the lid. 'I definitely recall you *trying* to prove their existence.'

'I got a high distinction for that essay.'

'And a lot of strange looks from the lecturer.'

'Not true, but have you ever considered the possibility that Dax is a—'

'I swear to God, if you say mermaid—'

'Mermaids are female. I was going to say sea creature.'

The water went the wrong way down Ella's throat, and she began coughing. Dax looked in her direction, even though he was too far away to hear. She breathed hard through her nose in an attempt to stop.

'How is that better?' she choked out.

'It's all-encompassing.'

Ella waited to catch her breath before speaking. 'I know you really loved *The Little Mermaid* routine you did as a teenager, but they're called fairy tales for a reason.'

Lucy sighed. 'I really did love that dance. It sucked there were no males to partner with back then.'

'You had a partner.'

'Yeah, I was paired with Sophie, who used to nervous-vomit before performances.'

Ella smoothed down Caleb's silky hair, which was sticking up in all directions. 'I think the absence of a fish tail shoots down your theory.'

Lucy gave her a tired look. 'They don't all have fish tails and carry magical tridents. There are *many* representations.'

'But no actual sightings, which kind of shoots holes in your theory, don't you think?'

'Merpeople, nymphs, nereids, oceanids, sirens, finfolk. Even the Aboriginal people have stories of spirits in watering holes and billabongs.'

'Oh my God. You're actually serious.'

'Deadly.' Lucy popped the last piece of sushi into her mouth and chewed. 'Forget about the representations portrayed in mainstream media. I know most of that is born of myth and legend. But think about all the creatures that now live on land that once lived in the sea. Why should humans be any different?'

'Should I check him for a tail, then?'

Lucy let out a noisy sigh. 'Even in mythology, they don't all have fishy parts. You know, sarcasm delivered in a sweet tone is still sarcasm. Remember what Miss Judy used to say in tap class?'

Ella shook her head. 'I only remember what Oscar Wilde said. "Sarcasm is the lowest form of wit but the highest form of intelligence."'

Lucy tilted her head. 'You do realise you're becoming your dad?'

Ella scrunched up her nose. 'I really am.' She noticed Lucy's expression collapse, the colour leaving her face. 'What's wrong?' She turned to see what her friend was looking at and her heart stopped dead. Standing in the middle of the lawn, with the sun angled like a halo above him, was Peter. 'Oh, for fu—'

'He hasn't seen you yet.'

Ella faced forwards. 'Just keep really still.'

'Won't that draw more attention?' Lucy whispered. 'Shouldn't we act natural?'

'*Fine*. Act natural.'

They sat staring at one another with slightly panicked expressions.

'Peter!' Caleb shouted, waving his little arm.

Lucy reached out to cover his mouth, but it was too late. Ella could tell because Lucy's panicked expression was replaced with an enormous smile suddenly.

'He's coming over, isn't he?' Ella asked.

Lucy nodded awkwardly. 'Peter.' She rose to her feet. 'What are you doing here?'

Ella drew a breath and stood, noting the surprise on Peter's face when he saw her.

'Ella?'

She smiled, but it felt stiff and unnatural. 'Small world.' Much, much too small.

He leaned in to kiss her cheek. 'Look at you.' His eyes raked the length of her. 'I'd heard you'd gone corporate.' He made a face when he said the word corporate, like a cat about to cough up a hairball.

Ella scrunched up her nose. 'I don't know if I'd call it corporate.'

Peter looked up at the tall buildings. 'Well, you do work for a corporation.'

'I couldn't leech off my father forever,' she replied, feeling like a traitor to the arts. She risked a glance in Dax's direction and found him watching her. As if the exchange wasn't uncomfortable enough.

'Tell me about the job,' he said, clapping his hands together. 'Advertising, did I hear?'

'Communications.'

'Nice.' He nodded. 'Well, we're getting ready to do *Giselle* over the summer. You should come watch me.'

And it was back to him—his favourite topic.

She swallowed. 'I love *Giselle*.'

'I'm playing Albrecht.'

Of course he was.

Ella nodded, and Lucy continued smiling while Peter

filled them in on all the details of his dancing life. When he was done, he looked down at Caleb.

'And how are you, Caleb?'

The toddler grinned up at him, his teeth coated with chocolate milk. 'Good.'

'What do you think of Ella having a new job in the city?'

He shrugged. 'If it doesn't work out, she's gonna be a stripper.'

Ella died a small death in that moment.

Lucy grabbed Caleb by the arm and pulled him to his feet. 'Why would you say that?' she whispered, marching him off in the other direction.

Peter's eyes returned to Ella, who was fighting hard to keep her sushi down.

'Caleb has a habit of remembering all the undesirable parts of a conversation and forming his own narratives,' she explained.

Peter nodded, visibly uncomfortable. 'Creative like his mother.' He removed the lid from the bottle of water he was carrying and took a sip.

'I think we're going to head off,' Lucy said, appearing next to them and literally pulling the blanket out from beneath Ella's feet.

'Now?' Ella asked.

'I promised to call in on Mum.'

'Okay.' Ella cleared her throat. 'Well, I should get back to work.'

'I'll walk you,' Peter said, stepping closer.

'No, that's okay.' She moved back. 'It's just that building there.' She pointed.

'It's on my way.'

Lucy kissed Ella goodbye, avoiding eye contact, then fled the scene with Caleb in one hand and the stroller in the other. Ella watched them until they were out of sight.

'How's the knee?' Peter asked.

Ella began walking towards work, her gaze drifting to Dax a final time. He was still watching her. 'The knee's fine.'

'I hear the scarring on those surgeries is minimal now.'

She blinked slowly. 'Only three incision marks.' A constant reminder of her shortcomings.

They continued their small talk all the way to the path, stopping at the edge of the lawn.

Ella found a final smile for him. 'Well, it was nice seeing you.'

He reached out and rubbed her arm. The gesture felt familiar but too intimate post-breakup. That was the problem when dance partners became bed partners—the lines were forever blurred. She didn't pull away.

'I was serious about the invitation,' he said. 'I'd love you to come. You can hang backstage.'

'You know I'm happy to be in the audience.'

His hand slid down to hold hers. 'You don't have to completely drop off the planet just because you're no longer performing.'

Ella swallowed back tears, hating that he was right.

She was about to respond when the water bottle in Peter's hand jolted, sending a spray of water over his face, neck, and down the front of his T-shirt. He let go of her hand and stepped back, staring down at the bottle with a shocked expression. Ella stood wide-eyed, unsure what had just happened.

'What the hell?' Peter wiped his face and shook his T-shirt as if that might help somehow.

Ella looked across the lawn and found Dax standing at the other end of the grass, eyes fixed on Peter. They mirrored the threat of the storm above. When he looked at her, she had the weirdest sense he was somehow responsible for the incident. Of course, that wasn't possible, but the pleased expression that settled on his face didn't exactly put her mind at ease.

Miller walked up to him and said something in his ear. Dax nodded and glanced in her direction before rejoining the group waiting nearby.

Ella turned back to Peter. 'Are you all right?'

'Yeah, I just… did you knock my water?'

She shook her head, noting his red neck, the only indicator he was embarrassed. She handed him one of the Sushi Tower serviettes she was still holding, and he took it without saying anything. 'I really have to get back to work. Text me the details for *Giselle*, and if I can make it, I will.'

'Will do.' He finished wiping his neck and bent to kiss her cheek. 'Nice seeing you.'

'You too.'

She pretended to watch him walk away, but she was really looking past him to Dax. He was at the back of the group, his broad shoulders filling the footpath and callused hands swinging slightly. She willed him to look back at her, but he never did.

CHAPTER 10

'Where are you going?' Miller asked, looking Dax up and down.

Dax paused with his hand on the front door, then turned to meet his brother's disapproving eyes. 'Out.'

'Where?'

'I have to tell you where?'

Miller didn't respond straight away. 'Normally you're off in the water, stirring up trouble, dodging cops. Now you're making new trouble for the pod.'

The keys jingled in Dax's hand. 'You got all that from "Out"?'

Miller inhaled and looked away. 'If you go down this path, you know what happens. She's already suspicious.' His eyes returned to his brother. 'You moved water today —right in front of her, out in the open, with no thought to who might see.'

'The guy spilled his drink.'

'*You* spilled his drink. And give that girl some credit. She looked straight at you when it happened. You're being reckless.'

'Easy, *Dad*.'

Miller didn't so much as smile. 'Why her?'

Dax didn't really have an answer, only a feeling. 'She works at Bass Fuel, you know.'

Nothing changed on Miller's face. 'So what, you're getting intel?'

'She works directly under Barry Taylor. Can't hurt to find out what she knows.'

Miller blinked and looked down. 'This is dangerous territory.'

'It might help the pod.'

'This isn't about the pod. You didn't throw water at that guy because of the pod. You don't look for this girl everywhere we go *for the pod*.'

Dax didn't deny it. There was no point. His brother knew him too well.

'I can't tell you not to see her,' Miller went on. 'But you better make damn sure you trust her before you take whatever this is any further.'

Dax shoved both hands into his pockets along with his keys. 'I can't stay away, and I need to know why.'

Miller rubbed at his forehead. 'There's really no one within the pod you could obsess over instead?'

Dax breathed out a laugh. 'I tried. It didn't work out so good.'

'I'm telling Mum and Dad.'

Dax pulled the door open. 'Snitch.'

'You can tell the pod. I'm not taking heat for your secrets.'

Dax was already through the door. 'What secrets?' He pulled the door shut behind him before Miller could reply.

~

ELLA TAPPED her finger on the mouse as she scrolled down the web page, pausing at a picture of Herbert James Draper's *Ulysses and the Sirens*. There was Ulysses, tied to the mast of the ship, helpless against the sirens seducing him. Ella glanced in the direction of Barry's office before opening a new tab and typing "merfolk without tails", shaking her head as she did so.

Lucy would love this.

Opening the first link, she browsed the female depictions, then jumped when the door to Barry's office opened.

'What are you still doing here?' he asked, bag in hand and jacket draped over his arm.

She clicked the browser closed and stood. 'Just wanted to make sure you didn't need anything before I left for the weekend.'

'Kind of you, but it's Friday night. Shouldn't you be out drinking with friends?'

She made a face. 'My Fridays tend to be quite tame.'

He chuckled.

'You were on the phone all afternoon,' she said. 'Everything okay?'

He nodded, but there was no hiding his fatigue. 'I'm probably going to fly out to Flathead Rig in the next few weeks, meet with the operators.' He paused. 'You should come with me, see the rig for yourself. I can organise a tour. Ever flown in a chopper before?'

She shook her head.

'Want to?'

'Of course.' She had zero interest in touring an oil rig, but if it helped her in the role, she'd do it. 'Sounds interesting.'

'Grab your stuff. I'll walk you downstairs. Your dad waiting for you?'

She glanced at her rose-gold watch, a present from her

father when she got accepted to do her master's. 'He's probably still working.'

They made their way down to the foyer, and as Ella stepped out of the lift, she saw Dax seated on one of the leather lounges. His hair was tied back, and he wore a black shirt rolled to the elbows with faded jeans and loafers. She'd never seen him in anything other than work gear before.

'You coming?' Barry asked, looking over his shoulder.

She hadn't realised she'd stopped walking. 'Yes.'

Dax stood, those potent eyes running the length of her. Then his gaze shifted to Barry, and he straightened. Ella noticed a change in Barry's posture also. She had forgotten they knew each other and understood the state of their relationship before they even exchanged one word.

'Here's trouble,' Barry said. 'Shouldn't you be outside waving a sign or something?'

Dax eyed him coolly. 'Would it do any good?' He looked at Ella. 'Miss Lewis.'

She suppressed a smile. 'Dax.'

Barry looked between them. 'You two know each other?'

Dax looked to Ella, letting her answer that one. But what to say? 'Dax is also a fan of the coffee next door. We've waited in many a line together.'

Barry watched Dax with a wary expression. 'That so?'

'How's things out at Flathead Rig?' Dax asked. 'I hear you still have issues with oil leaks.'

Barry laughed through his nose. 'And where did you hear that?'

'Just around. But hey, what would a simple construction worker know about the breach of environmental policies.'

'Don't believe everything you read in the papers,' Barry

replied. He turned to Ella. 'Want me to walk you to your father?'

'I can walk her,' Dax said.

Barry ignored him and waited for Ella's response.

'You go home to your family. Dax will walk me.'

Barry looked at Dax, a warning in his eyes. 'Make sure she gets there.' He glanced a final time at Ella. 'Have a good weekend.'

'You too.'

The pair watched him leave, and then Dax said to Ella, 'Do you want to get dinner?'

Excitement rose inside her. 'Dinner?' She tried to think through the logistics. 'I'm supposed to meet my dad, but I could call him and tell him I'll catch the train later.'

'I'll drive you home,' Dax said without hesitation. 'I'm not letting you get on a train alone on a Friday night.'

A few weeks ago, she would never have considered getting in the car with a man she barely knew, but she trusted him—stupidly, perhaps, but wholly. She couldn't explain it, but she knew if he said he would get her home safe, then he would get her home safe. 'You and Barry really have history, huh?'

Dax glanced in the direction of the door. 'You could say that.'

She would have to ask him about that later. 'Let me call Dad.'

Ella moved away to phone him, knowing he would have five hundred questions for her and not wanting to answer them in front of Dax. She watched him from the other side of the room as she reassured her father she would text him when she got home.

'Sorry,' she said when she returned.

'Don't apologise.'

Ella could smell his shampoo, something with coconut. She breathed it in. 'Where are we going?'

'That depends.' His eyes were warm on her. 'What do you eat besides cleansing juices?'

She liked that he asked her instead of just deciding as Peter would've done. 'This was your idea.'

He hooked a finger in his pocket. 'I'll be honest, I didn't think that far ahead because I didn't think you'd say yes.'

Her eyebrows came together. 'Really?'

'My blind optimism paid off.'

A smile stretched across her face. 'Bit early in the date to be drawing those kinds of conclusions.'

'Who said anything about a date?'

Her smile faltered. 'What would you call it?'

'*I'd* call it a date. Just surprised you would.'

She looked down. 'Let's just call it dinner, then.'

He shrugged. 'You can call it whatever you want. Makes no difference to me. Do you like vegan food?'

They began walking towards the exit.

'Do you?' she asked.

'Sure.'

'But you're not vegan.'

'Only vegans can eat vegan food?'

'No.' She watched her feet. 'Do I give off a vegan vibe?'

'I've seen you eat sushi and drink coffee with milk. At worst, you're a vegetarian.'

'At *worst*?' She laughed.

'Now I'm second-guessing myself. Would you rather a steak?'

Ella didn't care. She just wanted to sit across the table from him and not have to rush off like usual. She wanted to watch him read the menu and order, to know if he ate a burger with a knife and fork, if he liked his steak bloody, if he preferred pizza with or without pineapple. She wanted to see how he treated waiters, whether he would split the bill or insist on paying. He seemed like the kind of guy who just quietly paid on the way back from the bathroom and never brought it up.

She was impatient to know him.

'You know, I rarely eat out in the city,' she said. 'Why don't you pick. I promise I'm not as fussy as I seem.'

'Really? Because you seem pretty fussy.'

She was grinning like a fool. 'Lead the way, funny man.'

He thought for a moment. 'All right. I know a place.' He looked down at her shoes. 'You're wearing flats, even better. Wait. Weren't you wearing heels today?'

'That's very observant of you. They're safely tucked in my bag so I don't stand on anyone's feet.'

'I never did get that scuff off my boot,' he said.

The memory of that meeting smouldered between them.

'Serves you right for standing so close.'

Amusement flashed in his eyes. 'Every coffee drinker knows you step to the side when you're done. That's how I know you're a caffeine fraud.'

She couldn't stop the laughter.

At the corner of Collins and Seafare Lane, they stopped to wait for the green man while others passed them. She suspected he was on his best behaviour because he knew she was the kind of girl who followed the rules. A tram rang its bell at the intersection before whooshing past them towards the city. The red man turned to green, but as Ella went to step out, Dax caught her by the wrist and pulled her back. A cyclist passed so closely that Ella's hair went up in a swirl of wind.

'That's a red light, arsehole,' Dax called after him, keeping a hold of her wrist. She felt hot and cold all at once as she stared down at the hand wrapped around her. Only when he was sure the road was clear did he release his grip on her. 'Let's go.'

When they reached Bourke Street, Dax leaned across

her to press the button, eyes meeting hers. 'Better look before crossing this time. Not everyone follows the rules like you, Miss Lewis.'

'Wow, you really have me pegged. The good girl vegan.'

He leaned against the pole as they waited for the lights, regarding her with open amusement. 'Nah. Good girls don't work at Bass Fuel. Good girls care about the planet.'

'*I* care about the planet.' When he didn't reply, she added, 'I read Bass Fuel's 2019 sustainability report before I agreed to the interview.'

He laughed in response.

The light turned green, and she looked both ways before stepping forwards. 'Out of curiosity, Mr Environment, what do you drive?'

He glanced sideways at her. 'An Outlander.'

'And does it run on water?'

He continued to check for cars as they crossed. 'It's a hybrid, if that's your angle.'

He had to be lying. Tradies didn't drive electric cars. They bought the biggest petrol-guzzling utes they could afford.

'How do you feel about Vietnamese food?' Dax asked, changing the subject. He stopped in front of a narrow restaurant directly opposite the water.

Ella looked through the window at the small tables lit up by tea lights. 'It looks awfully romantic for a casual dinner.'

'I can tell stories from work and eat with my fingers if you think it'll help.'

She took in his playful expression. 'That could help.'

He stepped up to the door and held it open for her. When they entered, a smiling woman approached with menus in hand.

'Two people?'

Dax nodded, and the pair followed the woman over to a

table by the wall. Ella hung her handbag over her chair and removed her blazer before sitting. She wore a long-sleeve floral print shirt tucked into high-waisted trousers.

'Drinks?' the waitress asked.

Ella ran her eyes over the drink list. 'I'll have a Little Creatures Pale Ale.' When she looked at Dax, she found him watching her with an expression she couldn't read. 'What?'

'Nothing.' He glanced up at the waitress. 'I'll have the same.' When the woman left, he said, 'I hope you're not drinking beer for my benefit.'

'I didn't know you drank beer when I ordered.'

He smiled at the table. 'Fair point.'

'I've always liked it, just don't drink it very often.'

He studied her. 'It's been on the restricted list for a while?'

'Something like that.'

He pushed one of the menus towards her. 'Is there anything you don't eat?'

Her knees brushed his under the table. 'Preferably nothing labelled "meatball". I prefer to know what type of animal I'm eating—and what part.'

He laughed quietly. 'Well, I don't eat seafood, but you go ahead.'

Ella looked up at that. 'Really? No fish? Prawns?'

'Well, they're both seafood, so...'

Her cheeks coloured. 'I was just checking you meant all seafood. I once knew a vegetarian who ate chicken. Apparently poultry didn't count.'

Dax smiled, and her gaze fell to those pearly teeth of his. The waitress arrived with their beers and set the bottles down before rushing off again.

'Did you want a glass?' Dax asked.

Ella picked up her drink. 'I can drink from the bottle, but thanks.'

Dax clinked his drink to hers, and they watched each other as they took their first sip.

'Are you allergic?' Ella asked. She had come across an interesting fact about merfolk during her research earlier. They considered fish to be sacred.

He placed the bottle on the table. 'No. It's not an allergy.'

'Do your friends eat it?'

'You mean my fellow cult members? No.'

She smiled but watched him closely for signs of discomfort. 'What about doves? Do you eat doves?'

He angled his head, laughter in his eyes. 'Weirdly, no. And before you ask, none of my friends do either.'

'Is that because they're holy?' She had also read that merfolk ate all fowl except doves.

He leaned back in his chair, stretching his long legs out next to hers. She could feel the heat from them.

'Where are you going with these questions?'

Ella's heart sped up. She really wanted to just ask him, see his genuine confusion to the question so she could dismiss the ridiculous idea Lucy had put in her head, the idea that grew roots when she witnessed Peter spilling water over himself with no idea how it happened. And then there was the image of Dax *underwater,* watching her. But what was she supposed to say? 'Are you a sea creature? Do you have a water superpower?' He would think her crazy, get up from the table, and leave her there.

'I was just curious,' she replied.

Her eyes went to the glass jug of water sitting between them. Perhaps there were better ways to get answers. She reached for it, lifting it higher than necessary. Then, as it hovered near his empty glass, she drew a breath and let go. The base hit the table, then bounced. Ella braced for the spill—but it didn't come.

Dax's hand flew up, and the jug stilled without him

touching it. It teetered on its edge, the water inside contained as though covered with an invisible lid.

Ella's hand was still outstretched, frozen in place, the other gripping the edge of the table. Her eyes snapped to Dax, who reached out and pushed the jug down until it was flat on the table. His fingers rested on the rim. Slowly, he lifted his gaze to meet hers.

'Okay,' said the waitress, stopping next to their table. 'What can I get you to eat?'

CHAPTER 11

S hit.
Dax looked into Ella's panic-stricken eyes. Her breaths were coming fast. 'We're going to need a few more minutes,' he told the waitress.

She looked between them before wandering away.

Ella's gaze moved back down to the jug of water between them. He could see her trying to make sense of what she'd just witnessed. He should've let it tip, like he'd done so many times before. He was usually smarter. But he had a habit of forgetting himself around her, of *being* himself around her.

And now he'd messed up.

'Did you...' Ella swallowed, unable to finish.

Dax was standing at a crossroads. One direction was honesty, betraying his pod, then watching Ella flee the restaurant as fast as those dancer legs could carry her. The other direction was lying to protect himself and his pod and hoping like hell she would be satisfied by the spin he fed her. They were both ends of sorts.

'Ella...' His words stuck also.

She searched his face, needing more words from him.

Truth. He knew it was truth.

'How did you do that?' she breathed out. When he didn't respond straight away, she whispered, 'What are you?'

He shifted in his chair, and she flinched. *Flinched*. 'I can't…' He couldn't lie, but he couldn't tell her the truth either. He'd be betraying his pod for a human he barely knew.

Ella reached for her handbag with trembling hands, pulled out her purse, and took out a twenty, dropping it onto the table.

'What are you doing?' Dax asked.

'I have to go.'

He reached across the table for her hand, but she shot up and drew back from him so fast that her chair fell backwards. 'Ella.' He waited for her to look at him, but she just bent to pick up the chair. 'Stay and talk to me.'

Now she looked at him.

'So you can lie some more?' She threw her blazer over her arm and flew past him.

Dax watched the note flutter across the table as the restaurant door opened and closed, foot tapping as he sat there trying to decide what to do next. Ella was smart. She would draw her own conclusions. Remaining silent would only serve as confirmation.

'Ready to order?' asked the host, appearing beside him once more.

He rose. 'Sorry.' Then he went for the door.

Dax jogged along Cumberland Street towards Bourke, spotting her up ahead, arms wrapped against the cold air and back to him. 'Ella!'

She didn't stop or look back.

He sped up, trying to catch her before she reached the main road. 'Ella, stop.'

Her feet stilled, but she didn't turn, eyes on the footpath.

He moved in front of her. 'Don't run from me.'

Her hands went over her face, then fell to her side. 'Give me something honest or I'm leaving.'

'Look at me.' He waited for her to lift her eyes to him, then struggled with what to say next. 'I told you it was complicated.'

'And I told you I couldn't do complicated. So why didn't you stay away?'

He hated the feeling of her slipping through his fingers, like he couldn't grasp her in that moment. 'You're right. I should've stayed away.'

'Instead, you come to my work dressed like'—she gestured with her hand—'like that, and say things, and make me feel things, and then *do* things that make me question what I'm seeing—again.' She put her hands over her eyes once more.

'All right. Please don't get upset. I can't see you upset, and I definitely can't be the reason you are.' When he went to remove her hands from her eyes, she drew back, increasing the distance between them.

'What are you?' she said. 'Why can you move things?'

He swallowed, closing his eyes for a moment. 'Water. I can only move water.'

She remained perfectly still, not speaking for the longest time. 'Why can you move water?'

Drawing a breath, he looked around. 'Can we go back to the restaurant? You're freezing.'

She shook her head. 'I'm not going anywhere with you.'

Slowly, Dax stepped forwards, reached for her blazer and wrapped it around her shoulders. Ella threaded her arms through the sleeves, eyes never leaving his.

'I googled merfolk today,' she said, watching his reaction closely.

'Guess that explains the dove question.'

'So you know what I'm talking about?'

'Sadly, yes.' He exhaled. 'I know what you're talking about. You going to tell me why you were googling merfolk?'

She finally looked away. 'Lucy said something earlier that stuck.'

'Yeah? What was that?'

'That not all sea creatures have fishy parts.'

He nodded. 'You mean, like a tail?' Even in the dark, he could tell she was blushing. She looked down at the footpath again to hide the fact. 'What if I told you there's some truth to all the crap you read today?'

Her eyes returned to him. 'I'd tell you that I'm listening.'

He knew what he was about to do would get him into a lot of trouble with his pod. But she deserved to know the truth. 'What do you know about ondines?'

'Ondines?'

'Ondines.'

She thought a moment. 'I know Frederick Ashton produced it for the Royal Ballet in 1958.'

He breathed out a laugh. 'Of course you know all about the ballet. Never seen it, so I can't tell you how accurate it is.'

Ella moved her feet. 'An accurate depiction of what? Of you?'

He checked both ways down the street before continuing. 'Ondines have evolved over centuries. They mostly live on land now.'

'Is that what you are?' She seemed to be holding her breath. 'An ondine?'

He nodded, knowing his brother would kick his arse later. He heard her release the breath she'd been holding.

'And your friends?'

He'd really done it now. 'My *pod*.' He braced.

'Pod. Like a pod of dolphins?'

'Yeah, kind of.' He knew it could go either way at that point: she would either run or continue firing questions at him.

'Are you... similar to dolphins?'

'We're a lot closer to humans than dolphins. We certainly don't sleep in the water unless we have to.' He kept waiting for her to freak out and leave, but her feet stuck.

'But you can breathe underwater?'

'Yes.'

Her eyes moved over him. 'Where are your... gills?'

He couldn't help but smile at that question. 'They're not visible. We breathe through our skin underwater.'

A group of people turned down the street, and Ella moved out of their way. She crossed her arms and waited for them to be out of earshot. Dax resisted the urge to put an arm around her to keep her warm.

'Am I allowed to ask questions?' she said.

'No, but ask them anyway.'

She had to wait for another couple to pass before continuing. 'Some of them might sound stupid.'

'I'll allow stupid questions.'

She watched her feet a moment. 'Are your insides different?'

'You mean my organs?'

She nodded as she looked up.

'Sure, but most of the differences aren't visible. You'd have to be a doctor to notice anything strange. We have the same parts that you do.'

'Does your skin go wrinkly if you're in the water for too long?'

He bit back a smile. 'No.'

She looked down at his arm. 'Your skin feels warm, like mine.'

'It behaves like human skin out of the water, but I don't really feel the cold like you, and I'm more sensitive to heat in the summer. I can dehydrate easy enough.'

She took a moment to process that. 'What happens to your lungs when you go underwater?'

'Everything closes off—ears, nose, mouth.'

'What about your eyes? Do they have a special protective coating or something?'

He was actually impressed by that question. 'We have a second eyelid, but again, not visible to humans—unless you're an optometrist.'

'What do you do in that instance? What if you need glasses?'

'Ondines don't need glasses. Our eyesight is excellent. But in the case of an injury, there are two from our pod based in city hospitals.'

She watched him a moment. 'How many of your kind are there?'

'Around the world? Thousands. Bass Strait has around three hundred. Some live here in Melbourne, others in Tasmania. There are smaller groups in beach towns along the coast of Victoria.'

She frowned. 'So each pod has a section of ocean?'

'We all have territory we're responsible for.'

'You're territorial?'

He couldn't hold back the grin. 'Not in an aggressive way. We have friends in pods all around Australia and New Zealand, and they're welcome here anytime. It's more about being responsible for the water and its creatures.'

'Do they all look like you?'

He squinted down at her. 'What do you mean?'

'Like, do ondines in Africa look African?'

'It's not some white cult, if that's what you're asking.'

She didn't laugh.

'Just like humans, we travel, we meet ondines from

other countries, move, start families,' he said. 'Hurley's mother is originally from the South China Sea pod. She met his dad while travelling.' He skipped the part about them being mates because she didn't need more reasons to run.

Ella watched him with a thoughtful expression. 'Flathead Rig is in your territory.'

'Yes.'

She buried her hands in the pocket of her blazer. 'And you're responsible for the mess it makes.'

He nodded. 'That's right. We can taste the oil and VOCs in the water when there are leaks.'

'VOCs?'

'Volatile organic compounds. We don't need fancy testing equipment. We see the impact on marine life firsthand. Oil destroys the insulating ability of mammals and water repellency of birds, exposing them to hypothermia. Mammals, including us, inhale the oil and chemicals. It affects our lungs, immune function, even reproduction.'

Ella blinked at him for a moment, taking it all in.

'Bass Fuel keeps patching up holes,' Dax added, 'ticking all the boxes to pass the relevant safety inspections.'

'And what do you do that has Barry so wary of you?'

He gave a small shrug. 'Whatever we have to in order to protect the ocean. The rig should've been shut down years ago, but it's a cash cow.'

She nodded slowly. 'So Barry doesn't like you because you call him out on it.'

'I'm sure it's not the only reason.'

Ella watched him a moment. 'I guess that explains why your friends hate me. I literally work for the enemy.'

'They don't hate you. They're just worried because you... caught my attention.'

Her gaze moved over his face. 'Is that unusual for you?'

'It's unusual for our kind.'

'To mix with humans, you mean?'

He hesitated. 'To be drawn to a human in the way I'm drawn to you.'

'You mean *attraction?*'

The corners of his mouth lifted slightly. 'Attraction doesn't seem like an adequate word in this instance.'

She looked down again. 'Does Barry know what you are?'

Dax shook his head. 'Pretty sure he thinks I'm working with Greenpacific or something.' He watched as she processed that piece of information. 'Are you feeling better or worse now? I can't tell.'

'I don't really know.' She kept three feet between them. 'Can you move other liquids?'

'Depends on the water content.'

'Cordial?'

He laughed. '*Cordial?* Who drinks cordial nowadays?'

'I'm trying to get a sense of how much water,' she replied, colour in her cheeks again.

He didn't want to make fun of her questions or discourage her from asking them, so he tried to be serious. 'The lower the water content, the harder it is to move. It's also easier to move seawater than freshwater.'

She chewed on that lip of hers. 'The human body is made up of 60 percent water. Could you move me?'

'You? Maybe. Regular-sized people, not so much.'

She didn't laugh.

'We don't walk around pushing people over, if that's what you're asking.'

'You just make them spill water all over themselves?'

He looked away. 'The guy looked like he was hassling you.'

'His name is Peter. He's my ex, and I can handle him just fine without your help.'

Dax's eyes snapped back to hers. 'That guy's your *ex?*'

'Yes.'

He was quiet a moment. 'He looks younger than you, and that's saying something.'

She rolled her eyes. 'Here we go.'

'It's cool. When do you think he'll hit puberty?'

Ella's spine straightened even more, if that were possible. 'He's a dancer.'

'They don't grow facial hair?'

'It's called a close shave, and I still have more questions,' she said, feigning annoyance.

A smile tugged at his mouth. 'Fine. Go ahead.'

'Tell me about the rules. Will your pod be angry that I know about you?'

'Yes.'

She bit her lip again. 'So you'll be in trouble for telling me?'

He really wanted to ease that lip out of her teeth with his thumb. 'Honestly, I've been in trouble since the day you stepped on me in that cafe.'

She released her lip. 'Are you... allowed to be attracted to humans?'

'It's complicated.'

'Complicated.' She thought a moment. 'Tell me how it usually works with your kind. Do ondines tend to seek other ondines?'

'Yes.' That was his chance to explain the concept of mates, but he was sure it would scare her off.

'Is that to ensure the secret is kept safe?'

He nodded. 'That's one reason.'

'What are the other reasons?'

He sighed. 'There's not generally a need to look outside of the pod. Ondine females are... very alluring.'

'You mean beautiful?'

He squinted, growing uncomfortable with the shift in topic. 'Not just beautiful.'

'Good in bed? Strong swimmers? Temptresses of the sea?'

He suppressed a smile. 'Too much Wikipedia for you.'

Her expression remained serious. 'Are humans *less* alluring to an ondine?'

'I guess that depends on the ondine and the human.'

'Frankie is gorgeous.'

'She is.'

'All that blonde hair. And those legs.'

He watched her with open amusement. 'Sure, but she can't do jetés on the edge of the water.'

'Those were fouettés.'

'Right.' Frankie didn't make him laugh like Ella did, didn't smell like spring, didn't make his pulse race at the sight of her. No woman had ever come close to the tiny dancer interrogating him.

'Are there any of you—that is, ondines in the pod—in a relationship with a human?'

He wished he had a different answer. 'It happens from time to time, but they don't tend to be very successful.'

'You mean they break up?'

How to answer something she couldn't possibly understand. 'Let's just say the sea always calls its creatures back.'

'What does that mean?'

He thought about the best way to explain it. 'Think of it like karma, but instead of a balance between good and bad intent, it's a balance of sea and land.'

Ella nodded. 'And a relationship with a human throws that balance?'

'That seems to be the case historically. Doesn't mean it's forbidden.'

'Just strongly discouraged?'

When he didn't reply, she looked at him with a heavy expression. Dax's gaze fell to the goosebumps peppered across her neck and collarbone. 'I think I've laid enough on you for one night. Please let me feed you before you freeze to death. I know a place that does great dove.'

She wasn't even close to smiling. He wished he could crawl inside her mind and see all of her thoughts playing out.

'I want to go home,' she said quietly, arms still crossed tightly in front of her.

He gave her a resigned nod. 'Then I'll take you home.'

CHAPTER 12

*T*he smart thing for Ella to do was stay away from Dax Coburn. It would be better for both of them if she could, but she found herself unwilling to cut the cord. He filled her thoughts in the days that followed their almost-dinner, and new questions swirled in her mind until she felt compelled to ask them. She didn't do it face to face though. She didn't even pick up the phone. She sent them in a text—like a coward. He had put his number in her phone when he dropped her home, never asking her if she wanted it.

Ella: What happens if you stay out of the sea too long?

Dax: I combust into flames.

Ella: *rolling eyes emoji*

Dax: I start to feel unwell, tired, weak. Like if you were to not eat for a few days.

When she didn't respond, Dax texted with a question of his own.

Dax: Tacos. Soft or crunchy?

Ella: Soft. You don't want to see me eat crunchy tacos.

Dax: Now I do. Cats or dogs?

Ella: Dogs. Turtle or octopus?

Dax: You're a funny lady, Miss Lewis :)

It was a few more days before Ella received another text. She was sitting alone on the lawn outside of her building, choosing spring sunshine over queuing for food, when she heard her phone ding. It was from him.

Dax Coburn.

Construction worker, closet engineer, environmentalist, her boss's nemesis, driver of a hybrid, creature of the sea, and heart thief.

Dax: How brave are you feeling right now?

Ella knew if she just started ignoring such messages, she stood a chance at severing that cord.

Ella: Never very brave when it comes to you.

So why did she keep replying?

A phone beeped nearby, causing her to turn and look. And there was Dax, standing a few metres away, watching her.

'Have you eaten already?' he asked, not moving.

She pushed herself up to standing, her insides singing at the sight of him, drowning out the sound of alarm bells. 'I'm not hungry.' She looked him over, from his messy hair peppered with debris all the way down to his filthy boots. He was an alluring mess.

'Were you just checking out my disproportional calves?'

His grey eyes were as clear as the sky as they met hers. She felt the beginnings of a smile, but before it had a chance to take flight, she spotted his friends approaching, Frankie among them. The change in her expression made Dax glance over his shoulder.

'Ah, the pod effect.' He studied her face. 'I don't suppose you want to eat with us?'

Ella's eyes widened slightly. 'Oh.' That explained the text message. The answer was, of course, no. What she wanted was to avoid their scrutiny forever. She certainly wasn't feeling that brave. 'Okay.'

Clearly she was spiralling.

'Only if *you* want to,' Dax said, seemingly surprised that she agreed. 'Can't guarantee someone won't say something stupid.'

'And I can't guarantee I won't beat them to it.'

Light filled those eyes of his, and it thrilled her that she was the reason for it.

'Hey,' Miller called, food already in hand. 'You coming?'

Dax turned to the curious faces behind him, all focused on the human. 'We'll meet you there.'

Ella suspected Dax hadn't consulted them on his plus-one for lunch plans. She watched as the pod exchanged cautious glances, while Frankie looked only at her, eyes like two green flames. She clearly knew Ella had learned their secret—and she was not happy about it.

'See you down there,' said the other woman in the group, casting a sympathetic smile in Ella's direction.

It was the first nice gesture from any of them.

Ella stared down at the ground as the group headed towards the water.

'You're nervous,' Dax said quietly as he started walking slowly in the direction of the cafe. 'Don't be nervous.'

Ella looked up at him. 'This is a bad idea.'

'So why did you say yes?'

'For the same reason you asked me in the first place.'

They barely spoke as they ordered and waited for their food before heading down to the water. Ella's heart sped up as they descended the ramp to the small wharf, where the rest of the pod had stripped off their shoes and socks.

Miller looked up as she sank down beside Dax, then said with a sigh, 'I guess we better do introductions.' He pointed to the others. 'Adrian, Hurley, Greta, Frankie.'

'And this is Ella,' Dax said, getting comfortable.

Ella raised a hand. 'Hi.'

Frankie looked away. 'Can we eat now? I have to get back to the office.'

Dax shook his head, eyes meeting Ella's. They held an apology, as if Frankie's words were his fault somehow. She could feel them watching her every move. To make matters worse, Dax didn't remove his boots like normal, instead stretching his legs out on the wharf as he unwrapped his sandwich.

Ella leaned in and whispered, 'Are you supposed to put your feet in?'

He took a bite of his sandwich. 'It's fine. I'll swim after work.'

Miller stared hard at his food while the others looked away, except Frankie, who looked straight at them. 'This is how it starts,' she said, 'and we all know how it ends.'

'Jesus,' Dax said. 'Stop being so dramatic.'

He was trying not to make Ella feel like the odd one out, but the thought of him becoming unwell or tired because of her was ruining her already poor appetite. Putting her salad down, she slipped her shoes off and began rolling up her pants.

'What are you doing?' Dax asked, agitation in his voice.

She shuffled forwards to the edge of the pier and tentatively lowered her feet in the water. 'Just seeing if it's as cold as it looks.' She sucked in a breath. 'And the answer is yes.'

With a sigh bordering on a growl, Dax moved to sit beside her, took off his boots and socks, and dropped his feet into the water before snatching up his sandwich again. 'Take your feet out before they fall off.'

She shuffled back so they hovered above the water.

'Dax tells us you're a ballet dancer,' Greta said, braving small talk after an awkward silence.

Ella lowered her salad to her lap. 'I used to dance for the Melbourne Ballet Company.'

'And now she dances for Bass Fuel,' Frankie said, sounding pleased with her wit.

Dax straightened, but before he could say anything, Miller said, 'We all went and saw *Swan Lake* last year—even Dax.'

Ella was surprised he hadn't mentioned it. She tried to recall which company had done *Swan Lake* that year and came up blank.

'A different dance company,' Adrian said, grinning.

Greta shook her head.

'Which one?' Ella asked.

'Bambi Ballet in Port Melbourne,' Greta said. 'Our three-year-old daughter goes there.'

Ella smiled, relaxing for the first time. '*Swan Lake* starring toddlers must've been very entertaining.'

'Oh, it was entertaining all right,' Greta agreed.

Adrian chuckled. 'Ariel spent more time waving at us in the audience than actually dancing.'

'Your daughter's name is Ariel?' Ella asked.

Frankie looked in her direction. 'Is that a problem?'

Ella's cheeks heated. 'No. It's a beautiful name.' *The Little Mermaid* reference had just tripped her for a moment. 'I once played Ariel in a performance at uni.'

Frankie picked up her drink, eyes never leaving Ella. 'You playing a mermaid. Hard to imagine.'

Dax cast a warning glance in her direction.

'To be fair,' Miller said, 'there's some irony in that.'

'She's been dancing all her life,' Dax said. 'She's probably played all types of mythical creatures, princesses, and animals.'

Ella looked up at that. 'Animals?'

He shrugged. 'Swans and shit.'

Ella frowned as the others laughed. 'Swans and shit?'

'You know what I mean,' Dax replied, quieter this time. '*The Nutcracker* has a Mouse King.'

Miller and Hurley exchanged a look.

'Since when do you know shit about *The Nutcracker*?' Hurley asked, holding back laughter.

'I read it when I was googling ballet.'

That made Ella much happier than she cared to admit. 'I played the Mouse King when I was eight,' she said. 'I got tangled in my tail on stage and collided with the Sugar Plum Fairy.'

Everyone laughed—except Frankie.

'I'm sure you were the perfect mouse,' Frankie said, 'given your size.'

'Be nice or leave,' Dax said, his tone clipped.

Ella changed the subject. 'Do you guys do any water sports outside of swimming?'

'We all surf,' Hurley said. 'And jet-ski. Anything that can be done in the water, we've tried it at some point.'

'And we kayak,' Miller added. 'Mostly in summer, when it's too busy to swim far out without being noticed.'

'We like to paddle out until there's nothing but sea in all directions,' Greta said. 'It's bliss.'

'I get that,' Ella replied, nodding.

Frankie laughed through her nose. 'No you don't.'

Dax levelled a look at her.

'Everyone has their means of escape,' Ella said. 'Dance is to me what I imagine water is to you. A constant draw, an immersive experience, a daily baptism. Addictive. Medicinal. And a curse at times.'

Everyone was staring at her like she had spoken in tongues, except for Dax, whose face held pure affection.

Greta lifted her juice in a mock toast. 'I couldn't have described it better myself.'

Frankie's gaze slid to Dax. 'You have yourself a true poet.'

Ella let the sarcasm blow past her.

'Dax says you live in Williamstown,' Miller said. 'Great beach there.'

Ella poked at her salad. 'Yeah. It's pretty popular.'

'I'm surprised we haven't run into you there before.'

Ella reached for her drink, her mouth turning dry. 'I don't really swim there.'

'You don't?' Dax asked. 'Not even in summer?'

Ella blinked away the image of her lifeless mother laid out on a hospital bed. 'I'm not really a beach person.'

Silence rang out around her. Of all the things she could've said in front of a pod of ondines, that was probably the worst.

'Let me guess,' Frankie said. 'You don't like the way the sand sticks to everything?'

The doctor's sombre face flashed in Ella's mind, that moment when he pulled back the curtain and met her gaze before looking up at her father.

I'm so sorry.

Her father had caught her when her legs failed her for the first time in her dancing life. It wouldn't be the last time though.

Dax leaned in and whispered, 'Hey, you okay?'

She couldn't quite meet his eyes. 'Williamstown has a great outdoor pool.'

The others slowly returned to their food while Dax continued to watch her.

'Ella' came a voice from the path.

She knew it was Peter before she laid eyes on him. She sat frozen as he waved a beautifully defined arm at her. Then, drawing her legs in, she snatched up her shoes, knowing she needed to get to him before he reached her.

With her heart racing once more, she shoved her still wet feet into her flats. 'I should… It was nice meeting you all,' Ella said, grabbing her handbag and shoving the salad container into it.

'You too,' Greta said, eyes drifting in Peter's direction.

Ella flew up the ramp before Dax had even figured out what was happening and went straight up to Peter, ushering him in the other direction.

'What are you doing here?' She tried to keep her tone friendly, but it bordered on hysterical.

'I went to your work, hoping to catch you at lunch.' His gaze shifted to the pod. 'Are they friends of yours?'

'Yes.' A lie. She risked a glance at Dax and saw he was now on his feet.

Peter took a firm hold of her arms, visibly excited. 'How would you like to return to dance in a big way?'

Ella's mind tripped. 'What?'

'As artistic coordinator.' He said the words as if he were offering her the world. 'I literally just found out that Meaghan is pregnant and will be going on maternity leave in four months. They haven't advertised the role yet, and I told them not to bother because I knew the perfect person.'

Ella stopped walking, feeling sick and angry all at once. 'You want me to fit shoes?'

'It's such an important support role, as you know.'

Ella looked down. 'I already have a job.' She couldn't return to Melbourne Ballet for any other reason than to dance. It would be torture, and she was surprised Peter didn't understand that.

He tipped her face up so she was forced to look at him. 'I know it's not the same as being onstage, but you can't work in the fuel industry. It's laughable.'

She stepped back from him, though it was more of a stumble. A warm hand caught her arm, holding her steady. She looked up to see Dax.

'You okay?' he asked.

No, she was not okay. 'Fine.' She should've used another word. 'Peter, this is a friend of mine, Dax.' Friend seemed like an odd word, but it was all she had.

Peter looked Dax up and down like one does an ill-fitting suit before extending a hand. Dax reluctantly took it.

'I thought I knew all of Ella's friends,' Peter said. 'You an actor?'

Ella inhaled. 'Dax isn't a performer.'

Peter looked immediately suspicious. 'Writer?'

Ella closed her eyes.

'Construction,' Dax said, releasing Ella's arm.

She knew Peter would have a field day with that, so she added, 'He studied engineering at uni.'

Dax leaned away from her. 'But I work in construction.'

Peter nodded. 'Well, that must keep you fit.'

'Among other things.' Dax didn't sound particularly friendly. 'What brings you to Docklands?'

'I had a proposal for Ella.'

She suspected he was being intentional with his word choice, but Dax didn't react.

'It's confidential,' Peter added.

Ella drew a breath. 'Listen, can I call you later?' she said to Peter. 'I have to get back to work.'

He watched her a moment. 'You're really not going to jump on this?'

She shook her head. 'I'm really not, but I appreciate you thinking of me.'

Peter glanced at Dax as he shifted his weight. 'I haven't forgotten about *Giselle*. I'll send you a ticket when we open.'

Ella nodded. 'Great.'

Peter still didn't leave. 'Want me to walk you back?'

'I'll walk her back,' Dax said, making it very clear it wasn't open for debate.

Peter kissed Ella's cheek, then finally turned and left. She watched him until he was out of sight, then turned to face Dax.

'Who's Giselle?' he asked.

She suppressed a smile. 'It's a ballet.'

'Oh.' Dax uncrossed his arms and hooked his thumbs in his pockets. 'I'm still trying to get my head around you with that guy. He's a bit of a wanker.'

She laughed. 'You can't say that.'

'Why not?'

'Because…' She didn't really have a good reason. 'Because your ex is a bit of a wanker too.' She bit her lip. 'But please don't tell her I said that.'

Dax breathed out a laugh, relaxing again. 'I'm sorry about her. I was hoping she'd be better behaved.'

Ella waved him off. 'I've spent my entire life around competitive and jealous females. Dance schools are full of them. I've developed a rather thick skin.'

They were both silent a moment.

'Frankie and Peter in one lunch break was ambitious,' she said, attempting a smile. 'She's clearly still in love with you.'

Dax squinted at the ground. 'We were absolutely terrible together. Our parents are close friends, and they made no secret of the fact that they wanted it to happen.'

'So you gave it a go for them?'

'Obviously wish I hadn't now.' He paused. 'This is the part where you tell me Peter was a mistake and list all the reasons why so I feel better about hating him.'

'You don't even know him.'

'I know he's always got his fucking hands on you.'

It was wrong, but the jealousy pleased her. 'We did our master's together, were partners for years before we started dating. That kind of familiarity doesn't just go away.'

Dax's jaw ticked. 'Now I hate him even more.'

'Why?'

'Because he basically gave you dancing, and I can't compete with that.'

She bit back a smile. 'I gave *myself* dancing, and while I don't have a big list of faults, I can tell you the relationship was all about him and his career. I was just there to make him feel good about himself.'

Dax searched her eyes. 'That does make me feel better.'

She laughed quietly.

'If you belonged to me,' he said, expression serious now, 'you'd always be centre stage.'

Her smile widened. 'Oh my God. Did you just use a dance metaphor?'

'I had it saved up for this conversation.'

'The *ex* conversation?'

'The "what the hell are we going to do now" conversation.'

She was no longer laughing. 'Have you imagined it? What we would be like together?'

'Only most days.'

She reminded herself to breathe. 'And?'

He looked in the direction Peter had walked off in. 'And then I check myself.' He drew a breath before continuing. 'It's not only the human-ondine thing. Girls like you don't date guys like me.'

'You mean guys with big calves?'

He didn't laugh. 'Construction workers. That's why you told perfect Pete that I studied engineering, isn't it?'

She hadn't been expecting that.

'It's fine,' he continued. 'There's a hundred things against us, and your snobbery is quite far down the list.'

Her mouth fell open. 'I'm not a snob.'

'Yes you are, but that's okay. I happen to like that about you.'

She closed her mouth. 'So, where does that leave us? We just stay as we are?'

There was amusement in his eyes. 'Where's that exactly?'

A very good question. 'Friends?' It came out more of a question than a statement.

'You think we're friends? You think what I feel for you, how I *am* with you, can be reduced to friendship?'

So much for cutting ties. She was swooning like a twelve-year-old girl at a Bieber concert. 'I don't know. I mean, this past week, we've barely been talking—'

'*You've* barely been talking.'

'You kind of dropped a grenade on me.'

'You took it from my hands and pulled the pin yourself.'

Her hand went to her forehead as she drew a calming breath. 'I tend to think ahead—far ahead. It's a dancer problem. We've got no idea how to live in the present because our entire futures are planned out from puberty.'

'Why puberty?'

She shifted her weight. 'It's when you know what your body's going to do. Some girls go up, some out. Some get a little... top heavy.'

His gaze swept over her. 'And you got perfect?'

'Well, I certainly didn't get top heavy.'

He breathed out a laugh, and they both relaxed a little.

'I should go up.'

He nodded. 'For the record, I think ahead too. I know the logical thing to do here'—he brushed a finger down his nose—'but you're not easy to walk away from.'

Just the mention of him walking away made her stomach drop. 'As much as I'd like to stand here and pretend I'm all casual and go with the flow, I'm really not.'

'Okay.'

'I understand guys like you don't wait around for girls.'

'Guys like me?'

She didn't know why she said that. 'I just meant if you're seeing other people, or other ondines—'

109

'What?' He laughed. 'What are you talking about? I can't see past you.'

The relief was instant. 'Oh.'

'I'm trying to be careful, respectful, and not mess up that tidy little life of yours.'

'Too late.'

His eyes moved between hers. 'Honestly, I'm waiting for you to tell me to piss off, but you haven't said it yet, which gives me hope.'

'And I don't want to be the human who messes up an ancient culture.'

His eyebrows rose. 'That's what you're worried about?'

That and having her heart completely crushed by the man with a firm grip on it. What was it he said? The sea always called its creatures back. There were some things she couldn't quite grasp, so she would need to trust him.

She held her breath when he stepped closer, his enormous hand cupping her face. The sensation crawled along her scalp. She thought he might kiss her, then saw the torture of restraint play out on his face.

'Just don't go running back to pre-puberty Pete while we figure this out,' he said, hand falling away.

She released the breath she'd been holding. 'I'm not running.'

CHAPTER 13

*D*ax ate lunch with Ella every day for the rest of the week, just the two of them, because he didn't trust Frankie to behave around her. They sat in another part of the bay, where Dax's feet could reach the water. He asked her about Lucy, dance, and all the plans she'd made before her body had given up. He expected her to drill him with questions about ondines, but all her questions related directly to him: his experience growing up with such a big secret, whether he fit in at school, and if he ever cheated at swimming carnivals. He told her stories from his teen years, and one of them made her laugh so hard she actually cried. Dax sat captivated by the sight of her head tipped back, mouth open, and wind blowing her hair over her face. She didn't smooth it back like normal.

The ballerina had left the stage.

That was all they did that week: talk, watch each other, and laugh. By Friday, they sat with their thighs touching and arms bumping. It was like his body sought hers whenever they were together, and hers just played right along. He had no idea what it meant, what they were to each other—he just knew he didn't want it to stop.

Their week should've ended there, but after a swim and shower, Dax headed back to Docklands to wait outside Ella's building. He was heading to his parents' house for the weekend and was hoping to steal a few final moments with her before he left. They would be making plans for Flathead Rig—plans Ella would never be privy to.

He waited across the road, watching the automatic doors of her building open and close. She would head up Collins Street to meet her father; he knew because he'd been working later the past few days so he could catch her as she passed. He liked to make sure she got there safely, despite her telling him every time that she was quite capable of walking a few blocks without supervision. He would dispute that by bringing up the close call with the bicycle. Just the thought of her getting run down was enough to make him break out in a sweat.

The week had given Dax hope that maybe they could work somehow, but he was still trying to figure out what that would look like. It was a harsh life to inflict on her. A bit like dating a severe diabetic. The sea was his insulin, and the pod was his family—his *priority*. She would always feel like an outcast, like she was second to them. And the secret would weigh her down, possibly erode her other relationships.

It was inevitable.

She couldn't tell her father, her best friend, not even her shrink if she saw one. The possibility of the pod rejecting her for the smallest mistake would play constantly on her mind. There would be times he would be forced to choose, and he'd seen first-hand what happened to his kind when they chose wrong.

The doors across the road swung open once more, and Ella stepped through them. She looked both ways, her lip clamped between her teeth. He just watched her for a moment, wondering if she could feel his presence the way he seemed to sense her when she was nearby. She looked across the road, eyes meeting his, and a smile spread across that beautiful face. His temperature rose in response. The same thing had happened earlier that week at the mere thought of kissing her. She was ready, willing, but he knew there would be no turning back once he *tasted* her.

Dax didn't move straight away. He let the elation wash through him, savouring the intense magnetic draw Adrian had once described when speaking about mates. Dax had met more female ondines than he could count and had never felt anything more than mild attraction. Never anything like this.

He pushed off the wall and crossed the road towards her, jogging to beat an oncoming tram. She stood still in the middle of the footpath, waiting. That honey brown hair of hers was swept back into a neat bun, so she was all blue eyes and pink lips. He shoved his hands into his jean pockets to stop from reaching out and touching her face.

'Aren't you cold?' she asked, pulling the collar of her coat up against the sea breeze.

He noticed she didn't ask what he was doing there. She didn't need to. 'This weather's perfect for me.' He looked up the street. 'You meeting your dad?'

She nodded and started walking, accepting him as escort without any fuss. 'How was work?'

'Productive. You?'

'Also productive.'

'That's all I get?'

She glanced up at him. 'I'm not feeding you information about Barry or the company, if that's what you're holding out for.'

'In that case I'll head off.'

She jabbed him lightly with her elbow.

'For the record, I don't think your future's in fossil fuels,' he told her.

'That so?'

He watched her a moment. 'Surely there are jobs in the arts you'd be better suited for.'

'This might be hard for you to understand, but it's not easy working closely with people who are living out your dreams in front of you.'

'Like a former heroin user watching his friends shoot up?'

Ella laughed. 'That's a very dark example but fairly accurate.'

He loved the way her cheeks flushed in those moments.

Conversation bounced back and forth all the way to the LMDC building, where her father worked. Dax stopped short of the door, and Ella turned to him.

'Do you want to meet him?' she asked, sounding unsure.

'You want me to meet your dad?'

Her lip disappeared once more, the way it did when she was nervous or thinking. 'Not *meet him*, meet him, in that official way one meets the parents.' She cleared her throat. 'Just say hello because you're here and... actually, never mind.' She began backing away.

'Sure. I'll meet him.' Anything to stop her from retreating.

'Only if you want to.'

He wanted to make her happy, so that was close enough. 'Let's do this.'

They entered the foyer, and Ella texted her father as they took a seat. She was nervous, her finger tapping against her handbag as she watched the lift.

'You sure about this?' he asked.

She actually jumped when he spoke. 'What? Yes, of course. He'll be here in a sec.'

Her finger stilled when the lift opened and a man in his fifties stepped out, surveying the foyer. Ella stood, and Dax followed her lead, looking for similarities between the two of them and finding none. She must've looked more like her mother.

'There she is,' her father said before his gaze shifted to Dax. He managed to keep his smile.

Ella gestured to Dax. 'I thought I should introduce you to Dax since we've been hanging out a lot lately and you keep asking who he is.' Her tone was teasing. 'This is my dad, Michael.'

'Ah. So this is Dax.' Michael's eyes scanned the length of him. 'Do you work at Bass Fuel too?'

He likely already knew the answer to that by the way Dax was dressed. It was pretty clear he hadn't just come from an office job, but he played along for Ella's sake.

'Actually, I work for Coburn Construction.'

Michael's expression switched from curious to something else. 'I'm familiar with the company. How long have you been there?'

'Since I graduated. My parents own it.' He watched the colour leave Michael's face.

'Your parents own the company?'

'That's right.'

Michael blinked in surprise. 'Your parents are Irvin and June Coburn?'

Dax tried to predict where the questions were headed but came up blank.

'Do you know them?' Ella asked.

Michael found another smile for his daughter. 'Coburn Construction has been around for years. I think we pitched to them at some point.'

His eyes moved over Dax once more, as though searching for faults. Dax probably should've tied his hair back, but he hadn't planned on meeting Ella's father.

'I didn't realise you had friends in construction,' Michael said.

Ella's expression fell just a little. 'Dax is actually an engineer.'

Dax looked down as she tried to talk him up again. Clearly his occupation was an issue for her.

'Where did you study?' Michael asked.

He looked up. 'Deakin.'

'Which campus?'

'Burwood.'

Michael stared hard at him. 'What type of engineering did you study?'

'Dad,' Ella said.

Michael glanced at her. 'What? I'm not allowed to take an interest in your friends?'

Dax hated seeing Ella uncomfortable. 'Environmental engineering.'

'See?' Michael said. 'He doesn't mind.'

Dax turned to Ella, wanting to put her out of her misery. 'Listen, I have to head off.'

Her expression was apologetic. 'Thanks for walking me.'

'Anytime.' His eyes returned to Ella's father. 'Good to meet you.'

Michael nodded slowly. 'And you.'

When Dax arrived home, he found his parents seated on the couch opposite Miller. His mother rose and went to him, pulling him into a firm hug.

'We were just about to send a search party out. We've been waiting to eat with you.'

His dad stood to shake his hand. 'I told her we could eat without you.'

'Miller has just been filling us in on Melbourne news,' June said. 'He hinted at you having a new love interest but

116

wouldn't spill on the details.' She drew back to look at him properly. 'So it's really over with Frankie, then?'

Irvin shook his head. 'It's been over for some time, my love.'

June ignored her husband. 'So? Do tell.'

Dax glanced at his brother, who gave an innocent shrug. 'There's really nothing to tell. We're just friends.'

'Well, which pod does this *friend* belong to?' June pushed.

Irvin lowered himself back onto the couch. 'Why don't we wait until the boy is ready to share his news, hey?'

'Good idea,' Dax said, taking a seat next to Miller. 'How did it go out at Flathead?'

'Still leaking,' Irvin said. 'We could taste the change in the water twenty kilometres out from the rig. Plus, we came across some arctic terns and seagulls in the area with matted plumage and discolouring from oil.'

Dax looked between his parents. 'Sounds like it's time to step things up.'

'Meaning?' Miller asked.

'Meaning it's time to shine a spotlight on that piece-of-shit rig.'

His mother tutted.

Dax continued like she hadn't. 'Let's hit it so hard that VEPA and WorkSafe are crawling all over that joint like cockroaches.'

Irvin and June exchanged a concerned look.

'What?' Dax asked. 'You disagree?'

Irvin leaned forwards, resting his elbows on his knees. 'No one's disagreeing, but you can't afford to be spotted out in those waters. You need to stay on land and have an alibi outside of the pod. Any sniff that you were offshore when it happens and the police will be at your door.'

Miller nodded in agreement. 'You could hit the rig

Monday. Dax will be on-site, and there'll be a hundred workers to vouch for him.'

Dax hated that he would be making Ella's work life harder for a while. Maybe Barry would take his stress out on her.

He pushed the thought away. 'You need me there. My energy is stronger than all of yours combined.'

June's mouth flattened into a thin line. 'Excuse me?'

'It is.'

'It's grown, I'll give you that. But your father and I are still quite capable of making waves.'

'Sure, but we need the wave to reach the platform. You'll need help.'

'There are plenty of pod members able to lend a hand,' Irvin said.

'Hurley can go,' Miller offered. 'And I'm sure others will volunteer.'

June had fallen silent and was studying Dax closely. 'Something has shifted in you. I can sense it, a change in your energy. That can happen when a mate enters an ondine's life. It's like a testosterone surge.' She glanced sideways at Irvin. 'Do you remember our first few months as a couple?'

Miller brought a hand to his face. 'Can you not, please?'

'I second that request,' Dax said.

June leaned forwards. 'Now you *have* to tell us who she is.'

He thought about sidestepping the question again, but the problem with a pod was everyone knew everyone's business eventually—and there was no keeping it from his mother. He was dreading the look on her face that would follow his words. 'You don't know her.'

'We might.'

'You don't, because she's human.'

And there was the look.

'Human?' She glanced to Irvin, who stared down at the coffee table. 'Human?' she repeated. 'Why on earth would you get yourself mixed up with a *human*?'

Dax hated hearing Ella reduced to that word.

'Does she know what you are?' June asked.

Dax nodded, and the room fell silent for a moment.

'He didn't plan it that way,' Miller said, 'but it's done now. She's a nice enough girl, and Dax trusts her. That's the main thing.'

Irvin looked up. 'How long have you known her?'

'A few weeks.'

June's jaw dropped to her chest. 'A few *weeks*? You can't trust some girl after a few weeks.'

Dax drew a breath. 'The reveal wasn't exactly planned.'

More silence.

'How did you meet?' June asked.

Dax shrugged. 'We sort of just ran into each other.'

June crossed her legs and pressed her lips together. 'So you ran into a woman—a *human*—and weeks later, she knows our entire history.' She searched his face. 'It's not like you to be so reckless.'

That was true. It really wasn't.

'Not when you've kept that heart of yours so well guarded in the past,' June went on. 'Perhaps you're just upset things didn't work out with Frankie, not thinking clearly.'

Dax's head dropped. 'Christ, Mum. Let it go.'

'I'm just trying to understand. I mean, there's no future for the two of you. What's the plan when you come to your senses? Or when she does? Are you just going to hope she forgets?'

Dax exhaled. 'What would you have me do at this point?'

'End it,' June said. 'The sooner the better. Once there

119

are feelings involved, it gets messy very quickly, mark my words.'

Dax's feelings were so involved at that point he couldn't see past the fog of her. 'And what if she's my mate?'

Miller looked down at his hands, and his parents stared at him like he'd grown horns.

'You can't be serious,' June whispered. 'Your mate is still out there. Perhaps it's time you visited other pods, ventured out to sea for a while. You've been around humans too long.'

'Our kind have mated with them before,' Dax said.

June's expression was a plea. 'They're not love stories, they're tragedies. If you actually like this woman—which you clearly do if you're talking such nonsense—then the best thing you can do is walk away before she's left heart-broken, or worse, *grieving*.'

Dax stood. 'I think I'll go for another swim.'

'What about dinner?' June looked around the room for support.

He was already heading to the door. 'I'll eat later.'

CHAPTER 14

*E*lla had just slipped into leggings and a singlet when there was a knock at her front door. She had told Lucy she would meet her at the yoga studio, but it wasn't uncommon for her friend to get it wrong.

After tugging on a jumper, Ella tied her hair up as she walked. 'I said I'd meet you there,' she said as she pulled the door open and turned back to the kitchen. 'I just need to get my drink bottle. Come in.'

'I'm wet' came a voice that wasn't Lucy's.

Ella's feet stopped, and she turned slowly to look at the figure standing in the doorway. Sure enough, there was Dax, fully clothed and dripping. He rested an arm on the door frame.

'You going out?' he asked, pushing wet hair back from his face.

Her eyes travelled the length of him as she breathed out. 'Yoga.' She walked back towards him. 'Sorry. I thought you were Lucy.'

'Not Lucy.'

She stopped a few feet away from him. 'Do you normally swim fully clothed?'

'No.' He slid his arm down until his shoulder rested comfortably. 'What time does yoga finish?'

'Eight thirty, but I don't have to go.' She never missed scheduled exercise, but she also never had Dax show up like this. 'I'll get you a towel.'

He shook his head. 'Don't worry about it.'

She looked down at the pool of water forming at his feet. 'Is everything okay?

He was silent a moment. 'Do you want to come down to the beach?'

The correct answer was no. She hadn't stepped foot on that sand since she was ten.

'Yes.'

Then her traitorous mouth said that.

He extended a wet hand to her, an invitation to join him in the dark. She took it, and the contrast of warm skin and freezing water made her shudder. She slipped her house key into the inner pocket of her leggings and pulled the door closed behind them. She saw Dax glance back at the house as they exited the driveway.

'It needs a paint,' she said, reading his mind.

'These older houses come up great with a little love.'

She glimpsed his face as they passed beneath a street light. 'Lucy and I were going to do it last summer. Everything we need is sitting in the shed, covered in dust.'

He met her gaze. 'I can paint your house.'

She smiled at the footpath. 'I don't think I can afford you.'

'Don't tell anyone, but occasionally I work for food and beer.'

'I'll keep that in mind.'

They crossed Esplanade and walked over the soggy grass to the main beach. Teenagers sat in groups on the sand with half-drunk bottles of Coke and open parcels of fish and chips laid out on the sand between them.

Couples walked with dogs, and people jogged with AirPods tucked in their ears and phones hidden in secret pockets.

Ella looked down at Dax's bare feet, noticing them for the first time. 'Where are your shoes?'

'Port Melbourne Beach.'

Her eyes moved up his rolled pants and wet T-shirt sticking to his muscled body like a second skin. The man was in fine shape. Not surprising given his job. 'Hopefully they'll still be there when you get back.'

'Weirdly, not many people steal men's sneakers stuffed with dirty socks.'

'A dog might.'

He grinned and adjusted his grip on her hand. Her heart sped up when their feet hit the sand.

'Exactly how close to the water are we going?' she asked, trying to keep her tone casual.

He glanced down at her feet. 'You'll need to take your shoes and socks off.'

She slowed. 'We're going *in?*'

His eyes narrowed on her. 'You really hate the sand that much?'

'No one likes putting socks back onto sandy feet.'

He laughed quietly. 'Lucky for you, it's a short barefoot walk home.' He pulled up at the edge of the wet sand. 'Tide's going out. You can leave your things here.'

She looked out at the water, heart drumming away. It was probably time. She couldn't avoid the beach for the rest of her life.

'Are you… afraid?' Dax asked, angling his head to study her face.

It was terrifying how well he could read her.

'No.' Bending, she tugged her sneakers off and tucked her socks inside them. The sand was cold and unstable beneath her feet. 'Now what?'

Dax walked backwards into the water, gently pulling her along with him. 'You know you're safe with me, right?'

'I know.' Her feet just seemed to follow him, her eyes locked on his. She inhaled sharply when the water rolled up to meet her. Dax watched her with a serious expression but didn't stop. The bottom of her leggings soaked up water, and goosebumps prickled her skin.

'Exactly how deep are we going?' she asked as another wave rolled over them.

'Cold?'

Was she? Her fear seemed to warm her. 'I'm okay.' She matched him step for step until the water washed over her thighs, and then she stopped. 'I think that's deep enough for November.' It was deep enough for any month. She kept hold of his hand. 'Want to tell me why you swam to my door?'

He was still watching her with that serious expression. 'I don't think your dad likes me very much.'

She exhaled. 'Is that what this is about? He didn't like Peter either, and we were together for two years.' She tried to read him. 'Does it worry you? Because it shouldn't.'

'Not really.'

His expression was so troubled, she reached up to smooth the creased section of skin above his nose. His eyes closed when she touched him. When they opened, she saw a storm brewing in them.

'This doesn't make sense,' he said, fingers moving between hers.

'What doesn't make sense?'

He brought her hand to his chest. '*This*. This intense reaction to you.'

She flattened her palm against his chest and felt her own heart speed up in response.

'It's not just physical,' he went on. 'The way you fill my mind... it's distracting, consuming.'

Ella was no longer thinking about the water. She was completely focused on him.

'I'm not the jealous type,' Dax said, 'so why do I want to kick Peter's arse every time he looks at you for too long?'

'I feel it too—I just don't understand it.' She savoured the sensation of his heart beating against her hand. 'I thought it was lust, but now I'm not so sure.'

He moved closer, sending water swooshing higher up her legs. She sucked in a breath.

'I think lust is a symptom,' he said.

The only thing separating their bodies now was the hands between them. She let hers fall into the water. When she shivered, he drew her closer, and she leaned into the heat of his body.

Tipping her head back, she said, 'In dance, good partners can read each other's bodies, predict the other's moves, needs.' Her eyes sank shut as his large hands landed on her waist. 'This feels like that.'

'You're in trouble if you think I can predict your next move.'

A smile played on her lips. 'How are your lifts?'

'My *lifts?*'

She nodded.

He searched her face. 'I work with tools that weigh more than you.' Bending his knees slightly, he hoisted her up and out of the water. She squealed, then covered her mouth to hold it in. 'This seem right?'

She steadied herself. 'If you drop me, I'm never going into the water with you again.'

'I'm not going to drop you. Tell me what to do.'

She swallowed down her laughter and extended her arms. 'Okay. Can you move your hands to my hips?'

'Like this?' He tossed her slightly, catching her by the hips.

Another squeal escaped her, but she kept her body as straight as she could. 'Are you sure you have me?'

He lowered her slightly and rubbed his beard on the sliver of bare skin between her jumper and leggings.

'Stop! You'll drop me.'

'Never.' He raised her into the air once more. 'Now what?'

She pointed her toes and lifted her head. 'Now I fly.'

Her arms floated up and down, like elegant wings. She looked down at Dax and found him watching her with one of the most tortured expressions.

Her smile faded, and her hands went to his shoulders as he lowered her, gathering her in his arms instead of returning her to the water. There was no red face or shortness of breath from his lifting efforts, only desire.

Ella wrapped her legs around him, and she brought her face even with his. 'Why did you swim to my door?' she asked again.

His eyes reflected the dark water. 'I just... came for you.'

She ran her hands over the soft hairs at the base of his neck. Her gaze fell to his lips, so close to her own. Dax didn't move. He seemed to be waiting for her.

Slowly, she brought her mouth to his, brushing his lips lightly, then letting the sensation settle in her stomach, like hot tea on a freezing night. She licked her lips, tasting salt. He did the same, tasting *her*. She noted the change in his breath as he waited to see what she would do next. She kissed him again, firmer this time, drawing him closer. Dax's hand crawled slowly up her back, turning her spine to liquid. She pulled back to draw breath, to wait out the dizziness, but a heartbeat later, her mouth was on his again, her legs tightening around him. When his tongue brushed hers, her breath caught.

He stopped kissing her, pressing his forehead to hers as his breaths came fast.

'Sorry,' she said. 'It's a lot to feel all at once.'

'Do you want to stop?'

She shook her head.

Dax's mouth found hers again, opening as she curled her fingers like hooks in his hair. He bent his knees and lowered them into the water. Ella gasped as the cold swallowed her, pressing her body against his as she sought warmth. Strong arms encircled her, holding so tightly she could barely draw breath. But she never complained, willing him closer, fuller, hotter, harder. She wanted all of him, greedy for more sensation. If he had tried to strip her bare in the sea, she wouldn't have stopped him.

When Dax's mouth moved to her neck, she tipped her head back, encouraging him to explore the skin where her jumper hung from her shoulder. Her breathing changed the lower he went, and she struggled to keep her eyes open. At the same time, she wanted to watch his face, to gauge his desire. She needed to know if it matched her own. She straightened and met one storm cloud eye. The other was covered by hair.

Yes, his desire matched her own.

Dax tipped his head forwards, resting it on her shoulder. 'What are you doing to me?'

His warm breath made her shudder. 'I was going to ask you the same thing.'

They remained there for a moment, minds and hearts racing.

After a long time, Dax lifted his eyes to her. 'I don't think I can walk away now.' It almost sounded like an apology.

She loosened her grip on him. 'Did you want to walk away earlier? Is that why you came? To see if you could?'

He shook his head, but it wasn't overly convincing. 'No.'

'No?'

He drew her closer again. 'My parents are here. They said some things.'

'Oh.' She blinked. 'I gather they weren't good things.'

He looked ashamed, like he was somehow responsible for their reaction. 'Your lips are turning blue.'

She was shivering against him. Maybe from the cold, maybe from the possibility of losing him before she'd ever had him. 'The water's freezing.'

He kissed her forehead, her cheek. 'I'm going to walk you home, and then I'm going to leave.'

Her eyes searched his. 'You don't want to come in?'

There was that tortured expression again. 'Oh, I want to come in, but we need to tread really carefully.'

'Why?' She suspected she knew the answer but asked anyway.

He seemed to hesitate. 'Our kind aren't great at casual. Things can get serious very quickly. You just have to trust me on this.'

She buried her face in his neck and breathed out slowly. 'I trust you.'

CHAPTER 15

'Where were you on Friday night?' That was Lucy's first question shouted through the phone in place of a greeting.

'Sorry, I meant to call you back.' Ella kept her voice low as she stepped inside the foyer of her building. 'Something came up at the last minute. How was your weekend away with your aunt?'

'Good, I think. There was a lot of wine involved.' Lucy yawned through the phone. 'Were you, by any chance, with Dax on Friday?'

Ella's silence answered her question.

'I knew it. Did you... you know?'

Caleb must've been near her.

'No,' Ella replied. She wanted to though, even took a final try at luring Dax inside when they reached her house. 'Something big did happen though.'

'What?' The excitement in Lucy's voice was palpable.

Ella smiled into the phone. 'We went *swimming* at Williamstown Beach.'

There was a long silence on the other end before Lucy practically screeched, 'What? As in, you were in the water?'

'That is how one swims.'

'So for him you'll overcome your fears, but I have to swelter through every summer or brave the beach alone?'

'I didn't overcome my fear, I just… didn't feel it with him around.'

Lucy was quiet a moment. 'Is that your first beach swim since your mother passed?'

'Yes.'

'And you really didn't freak out in the water?'

'No. I mean, I was hesitant going in, but then he started talking. Oh, and he *lifted* me, just like we joked about.'

'He *lifted* you? Like a dance lift?'

'Yes.'

'And was it everything you imagined?'

Ella thought a moment. 'I mean, I would've rather not been facing one of my biggest fears at the time, or swimming in the very water my mother drowned in, and I would've preferred to have been on stage wearing pointe shoes and tulle, with Tchaikovsky playing… but it was pretty perfect, yeah.'

'I can hear you *smiling*.'

Ella stopped in front of the lift. 'I have to go.'

Lucy exhaled. 'I'm still adjusting to the idea of you smitten with a construction worker—'

'Technically he's an engineer.'

'Who works in construction. I know you like to pretend you're not a snob—'

'I'm not a snob.'

'All right, let's go with your version of the truth.'

Ella exhaled. 'I really have to go. I'm flying out to Flathead Rig today.'

'Just helicoptering about the place like it's no biggie?'

'To visit an oil rig, not attend a premiere.' She remained outside the lift because she knew her cell reception would cut out once she entered.

'Will you be at Pilates tonight? Or are you having another swim with water boy?'

Ella wished she could tell Lucy the truth about him, knowing she was the one person who would believe it. 'I'll be at Pilates.'

'Oh, before you go, did Dax reveal anything new about himself? Or is he still being cagey?'

Ella struggled to come up with a reply.

'Oh God,' Lucy said before Ella could say anything. 'Caleb found my mascara and has applied an astonishing amount to his lashes.'

'Ah—'

'And eyelids. And eyebrows. And cheeks. And all down the front of that T-shirt you bought him for Easter.'

'Which T-shirt?'

'It has two chocolate bunnies on the front. The one missing its arse says, "My butt hurts," and the other with no ears replies, "What?"'

Ella let out a disappointed sigh. 'Such a cute colour.'

'Agreed, but remember how disappointed he was when he opened the bag and found a T-shirt instead of chocolate? It really was such an Ella present.'

Ella paced in front of the lift. 'You told me the day before Easter you were worried about the amount of chocolate he'd eaten in the lead-up to the actual day. I was trying to be helpful.'

'Oh, is that your helicopter I hear flittering in the background?'

'No. And helicopters don't flitter, they whir. Kiss Caleb for me.'

~

'DO YOU HAVE A MINUTE?'

Dax looked up from his work and found Miller

131

standing there. He let the tape measure slide back into place and straightened. 'Yeah. Did you hear from them?'

It was the day their pod was due to swim out to Flathead Rig and bring some unwanted attention to Bass Fuel's star attraction. Dax wanted to join them but was forced to remain in Melbourne, in plain sight of other people the whole day. First sniff of trouble in those waters and the police always came knocking at his door.

'Just spoke to Dad,' Miller said. 'They're at White Beach. They're heading into the water soon.'

Dax exhaled and looked around. 'Okay. Keep me posted, would you?' He pulled his phone out of his pocket and dialled Ella's number.

'Who are you calling?' Miller asked.

'Ella.'

'Why?'

'Because we're sending a shitstorm her way, and I want to make sure she's okay before it hits.' He couldn't shield her from her job, but he could be there for her if she needed him. The guilt surprised him, the thought of making her life difficult weighing heavily on him.

'You can't say anything to her.'

Dax gave him a tired look. 'I know that.'

'She's a smart girl. She'll know something's up if you just call her in the middle of her workday for no reason.'

Miller was right, of course. 'I'm just checking if she's free for lunch.'

'She'll never make it to lunch. They're about to be in crisis control.'

Dax cursed when it went to voicemail. He dialled again and waited. Voicemail.

'She's at work,' Miller said. 'Just leave a message.'

Dax dialled again and left a message, Miller watching him the whole time. Probably fair. He couldn't be trusted when it came to her.

An uneasy feeling sat like lead in his gut, so he googled the number for Bass Fuel and rang the front desk.

'Bass Fuel, Susan speaking.'

'It's Dax Coburn calling for Ella Lewis.'

There was silence on the other end of the line. 'Did you say Dax Coburn?'

'That's right.'

'I'm sorry, Mr Coburn, Ella's out of the office today.'

He was immediately on edge. 'She sick?' They had texted the day before and she hadn't mentioned anything.

'They've flown out to Flathead Rig for the day. Barry had business there, and Ella's doing a tour of the rig.'

It was like someone had thrown ice over him. 'What?' Maybe he'd misheard.

'You're welcome to try her mobile, but the reception is terrible out at the rig. If you leave a message, she'll get it when she's back on land. Or I could leave a message on her desk if you like?'

'Ella's at Flathead Rig? You're sure?'

Miller shifted his weight.

'Just for the day,' Susan said, keeping a smile in her voice. 'Did you want me to leave a message?'

He was struggling to speak but knew it would look suspicious if he hung up or came apart on the phone. 'No. I'll… I'll leave a message on her phone. Thanks.' He hung up and immediately dialled his mother. No answer. 'Fuck.' He dialled his father. No answer. He tried Hurley, and then every other person he could think of who lived on King Island, but he knew they were already in the water.

'Don't get yourself worked up yet,' Miller said.

Dax handed the phone to his brother, then pulled his wallet and keys out of his pocket and did the same.

Miller looked down at the items in his hands, then back at him, his mouth pressed into a hard line. 'No you don't.'

'Ella's at the rig.'

'Yeah, I got that, but you can't go out there.'

Dax was already walking away, forcing Miller to jog after him.

'It's a two-hour swim. The others will beat you there,' Miller said.

'I can get there in an hour and a half.'

Miller grabbed his arm. 'You can't go out there without anyone knowing you're in the water. It's too dangerous.'

Dax turned, looking him straight in the eye. 'I don't expect you to believe me, but I think Ella's my mate.'

Miller blinked. 'She's not your mate. She's *human*.'

'You're just going to have to trust me on this.' He tugged his arm free and resumed walking, forcing Miller to run after him again.

'Can you just wait a second?' Miller said. 'Let me speak with Adrian. I might be able to come with you.'

'There's no time.'

'You can't go alone.'

He stopped walking. 'Will you just let me go before it's too late!' He let out a shaky breath. 'And keep calling the others. If by some miracle you get through, tell them it's off.'

CHAPTER 16

*E*lla held her breath as she was ushered out of the chopper and across the helipad. It took off again once they were standing in the safe zone. She watched it pass overhead, feeling oddly abandoned by the pilot.

'Don't worry. He'll be back,' Barry shouted over the noise as he guided her towards a waiting middle-aged woman. She wore red coveralls, her greying hair pulled back tightly, drawing attention to her weathered face. She greeted Barry with a warm smile before turning her attention to Ella.

'First time at the rig?' she asked.

Ella was put at ease by the motherly voice. 'Yes.'

'This is Karen,' Barry said. 'She's been with the Bass Fuel family for nearly twenty years. Best person to give you a tour of the place.'

Karen smiled appreciatively as she looked Ella over. 'Let's get you covered up. Though I'm afraid you're going to have to make do with rolled-up legs and sleeves. Tiny thing, aren't you?'

Story of her life. 'I'm used to rolling clothes up.'

'Right,' Barry said. 'I have a meeting in ten, so I'll leave you in Karen's capable hands.'

'Great,' Karen said, clapping her hands together. 'Follow me.'

They headed inside to a room where washing machines covered one wall and coveralls hung along another. Karen found the smallest size they had and handed it to Ella. 'This should do the job.'

Once Ella was dressed, they made their way out to the bridge connecting the two platforms.

'This sixty-metre bridge connects the two jackets of the rig,' Karen explained. 'There we have the wellhead platform, and the one we just came from is the central processing facility.'

Ella tried not to look down at the water. She wasn't afraid of heights, except when surrounded by nothing but ocean.

'The rig weighs seven hundred and fifty thousand tonnes,' Karen continued, 'and it's designed to withstand wave heights of over twenty-three metres.'

Ella could barely hear her over the noise of the rig and constant wind in her ears.

'It's pretty noisy here,' Karen said, reading her expression, 'but you get used to it. Barely notice it by the end of a three-week rotation.'

'Three weeks?' Ella asked. She couldn't imagine anything worse than being stuck in the middle of the sea for three weeks.

'There's plenty here to keep our workers entertained. Come. I'll show you.'

They left the bridge and made their way through a maze of corridors, where Ella got to see the gym, games room, and cinema room.

'Where do the workers sleep?' Ella asked.

'This way.'

They passed the muster station and foreroom on their way to the sleeping quarters.

'The rig has one hundred and eighty beds, but we're never at capacity.' Karen stepped aside to let some men pass. 'I'll show you the control room and meeting room, and then we'll head to the other platform, where the magic happens.'

When they were back on the bridge, Ella looked up at the tall crane perched above them. 'What's that used for?'

Karen looked up. 'It lifts large containers and drill pipes…' Her sentence faded out, and she stopped walking.

Ella stopped also, waiting for her to finish, but realised she was no longer looking at the crane. Her eyes were narrowed on something in the distance. Ella was about to ask if everything was all right when a loud siren rang out, causing her to jump.

Red lights flashed overhead.

'Let's go,' Karen said. 'We need to get off the bridge.'

All of Ella's senses seemed to heighten. 'Why?' Looking out, she saw what Karen had been transfixed on, and her heart stopped beating. A wall of water travelled towards the rig. 'Is that…' Ella couldn't even finish the question.

'It'll be okay,' Karen said, ushering her towards the wellhead platform. 'We're quite high up. I just need you to do exactly what I say.'

Ella recalled what she was told earlier. The platform could withstand waves of twenty-three metres. The Bass Strait never saw waves that high. So why had all the colour drained from Karen's face?

'Quickly now,' Karen said, moving faster.

'Is that a tidal wave?' Ella asked. 'Will it hit us?'

Karen's gaze kept returning to it. 'It'll likely flatten, but we need to be as high up as possible, just in case.'

Ella was slowed by the heavy coveralls. 'In case it reaches us?'

They made it to the wellhead platform, where men were running in all directions, securing equipment and shouting instructions. Ella's eyes were fixed on the wave, which only seemed to be growing taller.

'It's going to hit,' one of the men shouted as he ran past them.

Ella stood frozen, her heart pounding in her ears. She was going to die, to drown—just like her mother.

Karen tugged her over to one of the support beams.

'Hold on, and don't let go no matter what,' she instructed.

The siren continued to wail as Ella hugged the beam tightly and turned her face away from the wave.

'Incoming!' someone yelled.

'Where's Barry?' Ella shouted, but her voice was drowned out by the roar of water.

'Don't let go!' Karen said, one hand on the beam and the other on Ella.

Ella closed her eyes against the noise, wishing she could cover her ears. Her entire body shook as all shouting ceased, everyone holding a collective breath.

The steel beneath her feet began to hum, and a sob caught in her throat as she continued to hold tightly. Thunderous water rocked the platform, and Ella gasped as it pelted her relentlessly. She held her breath at first, but eventually she had to draw in air. Panic hit as water filled her nose and throat. An image of her mother laid out on bleached linen flashed in her mind, her long hair spilling over the edge of the bed, full of sand.

Ella reminded herself it couldn't go on forever.

It would end, and all the shaken workers would take care of each other. The helicopter would return and carry her back to land, and she would never go near the water again, no matter how divine the man luring her there might be.

A shout broke through the noise, and Ella dared a peek. She watched as Karen attempted to catch hold of something, slipped, and was washed across the floor at lightning speed. Instinctively, Ella let go of the beam and reached for her. Her own feet were washed out from beneath her just as she caught hold of Karen's coveralls. She slammed into the steel grate, and the fabric slipped from her hand as they were carried away by the water. Ella screamed when she saw Karen disappear beneath the rail of the bridge, maybe aloud or maybe only in her head. She reached for the rail as she was washed beneath it, but her fingers couldn't grip the slippery bar.

Her eyes widened as the floor disappeared beneath her and she fell towards the murky water below.

DAX WAS around a kilometre from the rig when he felt the shift in the water. His underwater calls had failed to reach his pod, and now it was too late.

The current began to change.

Dax surged ahead, his arms pinned to his sides and chest pressing forwards, propelling him faster. Fish darted away from him, and debris and seaweed swirled in his vision. It was the taste of the water that told him he was close to the rig—acidic and bitter. He thrust a hand out and watched as the water swirled violently in his path before rushing by him. Gritting his teeth as the steel frame of the rig came into view, he surfaced between the two platforms just as the sea collided with the structure.

Screams and shouts were absorbed by the blast of water. He raised a hand to guide it around him, creating a safe pocket as he looked around. He searched for her, listened for her voice amid the screams, felt for her with every sense available to him in the moment. The water level rose as the wave splintered around the rig. Dax used both hands to push back against it, kicking violently to get closer.

A scream made him look up at the bridge. And there she was, dressed in red coveralls, clinging to a beam like a frightened kitten. He had done that to her—and now his punishment was to witness her fear from afar.

His protective bubble broke simultaneously with his concentration, and the sea swelled, like it was raising him to her. He tensed as water pelted his face and smeared his vision. Then he lost sight of her. One second she was hanging tightly, and the next she was gone.

Gone.

He searched for her on the platform but knew there was no way she could move around in those conditions. He slipped beneath the surface, his hands cutting through the water as he tried to calm the angry sea. Something red caught his vision in the distance, and he swam towards it, knowing the risk. He should've swum in the other direction. If he was spotted, it would cause all kinds of trouble. But he couldn't swim away, because the something red was Ella thrashing in the water, hair ballooning around her as she was rolled by the wave.

Dax shot forwards, using all his energy to hold back the aggressive current carrying her away from him. He reached out and caught her by the leg, dragging her to him. Confused, she kicked out as tiny bubbles rose from her mouth. He took a firm hold of her face, forcing her to focus on him. Her wide eyes locked on his, and she stilled. Only then did Dax extend a hand against the current, creating a cocoon for them. He brought his face close to hers, frustrated he couldn't communicate with her. Ondines used pulses of sound that humans heard as a whistle. He only had eye contact in that moment.

One hand held her while the other controlled the water

around them. He brought his mouth to hers and exhaled long and hard. She coughed, panicked, clearly not under-standing what he was doing. Dax pulled back and looked at her, eyes pleading. He couldn't take her to the surface, couldn't be spotted. She nodded as though reading his mind. Again he brought his mouth to hers, and this time she breathed air straight from his lungs.

They stayed that way for a full minute, drifting along the sea floor, his lungs working as one with hers while his skin drew oxygen from the water. The push-and-pull of air was perfectly balanced, even, steady. Ella felt like an exten-sion of him, and the idea of her being his mate didn't seem so ridiculous suddenly.

They were one.

Her complete trust in him in that vulnerable moment fuelled his protectiveness of her. She wouldn't die. Never in the water. Not while he was alive to breathe for her.

As the water began to settle around them, Dax slowly withdrew his energy to test their surroundings.

The wave had passed.

He continued to breathe for her as he pushed gently off the sea floor, feet paddling slowly as he carried her to the surface. He needed to do it slowly, give her ears a chance to adjust to the change in pressure.

They emerged beneath the bridge, Dax searching the platforms above while Ella took her first breath without him. She drew greedy lungfuls of air, not because she needed it but because that was what humans did when they surfaced. He slipped below the water as he guided her to one of the support beams, her fingers holding tightly the whole time, like he might disappear without telling her. When the beam was within reach, Dax tried to pull her hands from him, but she held him tighter.

'No,' she pleaded above him.

He surfaced, glancing above to ensure no one was there. 'You're okay. Grab hold of the beam.'

She didn't move. 'Where are you going?'

His chest tightened at the fear in her eyes, in her voice. 'I can't stay. They'll see me.'

'Please don't leave.' A few tears escaped.

He cupped her face, keeping his voice low and calm. 'You'll be fine—I promise. You're going to call for help, and they're going to come for you.'

Her blazing blue eyes searched his. Finally she nodded. 'All right.'

'I'm going to wait beneath you. I'm not leaving until you're safely in the chopper. Understand?'

She nodded, just barely, a few more tears rolling down her icy cheeks. Her lips were blue, and there wasn't a damn thing he could do about it.

Ella sucked in a breath when she caught sight of something behind him. Dax turned and spotted someone floating face down in the water.

Shit.

'Oh my God,' Ella breathed out, pushing off the beam. 'It's Karen.'

Dax caught her by the waist and dragged her back to the beam. 'Hold on and don't move.'

He slipped beneath the water and swam over to the woman. Her eyes were closed, and she wasn't breathing. Gently, he rolled her over and waited to see if she would start breathing on her own. When she didn't, he pressed his fingers lightly to her back, channelling a small amount of energy that made her lungs contract and stomach spasm. The woman began coughing up water. He held her steady as he slowly guided her over to Ella.

'It's all right,' he heard Ella say as she pulled the woman to her. 'Somebody help us!'

Dax sank deeper and waited.

'Help!' Ella screamed, her voice raw and laced with fear.

Dax circled below like a shark, fighting the urge to go to her, get her to safety himself.

'Down Here! Help us! Please!' Ella shouted.

Finally, boots pounded on the bridge overhead.

CHAPTER 17

*D*ax waited at the front entrance of the Royal Melbourne Hospital, one foot resting on the curved wall, watching as cars pulled up to drop and collect patients. He was angry—mostly at himself. Ella had been traumatised by a disaster he'd personally orchestrated.

His parents stood on the other side of the door. They had met him at the hospital after they learned what happened at the rig. They were angry for a different reason. Dax had risked his own safety, and that of the pod, by showing up there.

'What the hell were you thinking? Someone could've seen you.' Those were the first words out of his mother's mouth.

He hadn't been thinking. Ella was in danger, and it was his job to protect her. No one had assigned him the role. It was an instinct, a reflex, a purpose that had been dormant in him until the day he met her.

Dax glanced over at his parents as a van pulled up to let a passenger out. His mother met his gaze.

'You don't have to wait,' he said. 'I'm just going to make sure she's okay, and then I'll head home.'

His father rubbed his forehead. 'We need to ensure this situation is contained.'

Irritation twitched inside Dax. 'Let me worry about that.'

'With respect,' June said, 'you're the reason we're in this situation.'

Dax couldn't argue that point.

He straightened when the doors opened, but it wasn't Ella.

'They'll just be checking her over as a precaution,' his mother said, seeing the state he was in.

He knew she was right because he'd waited in the water until the helicopter had taken off, then swam back to Melbourne in record time. According to the nurse, Ella's father had already been waiting at the hospital when she arrived, which was why Dax was outside.

The doors opened again, and this time Ella walked out with her father. Her feet seemed to falter when she saw him there.

'Dax,' she said, attempting a smile.

He looked her over. No plaster, stitches, crutches. No visible bruises. She looked wiped out, but at least she was dry with colour back in her face.

'I heard what happened out at the rig.' The lie was for her father's sake. 'You okay?'

Michael Lewis grew taller next to her, disapproval like a flashing sign on his face. 'I'm going to take her home to rest,' he said. Then he noticed June and Irvin standing there, and his face fell.

Dax noted the mutual shock on his parents' faces. He remembered Michael telling him they had crossed paths in the past, but this reaction didn't match that story. 'These are my parents, Irvin and June.'

They all stared across the walkway at each other, no one moving or speaking for the longest time. Ella cast a questioning look at Dax, who didn't have an explanation to offer.

'We know Michael,' Irvin said finally. 'It's been a long time.' Then he said to Ella, 'Glad you're okay.'

'Thank you,' she replied. 'I'd hoped to meet you under better circumstances.'

June just stood there, not speaking.

Michael's hand went protectively to Ella's back. 'You heard what the doctor said. You need to rest.'

'I just need a minute,' she said. 'Do you mind bringing the car around?'

Michael hesitated, then nodded. He cast a final glance in June and Irvin's direction that looked a lot like a warning.

Dax made a mental note to ask his parents about their history later, then moved in front of Ella, a physical barrier between her and his parents. 'What did the doctor say?'

'That I'm fine.'

'The doctor actually used the word fine?'

'Yes.' The word came out with weak laughter.

Dax was sceptical. 'Okay, good.'

Ella reached out and took hold of two of his fingers. He was relieved to find her hand warm. The need to hold her surged with the contact.

'Why were you out at the rig?' she asked, eyes on their joined hands.

It was a fair question, one he'd expected. And she deserved an honest answer—but he couldn't give her one. 'When I couldn't get in touch with you, I called the office. Susan said you were out at the rig.'

'So you followed me out?'

He wet his lips. 'I promised you'd always be safe in the water.'

Her brow creased as she thought. 'Did you know that tidal wave was coming?'

He searched for the right response, some form of the truth. 'Nothing happens in our home without us knowing about it.'

She nodded, seemingly satisfied with his reply. 'You saved my life.' She released his hand. 'And Karen's.'

Guilt churned inside him. She was painting him a hero. 'You spotted her.'

She took his hand again and squeezed. 'But you made her breathe.' She glanced in the direction her father had gone. 'I wish I could tell Dad that.'

'Because you want him to like me?'

'Yes.' A smile came and went. 'He's not normally that rude. I think today just gave him a fright. It brought back a lot of memories.'

Dax watched her chew her lip. 'Memories of what?'

'My mother.' Ella didn't look at him. 'She drowned when I was ten.'

He took a moment to absorb that new piece of information. 'I didn't realise it was a water accident.'

Ella drew a breath before continuing. 'She liked to swim away from the summer crowds. One day she went for a swim and just didn't come home. I remember my father tearing his hair out with worry. The lifeguards couldn't find her. The water police showed up and searched the area. Nothing.'

Dax waited for her to continue.

'Someone found her washed up on a beach in Torquay the next day. She was still alive at that point. The paramedics said she was breathing.' She paused. 'She died before we got to the hospital.'

'Jesus.' Dax raked a hand through his hair. 'Now I get why you hate the beach.'

Ella's eyes were a dull blue. 'Now I have two reasons to hate the water.' She attempted a smile, but it faded quickly.

'I'm sorry.'

'For what?'

For the tidal wave. For bringing up her grief. For her father's pain. For nearly killing her. He was sorry for all of it. 'For not being able to travel back in time and save her for you.'

She threaded her fingers through his as she peered up at him. Finally some light returned to her eyes. 'I'm standing here because of you.'

More guilt.

She looked past him to his parents, who had wandered away to give them privacy. 'That was a really awkward exchange earlier.'

'Agreed.'

'I'm thinking the business pitch didn't go well,' she joked. 'I gather your parents came to ensure I haven't spilled all your family secrets?'

Smart girl. 'Little bit.'

A corner of her mouth lifted. 'I had big plans to wow your family with my charm and wit if we ever met.'

He searched her eyes. 'What do you mean "if"?'

'I just meant...' She looked down. 'Everything's still up in the air.'

'No it's not. Not anymore.' He hooked a finger under her chin, forcing her to look up at him. 'Nothing's up in the air.'

She swallowed. 'Okay.'

He dropped his hand to his side when he heard a car pull up behind him. He could tell by the change in Ella's expression that it was her father.

She raised a fist and held it between them. 'Thanks for today. For everything.'

He stared down at the balled hand. 'Are we... fist-bumping?'

'My father's watching us. I panicked.'

Dax bit back a smile. 'I better not leave you hanging,

then.' He lifted a fist, bumping it lightly to hers. Turning to the car, he pulled the passenger door open and waited for her to climb in. 'I'll call you later,' he said before pushing it closed.

They watched each other through the glass until the car pulled away. Dax's chest tightened with the separation. He stared after the Audi until a hand landed on his shoulder. He turned to face his parents, looking between them.

'Well, that was awkward,' he said.

June swallowed. 'I think it's safe to say we believe you now.'

'About what?'

'Ella,' June said, her brow creased with worry. 'You might be right. She could be your mate.'

Dax crossed his arms. 'And what brought you to that realisation? Expert eavesdropping?'

June drew a shaky breath. 'Ella's father is Michael Lewis.'

'Yeah.'

'And her mother was Caroline Lewis.'

She said it like that was supposed to mean something to him.

'Did you know her or something?'

Irwin slipped an arm around his wife's waist, as if to steady her. 'We knew her as Carrie Abbott before she married.'

Dax sat with the name for a moment. 'Abbott. Why is it familiar?'

June was struggling to begin. 'As in the Abbotts who left our pod when you were a child.'

He shook his head. 'I'm lost.'

'You were a kid,' Irvin said. 'We always tried to shield you from pod drama.'

They still did.

'What drama? Stop feeding me clues and tell me.'

For a moment no one spoke. Then finally June said, 'The Abbotts left after their only daughter passed away. Carrie was my friend. She was also rebellious and reckless at times. Stubborn like her father. Always thought she knew better than our elders.'

Dax remained perfectly still, unable to speak.

'She fell in love,' Irvin said. 'With a life she was never meant to have.'

'And with Michael Lewis,' June added.

Irvin nodded, his expression sombre. 'She played human for too long, and she paid for it with her life.'

Dax's hands fell to his sides. 'Ella's mother was…' He couldn't finish.

'Ondine,' Irvin said. 'Ella's mother was one of us.'

CHAPTER 18

When Ella and her father pulled into the driveway, Michael turned off the car and sat back with an exhale.

'I'm going to organise for the house to be painted,' he said, eyes ahead.

She was so used to the sight of peeling paint now. 'I haven't even received my first pay yet.'

He turned and looked at her. 'I'll pay for it.'

'You paid for the house. I think that's plenty.'

'And you're paying me back.'

She tilted her head. 'At half the rate I'd be paying the banks. Please let me take care of the painting.'

He sighed and watched her a moment. 'Did you stay in Williamstown for her?'

She didn't need to ask who he was referring to. He always had trouble saying her mother's name aloud, even all those years later. 'I don't know. I grew up here. I danced here. Lucy's here.' She paused. 'And yes, all my memories of her are here.' Ella took in her father's expression. 'Did you leave because of her?'

He'd moved to Yarraville when Ella left home but had

hated the thought of her paying the little money she earned as a dancer to a landlord, so he'd made an offer on the house she was renting and bought it under the pretence of an investment.

'Yes,' he said after a long silence. 'All of my memories of her are here too.' He looked in the direction of the water as he held the steering wheel. 'Listen, I need you to do me a favour.'

'Okay. What's the favour?'

'I want you to stay away from Dax and his family.'

Ella's stomach contracted as his words landed. 'What?'

Michael worked his palm over the steering wheel. 'They're not the sort of people you should be hanging around with.'

Ella blinked, trying to understand. 'Is this about the pitch?'

'This isn't about business.'

She stared at him, needing more. 'I know Barry doesn't think much of Dax. Is this a loyalty thing? Did he say something?'

'No.' Her father touched two fingers to his temple. 'Though Barry's had his fair share of run-ins with the family, especially Dax.'

'Because Dax cares about the environment.' She was gripping the door handle like it was the only thing keeping her upright. Her father's approval was everything to her, so his disapproval hit hard.

'They're troublemakers, the lot of them. You don't want to get messed up in that.'

Ella opened her mouth to speak, then closed it. Swallowing, she tried again. 'You know, I really like Dax. I haven't felt this way about someone since... ever.'

Michael's jaw tightened. 'The family's so far left in their political views there's not even a word to describe it.'

Ella frowned. 'So is this about his political views or his family? I'm confused.'

'Both are a problem.'

'Well, you can't choose your family.' Ella moved back until her hip hit the car door. 'And since when do you discriminate because of someone's political views? So he doesn't support companies that contribute to ocean pollution. It's hardly a flaw.'

Michael looked taken aback. 'You don't think it's a problem he wants the company you work for *shut down*?'

She lifted her chin. 'I don't plan on staying there long enough for it to be a problem.'

Her father's hand stilled on the steering wheel. 'What are you talking about? You're excelling there from everything Barry's told me.'

'I can excel anywhere. And you know what? I don't appreciate being kept in the dark about important things. They've had ongoing leaks for months apparently, but the rig remains operational thanks to Barry's ability to dodge the media and feed them half-truths.'

'Can you hear yourself? That doesn't even sound like you. It's all Dax.'

'No, I witness it myself every day.'

Michael rubbed his forehead. 'That's Barry's job, and if he's shielding you from the ugly parts, you should be grateful.'

'*Grateful*? I'm not a child. If he'd been upfront about the issues, I wouldn't have accepted the role.'

Michael smacked the steering wheel. 'And you would've done what instead, Ella? You can't dance. You can't even be around dancers. The only reason Lucy makes the cut is because she blew her chance when she got knocked up by her director.'

Ella's hand slackened around the door handle. She had

never heard her father speak poorly of Lucy, and she had no idea how to respond.

'Sorry,' he whispered. 'I know how important she is to you.'

'She's family,' Ella said, her tone cold.

Michael sighed, nodded, and then sank back against his seat. 'I know.'

'And the man who *"knocked her up"*, as you so eloquently put it, failed to mention that he was married. He flew back to Sydney the second he heard she was pregnant and never contacted her again. That's not on her. That's *all* on him.'

Michael lifted his gaze, his anger gone. 'I'm sorry. She didn't deserve that. You're a good friend.'

Ella took a moment to rein in her emotions. 'I like Dax. We really click. Please don't ask me to walk away before I've even had a chance to know him properly.'

He looked exhausted suddenly. 'Let's finish this conversation another day. You're supposed to be resting.'

Apparently a pause on the topic was the best she was going to get.

'You want me to come in for a bit?' he asked.

'No need. I'm just going to be lying on the couch.'

He nodded. 'I'll call you tonight and check on you.'

Ella opened the car door. 'You don't have to do that.'

He exhaled through his nose. 'Ella.'

She looked back at him.

'What you do speaks so loudly that I cannot hear what you say.'

Her shoulders fell a few inches. 'Ralph Waldo Emerson.'

'Correct.'

She stepped out of the car and bent to look at him. '"Anyone who has never made a mistake has never tried anything new." Einstein.' She closed the door, lifted a hand in a wave, and went inside.

CHAPTER 19

*D*ax pulled the car door closed and started the ignition. He held the steering wheel with both hands, mind racing with all the information his parents had unloaded on him.

The clock read 3:53 p.m.

Normally he would've been packing up at work and heading for the sea, but he'd spent most of the day in the water, and he couldn't think past Ella.

His Ella.

His mate.

He had never been more sure of anything in his life.

Of course, he was still filling in the blanks, the bits he struggled to make sense of. Physically, Ella was nothing like him. The day had proven she couldn't breathe underwater.

'Because she's *human*,' his father had said when he posed the question.

Dax had shaken his head. 'But she's half ondine.'

'She might have an ondine mother, but she's not one of us,' June had said, sounding genuinely sorry for it.

Doctors had done all the tests on Ella after her birth. She certainly wasn't the first mixed child to be born, and it wasn't uncommon for them to throw to one parent.

'She definitely got her mother's beauty,' June had said, 'but the rest is every bit her human father. The fact that you're drawn to her, like a mate, is the only evidence that ondine blood runs through her veins.'

Dax turned the radio on to drown out his thoughts, then turned the volume up when it didn't work.

'Flathead Rig, a Bass Fuel-owned oil rig situated forty kilometres off the coast of Melbourne, is being evacuated this afternoon after a freak wave hit the construction. Two people were washed off the wellhead platform, but both have since been released from hospital. A full safety investigation will be carried out before its reopening. Communications manager Barry Taylor, who was at the rig when the wave hit, had this to say: "We're very fortunate that the rig's emergency procedures prevented any deaths. The safety of our workers remains our priority—"'

Dax turned the radio off and flicked his indicator on. He did a U-turn and headed to Ella's house.

When he pulled up out front, he checked to make sure her father's car was nowhere in sight before exiting. He was met with loud music pouring through the cracks and crevices of the flaky house. It was classical, so he didn't even hazard a guess at the composer. He walked up to the door and pressed his ear to it, listening for voices, signs she had company. All he could hear was the music.

He knocked, waited. No answer.

He pounded with a fist and waited for the music to stop, but it continued. Pulling out his phone, he called her, and when she didn't answer, he called again.

Now he was getting worried.

He tried the handle of the screen door and found it

unlocked. Shaking his head, he opened the wooden door behind it and cringed at the loud noise. He was surprised the deafening howl of the hinges didn't alert her to his arrival.

Dax looked around the small entryway with its peeling wallpaper, which would've once been a beautiful feature. Reaching out, he ran his fingers along it as he moved towards the music vibrating through the wall. He stopped when he came to a door sitting ajar and peered through the gap, surprised when he caught his own reflection. The wall was mirrored glass floor to ceiling. He shifted to a different angle until he spotted Ella, and the tightness in his chest eased.

She was fine.

And she was dancing.

She wore floral print leggings, pointe shoes, and a white T-shirt tied in a knot at the waist, revealing three inches of bare skin. Her hair was twisted up in a bun, loose pieces stuck to her face and neck. She wasn't just doing turns this time, she was using the full space of the room, leaping and spinning, rising and falling like a wave. Her eyes would sink shut at certain points in the music, and then they would open when she lifted, arms spreading like wings. She looked so happy and free. So beautiful. He didn't want to pull her from the moment, so he stood captivated at the door instead.

He should've left once he saw she was all right. It wasn't right to stroll in and invade her privacy in that way. But he didn't leave. He edged closer for a better view, studying her movements like he was learning the dance himself, committing it to memory so he could watch the replay later.

When the music finished, she folded over like a flower wilting in the heat, remaining in that position for some time. The only movement was the rise and fall of her ribcage. She straightened, eyes meeting his in the mirror before he had a chance to announce himself, and she spun around with a gasp.

Shit.

He pushed the door open and raised his hands. 'It's just me. Sorry. The front door was open. I tried to call you and panicked when you didn't pick up.'

Ella brought a hand to her chest. 'You scared me.'

'I'm sorry.'

Composing herself, she went to retrieve her phone from the floor and checked the missed calls. 'Oh. I didn't hear it ring over the music.' She wandered over to him. 'How long have you been there?'

He swallowed, eyes moving over her flushed face. 'Long enough to realise I might have an appreciation for the arts after all.'

She dragged a pointed toe across the floor. 'Are you just saying that?'

'No.'

Her eyes shone a little brighter. 'That makes me happier than you realise.'

He tore his gaze from her and looked around the room, surprised at what he saw. 'Wow. This is stunning.'

The rest of the walls were exposed brick and the floor polished timber. At the front was a large bay window with light spilling through it.

Ella looked around also. 'The studio was a house-warming present from Dad. This was actually two rooms. He had someone come in and take out the wall, strip the others back, and lay the floor. These older houses can be pretty dark, so they replaced the front window with a much bigger one that's still as charming as the original.'

Dax nodded appreciatively. 'It's really beautiful.'

Ella crossed her arms in front of her. 'When I left Melbourne Ballet, I didn't come in here for the longest time.'

His gaze returned to her. 'Why's that?'

'Too angry.' She paused. 'I came in here with a hammer once, ready to demolish it. I went straight for the mirror, then caught sight of myself with the hammer raised above my head.'

'Didn't like what you saw?'

She shook her head.

He loved that she was comfortable enough around him to show the ugly parts of herself, parts he didn't find ugly at all.

'I curled up on the floor and cried for an hour, then went to fetch the window spray. I cleaned every inch of it. It was like an apology to the mirror.'

'Bet it was clean by the end.'

'So clean.' She laughed as she turned back to him, looking him over. 'You're dry.'

'I drove.'

She nodded. 'So you came to check on me?'

That was part of it. He also wanted to know if her father had offered any truthful explanations about the encounter with his parents earlier. Dax was doubtful given Michael had kept the secret from his daughter for twenty-three years. 'Sorry things were so awkward at the hospital earlier.'

'Not your fault. I didn't realise my dad knew your family quite that well. Turns out he's not a fan of your politics.'

Dax forced a smile. 'That's it? That's his beef?'

'Honestly, he was being really weird about the whole thing. I think today just freaked him out, sent him into alpha-dad mode.'

As much as he wanted to spill the truth to her, he knew it wasn't his place. It had to come from her father. 'If I didn't know any better, I'd say he knew what I was.'

She dismissed the suggestion with a shake of the head. 'He's just being overprotective. We don't have much family outside of each other.'

Dax wondered what Michael had told Ella about her grandparents on her mother's side but knew prying would only raise suspicions. 'Aren't you supposed to be resting?'

Ella shrugged. 'I actually feel pretty good. Is that weird?'

He hooked his thumb in the pocket of his jeans. No, it most certainly wasn't weird for a half-ondine creature to feel better after being in the sea. It was interesting though. 'Better that than traumatised.'

She studied him a moment. 'I'm not going to say anything to anyone about you being there, if that's what you're worried about.'

'I know that.' He walked over and stopped in front of her, taking hold of her face as he dipped his head to kiss her. Touching her helped settle his scattered mind.

Ella held his wrists and backed up to the mirror, sucking in a breath when she hit the cold glass. He picked her up, sliding her up the mirror until her legs wrapped around him. A soft moan came from her as his hips pressed against her.

'I'm sorry you went through that today,' he whispered into her mouth.

Ella broke the kiss to look at him, slightly breathless. 'Will you stop apologising? You saved my life, and Karen is alive because of you.' She brushed her nose down his. 'I want you to keep kissing me instead of talking.'

He dropped his forehead to hers. If she knew he was responsible for that wave, she wouldn't be saying that. The confession sat on the edge of his tongue, but if he started on the truth, he wouldn't be able to stop—not with her. So he kissed her in place of confessing, and she softened in his arms. He traced a finger down her neck, breast, stomach, until he reached the bare skin he'd glimpsed earlier. She pulled back then, and he immediately withdrew his hand.

'I think you should carry me to the bedroom,' she whispered, heat pooling between them.

He wet his lips, struggling to think through his need for her. 'I don't know where the bedroom is.'

She smiled against his mouth. 'I'll direct you.'

He didn't move. 'That's not why I came.'

'I know.'

'You should sleep.'

She took hold of his hand and returned it to her stomach. 'I'll sleep after. I promise.'

He kissed her once, twice. 'You're a bad influence, Miss Lewis.'

'I can live with that.'

He walked his fingers along her ribcage, feeling goosebumps break out over her skin. He brushed his thumb over the thin fabric of her dance bra, and she shuddered, her hands going into his hair, guiding his lips down to the skin just above the neckline of her T-shirt. A shaky breath came from her, and he pulled back to see her face.

'I should warn you now,' he began, 'once I've explored your body, tasted every inch of it, lost myself to it, *buried* myself in it, there will be no turning back for me.'

Her lips parted, her breaths coming faster. 'I don't want you to turn back.'

'You'll belong to me.' There was a warning in his voice.

She gripped his hair tighter, eyes searching his. 'I already belong to you. Can't you feel it?'

It was all he felt—unhinged possessiveness and a dangerous need to hear her moan again.

Ella brought her lips to his ear. 'Are you going to take what's *yours*, Ondine?'

That marked the end of the conversation.

He crashed his lips against hers, devouring her mouth, his heart pressed to her pounding chest. She wrapped herself tighter around him as he lifted her off the glass and carried her from the room.

CHAPTER 20

I t was the first time Dax felt resentment towards the sea. It was taking him from Ella's bed, washing her scent from him too soon.

He turned his head to look at her in the grey light. She slept on her stomach like a child, hands tucked under her chin and face pouty. Her breathing was so quiet. He hated to wake her but didn't want her to think he'd bailed. Rolling onto his side, he pushed back the hair covering her face and watched her eyes blink open.

'Hey,' he whispered. 'I'm going for a swim.'

'Now?' Her voice was thick with sleep.

He kissed her warm face. 'Yeah. I need to.'

She pushed herself up onto her elbows. 'Are you sick?'

'I'm fine, just need a swim.' He kissed her furrowed brow, then her cheek, before sliding from the bed.

'I'll come with you,' she said, swinging her legs over the edge of the bed.

He watched her reach for her clothes on the floor and begin to dress, keeping her back to him for modesty, as if he hadn't just spent the entire night memorising every inch of her.

'It's freezing out. Why don't you stay in bed where it's warm?'

She looked over her shoulder as she pulled her T-shirt down. 'I'll be all right.'

He didn't argue any harder because he liked having her close. Dragging the knitted throw from the bed, he wrapped it around her shoulders, tucking it in tightly.

'I'm not going in,' she said, the corners of her mouth lifted slightly.

'Figure it'll be a while before I get you back in the water after yesterday.' He kissed her, breathed in her fruity scent.

'I feel safe with you. It's just a bit cold for us humans.'

He brushed a finger down her cheek. 'You'll always be safe when I'm around—in water and on land.'

She didn't respond. Didn't need to. Everything had already been said in the dark.

When they arrived at the beach, he watched her settle herself on the sand before stripping down to his boxers. He dumped his clothes in a pile beside her before wading into the water. When he was waist deep, he glanced over his shoulder at her wrapped in a blanket, knees pulled up to her chin and a blazing orange sky overhead. Her hair spilled in a tousled mess over the blanket. He took a mental photograph for later, then turned and dove in.

DAX HAD JUST PICKED up the circular saw when Miller whistled to him. When he looked over, he found Michael Lewis standing next to him. Dax placed the saw down and tugged off his gloves as the two men eyed each other.

Here we go.

Miller threw an "I told you so" look before wandering off.

'Morning,' Dax said as he approached Michael. 'Is Ella okay?' He needed that clarification first.

Michael nodded. 'She's fine. I was just hoping to have a word with you.'

Dax gestured for him to follow and took him somewhere safe and quiet. He turned, eyes sweeping over the man. Miller had given Michael a helmet and vest, which looked ridiculous paired with an expensive suit and designer shoes. 'I didn't tell her, if that's why you're here.'

Michael squinted at him. 'I know, because she's still speaking to me this morning.' He exhaled and looked around. 'Does she know what you are?'

Dax glanced around to ensure no one was within earshot. 'She's a smart girl. Didn't take her long to figure it out.'

Michael nodded. 'She is a smart girl, and she has a bright future ahead of her.'

Dax crossed his arms. 'I agree.'

'Listen. I'll try to keep this short, because we've both got work to get back to.'

'Okay.'

Michael looked him straight in the eye. 'I need you to back off. Do it respectfully, because I don't want her hurt, but do it *now* before this thing gets out of hand.'

Dax regarded him. 'This thing? You mean our relationship?'

'There's no relationship.' Michael's jaw ticked. 'That's not going to happen. I'm sure your parents explained why.'

Dax remained calm, because he knew getting worked up wasn't going to win him any points. 'Why haven't you told Ella about her mother?'

Michael shifted. 'That's none of your business.'

'Ella's half ondine, and she has no idea.'

'Ella's human. She's nothing like *you*, nothing like her mother.'

165

'She still deserves to know the truth. She has living grandparents she's never met.'

'Just hang on a minute,' Michael said, resting his hands on his hips. 'After the tests, once we knew for sure, we *all* agreed there was no need for her to know. No good would've come from it at such a young age. She would've felt confused, like a misfit, like there was something wrong with her.' He paused. 'What's the pod going to do with a human? What use is an ondine who can't breathe underwater?'

'Okay.' Dax nodded. 'She would've likely figured it out eventually.'

'She would've, but we wanted to wait until she was older. Being a kid is hard enough.' He swallowed. 'Then suddenly there wasn't a need to tell her at all.'

Dax ran a finger down his nose and dropped his gaze. 'I'm sorry about your wife.'

Michael swallowed. 'I don't need your condolences. I need you to stay away from my daughter.'

There was no chance of that happening.

'The thing is, I think Ella's my mate.'

Michael didn't seem surprised to hear that, but he shook his head all the same. 'Not gonna happen.'

'With all due respect, I think that's up to Ella.'

'With all due respect, *Dax*, you've barely known my daughter a month. Your pod has no claim on her, you have no claim on her, and the *sea* certainly has no claim on her.'

Dax glimpsed pain through the anger. 'It's not as easy as walking away. You of all people should know that.'

'Never said it was easy, but I'm not letting her waste her life trying to be something she's not.'

'You mean like her mother?'

Michael pointed a finger at him. 'Careful.'

'Do you know how hard it is for an ondine to drown?' Dax knew he was venturing into dangerous territory.

'Ella's mother must've been really weak when she entered the water.'

'Enough,' Michael said. 'My wife wasn't weak. She was one of the strongest women I've ever known.'

'She was also ondine.' Dax's parents had told him she'd go days without entering the water.

Michael took a small step back. 'Just stay away. It'll end badly. Is that what you want for *her*?'

'This isn't the same. Ella's half ondine.'

'No she's not.' Michael's tone left no room for argument. 'She had all the tests. *Your* doctors poked and prodded every part of her. I was there through all of it.'

Dax frowned. 'That doesn't erase what she is. You kept her out of the water.'

'Because she's *human*.'

'And yet we found each other. I had no idea who her mother was until yesterday.'

'Easy, Romeo. Just think of Ella for a moment. She's been through enough this past year, and if you think she's okay with it all, she's not.'

'I don't think she's okay at all, and me cutting her off isn't going to help.'

'Delaying will only make it harder. She'll be more attached.'

'I think that ship has sailed.' Dax drew a calming breath. 'What I will do though is keep your secret—for now. It's not for me to tell Ella about her mother.'

Michael studied him. 'Should I keep your secret too?'

'Okay, I'll bite. What are you talking about?'

'I'm talking about Flathead Rig getting hit by a freak wave. Does Ella know your pod was behind it?'

Dax's mouth flattened into a thin line.

'Did she tell you she was washed off the bridge?' Michael continued. 'She was lucky she didn't drown. Do you have any idea what would've been going through her head? Her mother died in that water, for Christ's sake.'

If he meant to make Dax feel guilty, it worked. 'Don't pretend we're the same. I plan on telling her the truth.'

Michael's expression didn't change. 'You know, aside from the fact that you're the wrong species, you're a bad fit for Ella.'

'Yeah. Why's that?'

'She lives and breathes the arts, for one. When was the last time you went to the theatre?'

Dax frowned. 'Really? I didn't go see *Jersey Boys* so I'm out?'

'She has ambition.'

'Not at the moment she doesn't. She's stuck in a job she hates, probably to keep you happy.'

Michael shook his head. 'You figure that out over a couple of dates?'

'Pretty much.'

Michael scoffed. 'Maybe you don't need me to interfere after all. It won't take Ella long to realise you're not right for her.'

The comment stung a little. 'Listen, if Ella tells me she doesn't want to see me anymore, I'll graciously step aside.' It might kill him to do it, but he'd do it if he thought it was what she wanted. 'You have my word on that. In the meantime, tell your daughter the truth before she finds out from someone else.'

'Don't threaten me.'

Dax resisted the urge to shove the guy in the direction of the exit.

'Stay out of my family's business,' Michael continued, 'like your pod promised.'

Dax sniffed and swallowed down his smart-arse retort, saying instead, 'Thanks for stopping by.'

CHAPTER 21

Dax: I have tickets to the ballet tonight? Wanna come with?

Ella: *laughing emoji* No you don't.

Dax: I really do.

Ella: I can't tell if you're joking.

Dax: I'm not joking. Come. But only if you feel up to it.

Ella smiled down at her phone.

Ella: What time?

Dax: I'll pick you up at 5.

Ella: 5pm for the ballet??

Dax: It's an early performance.

Ella: Hmmm. See you then x

'Why are you grinning like a weirdo?' Lucy said, strolling into the tiny lounge room.

Caleb was curled up beside Ella on the two-seater couch, his thumb jammed in his mouth, blinking at the TV.

Ella lowered her phone. 'Dax just asked me to go to the ballet with him tonight.'

Lucy laughed, then fell silent when she saw Ella's face. 'Oh, you're serious. I'd accuse him of trying to get in your pants if he hadn't already been in them. Are you going to go?'

'Of course. It's *ballet*.'

Lucy sank down on the other side of her. 'What are you seeing?'

'He didn't say.'

'You didn't *ask*?'

'I forgot to.' She didn't care which ballet. She was just excited to go with him.

'I can't remember the last time you smiled this hard.' Lucy watched her with amusement. 'Well, I'm going to the movies tonight, in case you were wondering.'

Ella's eyes widened. 'With who?'

'*Dad*, so you can stop looking so hopeful.' She sighed. 'No one wants to take a single mum to the ballet.'

'What are you talking about? Guys would be lining up if they knew you were accepting offers.'

Lucy gave her a tired look. 'Doesn't matter anyway because my bed is already at capacity.' She leaned forwards to look at Caleb. 'Should've kept your cot.'

He was too absorbed in the movie to hear her.

Ella glanced at the time on her phone. 'I have an hour. I should shower and find something to wear.'

'The knee-length black dress you wore to *Spartacus* with your pink blazer and the suede heels you wore to *Chicago*.'

Ella's brows rose. 'That's very specific.'

'Hair down. Goddess lips. Easy on the eyeliner.'

'When am I heavy on the eyeliner?'

'When you're nervous. Remember *Cinderella*? You looked like Lady Tremaine.'

Ella rolled her eyes. 'That was one time.' She bent to kiss the top of Caleb's head. 'Don't fall asleep now. Your mummy wants you to sleep *tonight*.'

ELLA'S HEART threatened to burst through her chest when she heard the knock at the front door. She forced herself to walk slowly.

Big mistake.

Caleb beat her to the door, pushing up onto his toes to open it.

'Hey,' Dax said when he spotted Caleb standing there.

Caleb regarded him for a moment. 'Why were you in Ella's pants?'

Ella sucked in a breath as she hurried for the door, scooping Caleb up with a nervous laugh.

'Let me guess,' Dax said. 'It was out of context?'

Ella glanced at him. 'He was supposed to be watching *Toy Story.*'

Lucy appeared behind them and cast an apologetic look in Ella's direction before turning her attention to Dax. 'So what's the ballet?'

'*Peter Pan.*'

Lucy's eyebrows came together. 'Where's it playing?'

'Port Melbourne Town Hall.'

Lucy's gaze slid to Ella, who was fitting the pieces together.

'Does this happen to be a reimagining by the Bambi Ballet School?' Ella asked.

Dax nodded. 'Yeah. Should be good.'

Lucy looked understandably confused.

'I think I might be overdressed for toddler ballet,' Ella said, looking down at her dress and clutch. 'Let me go change.'

Dax's eyes moved over her. 'You look beautiful. Don't change. Unless you want to. I don't want you to be uncomfortable.'

Lucy gave Ella a push towards the door. 'She's fine. Go have fun. I'll lock up.'

The moment his warm hand swallowed hers, Ella abandoned all notions of changing.

Outside, Dax opened the car door for her, and she slid in, rubbing her hands together as she waited for him to reach the driver side.

'You're cold,' he said, turning the heater up.

'I'm okay. Did you swim already?'

'Yep.'

She tugged the hem of her skirt towards her knees. 'How was your day?'

He went to say something, then stopped himself. 'Fine.'

'Fine? Fine's a bit underwhelming,' she said, quoting him. 'What were you going to say before that came out?'

He kept his eyes ahead. 'You don't want to hear about my boring work. Tell me about your day.'

Ella felt like he was holding something back but decided not to push the subject. 'Also boring. I'm going back to work tomorrow. I really don't need the rest of the week off.'

'You a doctor now?'

'No, but I am an expert on myself.'

Dax laughed deeply.

She cleared her throat. 'Just to be clear, I didn't share any details about last night with Lucy. I mean, she knows you stayed over...'

'I'm part of a pod where everyone knows everyone's business. I get it.'

He reached out and took her hand, threading his fingers through hers. The instant warmth made her relax into the seat.

Traffic was heavier once they crossed the Westgate Bridge, so they didn't arrive at the Port Melbourne Town Hall until a little before six. There was barely enough time to say hello to the rest of the group before they were ushered inside to take their seats.

'Thanks for coming,' Greta whispered as she took her seat on the other side of Ella.

Ella smiled. 'Thanks for the ticket.' At least one of them was warming to her. The others were polite enough for Dax's sake, except Frankie, who was still ice cold. He'd failed to mention she would be there.

The audience fell silent when a beaming woman in her mid-thirties trotted onto the stage. She introduced herself as the creative director of the school and talked about how hard the kids had been working on their pieces for the performance. The school taught classical ballet, lyrical, jazz, and tap.

Dax reached for Ella's hand as the curtains opened, revealing a hand-painted Netherlands backdrop and toddlers dressed as the lost children from *Peter Pan*. Ella smiled when they began to tap out of time to the music.

'Can you tap dance?' Dax whispered to her.

She glanced up at him. 'Of course. I can dance any style, even hip-hop.'

He looked like he didn't believe her. 'I'm going to need proof of that.'

She leaned closer. 'I even did a term of pole dancing to improve my core strength.'

'I'm *definitely* going to need proof of that.' He faced forwards. 'It's very confusing having those kinds of visuals at a children's performance.'

She squeezed his hand in place of laughter.

They watched the next three dances, applauding along with all the proud parents and laughing quietly whenever the children went rogue.

It was therapeutic for Ella to watch them. She wasn't critiquing the dancers like usual but was reminded of a time when dance was all about having fun. No pressure, just *fun*.

She tried to remember what age it had all changed. When had she started fretting over her technique, paying too much attention to those who could get more height than her, those who had better control? At what age had her feet blistered so badly she'd bled through her shoes? Before or after the hip pain began?

Before or after her mother's death?

'You okay?' Dax asked.

She jumped at the sound of his voice and looked up at his concerned face. 'Fine.'

His gaze fell to her white knuckles wrapping his. She hadn't realised she'd been gripping him that tightly and immediately relaxed her hand.

'Oh. Sorry.' She attempted a smile. 'I get excited whenever there's tulle in sight.'

The concern didn't leave his face.

Thankfully, Greta diverted his attention when she leaned forwards and said, 'Ariel's up next.'

They watched as a group of fairies fluttered onto the stage, all round-faced with wide smiles. There was a collective sigh among the parents as the dancers moved in a chaotic circle before taking their positions.

'Which one's Ariel?' Ella asked Dax.

He pointed. 'Third from the left.'

Ella regarded the beautiful dark-haired girl with large brown eyes. The happy toddler looked left and right, copying those either side of her, who were copying those either side of them, and so on and so on, meaning no one was ever in time.

Ella loved every misstep, every turn in the wrong direction, every tiny tutu and colourful sequin. She turned to Greta. 'Ariel's a total star.'

Greta laughed. 'Yeah, she's pretty damn cute.'

At that exact moment, Frankie leaned forwards in her chair to glare at Ella. At some point the ex was going to have to accept Dax had moved on, because Ella wasn't going anywhere.

They all faced forwards again to watch.

At interval, Adrian and Greta went backstage to see Ariel, and the rest of them made their way to the foyer. Hurley went to buy food, leaving Dax, Miller, Frankie, and Ella standing in a group.

'I think it's really nice you all came to watch Ariel,' Ella said. 'She's lucky to have such supportive friends.'

'Bit hard to say no when Greta just buys tickets and hands you one,' Miller said.

Dax nodded in agreement. 'Yeah, these things have a habit of magically appearing in our calendars.'

'I'm going to the ladies',' Frankie said, looking agitated.

Now was Ella's chance to clear the air. 'I'll come with you.'

Frankie levelled her with a look. 'I don't need supervision.'

'I know.' When Ella went to move, Dax caught her wrist. She looked up at him, but he didn't say anything, didn't have to. 'I'll be right back,' she reassured him.

Slowly, his grip eased, and she followed Frankie, who was striding ahead. When they reached the ladies' toilets, Frankie let the door swing shut behind her. Undeterred, Ella pushed through it.

'Hey,' she called to Frankie's back.

The ex marched into the first cubicle and locked it. Ella waited at the sinks, thinking through the best way to proceed.

'I understand why this is uncomfortable,' Ella said through the door, 'but I would really like to get to a point where you hate me a little less.'

The toilet flushed and the cubicle door swung open.

Frankie's gaze swept the length of her, then she checked the other cubicles to ensure they were empty. 'You do realise everyone in the pod is laughing at him.' She walked to the basin to wash her hands. 'You're a big joke. Everyone's just waiting for him to come to his senses.'

At least she was talking.

Ella kept her expression neutral. 'That's okay. I'm not going to be deterred by laughter.'

Frankie met her eyes in the mirror. 'What are you wearing? This isn't the Arts Centre.'

'Dax was a little light on the details when he invited me.'

Frankie wore skintight jeans and a suede jacket with black pumps. Her hair was back in a loose ponytail, the length of it reaching the middle of her back.

'It seems he's been light on a lot of details lately.' Frankie watched the running water.

'What does that mean?'

Frankie turned off the faucet and reached for some paper towel. 'You know, we have enough pod drama without outsiders creating more problems for us.'

Luckily for Ella, she had years of practice remaining composed in stressful situations. 'If this is about yesterday, I never asked him to follow me out there.'

Frankie's eyes appeared dark in the dim light. 'Didn't you ever ask yourself why he was there?'

'He was worried about me.'

Frankie turned around, a hand going to her hip. 'It's almost like he knew that wave was coming.'

Ella didn't so much as blink. 'He did know. It's an ondine thing.'

Frankie laughed harshly. 'You think we can predict tidal waves? Is that what he told you?'

Ella tried to think back to what he'd said. Something

about knowing everything that happens in his home. 'I don't understand.'

Frankie shook her head. 'I'm not getting in trouble for you.'

She went to leave, but Ella blocked her. 'How did Dax know that wave was coming if ondines can't predict them?'

Frankie made herself taller. 'Ondines can't predict tidal waves, but we sure can make them.' She leaned closer. 'Don't follow me into the ladies' again. I don't want to talk to you. We're not friends. You're not one of us. And next time you have questions, ask Dax.' With that, she stepped around Ella and left the bathroom.

The speakers crackled to life overhead, and a voice said, 'Please make your way to your seat in preparation for the second half. Thank you.'

Ella pressed a hand to the wall to steady herself as she thought back to the previous day.

'*I'm sorry,*' he had said.

And now she knew why.

Pulling the door open, she found Dax leaning against the wall on the other side of the corridor.

He took in her expression. 'What did she say that has you looking like you're ready to fall down?' He made no move towards her.

Ella swallowed. 'Was your pod responsible for the wave yesterday?'

He breathed out slowly, his defeated sigh speaking volumes.

Ella moved to the side so she wasn't blocking the door, even though the audience had already returned inside the main hall. '*Why?*'

Dax closed the distance between them, taking hold of her arms. 'We're not fighting over something Frankie dropped on you in the bathroom. This is what she does. If you have questions, I'll answer them, but not like this.'

177

She stared up at him. 'You told me you were worried when I didn't answer my phone.'

'I was.'

'Because you knew the wave was coming and that it would hit the rig.'

'Yes.'

'Because you *made* it.'

His hands moved to cradle her face. 'I didn't know you were there until the last minute.'

'But you knew *other* people were there.' She held onto his wrists. 'They could've died.'

'That was never our intention. We just needed to give VEPA a reason to get out there.'

Ella stepped sideways out of his grip. 'They have more than a hundred workers there at one time.'

He ran a hand down his face. 'Let's get out of here. We'll talk in the car.'

Her gaze fell to her feet. 'I can't be in a car with you right now. I'm going to catch an Uber home.'

'You're not catching an Uber.'

She looked up. 'Frankie was right. I'm not one of you.'

'Is that what she said? She's just stirring shit up.'

'She's blunt, but at least she's honest.'

Dax's jaw tightened. 'You think I'm not honest? I've told you more than I should've.'

She was too confused to argue sensibly. 'I'm going to leave, and I need you to not follow. Go back inside, and make sure your applause is loud enough for both of us at the end.'

Dax raked a hand through his hair. 'Sit in the back seat of the Uber, and text me when you're home or I'm coming over.'

She nodded as she stepped away.

'Goodnight, Ella.'

CHAPTER 22

*N*ine days. Nine days of silence, of unanswered texts, and missed calls. All he'd gotten from her in that time was one text message the night of their fight.

ELLA: I'm home safe.

LEANING against the wall outside of B for Brazil, Dax dialled her number for the second time that day. She had made an art of avoiding him.

Voicemail.

He hung up and shoved the phone back into his pocket just as Miller exited the cafe, eyeing him suspiciously.

'Tell me you didn't call her again.'

'Would it kill her to answer?'

'All you need to do now is start driving past her house at night to check if her car's in the driveway and you get the official title of stalker.'

Dax pushed off the wall. 'She won't give me a chance to explain.'

'Explain what? She already knows our family created a tidal wave and aimed it at her employer. What else are you going to say?' Miller handed him a coffee, and they began walking back towards the site. 'You can't expect her to understand. I hate to say it, but Frankie's actually right on this one. She's not part of our world.'

'Don't praise Frankie right now. She's the reason I'm in this situation.'

Miller's gaze slid to him. 'You can't be pissed at her forever.'

'Challenge accepted.'

Miller laughed quietly into his drink. 'We're heading out tonight, and you're coming with us. It might take your mind off her for a bit.'

Nothing had managed to distract him so far. 'Not really in the mood.'

'I'm not asking, brother.' He kept his eyes ahead. 'And make sure you swim beforehand.'

ELLA WAS JUST PACKING up at work when Susan popped up over her monitor.

'Are you avoiding Dax, by any chance?' she asked, keeping her voice low.

Ella jumped slightly, then glanced in the direction of Barry's closed door. 'Why do you ask?'

'He called the front desk this afternoon when you were in a meeting but didn't leave a message. I'm assuming he has your mobile number.'

Ella bit her lip. She'd been ignoring his calls since she fled Port Melbourne Town Hall, delaying their next conversation for as long as possible. The actions of the pod were inexcusable. As deep as her feelings were for Dax, she couldn't figure a way past her disappointment. The sensible thing to do was part ways, but she couldn't bring herself to suggest it. She was hoping for some miracle fix before she was forced to break her own heart, but it wasn't looking good.

'Thanks for letting me know. I'll call him later,' she lied.

Susan tapped a finger atop the monitor. 'I'm meeting up with the girls tonight for drinks. You should come with us.'

Ella continued packing her bag. 'I have yoga.'

'On a *Friday*?' Susan laughed.

Ella always did yoga on Fridays before heading home for fish and chips. Well, her version of fish and chips, which was pan-fried salmon, oven-baked sweet potatoes, and a leafy salad. 'I'm not a big drinker.'

'But you are a dancer, and Tram Bar has a dance floor. It's a really fun crowd.'

Ella recalled what Lucy had tearily told her the night before about feeling eighty in her twenties. Letting out a resigned breath, she said, 'Can I bring a friend along?'

Susan's face lit up. 'Of course. The more the merrier. We'll have a few wines, do a few shots, dance. Maybe find a hottie in the crowd for you, get your mind off Dax.'

Ella hooked her handbag over her shoulder as she stood. 'What makes you think I want to get my mind off Dax?'

'Because you're avoiding him,' Susan replied with a knowing smile. 'What happened? Did he cheat?'

Ella shook her head. 'No, nothing like that. I'll head home and change, meet you there later.'

Susan stepped back from the desk. 'Make sure you eat something beforehand.'

CHAPTER 23

'Are you sure this skirt isn't too short?' Lucy asked as they joined the queue to get into Tram Bar.

Ella looked her over. 'It's the same length as the last time you asked, which was only four minutes ago.'

It was the first time Lucy had gone out drinking since Caleb was born. Seeing she was nervous, Ella reached out and squeezed her hand. 'Honestly, you look absolutely stunning. You've always been able to pull off any length skirt with those legs.'

Ella had opted for black skinny jeans and the striped bodice top Lucy had given her on her birthday, along with the explanation that "Vertical stripes add height".

'What am I supposed to say if a guy actually talks to me?' Lucy asked.

'Say something back?'

Lucy rolled her eyes. 'Like what? "Oh, I'm a failed dancer and single mother"?'

Ella gave her a disapproving look. 'Don't say that. You're an incredible dancer and a rock star mum. You could still return to the stage later if it's what you want.'

'No, that ship has sailed. I'm going to need something a

little more family-friendly. I don't have a partner to fall back on.'

'You have me.'

Lucy pressed a hand to her chest. 'I love you for saying that, but one day you'll have your own kids to worry about.' She eyed Ella. 'Maybe with Dax.'

'Doubtful.'

'You're really not going to tell me what you fought about?'

'I'm really not.'

When they reached the front of the line, the bouncer looked Ella over. 'ID, please.'

Not entirely surprising. She fetched it from her clutch and waited a full minute while he looked between it and her before finally waving them inside.

The girls paused and looked around at the mirrored bar and polished-timber dance floor. They found Susan and her friends seated on tall stools at a table barely wide enough to fit all their wine glasses.

'Hi!' Susan said, slipping from her stool to greet Ella. 'Yay, you made it.'

'This is Lucy,' Ella shouted over the music.

'Nice to meet you,' Susan said. 'Come meet the girls, and I'll find some extra stools.'

Susan's three friends were hard to tell apart. They all looked like slightly different variations of Susan.

After introductions were made, Ella said, 'I'm going to the bar. Anyone need another?'

'Can you grab a bottle of rosé?' Carly asked. She held up their empty bottle so Ella could see the label.

Ella nodded, then made her way over to the bar, studying the bottled beers in the fridge. She was a light-weight on wine, and pre-mixed spirits always reminded her of undiluted cordial.

As she waited to be served, she looked around the

room. It was early, so the dance floor was empty. Her eyes stopped on the large booth in the corner, lit up by an over-hanging bulb. Ella stiffened. Packed into the small space were Dax and his friends.

Dax.

His hair was tied back, his blue shirt rolled to the elbows. He wore black faded jeans and a lazy smile as he chatted to Hurley across the table. Ella watched as he picked up the Peroni sitting in front of him and swung it up to drink.

'What can I get you?' the bartender called to her.

At that moment, Dax glanced in the direction of the bar, and the smile fell from his face.

DAX BLINKED A FEW TIMES, wondering if he had finally lost his mind after being separated from his mate for too long. But it was her all right. Unmistakably, achingly beautiful, Miss Ella Lewis. She was wearing jeans and a blue-and-cream strapless top, lips painted red and long hair out and falling in waves over her bare skin, the same skin he had buried his face in, kissed, traced his fingers over.

She looked equally as surprised to see him.

Placing his beer on the table, he slipped from the booth, ignoring the drink requests that followed him as he headed over to the bar.

'Ella.' Her name was honey on his tongue.

She finished ordering, then turned to face him, her brow creased with worry. 'Hi.'

'Hey.'

She looked nervously in the direction of the booth. 'I didn't know you would be here. Sorry.'

He brought a hand up, rubbing his jaw. 'I'm not sorry. Saves me another phone call.'

The bartender placed two beers and a bottle of wine on the counter in front of her. 'That's sixty-four.'

Dax pulled his card out of his back pocket and tapped it while Ella fumbled with her clutch.

She closed her eyes when she heard it beep. 'I can buy my own drinks.'

He was so desperate to take care of her in any way he could, he had done it without thinking. 'I know. How have you been?'

Ella tucked her clutch under her arm and reached for the drinks at the same time he did. 'I've got them,' she said.

He breathed out and looked around. 'At some point you're going to have to talk to me. If it's over, you need to say the words.'

She blinked back what appeared to be tears. Just the mention of separation and she looked ready to fall down. 'I haven't been avoiding your calls to be spiteful. I'm just having a bit of difficulty reconciling you… with all the other stuff.' She spoke the words to his chest as she held the drinks between them.

'I get it. There's logic, and then there's us.'

She lifted her gaze to him. 'And I'm usually such a logical person.' Her eyes were shiny with tears.

In those difficult moments, he was supposed to be her comfort, not the reason for her tears. Looking past her, he asked, 'Who are you here with?'

'Lucy and Susan from work'—she glanced in the direction of the other table—'and some of Susan's friends.'

Dax recognised some of them. They were regulars at the bar who liked to dance up a storm, flirt, empty the fridges of wine, then leave alone, much to the disappointment of their dance partners and the amusement of the pod.

'Normally I'd just leave, let you enjoy your evening,' Ella

said. 'But this is Lucy's first proper night out in a long time. I don't have the heart to end it early.'

Dax shook his head. 'I don't want you to leave.'

She was looking everywhere but up at him.

'Go enjoy your night with Lucy,' he said. 'I didn't come over here to ruin your fun.'

Ella nodded and bit down on that painted lip of hers. 'This is why I didn't want to see you. It's confusing. I feel this crushing disappointment and insane joy all at once.'

Something pulled in Dax's chest.

While they were staring at one another, a guy walked by, clipping Ella's shoulder on his way to the bar. The beers she was holding began to froth up.

'Watch it,' Dax growled at the man, prompting him to turn. Dax shifted his weight when he saw who it was.

It was Peter.

'Peter,' Ella said, eyes widening. 'What... what are you doing here?'

'Ella?' He laughed and bent to kiss her cheek. 'What am *I* doing here? What the hell are *you* doing here on yoga night?'

Ella's cheeks coloured. 'I don't always do yoga...' She pointed over to the table where Lucy sat chatting. 'Girls' night. You?'

'I'm here with the *Giselle* crew,' Peter said. 'We're doing drinks early so we're nice and clear-headed for next week's opening.'

Ella nodded and gestured to Dax. 'You remember my friend Dax.'

Friend.

'Of course,' Peter said, maintaining his smile. 'You having a girls' night too?'

Dax kept his cool gaze on him a moment, imagining how easy it would be to mess up that pretty face of his.

186

'Listen, I'll let you guys catch up.' He took a step back, not wanting to ruin Ella's night any more than he had.

'Oh,' Ella said. 'Okay. I'll come see you before I go.'

He nodded once before returning to the booth. A familiar energy stirred inside of him. It was never a good thing when he felt it everywhere. In his hands he had control. Through his entire body, not so much.

'Ella's here?' Miller asked when he slipped back into his seat. 'Did you invite her?'

'Nope.' Dax picked up his beer and took a large drink.

'Of course she's here,' Frankie said, running a finger along the rim of her glass.

Miller looked Dax over. 'You want to leave?'

'That's her ex-boyfriend standing with her,' Dax replied. 'What do you think?'

Hurley chuckled as he lifted his beer to drink.

Miller exhaled. 'As long as you're in control.'

'When am I not in control?'

The group exchanged looks but said nothing.

Frankie lifted a hand as though feeling something in the air. 'Your energy's off.'

'My energy's fine.'

'Anyone else feel that?' she continued, looking around. 'I can feel it from over here.'

His emotions were just running high after seeing Ella, that was all. Dax rubbed his hands together, trying to bring it under control, and the jug of water on the table slid a few inches in the other direction.

All eyes went to it, then to him.

'Do we need to leave?' Adrian asked, an arm stretched out behind Greta.

Ariel was having a sleepover at her grandparents' house, and the couple were making the most of it.

Dax shook his head. 'I told you, I'm fine.'

The jug slid half the length of the table before Hurley caught it. 'What the hell? Go outside and walk it off.'

Greta spoke up. 'Give him a break. He's allowed to feel protective.'

'Of his human crush?' Frankie said, rolling her eyes.

Only his family knew the truth about Ella and her mother. Dax had asked them all not to say anything until she knew.

Greta cast a sympathetic look at Dax before his gaze drifted back to Ella. The bar was filling up, impairing his view, but he saw Lucy now standing with Ella. She glanced in his direction, as though feeling his eyes on her. Peter had moved to her side and was pretending he belonged there. His elbow kept touching Ella's arm as he spoke to Lucy.

Feeling hot suddenly, Dax brought a hand to his head, and the various glasses of water around the table all scattered at once.

'Jesus,' Adrian said, catching his and Greta's glasses.

'All right, time to go,' Miller said, standing.

'Sit,' Dax said, closing his hands into tight fists in an attempt to gain control. 'I told you, I'll leave when she does.'

'And what if she leaves with Peter?' Frankie asked.

Dax cast a warning glance in her direction before turning back to Ella. Their group had grown to include Susan and her friends. They took the bottle of wine from Ella and began passing it around. Some of Peter's friends also wandered over. Lucy said something to the group, and everybody laughed. Then Peter hooked an arm around Ella as he gestured with his other hand. More laughter, Ella along with them. But it wasn't the laughter he'd witnessed over the weeks he'd known her, the kind that made her head tip back and blue eyes shine as bright as the sky. This laughter didn't quite reach those places.

Even still, he was forced to admit he was jealous. It was annoying, because he wasn't the jealous type—except with her. Jealousy was one thing, but witnessing her discomfort as she stood stiff beneath Peter's arm was something else. His vision blurred, and he blinked to clear it. The sound of glass breaking made everyone at the table jump.

Dax looked down to where his beer lay smashed on the ground after sliding off the table. He swore quietly.

'I'll get someone to clean it up,' Hurley said, slipping from the booth.

'Can you get me another beer while you're there?' He didn't want to brave a visit to the bar in his current state.

Peter returned to his friends once the DJ started playing, and Dax was finally able to relax. The dance floor started to get busy, and Ella's group made their way out onto it. From that point on, Dax couldn't take his eyes off her. She waved her arms and swung her hips, singing along to all the pop songs Dax hated. Though he didn't mind them so much when she was lip-syncing to them. He felt like a perv sitting there watching her, but he couldn't look away. When her hair fell to one side, revealing that creamy neck he'd spent so much time exploring with his mouth, he had to take a long drink.

A remix of 'Señorita' came on, and Peter looked over at Ella with his hands raised and a stupid look on his face. He made his way over to her, said something into her ear, and pulled her away from the group to where there was more space. She was protesting but mostly smiling. Dax suspected she was being modest, but he watched her closely for signs to the contrary.

A moment later they fell into step with each other, like they had rehearsed for this very occasion. Dax recalled what Ella had told him in the water about good partners being in sync. He had to push the thought away as his eyes followed every movement of Peter's hands, growing agitated by the way his fingers traced her waist whenever he turned her.

Frankie pulled his attention as she switched places with Hurley. 'You just going to watch her like a stalker all night?' she asked, reaching for her wine.

'Yep.' He took another sip of beer, relieved when Lucy dragged Ella from Peter's hands to go dance with the other girls.

Dax could breathe again.

'Two years we were together,' Frankie said. 'You never once looked at me that way.'

He eyed Frankie as he drank. 'I'm not doing this.'

'I'm just pointing out what a bad boyfriend you were.'

At least she had stopped using the word mate. That was progress.

Frankie's gaze drifted to the dance floor as a Taylor Swift song began to play. Her eyes narrowed. 'Just keep looking at me. We don't want any more broken drinks.'

Dax instinctively looked over at Ella and found some guy holding her elbow and talking into her ear. When his lips brushed her hair, she leaned away from him. Energy surged through Dax, causing his arms to twitch and fingers to grow rigid.

Frankie reached out and took the beer from his hand, placing it on the table. 'Relax. They're just talking.'

The bottle slid away, knocking into Miller's elbow. Miller picked up the beer and was about to say something when the bottle exploded in his hand, sending glass spraying in all directions.

Dax tore his gaze from Ella and shot up from the table when he realised what had happened. He'd done that. 'Shit. Are you okay?'

A few people dancing close by stopped and looked in their direction.

'We're going,' Miller said, gesturing for Hurley and Frankie to move.

Dax didn't argue this time. He wasn't in control, which meant it wasn't safe for him to stay. He wouldn't forgive himself if anyone got hurt.

Standing, Dax looked over at Ella and saw the guy was still holding her as she shook her head and tried to pull away.

'Dax, don't—' Frankie said as he stood, but she didn't get a chance to finish.

Light flashed in Dax's vision, and he closed his eyes against it. At that same moment, he felt a surge of energy jolt through him like he'd been tasered. Maybe he had. It wouldn't be the first time.

His eyes snapped open when the neat rows of spirits lining the mirrored wall behind the bar exploded simultaneously, sending shards of colourful glass in all directions. The bartenders covered their heads. People queuing for drinks ducked and screamed. The music stopped.

'Go,' Miller said, giving Dax a shove to get him moving. '*Now.*'

Dax looked down at his open hands as he was hustled towards the door.

CHAPTER 24

Screams rang out around Ella as she stared at the glass shelves behind the bar, covered in broken bottles and dripping liquor. Not one had survived. Everyone on the dance floor was looking around, confused, partially covering their heads because they didn't know what the noise meant. Those closest to the bar were pulling pieces of glass from their hair.

'Let's go,' Lucy said, grabbing Ella by the arm and dragging her towards the exit. 'If someone's breaking shit, I'm not waiting around to find out who.'

Ella barely heard her over the ringing in her ears, but she followed, looking over in the direction of the empty booth.

Where is Dax?

A bad feeling enveloped her.

Facing forwards, she spotted Susan and her friends ahead of them. Peter was nowhere in sight.

They were almost at the door when Lucy slipped on a piece of glass, landing on her hip. Ella slowed the fall, but when she tried to pull Lucy to her feet, she was swept away by the moving crowd.

'Lucy!' Ella pushed back against the people behind her. 'Move!' She reached for Lucy. 'Take my hand.' No one slowed or stopped to help. Every time Ella got close, someone knocked her back. Lucy tried to crawl towards her on hands and knees, but then someone stood on her, and she dropped onto her elbow. 'You're trampling her.'

Ella continued to push her way back but was stopped by a wall of chest. She looked up to see Dax, and relief pulsed through her.

'Stay close,' he said, holding Ella to him as he edged backwards, unapologetically shoving people aside. He picked Lucy off the floor in one clean sweep. 'You okay?'

Her hands were shaking as she brushed glass off them. 'I'm fine.'

Ella held onto Lucy's hand as Dax guided them through the door, his large body a physical barrier.

Once outside, Ella saw Susan and her friends climbing into a taxi. She looked around for Peter, spotting him standing with his friends. He made his way over when he caught sight of her.

'What the hell happened in there?' he said. 'Are you all right?'

'Lucy fell,' Ella said, annoyed he'd fled without a backwards glance.

'I'm fine,' Lucy reassured her.

'Peter!' called one his friends.

He looked over to a woman with one foot already inside an Uber, then back at Ella. 'You guys need a ride?'

'We're going with Dax,' Ella said, not bothering to check with him first.

Peter hesitated. 'Okay. See you ladies soon.' He kissed them both on the cheek and nodded once at Dax.

Ella watched him get into the Uber.

'Let's go.' Dax said. 'Miller's got a taxi waiting for us.'

Ella kept hold of Lucy. 'You sure there's room? You had a big group.'

'I'm sure.' His hand went to the small of her back as they made their way to the taxi rank.

Miller was leaning on the passenger side of the first car. He straightened and opened the back door when he spotted them. 'Everyone okay?'

Ella forced a smile. 'We're fine. Thanks for this.' She followed Lucy into the car.

Dax jumped in next and pulled the door shut, his knees touching the back of the seat in front of him. His arm rested against hers, and she didn't move away.

As they crossed the Westgate Bridge, Dax turned to her. 'I'm sorry,' he mouthed.

She didn't have to ask why. A part of her had known it was him the moment she'd realised what had happened. She placed her open hand palm up on her thigh. He took it and looked out the window. No one spoke for the rest of the trip.

When they reached Lucy's house, Ella let go of Dax's hand and went to follow her out of the car, but Lucy shook her head.

'I'm fine, and my bed's crowded enough, remember?' She smiled at Ella. 'I love you. I'll call you in the morning.'

'Love you too.'

Ella waited for her to go inside before pulling the car door closed. A seat now separated her from Dax, and she fought the urge to crawl to him and curl up on his lap. She wanted to press her ear to his chest and see if their hearts were beating in sync, but the drama of the past few weeks filled the space between them.

'Jesus,' Miller said when the taxi pulled up out front of her house. 'Think it might be time for a paint job.'

Ella let out a breath. 'It's on my to-do list.'

Dax got out to open her door, but by the time he got to the other side of the car, she was already standing.

They looked at each other.

'Do you drink tea?' she asked.

His eyebrows rose slightly. 'No.'

She nodded, having guessed that about him. 'There's a shop in Williamstown that makes custom blends. The lady's an iridologist. She claims to know what you need by studying your pupils.' She paused. 'I also had to poke out my tongue. Apparently you can tell a lot from them too.'

Dax shoved his hands into his pockets. 'So... she made you Ella tea?'

'She did.'

'Well, I'd drink Ella tea, if that was an invite.'

'It was.'

Dax closed the car door and walked around to his brother's window. Miller didn't bother putting it down. He just lifted a hand off his leg in a small wave.

Inside, Ella put the kettle on and filled a diffuser with tea leaves, sitting it in the pot her mother had once used. Dax leaned against the kitchen sink watching her.

'I lost control of my energy tonight,' he said. 'That's never happened before.'

Ella finished pouring the water before turning to face him. 'What does that mean?'

He gestured to the kettle. 'It means I boiled over.'

She was silent a moment. 'Was it my fault?'

'No,' he replied immediately. 'It was all me.' There was a long pause. 'And maybe a little bit the wanker handling you on the dance floor.'

She fiddled with the teapot. 'He said he knew me from somewhere.'

'Of course he did.'

She exhaled. 'Persistent but harmless.'

Dax didn't reply.

'I don't really know what to say or what to think about that,' she said. 'I don't know what's normal for your kind.'

He shifted against the sink and looked past her to the ink painting of a ballet dancer hanging on the wall. 'I warned you things can get serious very fast with an ondine.'

'You did.'

'That's because we don't really date. We wait for the right partner. Some of us don't get it right the first time.'

'Who does?'

Dax met her gaze. 'We call them mates.'

'The people you date?'

He shook his head. 'The partner we're meant to be with for life.'

Ella stared back at him. 'Oh. Like soulmates?'

He nodded.

'How do you know when you've found them?'

He thought on that for a moment. 'You just know. It's not logical or sensible. It can't be rationalised or reduced.' He paused. 'It's consuming, confusing, and as I realised tonight, it can scare the shit out of you.'

Ella picked up the teapot with unsteady hands and filled two cups. 'Can an ondine mate with a human?'

He tipped his head back, studying the roof. 'Most would argue no.'

She placed the pot down again. 'And what would you argue?'

'I'd argue I've never smashed a bar apart for anyone else.' He ran a hand down his face. 'I'd argue I'm losing my fucking mind struggling to manage what I feel while trying to do what's best for you.'

Ella chewed her lip. 'I know something of soulmates.'

He fixed his eyes on her once more. 'Let me guess, there's a *Romeo and Juliet* ballet?'

She angled her head. 'Harsh, but there is actually. What

I meant is it's not logical for me either. I've tried to rationalise it, reduce it to a fling.' She drew a breath. 'It's too much, too fast. All of it. It's more complicated than it should be, more dangerous…' She paused. 'I'm sorry Peter was there tonight. He just pops up at the worst times.'

'Don't apologise. Frankie was there too, and *you* didn't blow anything up.'

Ella slid a mug of tea towards him. 'What does it mean to be the mate of an ondine?'

Dax considered his words before replying. 'It means that no matter where life takes us from here, we'll always find our way back to each other.'

'Like an ondine to the sea?' Ella said, the corners of her mouth lifting.

Dax smirked. 'Like an ondine to the sea.' He watched her a moment. 'I don't want you to feel pressured by anything I've just said. You're not obligated to reciprocate or to say or do anything.'

Her eyebrows came together. 'What happens if one mate ends the relationship? Can an ondine find another mate?'

'If they were to end it permanently, then they probably weren't mates to begin with. The best an ondine without a mate can hope for is companionship. Plenty do it.'

'Like you and Frankie?'

'We're definitely better as friends.'

Ella thought. 'Does Miller have a mate?'

'Not that he's met yet.'

'What about Adrian and Greta? Are they companions or mates?'

A smile spread across Dax's face. 'Definitely mates.'

Ella cradled her tea in both hands and watched as Dax took a sip. 'Well?'

He set the cup down on the sink. 'It tastes like rank bathwater.'

'Should I be worried that you've drunk rank bathwater?'

He walked over and took hold of her face, making the tiny hairs on her neck stand to attention.

'I'm going to go home,' he said. 'Give you some space to think.'

She set her tea down and reached for his hands. 'What if I don't want you to leave?'

He brushed his thumb across her jaw. 'Well, we've just established that I'm completely at your mercy, so...'

She felt the sting of tears. 'The separation doesn't work. It's like I'm missing a lung or something. What am I supposed to do with only one lung?'

He brushed hair back from her face. 'You tell me when you're short of breath and I'll breathe for you. On land, in the water. It doesn't matter.'

Ella pushed herself up on her toes and kissed him. 'Please stay,' she whispered against his mouth.

'Do I have to finish the tea?'

'No.'

His arms enclosed her, lifting her slightly so he could bury his face in her neck. 'Then I'll stay.'

CHAPTER 25

*E*lla's eyes snapped open at the sound of a loud noise outside her window. She looked to the empty space in her bed where Dax had been, then pushed the blankets back, going to find some clothes before stepping into Uggs. As she exited the back door into the yard, she crossed her arms against the cold morning as she spotted him holding the electric sander she bought, dusty tins of paint sitting close by.

'What are you up to?' she asked.

He looked in her direction, eyes sweeping the length of her. 'There she is.' He placed the sander on the ground and walked over to kiss her. 'Did I wake you?'

'Yes.' But she didn't mind one bit. 'Are you trying to get me in trouble with the neighbours? No noise before nine o'clock.'

'It's nine thirty.'

'It is?' She hadn't looked at the clock. 'Then I guess I slept in.'

His mouth lifted a little. 'You're allowed to sleep in on weekends. It's not a shortcoming.'

He watched her in a way that made heat crawl up her neck. 'How's the sander?'

'It's not great.'

'Really? I bought the one from the online tutorial.' She looked past him to the paint. 'And I got masking tape for the testing.'

'Tutorial, huh?' He crossed his arms and eyed her. 'And what testing would that be?'

She gestured with her hands. 'First you take a Stanley knife, make an X on one of the weatherboards, then cover it with the tape.' She frowned at his amused expression. 'If the paint sticks to it, then the surface needs sanding.'

He laughed and turned to the house, rubbing at one of the boards with two fingers. Flakes of paint flew in all directions. 'You think I need a piece of tape to tell me your house needs sanding?'

She waved a hand in front of her face. 'This wall gets a lot of sun. You're supposed to test *all* the walls.'

'That what the man in the tutorial said?'

'Yes, actually.'

He kissed the top of her head. 'I called Miller to help. He's bringing my tools.'

Her arms fell to her sides. 'Honestly, I can't really afford it right now.'

'Afford what?'

'To pay you.'

There was that amused expression again. 'Do you see me putting my hand out for money?'

'It's at least eight thousand dollars' worth of work.'

He went to fetch the paint tins, carrying them closer to the house. 'How do you know that?'

'I got quotes.'

He laughed at that. 'That is ludicrous.'

'Three separate painters gave me similar quotes.'

He dropped the tins and returned to her, picking her up

off the ground like she weighed nothing. 'My beautiful, sensible Ella. You did the right thing getting multiple quotes.'

She snaked her arms around his neck. 'I feel a *"but"* coming.'

'But three separate painters were trying to rip you off.'

She felt invincible in his arms, even when he was poking fun at her. 'So you just woke up this morning and decided to paint my house?'

'Pretty much.'

She kneaded his wet hair between her fingers. He smelled all fresh and summery. 'You swam already? I would've come with you.'

'And sat freezing on the beach? I prefer you tucked up warm in bed.'

She touched his beard, remembering the feel of it on her bare skin. 'What if I had woken up and decided this isn't a good idea?'

'The painting?'

'That *we* were not a good idea.'

He drew her closer, if that was possible. 'What's that got to do with me painting your house?'

She couldn't stop the smile. 'I don't want to be left with a half-finished job.'

He released his grip on her, catching her a few inches from the ground. 'Have some faith, Miss Lewis. I'm a professional.' He gently placed her on the lawn.

'Professionals don't sleep with their clients.'

'I don't sleep with all of them,' he called over his shoulder. 'Do you mind making some coffee? Then you can help me out here.'

'I watched the tutorial on painting as well as prep. Bought the exact spray gun the man used in the video too.'

Dax chuckled in response.

'The coffee's instant,' she said, then heard him swear under his breath. 'There's always Ella tea.'

He met her gaze with a playful expression before she wandered back inside. Instead of making coffee, she rummaged through the fridge for smoothie ingredients. She found some coconut milk, threw in a handful of almonds, some chia seeds, a cucumber, a few handfuls of spinach, an apple, and a frozen banana she'd forgotten about. She blitzed it and poured it into two tall glasses, topping each with pepitas.

Pushing through the back screen with her shoulder, she found Dax poking around in the shed. 'Here you go,' she called from the door.

He straightened and brushed his hands on his jeans, taking one of the glasses from her and eyeing it suspiciously.

'Better than instant coffee,' she said.

He took a large gulp, let the taste settle, and then emptied the glass. 'You're right. Better than instant coffee.'

Ella took the empty glass from him. 'Don't you get brain freeze from drinking it that fast?'

'I swim in arctic temperatures. You really think a chilled smoothie is going to be problematic?'

'Fair point.'

Miller called to them from the side gate, and Ella went to let him through.

'Morning,' he said with a nod, arms loaded with tools. He dumped them at Dax's feet along with a backpack. 'Clothes,' he said by way of explanation.

Ella hadn't thought about clothes. All Dax had was what he wore the night prior. Hardly practical. He was also barefoot, the tops of his feet still covered in sand.

Ella stared down at her smoothie while he changed. It felt wrong to appreciate the view with his brother standing there.

'I'll go get the rest of the gear,' Miller said.

Ella looked up as he passed. 'I really appreciate you helping.'

Miller nodded. 'Do you think I could get a coffee?'

Ella bit her lip and glanced at Dax, now wearing khaki shorts with torn pockets and a Vans T-shirt. He smiled at the ground. 'Do you want a smoothie?' she called after Miller.

He paused, eyeing the drink in her hand. 'Thanks, but I'll just wait for the coffee. The others are on their way too.'

'Oh. I'll do a coffee run, then.'

Ella heard the gate open again, and Lucy and Caleb entering the yard.

'Just us,' Lucy called. She looked from Dax to Miller to the paint. 'Well, well. What's going on here?'

'Morning,' Dax said.

Lucy gave him a sly look. 'You're here early.' She knew full well he'd never left.

'Can I help?' Caleb asked, running straight over to Dax.

Dax wrapped a sanding block with sandpaper and handed it to him. 'Come with me. I'll show you which section's yours.'

Ella faced an open-mouthed Lucy.

'Um, did both brothers stay?' Lucy asked.

Ella flicked her arm. 'Very funny.'

Lucy looked at the freshly sanded wall. 'So they're just going to paint your house?'

'Apparently his friends are on their way.'

Lucy looked her up and down. 'Dax obviously had a *very* good night if this is what you get the following morning.'

'Say it a bit louder, I don't think he heard you.'

Lucy laughed and walked over to the wall, inspecting it. 'I need a handyman.'

'You need a house first.'

'Actually, I need a job first.' Lucy peered through the bedroom window. 'You haven't even made your bed.'

'So?'

Lucy looked over her shoulder. 'So you always make your bed. I think I quite like post-sex Ella. She's so chill.'

A clearing of the throat made them both look in Dax's direction. He passed between them without saying anything.

'Want me to stay and help?' Lucy asked, ignoring Ella's glare. 'I could make lunch for everyone.'

Ella couldn't stay angry at her for more than five seconds. 'Only if you have time.'

Lucy was already walking towards the back door.

Dax's warm arms wrapped around Ella the moment the back door slapped shut, and he rubbed his beard on her cheek. 'I'm going to get back to it.'

'I'll help,' she said, turning into him.

'I only have one sander.'

She tilted her head. 'I too have a sander. And gloves. And safety glasses.'

'I saw that.' He let go of her. 'Sounds like you paid close attention to that tutorial.'

'That's kind of the point.'

He laughed. 'Go get some proper shoes on, and I'll show you what to do.'

'I already know.'

He shrugged. 'Okay. Then maybe later I'll go watch a tutorial on how to become a ballet dancer, then put on a flawless performance for you.'

Her head tipped back with laughter. 'I'd actually really like that.'

He stepped back and nodded at the smoothie in her hand. 'Drink it. You haven't had breakfast.'

She wondered whether that protective streak was part

of being a mate. What would happen if they got a year down the track and he realised he was wrong?

'What's the matter?' he asked.

No one could read her like he could. He seemed to sense her shift in mood. 'Nothing's the matter.'

'Liar.' Reaching up, he brushed his knuckles down her cheek. 'Now go change your shoes.'

~

DAX WAS GOING AT HALF his usual pace thanks to the welcomed distraction of Ella sanding a few metres from him. He could get used to having her in constant sight while he worked. He liked her dressed down: old sneakers, over-sized jumper, make-up free, and hair bundled carelessly on top of her head. She looked like a very cute blowfly with those safety goggles on.

Ella straightened and looked over, comparing their work. 'How is it you've managed to sand twice the area when you've spent half your time watching me do the work?'

So she had noticed. 'I've done this a few times, and I've got better tools than you.'

He bit back a smile when Ella removed her goggles, revealing a clear outline of white dust covering the rest of her face.

She scowled. 'What are you laughing at?'

He shook his head and resumed working, conscious of the rest of the pod watching them. Hurley, Greta, Adrian, and Ariel had joined the painting party. Unsurprisingly, Frankie had declined.

Caleb and Ariel went running by, causing Ella to smile after them.

'Instant friends,' Dax said.

Ella nodded. 'Looks that way.'

Caleb found the radio Hurley brought with him and turned the volume up. Men at Work's 'Down Under' came on just as Lucy emerged from the house carrying a tray of wraps. She placed them on the small table she'd wiped down earlier.

'Has Ella told you about her obsession with watching eighties music clips?' Lucy said. 'The cornier the better. This is one of her faves.'

Dax eyed Ella. 'A little before your time, isn't it?'

'So what? I'm not allowed to be amused by it?'

Greta wandered over to Adrian, hugging him around the middle. 'It was a little before your time too, wise old man,' she called to Dax.

He never looked away from Ella. 'You trying to tell me you know *this* song?'

'Every word.' Ella removed her gloves and wandered over to the tap to wash her hands.

Dax followed, leaning against the house. 'Prove it.'

She straightened, looking up at him in a way that made his breath catch, then began to sing along. She sang about bread in Brussels, six-foot men, and Vegemite sandwiches, mostly out of tune and not caring at all.

Lucy wandered over and took her by the hand, turning her elegantly four times to the bogan song. Everyone laughed, even Dax. He liked that she wasn't shy around his friends, even though she had reason to be. Greta and Adrian joined in the singing for the chorus, prompting the kids to start dancing.

Miller and Hurley watched the confusing scene in front of them, heads shaking. Ella collected the plate of food and danced over to them, never missing a lyric as she handed the wraps around. She finished at Dax, singing the final chorus directly to him as she offered him a beef one, knowing he wasn't one for falafels.

He took a bite and kissed her with a full mouth of food

just as the song finished. 'Very impressive, Miss Lewis. I won't doubt you again.'

Ella looked fairly pleased with herself as she took a wrap before returning the plate to the table. She turned the music down on her walk back, and the pair sank to the ground, their backs against the warm wall. They watched Lucy and Greta chatting away as the kids ran in circles around them.

'That scene gives me hope,' Ella said.

Dax looked in the direction of the screaming kids. 'Hope for what?'

'That our worlds could merge.'

Dax stopped chewing. 'Sure, they can merge.'

Ella looked up at him. 'I'd still be keeping this enormous secret from Lucy. I've never kept anything from her before.'

Dax rested his wrists on his knees and watched the guilt play out on her face. He hated being the reason for it. 'I'm sorry. The leniency of the pod only stretches so far, otherwise where does it end?'

She stared ahead once more. 'I get it. I'm not trying to change your mind, I just want you to understand that it's different for me. Your friends know what I am.'

That wasn't entirely true.

'The secret will be a permanent thorn in our relationship,' she added.

It was becoming clear to him that Michael Lewis had no intention of telling Ella the truth about her mother, forcing Dax to keep secrets of his own.

That wouldn't do.

Ella turned back to him. 'If we do this, properly do this, we'll be honest with each other, right?'

He nodded. 'Of course.' Guilt reared up inside of him again.

'I'll be honest with you—always.'

207

He never doubted it for a minute.

The truth about her mother sat on the tip of his tongue, and he wondered if he should just come out and say it. He knew it would bite him on the arse later if he didn't.

Fucking Michael Lewis. He probably thought he'd dodged a bullet.

Dax decided to give him one more chance to come clean. Once the man realised the pair were in fact mates, he'd have no choice but to tell her the truth. 'Next time we fight—and we will—don't ignore my calls for nine days and expect me to be sane at the end of it.'

'And *you* can't be blowing up bars.'

He laughed, then fell quiet. 'You sure about this?'

Ella relaxed against the wall, still watching him. 'Yes.'

He reached for her hand, flattening his palm against hers. He marvelled at the softness of her skin, and his blood stirred at the memory of her naked and pressed against him just hours earlier. Spent, she had curled against him like a cat and fallen asleep. He'd watched her for hours before giving up on sleep and sneaking out to swim. As he dressed, she'd felt for him while she slept. As if he needed more proof they belonged together.

The downside of finding your mate was the dependence that developed—and fast. He'd seen it happen with Adrian and Greta and many couples before them.

'It won't be easy,' he said, offering her a final out.

'Hasn't been so far.' There was a mischievous glint in her eye.

Leaning to kiss her, he whispered, 'Time to get back to work, Miss Lewis.'

CHAPTER 26

*E*lla was in the car with her father on Monday morning when her phone rang. 'It's work,' she said before answering it. 'Hello?'

'Hi, it's Susan. Did you get home all right on Friday?'

Ella glanced at her father, who knew nothing about her weekend other than that her house had been miraculously painted at some point.

'House looks good' was all he'd said when she climbed into the car.

He didn't ask who was responsible—didn't need to. In fact, he hadn't said one more word about it.

'Sure did,' Ella said into the phone.

'I don't think even the owners know what happened. Luckily there are plenty of bars in the area. We just went to another one.'

Ella looked down at her lap, aware her father was eavesdropping. 'Great.'

'Now,' Susan began, 'I've just emailed the statement for the press conference this morning. Barry's still in the meeting with the lawyers. They've been at it since seven thirty. He's asked if you could read it.'

Ella put the call on speaker so she could open the email. 'He wants *me* to do it?'

'You literally just have to read it out,' Susan assured her. 'Barry has complete faith in you.'

'Can't I just send it as a press release?'

Ella's father looked over when they pulled up at a set of lights.

'I know Barry,' he whispered. 'He wouldn't ask you to do it if he wasn't a hundred percent sure you could.'

'Only a few journos usually show up,' Susan continued. 'They take a picture and leave. You don't have to answer their questions. It says at the bottom of the attachment "Please direct any follow-up questions to Barry Taylor." So you're literally reading this out and walking back inside.'

Ella glanced at her watch. 'What time?'

'Nine. I'll leave a printout at the front desk for you. I'm doing a coffee run for the boardroom, so good luck if I don't see you.'

'Thanks.'

The line went dead.

Michael's thumb tapped the steering wheel. 'You can choose courage, or you can choose comfort, but you cannot choose both.'

'Brené Brown,' Ella said absently.

Her father nodded. 'I'm going to drop you out front, park, and then come back for the conference.'

'You don't have to do that.'

'I've never missed a big moment in your life. I'm not about to start now.'

Ella expected nothing less from him.

As she read over the statement, a hollow feeling settled inside her. It was all clever wording and vague comments. She wondered if that was who she was now.

Dance had been honest. There was no deceiving your audience onstage. A dancer was completely exposed, raw, unfiltered. And now she was replacing that expressive ritual with carefully selected words.

'You'll be amazing,' her father said. 'Trust me.'

She pushed the doubt down and focused hard on the words in front of her.

~

SUSAN HAD BEEN RIGHT. Only four journalists waited for her on the lawn outside their building. Her father stood some distance back, wearing the same proud expression he'd worn at every performance he had attended. She felt thirteen again.

Ella glanced down at her notes.

'Thank you all for your time this morning. As you're all aware, the Bass Fuel-owned Flathead Rig was hit by a tidal wave on November 28. Following the incident, safety inspections were carried out, including testing, which revealed gas in the atmosphere and oil in the surrounding waters.'

She swallowed before the lie.

'This is likely a result of damage from the wave. Repairs are now underway to ensure the site is safe for both our workers and marine life.'

She drew a breath before continuing.

'Bass Fuel plans to reopen the rig on December 15 and looks forward to welcoming workers back very soon.'

Ella glanced in the direction of her father and stilled when she spotted Dax leaning against one of the nearby sculptures. Their eyes met briefly, and even from that distance, she could feel his disapproval.

A reporter from *The Age* spoke up, pulling her attention back. 'What impact have these leaks had on marine life so far?'

'I'm afraid I don't have that information on me, but I will have Barry email you the details.'

A young reporter from the *Herald Sun* then asked, 'The environmental group Greenpacific have suggested the leaks were happening before the wave hit. According to the media relations officer, and I quote'—she referred to her notes—'"Gas and oil have been leaking into the water and atmosphere for months." How do you respond to that?'

Panic crawled up Ella's throat. 'I assure you employee safety is Bass Fuel's first priority. The rig would've been closed earlier if there was any danger to its workers.'

'My question is about the danger to marine life.'

In her peripheral vision, Ella saw Dax push off the sculpture and walk off. 'I've included contact details on the printout. Please feel free to send through any follow-up questions to the email address listed, and we'll make sure we come back to you today. Thanks, everyone.'

Ella turned away from the disapproving faces and walked across the lawn to the safety of the foyer. She stopped inside the doors, her stomach churning as she waited for her father to reach her.

'You did great,' he said as he stepped through the doors. His pride dissipated when he saw her expression. 'What's the matter?'

'The oil and gas leaks *have* been ongoing. The air might be safe enough for workers, but the surrounding water is toxic for birds, fish, seals, and—' She stopped herself. 'I just feel like a big fraud.'

Michael's eyebrows lowered. 'You did your job. Focus on that, and be proud.'

'None of it feels genuine.'

'What are you talking about?'

'I'm only here because of you. You got me this job.'

'No, I got you the interview. *You* got the job.'

Ella rubbed her forehead, where a headache was starting.

'You know what I think?' her father said.

'What?'

'I think you're letting that Coburn boy get in your head. One weekend with him and you're doubting yourself.'

She blinked. 'I'm not doubting myself. I'm second-guessing all of this.' She gestured around her. 'This isn't me.' She covered her face. 'What was I thinking?'

'You weren't thinking. You were mourning your career, which is why I stepped in. Ella, you had to do *something*. Self-pity can't be your profession.'

'I just needed time.'

'You had time.'

'Well, I needed more, but you just kept at me.'

'I'm not going to apologise for helping you find employment. You want to get a different job? Go ahead. Just don't do it because your fish fling doesn't understand how the real world works.'

A cold sensation passed over Ella, and she dropped her hand to her side. 'What did you say?'

Michael stilled, realising what he'd said. 'I just don't want that boy getting in your head.'

'You said "fish fling". Why would you say that?' Her heart thudded in her throat as she waited for his reply.

'Because he's... always in the water—the lot of them.' He didn't look her in the eye when he spoke.

Ella's mouth went dry. 'Oh my God. You know.' She pressed her palm to her brow. 'Of course you do. That makes perfect sense. The reaction at the hospital. Your unbridled hate for him.' The folder fell from her hand, slapping against the floor. Neither of them moved to pick it up. She stared hard at him, waiting. 'How long have you known?'

Michael swallowed repeatedly. 'Longer than you.'

213

She nodded slowly and bent to pick up the folder. 'I have to go. I can't do this now.'

He swore, which was out of character. 'Don't leave like this.'

'You should've told me.'

'It's not my secret to share,' he whispered. 'You *know* that.'

That was true, but even still.

'At least you understand now why I'm against it,' he said.

She backed away. 'I'll call you later.'

'Ella—'

She turned and headed for the lift. 'I said I'll call you later.'

CHAPTER 27

'I don't get it,' Frankie said, handing him a coffee from the takeaway tray. 'She doesn't make sense for you.'

Dax looked over his shoulder to where the media was now dispersing. He hadn't stuck around until the end. It was like watching someone else, and it was unsettling. The only good thing to come from it was a chance encounter with Michael Lewis. Dax was hoping to catch him on his way back to work.

'You don't have to get it. You just have to accept it,' he told Frankie.

She tucked her hair behind her ear. 'It doesn't bother you that she lied to the media?'

Of course it did. 'It's her job to lie to the media.'

'Well, it should bother you.'

'Why? Because it bothers you?'

'Because it makes her the enemy. You are literally sleeping with the enemy.'

He exhaled. 'Can we skip the drama today?'

'The fight's still going. We have a responsibility to protect that water—and ourselves. Fertility issues are rife

215

across the pod because of water quality. Fewer ondine babies born each year will eventually lead to our extinction. We don't just give up and say, "Oh well, our plan didn't work," and move on.'

'I know all this.' Their next move would need to be bigger than their last.

Another glance over his shoulder, and Dax spotted Michael Lewis striding along Collins Street. This was his chance. 'I need a second. I'll catch up.'

Frankie stopped. 'Do I need to be worried?'

'It's not your job to worry. I'll see you in a bit.'

Frankie glanced in Michael's direction. 'I really hope you know what you're doing.' With that, she walked off.

Dax stood in the middle of the footpath and waited. Michael looked annoyed before Dax had even spoken a word.

'I'm late for work,' Michael said, passing him. 'What do you want?'

Dax fell into step with him. 'You need to tell Ella about her mother.'

Michael glanced sideways at him. 'I thought I told you to stay out of my family's business.'

'Well, Ella's my business now.'

They stopped at a set of lights, and a car honked when someone crossed on the red.

'I saw the house this morning,' Michael said. 'That's some paint job. Ella pay you for it?'

Dax drew a long breath. 'For the painting? No. She already had the materials.'

Michael glanced sideways at him. 'What about the labour?'

'It was a favour.'

He nodded. 'I'll fix you up. I'd rather she not owe you one in return.'

The light went green, and Dax followed him across the

road. 'I don't want your money. Ella doesn't owe me anything. Never has. Never will.'

When they reached the other side, Dax stopped walking. Michael looked back, then, with an exaggerated sigh, turned to face him, smoothing down his expensive suit jacket.

'I don't answer to you when it comes to my daughter,' he said. 'I want to be very clear about that.'

Dax looked around. 'You have to tell her, because I'm not lying to her about this. It's better if it comes from you.'

'And I'm not working to your timeline.'

Dax straightened. 'I promised Ella honesty, and I intend to keep every promise I make to her.'

Michael looked both ways down the street. 'You want me to be the bad guy so you can swoop in and pick up the pieces? Is that it?'

'If you leave her in pieces, then we're going to have a much bigger problem.'

If looks could kill, Dax would've dropped dead.

'Listen, I've never been afraid of your kind, and I certainly don't intend to start now.' He looked Dax straight in the eye when he added, 'I'm going to tell her everything, but I'm going to do it in my own time and in my own way. So don't chase me down the street again.'

If he hadn't been Ella's father, Dax might've punched the arrogant prick in the face. 'You have until tomorrow.' He nodded once. 'Have a good day, Mr Lewis.'

CHAPTER 28

The day passed in a blur. Ella had texted Dax to let him know she was working through lunch. Truthfully, she was still processing the conversation with her father and hadn't been ready to talk about it. By the time she stepped out of the foyer at six thirty, her mind full and her stomach empty, all she wanted was to feel the weight of Dax's arms, to see her own shock mirrored back at her when she told him the news.

But he wasn't there.

She pulled her phone out and texted him, asking if he was at home.

Two seconds later, her phone rang.

'You okay?' Those were the first words out of his mouth.

She bit her lip. 'Yeah. I just wanted to check in before I…' Before she what? Went to her father's work? Had it out with him in the car? She wasn't ready to confront him and wondered if she should catch the train home instead.

'What's going on?' Dax asked.

She looked around. 'Nothing, I was just hoping to talk to you about something.'

'Okay. About what?'

'Something my dad said today.'

There was a long silence before he said, 'Wait there. I'll come pick you up.'

'Don't do that. Traffic is horrible.'

'Then jump in a taxi. That'll halve the time. My parents are here, but we can take a walk.'

She shook her head. 'That's okay—'

'Ella.'

The way he said her name made her still.

'I'm texting you my address,' he said. 'I'll see you soon.'

She was already walking to the taxi rank. 'Okay.'

Dax was waiting out front when the taxi pulled up. He opened the passenger door and paid the driver before she had a chance to pull her wallet out.

'You don't need to do that,' she said once she was standing on the footpath with him.

His eyes moved over her. 'Have you eaten today?'

She was about to lie but thought better of it. 'I'll eat later.'

He took her hand and tugged her in the direction of the house. 'Mum's at Frankie's, but she made up a plate of food for you.'

Ella glanced down the street at the group of town-houses where she knew the rest of the pod lived—including Frankie. 'That was really nice of her.'

As she stepped inside the house, she looked around at the stylish furniture and modern art before following Dax to the dining table, where his father sat reading the paper. Opposite him was a plate covered with another plate. They were obviously not Glad Wrap people.

'Sit,' Dax said. 'I'll get you some water.'

She met Irvin's gaze as she took her seat. 'I hope you don't mind me crashing your dinner.'

He folded the paper and dropped it on the table in front

of him. 'Not intruding at all. We've been looking forward to meeting you properly.' He gestured to the food. 'Eat up. It's still warm.'

Ella removed the cover and looked down at the enormous steak bleeding out on her plate. A pink pool of fatty liquid surrounded her mashed potato and stained the carrots. 'Wow.'

Dax placed a glass of water in front of her as he sank into the chair beside. 'You don't have to finish.'

'You like beef?' Irvin asked, watching her pick up her cutlery.

Ella looked up from her plate. 'Yes.' Steaks the size of a man's head not so much, but she would give it a red-hot go for Dax's sake.

'We burn a lot of calories,' Irvin said, 'so we need a lot of protein.'

'I've noticed. Seems you drink a lot of coffee too.' She glanced sideways at Dax. 'Or is that just you?'

Dax rested his elbows on the table. 'Oh, that's a pod-wide problem.'

'Dax tells us you danced for Melbourne Ballet before moving over to Bass Fuel,' Irvin said.

Ella sawed through the meat. 'Yeah, I was with them a few years. I was getting injured a lot. The training's quite intensive. Turns out I'm better suited to dancing as a hobby.'

Irvin studied her. 'Can't be easy giving up your passion.'

Ella chewed and swallowed. 'No, it wasn't.' She saw the men exchange a look and wondered if Dax had said something to his father about her reason for coming. He had warned her there were no secrets within the pod. Swallowing her food, she decided to broach the topic with Irvin around since it affected him also.

No time like the present.

Laying down her cutlery, she said, 'Listen, I spoke with Dad today. It seems he's been keeping a secret.'

Dax's hands came together in front of him, and he exchanged another look with his father, one that made her stomach feel uneasy, like they knew what was coming.

'Would you prefer to chat in private?' Dax asked.

Ella read his expression, noting the lack of eye contact that looked a lot like guilt. Her hands went slack around the cutlery. 'Do you already know what I'm about to say?' Her gaze went across the table to Irvin. 'Do you all know?'

The silence was nauseating.

'Oh,' Ella said quietly. 'So it's just me playing catch-up here.' She fixed her eyes on Dax. 'And how long have you known?'

'Not long.'

'Did you know on the weekend? *Before* we had a conversation about honesty?'

Dax searched her eyes, then looked over at his father. 'Can you give us a minute, please?'

Irvin slowly rose and went out back.

Ella placed her cutlery down on the bloody plate.

'He wanted to tell you himself,' Dax said, 'so I gave him the chance.'

'Oh, so you decided it together. It doesn't even make sense why you'd keep it from me. Him knowing makes life so much easier, don't you think?' She looked up at him and saw the confused expression on his face.

He shook his head. 'Him knowing?'

That was the moment Ella realised they were talking about different things.

Dax leaned back in his chair, regarding her. 'What exactly did your father tell you?'

Her heart began to race. 'Everything.'

His eyes never left her face. 'Ella, what did your father tell you today?'

She raised her chin. 'First you tell me everything you know, and then I'll tell you if it matches.'

'Ella,' Dax said, a warning in his voice. 'This isn't a game.'

She opened her mouth, but before she got a word out, the front door burst open. Ella jumped half a foot, and Dax shot up out of his chair when Frankie marched into the room. Her lips were bare, her eyes mascara smudged. She looked between them before her gaze settled on Dax.

'You should've told me sooner,' she slurred. 'It would've saved me so much unnecessary pain.'

The smell of wine hit Ella as she sat frozen in her chair.

'Jesus, Frankie,' Dax said. 'You're a fucking mess.'

June rushed through the door, out of breath. She went straight to Frankie, taking her gently by the arm. 'Let's go into the kitchen and make you some coffee.'

Frankie tore her arm free. 'No! He owes me an explanation. Why did you wait?'

'I've already explained why,' June whispered, casting an apologetic look in their direction.

Ella looked up at Dax. 'What's she talking about?'

'Get her out of here,' he said, moving around the table towards them. 'She doesn't know.'

'Know what?' Ella asked.

Frankie's wild eyes locked on hers. 'She doesn't know about her *mother*?'

Dax stopped dead in his tracks, eyes closing.

'Your traitorous whore of a mother who thought she was *so* special.' Frankie practically spat the words at Ella. 'She rode off into the sunset with her human. Well, guess what? The sea *took her back*.'

Dax fixed his dark eyes on his mother. 'Get her out of here. *Now*.'

June guided a teary Frankie from the room, casting a look of pity at Ella before they disappeared from sight.

Slowly, Ella stood, one hand pressed to her hammering heart as her chair screeched along the floor. 'The sea took her... *back*?' Her legs wobbled beneath her as she waited for Dax to look at her. 'What does that mean? What is she talking about?'

He gripped the top of a chair with both hands and lifted his gaze. 'I don't think your father told you everything.'

That was becoming very clear. 'Then *you* tell me.'

He looked torn.

'Tell me,' Ella pleaded.

He released a resigned breath. 'Your mother was ondine. She was one of us.'

'*What?*' Her voice rang in her ears.

Dax moved towards her, hand outstretched. 'Ella.'

That was the last word she registered as the room tilted. After that it was just images flashing in her vision and noises cutting in and out like a faulty microphone. Then Dax's face was above her, so close, his mouth moving. She watched it, wanting to comprehend but unable to. The downlight was angled like a halo above him, casting strange shadows across his face.

Her eyes sank shut.

She was lifted, carried, breathing in Dax's familiar scent. She held on to it with every mental capability she had left as she leaned into his warmth.

'It'll be all right,' she heard him whisper into her hair.

That was the last thing she remembered.

～

ELLA BLINKED against the light streaming through a gap in the curtains—curtains she didn't recognise. She pushed herself up and looked around the unfamiliar room. She knew it was Dax's by the smell and the few items of clothing thrown over the chair in the corner. She glanced behind her at the empty bed. Dax was likely swimming already.

Swinging her legs over the edge of the bed, she reached for her bag and pulled out her phone to check the time. There were fourteen missed calls from her father. The memories from the day before came crashing down on her. She took a few slow breaths before dialling his number, and he answered on the second ring.

'Are you okay?'

Tears pricked her eyes. 'Is it true? Was Mum one of them?'

The silence on the other end of the phone was her answer. She blinked, and a tear escaped. She hung up before brushing it aside. The betrayal was too big to grasp.

Covering her mouth, she held in a sob, afraid someone would hear her. She breathed slowly in and out until she had her emotions under control, then rose from the bed and stepped into her shoes before snatching up her handbag. Her legs threatened to give way at any moment, but she knew she would drag herself down the stairs if need be.

Opening the door, she looked both ways before stepping out onto the landing and creeping down the stairs like an intruder. She made it all the way to the front gate before coming face to face with a dripping Dax. He looked her over before speaking.

'You're up. How are you feeling?'

She was surprised by how hard the anger hit her, how enormous the betrayal felt. 'I'm going home.'

'Okay. Just let me throw some clothes on and grab my keys.'

Ella shook her head and stepped past him out onto the footpath. 'No.'

'What do you mean, *no*?' he said, turning.

'Just no. I don't want to be in a car with you or anywhere near you.' The ice in her tone surprised even her.

Dax followed and reached for her. 'Wait.'

'Don't touch me.'

He immediately let go, raising his hands. 'You need space. I get that. Just let me get you home safely, and then you can hate me all you want.'

She pushed her hair back from her face. 'You should've told me.' Her eyes began to burn.

'It wasn't my secret to tell.'

She emitted a harsh noise that resembled a laugh. 'Yes, it was so much better coming from *Frankie*.'

Dax lowered his hands. 'Your dad was supposed to tell you.'

'Didn't you hear? He's a liar too.' Her voice broke, and when Dax reached for her again, she stepped back. 'No!' Her handbag fell to the ground between them, its contents scattering. 'You don't get to pretend to care about me now.'

'What are you talking about?'

'You're a *liar*. You fed me all that bullshit about mates, and trust, and honesty, all while lying to my face.'

He didn't move. 'Okay. I'll cop to that.'

'We're done. Over!'

He ran a hand down his face. 'It doesn't work like that. You can't just switch it off.'

'It doesn't work like that for *you*, but don't pretend to know me.'

'You can stand here and tell me you hate me until you're blue in the face, but it doesn't change what we are.'

'It changes *everything*.'

'We're mates.'

She stepped towards him, nearly tripping over her handbag. When he reached out to catch her, she pushed his hand away. 'I'm not your *mate*. I'm your *ex*.'

That last part got to him, because he threw his hands up

and walked back to the gate. 'Go on, then. Walk off your mood. I'm not going to stand here and be a punching bag for your daddy issues.'

She bent, gathering the contents of her handbag. 'I think I'll swim home.'

He paused, one hand resting on the gate as he looked back at her. 'You're going to *swim* to Williamstown?'

She was barely aware of the words spilling out of her mouth. Straightening, she looked across the road to the water. 'My mum was ondine, so I guess that makes me half fish.' She laughed despite nothing being funny. 'I'm probably a really good swimmer and just never had a chance to realise it.'

Her feet were moving then, but the second they hit the bitumen, a hand caught her arm.

'Ella, stop it,' Dax hissed. 'You can't swim that distance. You'll drown.'

She tore her arm free with such force that she fell backwards into the path of an oncoming bicycle. It would've hit her had Dax not yanked her out of the way.

'Jesus, Ella. Get off the bloody road,' he said, dragging her back onto the footpath.

She pounded his hand with a closed fist. 'Let go!'

'I'll let go when you calm down.'

She continued to struggle. 'I'll calm down when you let go!'

'You're behaving like a fucking child.' He released her as he said it.

They stood there panting, Ella brushing tears off her cheeks.

'Why can't I swim like you?' she blurted out.

He watched her carefully. 'Because you're human.'

'No. I'm half ondine.'

'Your mum might've been ondine, but *you're* human. That's why your dad never told you. There was no need for

226

you to know after your mother passed.' He raked a hand through his wet hair. 'I guess he thought he was protecting you from this.'

Ella was still panting. How was it that she was 50 percent her mother, yet the only parts she had inherited were her hair and eye colour?

She hugged her handbag close, her mind splintering as questions crashed down on her. The weight of them was too much. 'I'm going home. I'll catch a tram, then the train. If you follow me, then I'll swim it just to piss you off.'

She really did sound like a child, but she didn't care.

He stared at her for the longest time until finally he nodded. 'I'm not going to chase you. You'll come back to me when you're ready.'

She fought back tears. 'I'm not coming back. Whatever this is'—she gestured between them—'it doesn't work without trust. I'd rather live my life with an empty heart than a shattered one. You've done enough damage.'

Slinging her handbag over her shoulder, she left Dax standing in the middle of the footpath.

∼

A TRAM AND A TRAIN LATER, Ella finally made it home. She expected to find her father's car parked in the driveway, had even readied herself for another fight on the walk from the station, but it wasn't there.

When she unlocked the front door, the smell of tea hit her, the smell of comfort. Ella walked into the kitchen in search of Lucy. Sure enough, there she was, seated at the kitchen table with a mug nestled between her hands.

'Where's Caleb?' Ella asked, her voice barely carrying the distance between them.

Lucy rose from her chair, setting the cup down. 'With Mum.'

'What are you doing here?' Ella asked. 'And please don't lie. It'll finish me.'

Lucy nodded. 'Dax phoned me. He thought you might need someone waiting for you at this end.'

Ella's face collapsed. The tears she'd been holding in on the train now poured freely down her cheeks. She dropped her handbag and covered her mouth with both hands.

Lucy went to her, pulling her into a hug. Ella cried heaving, ugly tears.

'He said he would leave it to you to tell me everything,' Lucy whispered.

Ella pulled back. 'He did?'

Lucy searched her eyes. 'He told me to believe every word you told me. What does that mean?'

'I can barely process it. I've got no idea how you're supposed to.'

'Oh shit. This isn't some regular couple fight, is it?'

Ella shook her head. 'It's all a mess. I feel so broken right now.'

Lucy pulled her into a tight hug. 'It's okay. We'll piece you back together, just like last time. It's what we do. One piece at a time. One cup of tea at a time. One dance movie at a time.'

Ella's eyes sank shut. 'It involves Mum.'

Drawing back, Lucy stared at her. 'Your mum?'

A nod.

'Then I guess we'll start with *Save the Last Dance*. That's always been the one for mum feels.' Lucy guided her to the couch and lowered her onto it. 'In the absence of comfort food and wine, because you live like a masochist, I guess we'll hit up Caleb's stash of Tiny Teddies. Then you're going to tell me everything.'

Ella hung her head in her hands. 'Make sure you're sitting down.'

CHAPTER 29

*I*f Dax was asked to define torture, it was days with not one word from Ella.

No texts.

No missed calls.

Not that there was an opportunity for missed calls with him whipping his phone out of his pocket on the first ring.

She was his mate. She would find her way back to him eventually. In the meantime, he needed to settle in for a long wait.

He thought a lot about all the unanswered questions she would have. That was one way he could've been useful. He could've given her an ondine perspective her father would only have been able to guess at. But it seemed Lucy was the only person she truly needed. That was why he'd caved and pulled her best friend into their mess. He could live with an angry pod, but he couldn't sleep knowing Ella was alone in this.

Despite the logic, knowing she needed space and time, he still watched the footpath in the mornings, waiting for her to pass by on her way to work. He didn't see her once.

He was fairly sure she was walking the long way around in order to avoid him, so he volunteered for every coffee run, even found himself hanging with the smokers in hope she might randomly pass by during the day. Was it too much to ask for just a glimpse of her? He could tell plenty from a glimpse.

When November turned into December, Dax knew he needed a different strategy in order to keep sane, so for the next few weeks, he threw himself into his work. He swam at five every morning and was on-site just after six. He skipped breaks and let the others do the coffee runs, because he knew any sight of her would send him spiralling into stalker mode. During his lunch breaks, he wandered to different parts of Docklands and ate by himself.

It worked well enough for a time.

Then a couple of weeks before Christmas, Dax got home from work and found his parents seated at the kitchen table.

'Hey,' he said, dropping his keys on the bench before going to greet them.

'How are you, love?' his mother asked, kissing his cheek. She knew better than to ask after Ella.

'Good,' he lied.

His parents had been travelling between Melbourne and King Island over the previous few weeks, keeping a close eye on the happenings of Flathead Rig. It was due to open the next day.

'Well?' Dax said. 'What's the latest?'

His father wore a solemn expression. 'The rig will reopen as planned. Emissions are supposedly at a safe level. No one seems to care what's happening below the water's surface.'

Dax cursed, then apologised to his mother, but she didn't appear to care.

Miller leaned against the kitchen bench. 'Do we have a plan B?'

'There's always a plan B,' Dax said. 'It's just a matter of whether we're prepared to implement it.'

June tapped a finger on the table. 'I don't know about this particular plan. There's a good chance someone will get hurt.'

'Not to mention the high risk of an oil leak,' Irvin chimed in.

'You don't think two tidal waves hitting the rig in a matter of weeks is going to look suspicious?' Miller asked.

'We're not hitting it with a wave,' Dax said. 'We're sinking it.'

Miller frowned. 'So your plan is to swim out there with your circular saw and just start cutting through the supports?'

'Very funny,' Dax said. 'Since no one's focused on what's happening underwater, we can weaken the support beams and let gravity do the rest.'

'A structural collapse will prompt an even bigger investigation,' Miller said. 'What are the support beams made from?'

'Steel and concrete,' Dax replied. 'Both corrode over time. We're just going to help the process along.'

If anyone knew what they were doing, it was a bunch of ondines with expertise in construction.

'My energy's grown considerably these past few months,' Dax added. 'I'm coming out for this one.'

Irvin shook his head. 'Absolutely not. You'll stay on land.'

'Not your decision,' Dax replied. 'Besides, I have a good idea for an alibi.'

June perked up at that. 'Ella?'

Just her name spoken aloud stung. 'No, Mum, not Ella.'

'When would you do it?' Miller asked.

'We pick a quiet time at the rig,' Irvin said. 'Like Christmas Eve. Less risk of someone getting hurt.'

Dax turned to his father. 'That's a pretty dark suggestion from you.'

June tutted her husband. 'We're not ruining everyone's Christmas. When's their Christmas party?'

Miller looked between his parents. 'Ah, we're going to ruin that instead? Very considerate.'

'That's not a bad idea,' Irvin said. 'They do a big thing in the city with just skeleton staff out at the rig.'

'Maybe they've already had it.' Miller looked to Dax. 'Ella mention anything about a party?'

Dax shook his head. 'Nope, and I'm not dragging her into it. I'm supposed to protect her from this shit.'

June let out a heavy breath. 'I think you've protected her a little too well. That's why you're in this boat.'

Dax looked up at the roof. 'Here we go.'

'All I'll say—'

'On top of the things you've already said.'

'—is that perhaps she's not as fragile as you think. A child who experiences grief like that, at such a young age, is usually built of something solid by the time they reach adulthood.'

'Just casually run into her,' Miller said. 'Mention the Christmas party amid other meaningless small talk. You don't have to bring her into anything.'

Dax wasn't convinced. 'And how do I run into her if she's avoiding me?'

'She'll have to show up at work eventually. She's not going to run from you.'

'She might.'

Miller was undeterred. 'One awkward conversation for the good of the pod, and then you're done.'

Dax rose, needing that afternoon swim suddenly. 'Perfect. More deceit.'

'She's your mate.' His mother's voice followed him out of the room. 'She has to forgive you eventually.'

CHAPTER 30

*E*very morning, when Ella pulled herself from sleep, she would lie with the unbearable weight of betrayal on her chest for a few minutes. Eventually she would be forced to sit up and draw greedy breaths. It wasn't the first time in her life she had found herself in that state, so she knew what to do.

Keep moving.

Do the next thing, then the next, until another day was behind her.

It was several days until she was calm enough to hear her father out. He had come to the house to tell his story, and she had listened in silence. The following day, he came back with photos she'd never seen before, and she sat staring at the images.

One of them was of her mother wading in the sea with her hands outstretched, her belly enormous and hair wet. The water was rising, moving. She looked happy. Ella had always remembered her happy. But then again, that was what mothers did. Ella always marvelled at Lucy's ability to smile in front of Caleb no matter her internal state.

'The thing is, she never really belonged to us,' her father had said, head in his hands.

Ella had continued to stare at the photograph while her father spoke about the time before her death when she stopped going down to the sea.

'She didn't want to be one of them after your birth. She wanted to be like you.'

Carrie Lewis had grown sicker and weaker until the night Ella's father pleaded with her to return to the sea for a few days, to get better, stronger—because Carrie Lewis had belonged to the sea.

Perhaps she interpreted the fact that Ella was human as a false sign, like she could suddenly evolve to match her family.

Michael had called Ella every day since that visit, but every time, she just watched it ring out. Yes, those initial conversations had helped carve a path forwards for them, but she wasn't ready to walk down it yet.

Do the next thing.

The next thing.

The next thing.

She ran every day. She did extra Pilates classes, more yoga, took care of Caleb while encouraging Lucy to go out into the world when she couldn't. She did meal planning and food prep, anything to fill in the gaps of each day, because if she stopped, she would start thinking about Dax. There was only so much grief and resentment she could hold in that battered heart of hers. So much for being her mate, her protector. He was just another person poking holes in her.

Ella managed to avoid him. She brought her lunch every day, which meant the only time she had to go to B for Brazil was for coffee runs. He was never there though. She suspected he was avoiding her also.

It seemed to work—until the morning she found him waiting outside her building.

He was dressed in his work clothes, hair out, and one boot resting on the wall behind him. She marvelled at his ability to look so much cooler than every man in a designer suit passing him.

That was Dax.

She stopped some distance away, watching him, annoyed by her response. Her spirit seemed to soar, and the tension she'd carried for weeks dissipated in the breeze. It was like seeing home for the first time after being away for months. Swallowing thickly, she willed her heart to slow down, but it seemed to call to his. She knew that because he looked in her direction that very moment, and both feet returned to the ground as he buried his hands in his pockets.

He made no move towards her, just waited to see what she would do. He needed something, she could feel it. Her feet moved forwards, like he was reeling her in by an invisible cable attached to her chest. Then she was standing in front of him, wishing she had worn heels. He suddenly seemed impossibly tall.

As his eyes moved over her face, she wondered if she was supposed to ask him what he was doing there, perhaps reprimand him while maintaining a cold facade. The problem was they were beyond games, and while she could choose not to be with him, she couldn't stop loving him.

'Are you okay?' she asked.

He nodded. 'You?'

'Fine.' She breathed out. 'What are you doing here?'

'I'm not here to hassle you. I just wanted to check in.'

'Okay.'

He sniffed. 'I realised the other day I never congratulated you on your first press conference.'

Ella had been trying to forget about it, but Barry kept

bringing it up, reminding her how well she was doing at Bass Fuel. She had started browsing other opportunities, wondering where else she might fit in the world. 'So you came to congratulate me?'

'No,' Dax said.

She looked down. 'I think we were both frauds that day.'

He didn't respond to that.

'How's your work going?' she asked, looking up again.

He seemed to think on it a moment. 'Pretty good. Had our Christmas party last week. We hired out a lawn bowls club for the afternoon.'

She felt the pull of a smile. 'That actually sounds really fun. Plus cheap beer.'

'There's that.'

Dax took a step back from the door when he saw Barry approaching.

'Morning,' Barry said, eyeing Dax.

'Morning,' they said in unison, like two kids caught doing something wrong in the schoolyard.

Instead of continuing past, Barry paused in front of Ella. 'Can I see you in my office when you come up?'

Ella wondered whether the authoritative tone was for Dax's benefit. 'Of course. Be there in a sec.'

When they were alone again, Dax said, 'Friendly bloke.'

The corners of her mouth lifted, using muscles she'd forgotten about. 'I should go up.'

'Wait, you didn't tell me about your Christmas party.'

She thought that was a weird reason to stall her but figured he was just trying to extend their conversation. 'It's this Friday, at some rooftop bar in the city I've never heard of. Susan convinced me to get ready with her. She's treating it like her debutante.'

Dax laughed quietly, and the noise rolled over Ella, warming her.

'Well, enjoy.' He pulled his hands from his pockets as he stepped back. 'Be safe.'

She fought the impulse to follow him. 'Seeing you always feels good right up until the moment you leave. Then it's like this enormous storm cloud arrives, and I'm just left standing in the rain.'

His throat bobbed as he looked away. 'Well, that same storm cloud has followed me around for weeks, if that makes you feel any better.'

'A little.'

He laughed again, but it died quickly. 'I've only ever wanted sunshine for you.'

'I'm searching for it.'

'I promise you one thing.' He gestured above him with a nod. 'Bass Fuel is not your sunshine.' With the faintest smile, he added, 'See you around, Miss Lewis.' Then he left her on the footpath clutching her stomach.

～

'You wanted to see me?' Ella said, poking her head into Barry's office.

He waved her in. 'Yes. Close the door and come over here. I want to show you something.'

Ella thought nothing of it until she wandered over and stood behind him. Her breath caught when she saw what was on his computer screen. It was security footage from Flathead Rig date-stamped November 28—the day the tidal wave hit.

'What's all this?' she asked, hoping her voice didn't give her nerves away.

Barry pointed to the screen. 'This is a visual of the bridge that connects the platforms. You can see right down to the water below.'

Ella stared at the screen. 'So you can.'

'Keep watching. I want to show you something.'

At first, there was nothing. Then Karen and Ella appeared on the bridge as they rushed towards the well-head platform. Ella held her breath. A moment later, water burst across the bridge, and her blood turned cold at the memory of the freezing sea pounding her before sweeping her away.

'This was 10:14 a.m.,' Barry said, noting the time stamp.

Ella stood frozen next to Barry, willing him to stop the video, but it didn't stop. They continued watching until the water settled and the bridge was visible once more.

'There,' Barry said, pausing it and leaning forwards in his chair. He pointed to a black smudge in the water. 'At 10:18 a.m. You surface and swim to the support beam.'

Ella's heart beat a little harder.

'Almost *four minutes* after you were swept off the bridge,' Barry added, turning to her. He was silent a moment as she continued to stare at the screen. 'Do you know how long the average person can hold their breath?'

She shook her head. 'No.'

'It's not four minutes.' He faced the computer, clicking Play again. 'It's difficult to see, but this is you hanging on to the bridge.' He pointed. 'And over here, Karen appears on-screen.'

Ella's heart pounded in her ears as she stared at the black mark floating nearby.

'And what's this?' Barry asked, pointing to another black smudge next to Ella.

Dax's familiar form came into view.

'Someone else is with you.' Barry paused the video once more. 'There are three of you in the water.' He pointed before hitting Play, showing the part where Dax disappears to get Karen. She coughs up water before floating mysteriously towards Ella.

Barry finally closed the video and turned to her,

looking betrayed. 'Care to tell me what really happened in the water that day?'

She swallowed multiple times in place of words.

Barry released a breath and rubbed his forehead. 'It's not the first time we've had unauthorised people in the water out there. We know of certain groups, for lack of a better word, who are working very hard to shut that rig down.' He looked up at her. 'Your boyfriend, for one.'

She couldn't think, couldn't breathe.

'I know it was Dax. That's why you never mentioned it. You want to tell me what he was doing out at the rig that day? Or shall I have the police go ask him?'

She pressed the tips of her fingers onto the desk for balance. 'They test the water, that's all. They don't trespass. They just take their samples and leave.' She knew it was a fine line between saying too much and not saying enough.

Barry swivelled in his chair. 'Dax bloody Coburn. Troublemakers, the lot of them. He had his boat and scuba licence taken off him, you know? He's not allowed to be out there.' He tapped the arm of his chair. 'I could go to the police and have him hauled into court *again*.'

'I'm alive because of him. *Karen* is alive because of him. Two deaths might've resulted in the rig being shut down permanently.'

He thought on that for a moment. 'So I'm supposed to thank him?'

'No, of course not.' She calmed herself as best she could. 'I just think Bass Fuel has had enough media attention of late. If this gets out, everyone's going to ask why he was out there testing the water to begin with.'

Barry shook his head. 'You should've told me. You should've said something your first day back in the office.'

'He wasn't on the rig. He was in the water.'

'Doesn't matter. You chose to protect your boyfriend instead of coming to me.'

Ella swallowed back tears.

'He's using you, you know,' Barry said. 'You'll realise that soon enough.' He exhaled. 'Go pack up your desk. I'm going to have to let you go.'

That statement should've crushed Ella, but instead, she felt a strange sense of relief. 'Oh.'

'I'm sorry for it. You know how I feel about you, but I need to know your loyalty is to Bass Fuel, not the leeches trying to shut us down.'

'Okay.'

'That's all you're going to say? Not going to ask for another chance?'

'No.' She didn't want another chance. 'Dad's going to be so annoyed with me.'

'Given you're still within your three-month probation period, we can part ways with minimal fuss.'

'Right.' Ella nodded, walked around his desk, and then paused. 'I'm really sorry I broke your trust. I understand that kind of disappointment all too well.' She continued towards the door, feeling both sick and relieved all at once.

'Ella,' Barry called.

She stopped.

'Let's tell everyone it was your decision. I think we both know it would've come to that eventually. Am I wrong?'

She shook her head. 'Again, I'm sorry. You gave me every opportunity to succeed here. I let you down.'

Linking his hands in front of him, Barry said, 'Good luck with your next role.' He paused. 'And best of luck with your father.'

CHAPTER 31

*D*ax had just finished packing up for lunch when Miller whistled to him. He removed his gloves and wandered over.

'Yeah?'

Miller glanced over his shoulder. 'Ella's here. I think something's up.'

Dax brushed past him. 'Where is she?'

'I put her in my office.'

He zigzagged through the workers, tools, and debris, then stepped into the office, where he found Ella standing by the window. 'You okay? What happened?'

She turned in his direction, looking pale and exhausted. 'Barry knows.'

'Knows what?'

'That you were out at the rig on the day the wave hit. He has security footage.'

His first instinct was to go to her, soothe her in some way, but her body language made it clear she preferred the space between them. He remained by the door. 'He knows it was me?'

'It was blurry, but he put two and two together.'

'With the help of a calculator?'

Not even a hint of a smile. 'Did you know I was under-water for four minutes? No one can hold their breath that long.'

Dax leaned against the wall. 'So he'll call the cops, like he always does, and I'll handle it. If the footage isn't clear, he doesn't have a leg to stand on.'

'He knows it's you,' she said, hand going to her fore-head. 'He'd already drawn his own conclusions. Lying seemed pointless.'

He stared at the desk against the other wall. 'Well, it's my mess. I don't want you to worry about it.'

She looked over at that. 'He fired me.'

'He what?' Dax pushed off the wall and walked around to her. 'On what grounds?'

'Oh, I don't know. *Lying*, maybe.' She shook her head. 'It's not unreasonable to expect honesty from employees.'

His blood was running too hot to heed the moral lesson. 'I'll go speak to him, tell him it's on me, that I forced you to keep the secret.'

She watched him, arms crossed in front of her like a shield. 'I don't even care about the job. I'm just embar-rassed. You said it yourself, I don't belong there.'

'I thought the old fucker liked you.'

She blinked her disapproval. 'He does, which is why he's telling people I left.'

Dax relaxed a little. 'First decent thing he's done in his life.'

She exhaled and looked out the window again. 'He won't go to the police. He wants to protect the company from further scrutiny. But he'll be watching you closely, so tread carefully.'

'If he comes after me, we have pod members who can help.'

'Lawyers?'

'Lawyers, cops.'

She frowned at that. 'So you just live by your own laws and have dirty cops clean up your messes?'

He couldn't help but laugh. 'Our own laws? We don't walk around holding up 7-Elevens.'

She looked down. 'I think in his own way, Barry appreciates what you did. Take his silence as an expression of gratitude.'

'He might feel differently if he knew we made the wave.' He breathed out. 'Still can't believe he walked you.'

'It's the push I needed.'

They were silent a moment.

'So, what now?' he asked.

She looked around as though the answer lay somewhere in the office. 'I go home, have a cry, and then make a plan.'

The thought of her in tears turned his stomach. 'Let me drive you home.'

She shook her head. 'I can't crawl back to you for comfort at the first hurdle.'

'Why not?'

'Because I'll end up inviting you in and hate myself in the morning.'

His eyebrows rose. 'Whoa. I just offered you a ride home. Didn't say anything about coming in.'

Her cheeks coloured, and it was the most striking thing he'd seen in weeks.

'I'm going,' she said. 'Can you just promise me you'll stay away from the rig?'

He couldn't make that promise. 'Careful. I might start thinking you give a shit.'

She tilted her head. 'I don't want to see you in jail. I mean, how long can an ondine survive locked up?'

'The pod's very good at handling these things.' He really

wanted to hold that troubled face of hers. 'You look worried.'

'Of course I'm worried.'

He understood that better than anyone. 'It's a curse of sorts.'

Ella nodded as she stepped past him. It took all his willpower not to reach for her as she walked by. At the door, she paused.

'In every fairy tale I've ever danced,' she said, 'there's always a way to break the curse.'

CHAPTER 32

*I*t was the first warm evening of summer and Ella's first day of being unemployed. On her way back from yoga, she turned right at her street instead of left, finding herself down at the water. A group of boys played soccer, and a pair of women stood talking with their dogs on leads. Ella removed her shoes and socks before wading into the sea, not caring that her leggings got wet in the process. Her entire body broke out in goosebumps, and her feet ached from the cold, a reminder that she was very much human.

She faced away from the shore, imagining her mother swimming far out in the distance. It was different now though. She used to picture her mother drowning, kicking her feet as she tried to reach the surface. Now she envisioned her mother serene and breathing water.

She blinked back tears as a small wave wrapped her legs. 'She came back.' Ella spoke the words at her own shadow. 'She came back, and you just spat her out.'

The setting sun disappeared behind a cloud, taking her shadow with it.

Ella's phone vibrated in her pocket, and she pulled it

out. It was her father, likely trying to pitch a new job opportunity. She watched his name until it stopped ringing, then shoved it back in her pocket as she returned to shore.

Scooping up her shoes, she walked barefoot home, pausing out front of her house to admire the paintwork. She remembered the weekend fondly. It had felt too soon to say 'I love you', but the words had sat on the edge of her tongue. She was too sensible to say them aloud. Too safe. Too afraid.

Inside, she dropped her runners next to the door and brushed her feet off with her socks before heading into the studio. She walked the length of the mirror, assessing herself until she spotted a smudge that stopped her. She used her elbow to remove it, then stepped back to ensure there were no more like it. It was such a ridiculous set-up for a failed ballerina. She'd thought about renting the space out or turning it into a Pilates studio, but she always chickened out the moment the thought got too serious.

Walking over to the wall, she plugged in her phone and selected an Ed Sheeran song. She began to dance to it, watching herself closely as she moved in front of the mirror. No one was watching. No one was there critiquing or judging her. No one cared if her extensions weren't high enough or her turns were a little heavy. And yet her extensions *were* high enough, and her turns were faultless.

When the song ended, she remained in front of the mirror, breathing hard. An idea had come to her during the song, and she wondered why she hadn't thought of it before. Rushing over to her phone, she tugged the cord out and fumbled to unlock it, dialling Lucy's number.

'Hey' came Lucy's voice. 'What's up?'

Ella smoothed her hair back, a wide smile breaking across her face for the first time in weeks. 'I have an idea, and it might be a good one.'

'Okaaay.' Lucy sounded instantly wary. 'But before you speak, I just want you to remember that you only very recently lost your job and broke up with your soulmate, so what might seem like a good idea might in fact be a reaction to some serious stress.'

'How would you like to go into business together?'

'Oh God. I can already tell this is going to be bad.'

'Hear me out,' Ella said, pacing the room as the plan came together in her mind. 'A ballet school for pre-kinder, kinder, and primary-aged children.'

'Right—'

'We teach them through the *fun* years, then hand them over to someone else for the part that will break their bodies and crush their little spirits.'

Silence.

Ella took it as a good sign and carried on. 'I have this beautiful studio just sitting here. We're more than qualified. It's a good idea, isn't it?'

More silence.

'Toddlers in the morning, primary-aged children after school. We could even offer adult classes at night that are just for fun and fitness.'

'I thought you said it was pre-kinder to primary school.'

'I'm thinking on the fly here.' Her heart was pounding from excitement, an emotion she hadn't felt in such a long time. 'Please tell me it's a good idea.'

'I'm still processing it—'

'And that you're on board.'

'I'm supposed to answer you *now*?'

'There's no one else I'd rather do this with, and whether you admit it or not, it's time for you to get back to work.' More silence. 'Ballet, contemporary, jazz, tap—'

'I hate tap.'

'—and *hip-hop*.'

Lucy sucked in a breath. 'Hip-hop?'

'Hip. Hop.'

A sigh came through the phone. 'Please tell me I'm not going to regret indulging your nervous breakdown.'

'You won't.'

Lucy was silent a moment. 'You know I hate tap. I'm not teaching it unless one of your legs falls off, and even then, I'll complain the entire time.'

Ella covered her face and held in a squeal. 'Deal.'

CHAPTER 33

*D*ax flew to Adelaide the afternoon Ella came to see him at work, then took a taxi from the airport to a friend's house in Glenelg. Most of the St Vincent Gulf pod were based there, and he knew many of the families. It was the ultimate alibi if cops showed up at his house wanting to know where he was the night Flathead Rig collapsed.

The Davis family had a son, Dillon, a few years younger than Dax, and a fifteen-year-old daughter who they literally couldn't keep out of the water.

'It's not the worst problem for a young ondine female to have,' Dillon's mother told Dax.

The family took him out to Kangaroo Island to play tourist. He made sure to take lots of photos as evidence. From there he swam to Normanville, where the Brown family lived. They owned a small fishing boat that transported him overnight to Port McDonnell. He slept below, waking just as the sun broke over the horizon. After having something to eat, he swam nine hours to Warrnambool. Someone from the Southern Ocean pod, one of the largest in the region, then took him by boat part way to

King Island, where his family and friends were waiting. Miller remained in Melbourne with Adrian and Greta to manage the company and ensure the pod had a strong presence on land.

'There he is,' his mother said as he entered the small house. She grabbed a towel from the hook by the door. 'We were beginning to think the sharks got you.'

He dried off before entering the kitchen. His father stood at the sink washing dishes. Dax squeezed his shoulder as he passed before sinking down onto a stool. His mother turned the hotplate on and pulled a steak from the fridge along with a salad.

Hurley came in from the lounge room, clapping Dax's back before fetching a beer from the fridge. June shooed him away.

'We need you sober,' she tutted. She looked over at Dax. 'Have you heard from Ella?'

Dax closed his eyes. 'I literally just walked in, but no, I haven't.'

'She won't wonder where you are?'

Dax pulled Hurley's beer out of his hand as he passed, took a long drink, and then handed it back to him. Hurley gave him a knowing smile before fleeing the room. 'She won't even know I'm gone, and I prefer it that way.'

Irvin turned in his direction. 'I heard Barry fired her over some grainy security footage.'

'Yep.'

The pan hissed as June dropped the meat into it. 'She should've just denied it. He wouldn't have had a leg to stand on.' She filled a glass with cold water from the fridge and placed it in front of Dax.

'Lying doesn't come natural to her like it does us. He knew, and she handled it as best she could.'

June crossed her arms and leaned on the bench. 'At least

she's out of that place. Maybe we could find her something to do for us?'

Dax quirked an eyebrow. 'You want to take the ballet dancer from the fuel industry and stick her in construction?'

Irvin resumed washing dishes. 'What will she do for money until she finds something?'

Dax knew she wouldn't let him help her in any way. He was about to say as much when Frankie entered the kitchen. She glanced once at Dax before tugging the tea towel off the oven door and walking over to dry the dishes.

'Frankie,' Dax said.

'Dax.' Frankie turned and met his gaze. 'I heard Ella dumped your arse, then sold you out.'

Dax heard the pan hiss as his steak was flipped. 'She dumped me because you walked in, wine up to your eyeballs, and turned her entire world upside down.'

'It was sangria.'

'It was selfish.'

Frankie's hand flew up, sending the glass of water on the bench sliding towards Dax. His went up too, a reflex, and the glass halted. They stared at each other as the water shook between them, hit with energy from both sides. Frankie's face set in determination, her fingers straining, but it was no good. It slid towards her. With a growl, she gave up and caught the glass, water splashing up her arm.

June walked over and began angrily wiping the bench. 'Really, you two.'

'She started it,' Dax said, aware he sounded like a five-year-old.

'He's just spent two days in the water,' Irvin said, patting Frankie's shoulder. 'He has an advantage.'

'It's not just that.' Frankie glared in Dax's direction. 'His energy has grown.'

June slid the steak onto a plate and sat it in front of

Dax. 'Good. We'll need it tonight.' She wiped her hands on the tea towel Frankie was holding. 'Do you think you two can just focus on the task ahead?'

Dax and Frankie glanced at each other and reluctantly nodded.

'Good,' June said. 'Rest up. Then we're going to sink that rig.'

≈

'I THINK IT LOOKS PRETTY GOOD,' Lucy said, leaning back in her chair and studying the printed timetable. 'We've even managed a three-day weekend.'

Ella stared down at it, her fingers digging into her thighs. She felt excitement and paralysing fear all at once. 'We may need to open up Saturday mornings if there's demand.'

She touched the screen of her phone to check the time —9:12 p.m.

It was the night of Bass Fuel's Christmas party, and she knew they would be in full swing by now. Susan had been utterly perplexed by her decision to leave *before* the party, while Ella felt only relief. It was like stepping into daylight after a long winter spent indoors, or removing high heels after a day at the races. It was that first inhale when emerging from the water.

If she were being honest with herself, she wasn't only checking the time. A part of her had expected Dax to call or text, check in, even if she did slap the olive branch from his hand during their last encounter. She kept telling herself she'd done the right thing ending it. The relationship couldn't work without trust.

But there were no missed calls.

No texts.

Lucy looked over at her. 'I can't tell if you're desperate for that thing to ring or praying he leaves you alone.'

Ella placed the phone back on the table. 'Both?'

'Well, just keep me updated as to whether we love him or hate him. I can't be sitting here hating his guts while you sit next to me pining. It feels off.'

'Can you not just be indifferent?'

'Can *you* not just be indifferent about *Dirty Dancing: Havana Nights?*'

Ella looked down at the timetable again. 'Fair point.' She ran a finger over their new logo printed at the top of the page. Happy Toes Dance Studio. It was a place to incorporate dance into childhood instead of the other way around.

'I still think Ella Lewis School of Dance was better,' Lucy said, 'but this is your baby.'

'It's *our* baby, and we're selling fun here.'

'I honestly don't mind, as long as every child calls me Miss Lucy and falls silent the second I clear my throat. Some fear is healthy.'

Ella held up her hands. 'Fine by me.'

Her phone rang, and she immediately picked it up, adrenaline coursing through her. She exhaled when she saw who it was. 'It's Dad.'

'I gather from that reaction you were hoping it was Dax.'

Ella didn't bother denying it. 'I'm not answering while we're in a meeting.' She rejected the call and put the phone down on the table.

'So you're still not talking to him?'

'I heard him out.'

Lucy made a face. 'So that's it? You're all caught up on your past and no longer require a father?'

'He knows I've left Bass Fuel, and I'm not up for the lecture disguised as an inspirational talk.'

'He's probably chasing overdue house payments from you.'

'Even more reason not to answer.'

Much to Ella's surprise, Bass Fuel had paid her out until the end of December as well as a Christmas bonus. She had called Barry that afternoon because she assumed it was a mistake, but he'd assured her it wasn't.

Her phone rang again, *Dad mobile* flashing on the screen. She silenced it and picked up her wine glass. 'Let's toast.'

Lucy clapped her hands excitedly before picking up her glass. 'What shall we drink to?'

'How about two tragic ladies and one rocking dance school?'

Lucy clinked her glass to Ella's before drinking. 'So now that we've concluded business for the evening, I would like to talk about what I saw today.'

'Okay. What did you see?'

'I saw you *dance*.'

Ella gave her a confused look. 'You've seen me dance so many times.'

'Not like this. I heard "Dance of the Sugarplum" playing and came to spy at the door, because I know it's one of your favourites.'

'Can you imagine all those tiny tutus flitting across the stage at the end-of-year concert?'

'Yeah, yeah, very cute. I've seen you do that dance at least fifty times, but this was your best version by far. I think those extra Pilates classes are really paying off.'

Ella drew a pattern in the condensation on her glass. 'It's probably just because the pressure's off now.'

A knock at the door made both girls jump. They stared at one another for a moment, not moving.

'Fifty bucks says it's your dad,' Lucy whispered.

Ella rose. 'I don't have fifty dollars to lose, so I'm not

making any bets. I need every cent to put towards the open day.'

'You want me to referee, or can I abandon you and go home?'

'Go home to Caleb. I've got this.'

They walked together to the door and peeked through the spyhole. Ella's father waited on the other side.

'Remember, he's still your dad,' Lucy whispered before tugging the door open and stepping out. 'Good luck,' she said to Michael as she passed him.

He nodded. 'Thanks.' Then he looked at Ella, not moving.

Slowly, she stepped back from the door and opened it wider. 'Come in.'

CHAPTER 34

*T*orches were not an option. The pod relied on echolocation, the reflection of sound off objects, to navigate their way around the support beams. The erosion had been helped along in the days leading up to the big event, pod members having swum out under the cover of darkness to get a head start and assess the employee situation at the rig. It was a tricky balance between being ready to go when the time came and ensuring the structure was able to withstand strong currents until then.

Frankie was right. Dax's energy was the sharpest it had ever been. He could've bent the steel past the yield point if he needed to, but that would raise suspicions, making it look like something crashed into the frame when they were trying to sell erosion.

Every pod member had a task, a plan, and a timeline to ensure they all got out safely. As for the humans, that was up to them. They were always banging on about their safety processes—now was their chance to show them off to the world.

Dax circled one of the beams, examining it for vulnerable points, then drew back, arms extended towards it. He felt a familiar lift inside, and then the water began churning in front of him. He stretched his fingers, and the water hit the beam like a thousand tiny blades. The damage was uneven and messy, resembling nothing one would expect from a tool.

He stopped when he heard the metal groan. Swimming back a little, he watched the structure for a moment, trying to read its next move. He could hear his mother working twenty feet away, so he held off until she was done. They were aiming for a healthy lean that would prompt an emergency shutdown. There would be plenty of time for evacuation before the dramatic conclusion.

When the structure didn't budge, he raised his hands and did a little more damage. Soon, the beam buckled. The shift had a domino effect, and the moan of bending steel rang out around him. An alarm sounded, and red lights blinked overhead, illuminating the ocean with eerie flashes.

It was almost time to leave.

Dax surfaced under the wellhead platform and waited for the crew to hit the emergency shutdown button. He knew from their prior investigation of the rig that there were no security cameras in that part of the water, so it was safe to wait there. Above him, men shouted, but it was another noise that caught his attention—a noise from the well, a kick, which happened when the pressure was out of balance, forcing fluids into the wellbore. He held his breath, waiting for the blowout preventer to kick in.

Mud and gas were now spurting out.

'Cut the pipe!' he heard someone shout. 'Now!'

There was only one reason for that instruction—the blowout preventer had failed.

His father emerged next to him, wearing the same anxious expression as Dax. 'There's a kick. What the hell are they doing?'

Dax wiped a hand down his face. 'They're cutting the pipe.' Above them, mud and gas continued to spew out all over the platform. 'We can't leave until that well is sealed. You head to the bottom in case there's a leak. The second it's sealed, we all leave together.'

Irvin nodded and slipped below the surface, disappearing into the inky water. Dax heard someone shout, his words cut short by an explosion that lit up the sky like fireworks. Dax's eyes widened as the platform groaned above him and began to close in. He made a dash for the open water but came to a swirling stop when something splashed overhead. He looked up to see a fully clothed man thrashing in the water above him. When he made a move for him, someone grabbed hold of his leg. He looked down and saw Frankie, her eyes reflecting the red sky. She tried to pull him down, but he kicked free.

A whistle echoed. 'No,' she was saying, but Dax knew he could never look Ella in the eye again if he let the man drown. So up he swam, praying the man would be too disoriented to recall the details of that moment. Dax guided him to the surface by one of his boots as men shouted and torches flashed.

Boom.

Another explosion shook the water. Dax's hands flew to his ears, eyes closing against the noise. An ondine's hearing was far more sensitive than a human's underwater, and now his ears rang like a gun had gone off next to his head.

Men dropped into the ocean around him, forced to jump to escape the flames. Dax could taste the gas and see the oil spreading on the surface. He should've fled to safety, but instead he dove down, descending into the darkness below, chased by the desperate screams of men.

ELLA AND HER father sat on the couch holding mugs of tea. Michael's eyes went to the empty wine glasses on the table.

'I know what you're thinking,' Ella said. 'I'm allowed to have a drink with my best friend on a Friday night.'

Michael met her gaze. 'Not judging, just surprised is all. You normally do yoga on a Friday.'

Ella shrugged. 'Maybe it's time I started enjoying my Fridays.'

Her father studied her closely for a moment. 'Barry phoned me.'

'I figured he would.'

'The lawyers two floors down are looking for admin help, you know.'

She sighed inwardly. 'Are they?'

Michael rose and walked over to the table, picking up the printed sheet. 'What's all this, then?'

She drew a breath, preparing herself for criticism. 'Lucy and I are opening a dance studio in the new year.' She braced as he stared down at the timetable.

'Happy Toes Dance Studio,' he read aloud. '"Beginner through to advanced. Ballet, contemporary, jazz, tap, and hip-hop." This Lucy's idea?'

Ella shook her head. 'All me, actually.' It was like he refused to see his daughter in any other light than the one he had selected for her as a child. Michael Lewis's daughter was driven and sensible, committed and safe. She could see him trying to reconcile that person with the owner of Happy Toes. 'I don't know if it'll be successful, but I'm going to throw everything at it. The worst that can happen is that I end up exactly where I started—unemployed and miserable.'

He placed the timetable down. 'I think it's a great idea.'

She lowered her mug. 'You do?'

'I do. You're combining business and dance, and we now know you can succeed at both.'

Ella swallowed. 'Thank you.'

He wandered back to the couch. 'Do you need a business loan?'

'You mean from the same place I got my house loan?'

'Michael Lewis Banking,' he said with a grin.

Before Ella had a chance to decline the offer, her phone rang. She pulled it from her pocket and saw Lucy's name on the screen. 'Lucy. Probably making sure I'm being nice,' Ella said, only half joking. She rose and walked into the kitchen as she answered. 'Hey. Everything okay?'

'Have you seen the news? Has Barry called you?'

Ella froze. 'No and no. Why?' She pivoted and went to the television, snatching up the remote.

'Channel twenty-four,' Lucy said. 'There's been some sort of accident out at the rig.'

Ella's heart sped up. 'What?' It came out as a whisper. She flicked to the channel, sucking in a breath as flames filled the screen.

'What's going on?' Michael asked, back on his feet. 'Is that Flathead Rig?'

Before Ella could form words, a loud *bang* came through the television, and the flames grew, lighting up the sea as the rig began to collapse.

Ella stilled as she recalled something Dax said.

'You didn't tell me about your Christmas party.'

She had thought it an odd conversation point at the time but hadn't thought about it since. Now she wondered if he had been getting information out of her.

'Christ,' Michael said. 'What a mess.'

Ella stared at the TV. 'I have to go,' she told Lucy, hanging up. She immediately dialled Dax's number.

No answer.

She dialled again, but he didn't pick up.

'Who are you calling?' Michael asked.

'Dax, but he isn't answering. I don't know Miller's

number.' Thinking, she dialled Greta while her father stood with his hands resting on his hips, watching her.

'Want to tell me what's going on?' Michael said. 'Please tell me this isn't the pod's doing.'

Greta answered her phone. 'Ella?'

'I'm sorry to call so late. I was just wondering if you know where Dax is?'

Silence.

'It's really important I talk to him.'

'He's… in Adelaide with friends.'

Ella could hear the lie in her voice. 'He's not answering his mobile. Can I have his friend's number?'

There was a pause before Greta said, 'I have to go. I'm so sorry.'

Greta hung up, and the phone fell from Ella's hand.

'What's going on?' Michael said, taking a step towards her. 'Speak to me.'

Ella didn't know, that was the problem. She only knew he was out there in the water, could suddenly feel it in every fibre of her body. She pressed a hand to her thudding heart.

'Tell me what's going on so I know how to help,' her father said, his tone firmer this time.

She opened her mouth, closed it again. 'I have to go to him.'

'Who?' Michael shook his head, confused. 'What are you talking about?'

Ella headed for the front door, not even bothering with shoes.

'Ella!' he shouted.

She didn't have time to explain. She needed to find Dax. Yanking the front door open, she took off at a run.

'Ella!'

Her father's voice spilled out onto the road, but she didn't stop or slow. She sprinted along the footpath, down the poorly lit street towards the beach, towards the water, like she was responding to a call for help no one else could hear.

A car horn sounded, and tyres screeched.

'I'm sorry,' she shouted at the blinding headlights, unaware she'd crossed the road. A moment later, she felt grass beneath her feet, then the sand, then water. She didn't stop, plunging into the icy sea, barely registering the cold as it swallowed her whole.

'Dax!' she screamed, as if expecting him to rise up in front of her.

Then she was underwater, plunged into darkness. There was no surf at that beach, but the water still roared in her ears. A warning, a reminder that she didn't belong there, that she had ventured too far from land. Her mother's beautiful face flashed in her mind, or in the water—she couldn't tell. That calm face, her sun-kissed hair swirling around it like a halo. Of course she looked peaceful. It was easy to remain calm when you could breathe water.

In Ella's confused state, or perhaps it was a moment of rebellion, she inhaled. Water filled her nose, mouth, and ears, and her throat closed in protest. Pushing off the seafloor, she propelled herself out of the water, coughing and spluttering. She gasped, humiliated and angry. Her bloodlines had failed her in the cruellest way.

'Dax!' she tried to call out, but it came out as a croak, followed by more violent coughing as the water rocked her, like one did when soothing a hysterical child. She heard splashing nearby, and hope soared within her. 'I'm here!'

Arms wrapped around her middle, and her eyes sank shut with relief.

Dax.

'What the hell are you doing?'

Her eyes snapped open at the sound of her father's

voice, and she pushed at the arms around her. They were no longer comforting but suffocating. 'Let me go.'

'Stop struggling,' he barked.

Her eyes searched the black water as he pulled her back towards the shore, listening for Dax, feeling for him.

Where are you?

He promised he would always be there, that he would protect her, *breathe* for her. She pressed her eyes shut as her body came out of the water. He would die believing she didn't care, and it was so far from the truth.

She struggled to remember their last conversation. He'd told her their bond was a curse of sorts. What had she said in reply?

'In every fairy tale I've ever danced, there's always a way to break the curse.'

Those were her last words to him, a bold declaration of her ability to detach.

'Let me go,' she pleaded.

Michael scooped her up in his arms like a child and carried her all the way to the dry sand. He set her down before bending to rest his hands on his knees. 'Do not move from that spot.' He was blocking her view of the sea.

Ella pulled her knees up, hugging them tightly as she buried her face in her arms.

Dax.

CHAPTER 35

*E*lla only agreed to go home so she could get her phone and try Dax again. When he didn't answer, she left a voicemail for him. She told him she felt sick. She told him she was sorry for things she had said. She told him to call her as soon as he was able. Ella then tried Greta's number again, but it also went to voicemail.

As soon as she changed out of her wet clothes, she told her father she was going back to the beach. She expected him to try and stop her, but instead he quietly filled a thermos with tea and grabbed blankets from the linen cupboard before joining her at the door.

'Are you putting shoes on this time?' he asked.

She tugged on sneakers, not bothering with the laces.

When they arrived at the beach, Ella sank down onto the sand and sat shivering next to her father, a blanket pulled around her and a lid full of tea in hand as she watched the black water.

Michael glanced at her. 'You could've drowned.'

She wanted to believe that wasn't possible while Dax was alive. And he *was* alive—he had to be. 'Was this what it felt like waiting for her?'

Michael didn't ask what she was talking about. 'I reckon I was just about sitting in this same spot.'

'Why don't I remember?'

'You slept at Lucy's that night.'

'Oh.'

He wrapped the second blanket around both of them, and Ella rested her head against his shoulder. They sat in silence for hours, listening to the water and sipping tea. Eventually Ella's eyes sank shut.

'Will you watch for him?' she whispered as exhaustion took over.

'Yeah, I'll watch for him.'

When she woke, she found her father still awake as promised. Straightening, she glanced down at her phone— 4:30 a.m.

No missed calls or messages.

She pulled the blankets tighter around her while Michael poured the last of the tea and handed it to her. She sipped at it, letting the liquid warm her insides.

'It's a frightening moment when you realise you need another person more than you need oxygen,' she said, staring ahead. 'What am I supposed to do with feelings like that?'

He was silent a while before replying. 'It was like that with your mother. No one believed us though—certainly not her parents. Her mate was supposed to come from the water, not the western suburbs.' He released a long, slow breath. 'God, I felt it though. In my gut, my mind, my bones. It was like a fog arrived the day we met, covering everything else. I couldn't see my own hand in front of my face, but I saw her.'

Ella looked up at him. 'If you understood, then why did you tell me to walk away?'

He met her gaze. 'I was trying to protect you from moments like these.'

Glancing down at his expensive watch, he tapped it. It didn't light up. 'It wasn't waterproof.' Removing it, he tucked it into the pocket of his hoodie. He always kept a bag of gym clothes in his car. 'The sea always gets its way in the end,' he said, facing forwards again. 'I hope you realise that.'

Ella blinked back tears. 'I wouldn't survive his death.'

'You're stronger than you think.' He paused. 'You remind me so much of her, you know. With your impossibly high standards and ridiculous expectations you put on yourself.'

'I thought you liked that about me.'

'I admire it at times. I admired it in your mother too. As long as you realise you can't bend reality to fit your own narrative. That lesson cost your mother her life.' He looked down at her. 'You belong to this world, so you need to find a way to be happy on land. The sea doesn't get you too.'

Ella rested her head against his arm again, and they listened to the gentle shush of water lapping the sand as the tide drew closer. The sound was an intoxicating lullaby, and she lost the battle against sleep once more.

~

'ELLA.'

Her eyes snapped open at the sound of her father's voice. Soft light now painted the sea, making it appear less threatening. She blinked a few times as she sat up, and her vision snagged on movement in the water ahead. She was on her feet in an instant, the blankets sliding off her as she rose. Fifty metres from shore, she thought she saw a head bobbing in the sea. Her heart sped up, and her feet moved in that direction just as it disappeared from sight. She walked ankle deep into the water as she searched.

Nothing.

Exhaling, she looked over her shoulder at her father, who offered her a tired smile.

'I'm going home for a shower,' he said, turning and walking up the beach.

She sensed Dax before she laid eyes on him. Her head whipped around, and she found him waist deep in the water just ten metres from her, his bronze skin glistening in the early morning sun.

Her breath hitched at the sight of him, and her hands went over her mouth. He watched her through ribbons of wet hair, his shoulders rounded with exhaustion. She went to him, her strides messy and uneven, eyes never leaving his. When she was close, he opened his arms. Any reservations she had vanished, along with the anger and resentment she'd worn like a badge of honour for weeks. The only thing that mattered was him standing there—alive.

As his arms closed around her, a sob rose up so fierce she was unable to hold it in. He lifted her from the water, cradling her head as she cried into his neck, the kind of unhinged tears that would drive a sensible human away.

'Shh,' he whispered into her hair. 'Shh. It's all right. I'm here. You're okay.'

She pulled back to look at him properly, searching his face and body for injury, anything to justify the embarrassing display of emotion. She found a small cut above his eyebrow when she pushed his hair back.

'I'm fine,' he assured her. 'Really.'

She was crying again. 'I saw it on the news, and I just knew...'

He kissed her hair. 'We're all fine. And all the workers made it out alive.'

'Fine is underwhelming.'

A smile flickered on his tired face. 'Then replace it with any word you like, any word that makes you feel better. Just please stop crying.' He pushed her matted hair back

268

from her face, frowning at the sand in it. 'Were you in the water?'

She breathed in his salty skin. 'You didn't answer your phone. You *left* me.'

He was so much calmer than she was, or perhaps just too exhausted for big emotional displays. 'I'm here now.' He began walking. 'You should've waited at the house. It's too cold out here.' Instead of placing her on the ground, he guided her head to his shoulder. 'Let's get you home.'

~

Dax didn't want to put her down. It had been too long since she'd been in his arms, and he could feel her fear and relief like it was coursing through his own veins. But when they reached the road, she sensed his fatigue and insisted on walking.

It had taken the entire pod to seal the well and prevent a disastrous oil leak, plus careful consideration to ensure the end result was not suspicious. Dax and Hurley had remained behind until every worker was accounted for, until large boats surrounded the half-submerged rig, extinguishing the remaining flames just before the structure collapsed into the sea.

The plan had worked—sort of. No one could've foreseen just how flawed the technology was. Dax had overheard one of the workers explaining to someone that the blowout preventer had failed. If the pod hadn't acted when they did, the oil spill would've been one of the worst in Australian history.

When they arrived at the house, Dax hesitated at the door before entering. He was supposed to be on his way back to Adelaide. That was how he protected himself and his pod. And it was also how he protected Ella.

269

'Go take a shower,' Dax said, smoothing her hair down. 'You're freezing.'

She held on to his arm. 'You'll be here when I get out?'

Nodding, he watched her walk down the hall, then pulled his phone out to see what the news outlets were saying about the incident. Nothing suspicious mentioned, much to his relief. He listened to his voicemails, closing his eyes when he heard Ella's emotional apology. He deleted it on his way to the bathroom, leaning his head against the door and closing his eyes. He couldn't have left in that moment if he'd tried.

Turning the door handle, Dax found Ella seated on the shower floor with her knees pulled up and forehead resting on her arms. Hot water pounded her back. She looked up when she heard him close the door. Resting her chin on her arms, she watched him remove his board shorts and pull the glass door open, then moved over so he could fit next to her. He leaned against the tiled wall, letting her have all the heat.

They sat for a number of minutes, Ella thawing while he traced his fingers along her back. Eventually she reached for the shampoo and turned to face him. Squeezing some onto her hand, she worked it into a lather before reaching up and washing his hair. He never looked away from her, his affection growing with each passing moment. He wondered how that was possible. His feelings couldn't just keep growing and expanding until she dominated every part of him.

Could they?

After Ella finished rinsing his hair, he pulled her onto his lap and picked up the shampoo while she studied the cut above his eye with tentative fingers.

'It's just a graze,' he said.

Her hand fell away. 'I called to you last night, in the water. Did you hear me?'

'From forty kilometres away?'

She didn't smile. 'Did you?'

His first instinct once the danger had passed was to go to her. At some point he'd *felt* her. 'I came, didn't I?'

Ella reached up and turned off the faucet, then went to fetch towels. As he took one from her, she looked up at him with enormous blue eyes, full of adoration. He didn't feel worthy of it.

'I love you,' she said quietly. 'I've loved you for a really long time. Seems foolish not to say it.'

He ran the tips of his fingers along her cheek and swallowed down all the emotions rising inside: love, guilt, lust, and overwhelming possessiveness that scared the shit out of him. Before he could form any coherent words for her, she pushed up onto her toes and kissed him, deep and demanding. She tasted like the beach and smelled like fresh-cut flowers. His hands went to her face, and she melted against him, the change in her breath making his own falter.

Ella led him to her bedroom, where towels fell and mouths collided. Their hands were careful and urgent all at once. She was in complete control of him, but not in control of herself. He watched her carefully as the intensity built between them, watched her fall over the edge of her pleasure—and followed her.

She was such a beautiful mess in those moments after, even with tears falling down her cheeks. He drew her closer and cradled her while she fought off sleep.

'I have to go,' he whispered.

Her fingers wound around his so tightly he questioned his ability to leave.

'Where?' she asked.

'Adelaide.' He hesitated. 'I hate to ask this of you—'

'I never saw you. You were never here. It's okay.' She blinked up at him. 'When will you be back?'

'The less you know the better. Just in case.'

'Just in case of what?'

He rubbed his nose against her warm cheek. 'Just in case.'

Her eyelids sank shut. 'I don't want you to go back in the water. I want you to stay on land with me.'

Dax closed his eyes. 'I know.' She wanted human things from him. 'But I have to stay away for a little while. You can't follow me.' He kissed her cheek, then buried his face in her hair. 'I need you safe on land.'

Her body twitched with sleep, and she slipped away from him again.

CHAPTER 36

*E*lla woke to a knock at the front door. She had come to recognise the knocks of those closest to her over the years, and this wasn't Lucy's joyful tap or her father's familiar rhythmic rap of the knuckles. This knock was firm and authoritative.

She leapt up and threw on some clothes, smoothing down her hair as she made her way to the front door. When she opened it, she found two policemen standing there. She felt the colour drain from her face. This was a first for her.

'Are you Ella Lewis?' asked the taller one. She guessed him to be around thirty.

'Yes.'

'I'm Officer Williams,' said the older one with the deep scowl lines, 'and this is Officer Garcia. We just need to ask you a few questions.'

She invited them in because she knew not doing so would seem suspicious. Glancing at the clock on the wall, she saw it was a little before ten. 'What's this about?' She gestured for them to take a seat.

They looked around the room as they sat.

'Did you hear that Flathead Rig burned down last night?' asked Officer Williams.

She nodded. 'I saw it on the news. It was pretty shocking. I'm glad no one was hurt.'

Officer Garcia looked enormous at the small dining table, like Dax always did when he sat there. He faced her and began asking a string of questions about where she was the night prior.

'My father was here. We went to the beach after we saw the news, but we couldn't see anything.'

'What were you expecting to see?'

She shrugged. 'I thought I might see the flames from the shore.'

Officer Garcia continued to look around the room. 'When was the last time you saw Dax Coburn?'

'A few days ago.' She surprised herself with the confident lie.

'Is it usual for the two of you to go days without seeing each other? Mr Coburn is your boyfriend, is that right?'

She could hardly tell them it was complicated. 'The relationship ended a few weeks back.'

'Why?'

She shrugged. 'Couples fight.'

'What did you fight about?' asked Officer Williams.

Ella attempted a smile. 'What do most couples fight about? Things that seem important at the time.'

'So you broke up weeks back but saw him a few days ago?'

'I had just quit my job and needed someone to talk to. He works around the corner from Bass Fuel.'

'And what did Mr Coburn have to say about you leaving?'

She wet her lips. 'He wasn't overly surprised. He didn't think the job was a good fit for me.'

Officer Williams wrote a few things down. 'And you haven't seen or spoken to him since?'

She thought back to the voicemail she'd left the night before and tried to remember what she said. 'I tried to call him last night, but apparently he's in Adelaide.'

'He tell you that?'

'No, a mutual friend did.'

They asked a few more questions about her time at Bass Fuel and her decision to leave. Then they walked to the front door, telling her not to venture too far in case they had any follow-up questions.

As they were pulling away from the house, her father stopped in the driveway. He rushed inside and made her repeat every part of their conversation. He didn't like that she'd lied to them about seeing Dax the night before, but if Dax needed people to believe he had been in Adelaide, that was the story she would stand by. No texts, no calls. That was what he'd asked of her in her half-asleep state. She would wait for him to return.

Her father made her promise she wouldn't contact anyone from the pod. He reminded her that every text message was evidence, that every call could be recorded or traced. If the group was being treated as suspicious, she needed to remove herself from it. She agreed, because she knew that was what Dax wanted also.

'It won't be forever,' Michael reminded her when he saw her face. 'Just let them ask their questions and carry out their investigation. Once everything's quietened down, you can decide if you want to invite that trouble back into your life.'

She was disappointed by that last remark, had thought he finally understood.

Reading her mind, Michael added, 'You can still feel all of those things and choose another path for yourself.

There will be other relationships. Maybe a few less sparks, but a lot less drama too.'

She didn't blame her father for his assessment. All he'd seen were the negative aspects. He'd never witnessed the laughter, the jokes, the love, the fleeting moments of feeling invincible. He didn't know the reason she was returning to dance, to the things she loved, to *herself* was because Dax cared enough to challenge her choices.

'He didn't tell me anything. I don't even know when he'll be back,' she said. 'Should I be worried?'

'That's the smartest thing he's done yet.' Michael patted her shoulder. 'Just keep focused on that dance school of yours. You can't put your life on hold for him.'

She had waited twenty-three years to be with him. What was a little longer?

CHAPTER 37

'The police have been here asking questions,' Miller had told Dax on the phone that morning as he fled Ella's bedroom. 'They wanted to speak to you.'

Dax had gone to the bathroom, picked his shorts up off the floor, and stepped into them. 'What do they want?' He'd known the answer. The question was for the benefit of anyone listening in on their call. Better to be overcautious than sorry.

'I'd say they're looking for someone to pin Flathead Rig on.'

That was his prompt to flee Melbourne and get as far away from Ella as possible before she was implicated.

He had paused at the doorway of Ella's bedroom, holding on to the frame for a moment. If the cops came knocking, she would be forced to lie. The best thing he could do for her at that point was leave.

His return to Adelaide was uneventful, which was a good thing. He travelled day and night, long stretches of swimming occasionally broken up by boat. After saying goodbye to the Davis family, he made his way to the airport and arrived back in Melbourne a few days before Christmas.

He didn't call Ella, but he did head down to the police station per their request.

Officers Williams and Garcia asked their questions and searched for gaps in his story, staring hard at the receipts and plane ticket stubs he handed over. When Dax asked them why he was being questioned, they replied that Bass Fuel was treating the incident as suspicious.

'The CEO says your family has been taking aim at the company for years,' Garcia said.

'Maybe because it's been leaking gas and oil into the water the entire time,' Dax replied. 'I won't sit here and pretend I'm not happy it's destroyed. Can't take credit for it though.'

The men eyed him coolly.

'You seem to know a lot about the rig,' Williams said.

Dax met his gaze, unblinking. 'I read the papers. Not too many people are going to be saddened by the news.'

The officers exchanged a glance.

'We went and saw your girlfriend,' Garcia said, watching his reaction.

It wasn't Dax's first time dealing with the police. He knew the game. 'Which girlfriend would that be?'

'Ella Lewis.'

Her name from their lips made him uncomfortable. 'I don't know what she told you, but we broke up a few weeks back.'

Garcia nodded. 'We've been trying to figure out if you split with Miss Lewis because of her connections to the company or if you pursued her because of them?'

Dax fought to keep his expression neutral. 'Sorry to disappoint, but Ella's employer didn't factor.'

'It's not the reason the two of you fought?'

'We didn't fight.'

Williams nodded slowly. 'Really? Ms Lewis had a different view on things.'

'Exes normally do.'

'So you just… broke up?' Garcia pushed.

They were fishing, and Dax had no interest in biting. 'I'm not even going to pretend to understand where you're going with this one. My past relationships are none of your business.'

'The timing's interesting is all,' Williams said. 'Miss Lewis left the company just before things got really messy for her team.'

Dax never looked away from him. 'Exactly how many people is Bass Fuel trying to pin this on? They're going after the girl who fetched the coffee now?'

Garcia spoke up then. 'No one's pinning anything on anyone. Let's just wait and see what the Incident Analysis Team come back with.'

If they were trying to spook him, it wasn't working. Dax stepped back from the desk. 'Great. Are we done here?'

Williams nodded. 'Appreciate you coming down to the station. Maybe hold off on any interstate travel for a while.'

Dax looked between them, nodded, and then left without another word.

CHAPTER 38

*I*t was the first week of January, and the sun was melting the roads. Ella walked to the letterbox and glanced in the direction of the water as she opened it. She was waiting for him to return to her. She hated not knowing where he was, if he was okay, hated that she couldn't call anyone to find out for fear of making the situation worse.

Straightening, Ella flicked through the envelopes and paused when she saw Peter's handwriting. As she wandered back towards the house, she opened it and peered inside. It was a single ticket to *Giselle* and a hand-written note which said *Please come.*

She pulled open the new security door, marvelling at how quiet it was as it swung shut behind her. It was such a small thing, but it brought a smile to her face. They were one step closer to opening.

Lucy was seated at the kitchen counter with her laptop open, all serious-faced as she played with an Excel spreadsheet. Ella had decided to keep her head in the sand with regards to finances. She knew the business would be broke for some time. That was enough information for her.

Caleb was seated at the table next to his mother, absorbed in the Spider-Man colouring book Ella bought him. She ruffled his hair as she passed by and dropped the envelope in front of Lucy.

'What's this?' Lucy asked, opening it. 'Oh.' She watched Ella take a seat. 'Are you gonna go?'

'I don't think so.'

Lucy leaned back in her chair and released a breath. 'Now, you know I'm not a big fan of Peter's, but I actually think you should go.'

'All right,' Ella said, indulging her. 'Why?'

Lucy slid the envelope towards her. 'Because you love the ballet, it's a free ticket, and you need to leave the house for reasons other than groceries.'

'Pfft,' Ella said. 'I can't afford groceries.'

'Why do you think I keep inviting you over to my parents' house for dinner?' Lucy gave her a knowing look. 'Peter's safe company.'

'What does that mean?'

Lucy rolled her eyes. 'You know exactly what it means. It means you go into an evening knowing what to expect and come out in the same condition you went in.' She sighed. 'I know you love Dax. Hell, *I* love Dax. But every time you see him, he takes another piece of you. At this rate, soon there will be nothing left for the rest of us.'

Ella leaned over and squeezed her hand. 'There is plenty of me left.'

'What about next time? And the time after that?'

How to explain that it was no longer her heart to divide. Ella knew Dax would never intentionally chip away at her—quite the opposite. He would take her suffering if it were an option.

'Just go,' Lucy said. 'It's gonna be a long time before you can afford an A-reserve ticket to anything. You love *Giselle*, plus imagine the enormous satisfaction you'll get sitting there picking faults in Peter's performance.' She paused. 'If a night at the ballet restores a tiny piece of you, then it'll be worth it.'

Ella stared down at the ticket. Weirdly, it felt like a betrayal to Dax. 'He's coming back, you know. That's how it is with mates.'

'That's how it is between *ondines*. Humans get to choose.'

Ella remained quiet.

'I can't believe he only sent one ticket,' Lucy said, picking up the envelope again. 'I wouldn't have minded seeing *Giselle*.'

'He was probably worried I'd bring Dax.'

'Valid point.'

Ella reached for her phone. 'I'll text him and let him know I'm coming.' When she unlocked her phone, she saw a Google Alert she had set up for news on Flathead Rig. It was a link to a newspaper article.

THE INCIDENT ANALYSIS *Team (IAT) established in December 2019 undertook a two-week comprehensive analysis of both the oil rig and management of the incident to assess the cause and adequacy of the response. The team conducted on-site inspections and personal interviews with on-ground responders and environmental groups. The IAT has identified damage to support beams caused by long-term corrosion further weakened by a tidal wave that hit the rig on November 28. The team has also identified a number of equipment failures which may have caused the fires.*

ELLA'S EYES closed with relief. It wouldn't be long now until Dax returned to her; then they could fix whatever was broken between them.

'It'll be a treat to see you in something other than leggings,' Lucy said as she returned to her spreadsheet.

Ella sent a text to Peter thanking him for the ticket, then rose from her chair. 'I'm going to give the studio floor another polish.'

'The open day isn't for another week, and if that floor is any more polished, the kids are going to slide straight off it. Oh, and stop cleaning the mirror. You're starting to wear through the glass.'

Ella scrunched up her nose. 'Have you thought about what you'll do for your hip-hop demonstration?'

Lucy nodded. 'Already sorted.'

Caleb looked up at that. 'The song says "shit".'

'I'm going to clean up the language in the track before the performance,' Lucy said, poking him in the ribs.

He giggled.

'I thought I might do a contemporary piece,' Ella said.

Lucy looked up in surprise. 'Really? I thought you'd want to show off all that classical training.'

'Well, I'm feeling rebellious.'

'I barely recognise you anymore,' Lucy said, holding back a smile. 'Go on, Cinderella. Go polish your floor.'

CHAPTER 39

The reporting of the rig got smaller and farther back in the paper with each passing day. The police were no longer interested in Dax, at least not for that reason, but he continued to lie low because he was terrified one wrong move on his part would have them crawling all over his life again.

'When are you going to contact Ella?' Greta asked him one night. 'It's been weeks.'

Dax had gone cold turkey on Ella when he'd learned the cops showed up at her house and questioned her. It was exactly what he'd been trying to avoid.

'He's allowed to be cautious,' Adrian said, coming to his defence. 'I'd be the same with you. Better to let things breathe. She's not going anywhere.'

Greta's eyebrows rose. 'Says who?'

'Says fate,' Adrian said with a shrug.

Dax rubbed his forehead. 'Maybe I should've stayed home.'

'You've been in your house for weeks,' Adrian replied. 'Why don't you come into the city with me tonight? A few of the Beagle Gulf boys are down from Darwin. We're getting dinner.'

Greta nodded in agreement. 'That's a good idea. Then you can make sure he doesn't drink too much.'

'Right,' Dax said. 'So not for my mental well-being, then?'

'That too,' Greta said as she picked Ariel up and kissed her face.

Dax let out a resigned breath, knowing the distraction from Ella would do him good. 'Fine.'

That night, they caught the 109 tram into the heart of the coffee capital, known for its laneways, street art, and diverse food, then wandered up to an Italian restaurant buried in Flinders Lane. They met up with Beck and Gordy, ondines Dax had met on a trip up north a few years back. He had found them to be easy company in the past.

Adrian and Beck were both AFL enthusiasts and spent most of the evening talking football. Dax spoke to Gordy about his job as a marine engineer. It was a career he'd once imagined for himself before focusing his time and energy on Flathead Rig. He had no idea what to focus on now that the rig was gone. Gordy believed if large corporations insisted on building structures in the water, then he was at least going to make sure those structures were sound. It also enabled him to spend plenty of time offshore without raising suspicion.

'I don't know how you survive up there in that heat,' Dax said. 'I always feel like I can't breathe that far north.'

Gordy chuckled. 'You get used to it. Plus humans don't brave the ocean up there—not smart ones, anyway—so we have the water to ourselves.'

'Don't blame them. Between the jellyfish, sharks, and saltwater crocs, the beaches aren't very appealing.'

'You'll have to swim up and stay with us,' Gordy said. 'It's been a while.'

Dax nodded non-committally. He knew he couldn't be that far from Ella for too long.

'We're going to find a bar,' Adrian said, rising on unsteady legs.

So much for not drinking too much.

Dax took some cash from his wallet and slipped it in the black folder on the table. 'It's getting late, and your wife is waiting for you.'

Adrian and Beck exchanged a smirk.

'Don't mind him. He's missing his mate,' Adrian said by way of explanation.

Gordy rose. 'Where is she?'

'It's a long story,' Dax replied.

Beck clapped him on the shoulder as he passed. 'One drink.'

'It's never just one drink.'

Two hours and five beers later, they emerged from a pub in Federation Square, perched above Melbourne's busy railway lines. The Beagle Gulf boys said their goodbyes before parting ways. Dax and Adrian decided to head over the bridge to the Arts Centre in search of a taxi, hoping to skip the growing queue at Flinders Street Station. They crossed St Kilda Road and neared the bridge, the large spire of the centre coming into sight.

Dax stopped.

'What's wrong?' Adrian asked.

Dax blinked to clear his beer vision. 'I must be drunk, because that looks like Ella.'

Adrian followed his gaze. 'Oh shit. I think that *is* Ella.'

Dax's eyes shifted to the man standing beside her. It was Peter. Peter with his skinny jeans and designer jacket.

Peter with his hair gel and immaculate shoes. Peter with his… make-up?

Maybe he was drunker than he realised.

'What do you want to do?' Adrian asked.

Dax was already heading for them, eyes moving over Ella as he walked. She wore a checked coat over a grey dress with brown boots. Her hair was pulled back in a low bun.

He could guess at the colour of her lipstick, even in the dark.

She was leaning against the bridge with her back to the water, watching Peter. Jealousy surged through Dax like electricity, the reaction not matching the scene in front of him. They were just two people having a conversation. But seriously, what the hell was she doing out in the middle of the night with *Peter*?

Ella looked in his direction as he approached, her eyes widening when she recognised him.

'Shit,' he heard Adrian say behind him. 'Dax, wait.'

But Dax didn't stop until he was standing in front of her.

ELLA FELT THE AIR SHIFT, or maybe it was the water below. Whatever the feeling was, it pulled her attention from Peter and made her stand up straight. Looking around, her eyes narrowed on a tall, broad-shouldered man walking towards them. She knew it was Dax before she saw his face, had committed his shape to memory long ago.

When did he get back?

The thrill of seeing him vanished when she registered his dark expression. He immediately dominated the space. She would've stepped back from him if her spine hadn't already been touching the wall. His eyes were two black pools fixed on Peter.

'Dax,' she said, trying to hide her shock. 'I didn't know you were back.'

He looked at her then. 'Clearly.'

She swallowed, wilting under his glare. Her eyes went to Adrian, who stood a few feet away. He gave her an apologetic smile.

'Dax,' Peter said by way of greeting.

'Peter.'

Ella tried to make herself taller. 'How long have you been back in Melbourne?'

'A few weeks.'

She searched his eyes. 'A few *weeks*?'

'Looks like you've been keeping yourself busy.'

He had no right to be angry at her. She hadn't done anything wrong, while he'd been home for weeks and hadn't made any effort to contact her.

'Let's go,' Adrian said, stepping up and clapping a hand on his shoulder. 'You can call her tomorrow.'

Ella looked down at Dax's hands, which were balled into fists. 'I think that's sensible.'

'You two on a date?' Dax asked, his voice even.

Ella felt a surge of annoyance at the implication. A few weeks ago, she'd told him she loved him. Did he really think she would go running to someone else—back to *Peter*, of all people?

'I don't think Ella has to answer that,' Peter said, poking the bear.

Dax rounded on him. 'Was I talking to you, pretty boy?'

'*Dax*,' Ella said, moving in front of him. 'What the hell is the matter with you?'

'Let's go,' Peter said, placing an arm around Ella's shoulder. 'You've probably missed your train now. I'll drive you.'

Dax leaned across Ella, getting in his face. 'You were

288

going to let her take the fucking train? In the middle of the night?'

Ella pushed Dax's chest, but he didn't budge. 'I don't need his permission to catch the train.'

'You're drunk,' Peter said. 'Why don't you go home and sleep it off? You can talk to Ella when you've sobered up.'

Dax strained against Ella's hands. 'You think she needs protecting from *me*?'

A strange whirring noise made Ella look over her shoulder. The usually slow-flowing Yarra River was shifting and rocking like a swimming pool after an earthquake. Adrian noticed also.

'Dax, let's go—now,' he said, raking a hand through his hair.

'Yeah, take him home before I do something I regret,' Peter said.

Dax reached out and grabbed Peter by the shirt. 'That's tough talk for a guy wearing eyeshadow. Should we add some more colour to your face?' He raised a fist, but the noise of the river made him look in that direction.

'Walk away,' Ella said, both palms flattened against his chest. 'Please.'

He looked down into those blue eyes of hers, now alive with fear. He didn't know if she was afraid *for* him or *of* him.

'If you hurt him, he won't be able to dance,' she said, breathing hard. 'I won't let you do that to him. *Walk away.*'

It was a sobering moment for Dax, standing over Ella with his fist raised while the river churned below them. Lowering his hand, he released Peter with a shove and stepped back.

'I'm sorry,' he said to Ella. He looked over at Peter, whose hands were two ready fists. 'Make sure she gets home safe.'

Then he left with Adrian jogging after him.

he afternoon before Happy Toes open day, Ella sat at the kitchen table with a mug of instant coffee and her laptop open. She was reading an article in *The Age* that wrapped up the findings of the Flathead Rig blowout. The reason there was no major oil spill was because one of the explosions had buckled the pipe, cutting off the supply of gas and oil. One of the rig workers had described it as an act of God, saying that when he was forced to leap into the water to avoid the flames, Jesus had appeared. He claimed the hand of God guided him to the surface.

Ella smiled to herself, imagining Dax's reaction to that part of the story.

She hadn't heard from him since their run-in on the bridge in the city. She had expected him to call and apologise, but he'd remained completely silent and distant, and she'd lain awake many nights trying to figure out why.

A few times she thought about calling him. She would unlock her phone, her thumb hovering over his name. But then Lucy would remind her that Dax was in the wrong, and it was up to him to fix what he'd broken.

Ella didn't know the game they were playing, let alone the rules. She could love him and love him, but it didn't mean she could make it work between them. She was human, an outsider, and there would always be things she couldn't understand.

Dax was right. Their love was a curse, and perhaps he was tired of carrying the burden.

'Let's just get through the open day,' Lucy said. 'He doesn't get to take that from you too.'

Ella placed her coffee cup down and rose, knowing Lucy was right. She had to get through the next day, and as soon as they were done with that, she would call him, insist they meet, and find out what was going on with him.

Entering the studio, Ella scrolled through her phone until she found The Sweeplings' song 'Chains'. She plugged her phone into the speakers and ran through her piece for the open day. Lucy had seen it for the first time that morning. When the song ended, she'd stood with tears rolling down her cheeks.

'I'm so angry at him,' she'd said as Ella pushed herself off the ground, sweating and breathless.

Ella had only nodded before exiting the room.

The dance was an outlet, a pouring out of her pent-up hurt and frustration. Dance was her first language. While the story was as difficult to perform as it was to watch, it was the only story Ella was interested in telling. She hoped it moved people at the open day.

She ran through the entire thing twice, finishing on the floor with her arms curled protectively over her head. Instead of getting up, like she should've done, like she'd done so many times before, she brought her knees up, curled into a ball, and cried.

❧

DAX'S PARENTS were staying at his house, so in order to avoid their endless questions and disapproving glances, he'd spent the last few nights at Adrian and Greta's. The couple took full advantage, using him for babysitting and bedtime stories in order to steal a few moments alone together. It was Friday night, and the pair were getting ready to head out for dinner and drinks with the pod. Normally Greta's mother watched Ariel, but since Dax had no interest in going out, he'd offered to babysit for them instead.

He was seated at the bench flicking through the paper, not really reading it, because his thoughts always trailed back to Ella. He'd really messed things up, and he had no idea what to do about it. Greta, his mentor on the workings of the female mind, was telling him to lie low for a while. He was having difficulty gauging how badly he'd messed up.

'On a scale of one to ten? Ten,' Greta had said, sounding like a disappointed parent.

Closing the paper, Dax pushed it away. It slid across the bench and hit the pile of mail stacked at the end. He watched it fall to the floor. Standing, he went to pick everything up and paused when he noticed a flyer.

You're invited to join the fun at Happy Toes Dance Studio's Open Day.

Dax snatched it up and straightened, scanning the contents of the page. His gaze snagged on Ella's name printed at the bottom.

Miss Ella Lewis teaching ballet, contemporary, jazz, and tap.
Miss Lucy Anderson teaching ballet and hip-hop.

He sank down onto a stool and read the entire thing again.

Saturday, January 9. Meet the teachers. Kids entertainment and performances by Miss Ella Lewis and Miss Lucy Anderson.

He felt both proud of Ella and furious that no one had told him.

Greta walked into the kitchen at that moment, and Dax raised the piece of paper. 'What the hell is this?'

She slowed when she saw what he was holding up. 'A flyer.'

'I see that. Where did you get it?'

Greta busied herself in the kitchen. 'I took it from Ella's house when I went by to check on her last week.'

'You failed to mention that to me.'

She looked suitably guilty. 'I was worried about her. You're not the only one separated from your mate right now.'

Dax dropped the flyer onto the bench. 'She's opening a dance studio?'

'She is.'

'She didn't say anything to me.'

'You mean she didn't think to bring it up the night you almost died? Or was she supposed to interrupt your fight with Peter to let you know the good news?'

'That's a lot of sarcasm at once.' If he was being honest, he'd assumed she would live off her father for a while until he eventually found her another job she wasn't suited for. Catching that thought, he realised he should have had more faith in her. He was proud of her. 'Are you going to this thing tomorrow?'

She shook her head. 'It's a big day for her. I thought it best to stay away.'

'Is that why you've changed your tune and you're now telling me to give her space?'

Greta filled a glass with water. 'The last thing she needs is a scene.'

'I wouldn't make a scene.'

'Just like the scene you didn't make outside Flinders Street Station the other night?'

Dax looked down at the flyer. 'She was just standing there with him, in the middle of the night, dressed like a bloody goddess. A switch in my head flipped.'

'You forgot the part where you were drunk. I understand your perspective, by the way. I just hope you can see hers. You go cold for weeks, then just show up and almost unleash the river on the city while beating up her friend.'

'Her *ex*.'

'The point is, neither of them were doing anything wrong.'

Dax leaned his elbows on the bench and rubbed his face with both hands. 'I feel like I should be there tomorrow.'

Greta set her glass down and crossed her arms. 'And if Peter's there?'

'I'll beat his arse.'

'Not funny.'

'You know I'll behave.'

'If you're sober,' Greta said under her breath. 'Look, go if you want to be supportive and think she'd want you there. Just behave like the man she deserves.'

He sat with that for a moment. 'Her father said from day one I'm not good enough for her. Is he right?'

Greta rolled her eyes. 'No you don't. No pity parties on my watch. Only you and Ella get to decide what's best for you and Ella.'

'I've made a lot of mistakes.'

'Oh, I know.'

'But everything I did, I did for her. Sure, I could've shown up at her house when I got back from Adelaide, but the police were ready to pounce. They would've had a field day with her. Ella's never broken a law in her life. Then I come along and suddenly she's lying to the police to save my arse.'

Greta reached across the bench for his arm. 'There's middle ground here. No one's expecting you to be perfect, least of all Ella. But you need to let her decide what risks she is or isn't willing to take. You're robbing her of that choice and doing more damage. She doesn't feel protected, she feels abandoned.'

'Did she say that to you?'

Greta straightened and shook her head. 'No. *I'm* saying it. You want to be there tomorrow, be there. You're right, you should support her, but you should support her *all* the time.'

Dax rubbed at his beard, then nodded. 'Point taken.'

CHAPTER 41

*D*ax couldn't get a car space near Ella's house, so he parked near the beach and walked. He barely recognised her place when he reached it. She'd cleaned up the garden, mulched, and had new stones laid in the driveway. She'd even painted her letterbox the same colour as the house.

A few families stood out front talking, their kids clutching yellow balloons with *Happy Toes* printed on them. He spotted Lucy chatting among them. She glanced in his direction, falling silent when he raised his hand in a wave.

'Anyway,' she said, returning her attention to the adults she stood with, 'it's time for Miss Ella's contemporary performance. Why don't you head on into the studio and find a good spot before it fills up?'

The families went inside, and a moment later, Lucy was standing in front of him like a pissed-off bouncer at a nightclub.

'What are you doing here?' she whispered. 'You can't be here. Ella's about to perform.'

He raised his hands in mock surrender. 'I just came to show my support.'

Lucy smiled as someone walked by, but then her expression darkened once more. '*Now* you choose to be supportive? Where was your support a few weeks back when the cops were knocking on her door warning her not to go anywhere?'

Dax swallowed. 'That's exactly why I stayed away. You think it was easy?'

'Nothing's easy with you,' she whisper-shouted, eyes darting around to ensure no one was listening. 'I should just tell you to get the hell out of here, but now I'm thinking you should stay and see this dance.'

'You want me to stay... for the dance?'

Lucy glared up at him. 'You'll understand why when you see it. I'm warning you though, it's not easy to watch. It says everything Ella can't. She can't fake anything when it comes to dance. It's all there for everyone to see—the whole messy truth.'

Dax shifted his weight. 'I don't really get the whole artistic expression thing. If there's a point, I'm sure I'll miss it.'

'You won't miss it, trust me.' Lucy's tone was firm on that point. 'You can watch from the door—out of sight.' With that, she turned on her heel and marched inside.

Dax buried his hands in his pockets and looked around before following her.

He remained in the entryway while others passed by, finding a space inside the studio. There were only a handful of chairs, so most stood. Lucy kept guard at the door, casting warning glances in his direction.

He waited for the room to fall silent before stepping closer so he could see in. The people blocking the doorway provided cover, and he watched over their heads as Ella stepped away from her father and walked out into the middle of the room. She was wearing some sort of leotard and pink tights. Her feet were bare, her hair wavy and dishevelled. Her eyeliner was thick and eyeshadow heavy. Nude, glossy lips completed her slightly unhinged look. She smiled and clasped her hands in front of her as she looked around the room.

'For those of you wondering what contemporary dance is, or if you're trying to decide if it might be a good fit for you or your child, you'll see it's a very expressive style. It combines elements of other genres, like ballet, lyrical, and even jazz. It focuses on footwork, balance, floor work, and jumps. You'll notice it's very fluid, and it doesn't require painful shoes, which makes it an appealing choice for some.' She lifted one of her bare feet and wriggled her toes as her audience laughed. 'It's not about perfection but emotion, so it can be very useful for releasing stress.' She drew a long breath. 'So watch the performance and take note of how you feel as the story unfolds. You can ask me questions at the end. We're also offering a free trial class for both children and adults looking to dance for fitness and fun, so make sure you grab a copy of our term one timetable on your way out.'

Someone pulled the heavy curtain closed at the end of the room, revealing a lit section of floor. Lucy wandered over to start the music while Ella positioned herself beneath the light, one arm stretched overhead and back bent at an unnatural angle. Her eyes closed.

Dax stood so still, feeling too much already, and she hadn't even started dancing yet. He didn't recognise the song, but that wasn't really a surprise given he listened to Triple M at work. It was a ballad of some sort, maybe folk. He made a point of listening to the lyrics so he could understand why she chose it. If music was a way to see inside her mind, then he would pay attention.

This was nothing like the dancing he'd seen her do

before. It wasn't all straight lines and elegant turns. Yes, at times it was beautiful, but it was also dark and ugly. Raw. It told a story he hadn't been prepared for. There was one moment when she was on her back, sliding in a way that made it look like she was being dragged. He had to look away, because he was ready to push through the people separating them and scoop her off the floor.

There were moments she fought an invisible demon.

There were moments she submitted to it.

A silent scream came from her, and then she turned like she was looking for help—but nobody came. Leaping high into the air, she tucked her body at the last minute, rolling across the floor before rising on her toes again. Dax held his breath, certain she was going to accidentally kill herself. But every fall was intentional, and every time she rose again, she seemed stronger, taller, braver. She beat her chest at one point, and he felt those fists as though they were pounding on his own ribs.

He liked to think he was in tune with his mate, but watching her in that moment, it was clear he'd missed things. It was difficult to see her pain played out for the enjoyment of others, so vivid, beautiful, and disturbing. She'd warned him about the power of dance, and he'd always just smiled and kissed her. He saw how condescending that response was now. She had certainly made a believer of him.

Dax watched Ella for a few more counts, a few more lyrics, then turned and headed for the front door just as the applause began. If he left now, she wouldn't even know he'd been there.

'Dax,' Lucy called as he pushed through the screen door.

He stopped and waited, feet shuffling. He wanted to get out of there before Ella saw him. 'Yeah?'

'You're leaving?'

He didn't really have a clear reason why, only a strong

sense he was doing the right thing. 'You were right. She needs to focus on this, not me. I don't want to mess up today. I've messed up enough. I'll get out of your way.'

Lucy looked far from pleased. 'So, you're going to bail again?'

'*You* told me to leave.'

'You know, there's only so many times I can piece that girl back together.'

The door opened behind Lucy, and a child burst through it, followed by her parents. Lucy smiled in their direction.

'Thanks so much for coming. Did you get a timetable? Great.'

As she was waving them off, Ella stepped through the door and froze when she caught sight of Dax. One look at her face confirmed that he shouldn't have come. It had taken seeing her again to realise that the best thing he could do for her was leave her alone. She was quite capable of finding happiness if he could just manage to stay out of her way.

Lucy let out a breath and returned inside, touching Ella's arm as she passed. Ella never looked away from Dax as she stepped out to join him on the lawn. Without saying a word, they both headed for the footpath where they could speak in private. She stopped a few paces from him, still wearing the same leotard but with boyfriend jeans over her tights.

'Did you just get here?' she asked, sounding nervous.

'No. I got here before your dance.'

She searched his eyes. 'And now you're leaving?' She laughed. 'Was it that bad?'

He shook his head. 'No, you were amazing. If every parent in there doesn't immediately sign their kid up for your class, they're mental.'

Ella glanced in the direction of the house. 'If you can

wait, I'll be done in a few hours. I just need to finish up here.'

He stepped back from her. 'Go. I shouldn't have come. I had this stupid idea that I was supporting you by showing up, but I'm just distracting you.'

'You're not distracting me,' she replied quickly. 'Can you come back at two? There'll be leftover balloons.'

He narrowed his eyes at her. 'You're luring me back with balloons?'

She shrugged. 'We can inhale the helium and argue in funny voices.'

He didn't deserve her kindness or her jokes, but she gave him both anyway. As if he needed more reasons to worship the ground she walked on. 'I don't want to argue with you.'

'Okay.' Her lip disappeared between her teeth for a moment. 'We'll just talk, then.'

His chest felt like it was tearing in two, and he didn't really understand why. She was spoon-feeding him hope. So why was he turning away from it? 'I'm ridiculously proud of you, by the way. This is a great idea. The dance school, I mean.' He looked back at the house. 'You really figured shit out and went for it.'

She slid her hands into her back pockets. 'Thanks to the much-needed push you gave me.'

He shook his head. 'No. This is all you, Miss Lewis. Your clever mind, your talent, your brand-new dream. This is the simple life you were searching for when we met, remember?'

'A lot's changed since then.'

'You've got this clear path back to dance, and every-thing's as it should be.'

Ella stared at him a moment. 'Stop talking like that.'

'Like what?'

'Like you're... like you're saying goodbye.'

He swallowed. He certainly hadn't arrived with that intention, but it did seem to be turning into that. It was the first moment of clarity he'd had in a long time. 'You should go inside.'

She didn't move. 'I had this entire dramatic scene planned out in my head of how it would all go down between us. You would show up at my door, and I wouldn't invite you in. That would speak volumes. Then you would tell me how sorry you were, about everything. You would say you wished you'd told me the truth about everything from the start.'

He didn't interrupt her, understanding she needed to get this off her chest.

'You would apologise for the secrets,' she continued, 'for using me to get information about the Christmas party. You would tell me that what happened in the city with Peter would never happen again, that you were drunk, not yourself.' She paused to collect herself. 'I would tell you that's not an excuse, and that if you ever raised a fist at one of my friends like that again, it would be over between us, knowing all the while that it can never really be over between us.' She laughed and pressed her lips together. 'Somehow, you would fix us.' She looked up at him expectantly. 'That's why you came here, isn't it? To fix us?'

His arms hung heavy at his sides. 'I think—' His throat closed, and he had to clear it. 'I think I came to see how you were doing without me. Pretty well, it turns out.'

She shook her head. 'No, don't do that. Don't justify leaving again.' She pointed at the ground between them. 'You stay, and you fix us.' Her voice cracked with emotion. 'Please.'

The burn in his throat spread to his entire body. He blinked back tears. 'I love you. You deserve this life.' He pointed to the house. 'The one you've built with the help of Lucy and your father.'

'You're a part of this too.'

He didn't respond.

'You need to come back at two o'clock.' Her eyes held a plea. 'We'll talk then. You can say everything you want to say then.'

His face must've communicated his despair, because she took a few unsteady steps back as she brushed tears off her cheeks. She looked down at the black streaks on her hands. 'I have to go in.' She wiped them on her jeans. 'I'll see you at two.'

With a forced smile, she turned and strode off across the lawn without a backwards glance.

CHAPTER 42

By two o'clock, everyone had gone home. A few balloons bobbed against their restraints by the door, and a single iced cookie in the shape of a ballet slipper sat on the table. Ella and Lucy packed up the chairs and swept the studio floor. Michael had offered to stay behind and help, but Ella insisted they were fine. Truthfully, she wanted him gone by the time Dax returned. She didn't want anything scaring him off.

The studio curtain was pulled back, offering a clear view of the road. Ella sat on the window ledge looking out. She held her breath every time someone passed, but it was never him. Maybe he was giving her extra time to clean up, to ensure everyone had left so they could have the privacy they needed. She replayed their previous conversation in her mind, the look on Dax's face now burned into her memory. She blinked it away.

Lucy tinkered in the kitchen. They were supposed to be drinking champagne.

At four o'clock, she wandered in and sat opposite Ella.

'He'll be here,' Ella said, not looking away from the road. 'He'll come.'

Lucy rose and picked up the untouched cup of tea she had brought in earlier. 'We filled four of the junior primary classes today. That's amazing. Today was amazing. You should be smiling.'

Ella looked up at her. 'I'm thrilled about today. Thank you for everything.'

Lucy stared back at her. 'He's not coming. You know that, right?'

Ella turned back to the window and pulled her knees up. 'Why don't you go get the champagne out of the fridge? I'll join you in a minute.'

Lucy hesitated, then left the studio.

It was five o'clock when Ella finally wandered into the kitchen. Lucy was seated at the table looking at her phone, an empty champagne flute in front of her. A second flute sat nearby, the occasional bubble rising.

'I'm sorry,' Ella said, her voice breaking. 'You're right. He's not coming.'

Lucy rose and pulled her into a hug. Ella stood with her arms limp at her sides, feeling hollow.

'Screw this,' Lucy said, releasing her. 'You need closure. You *deserve* closure. So let's go get you some.' She snatched her jacket off the back of the chair. 'I'll drive you.'

'What about Caleb?'

'I'll call Mum in the car. She won't mind.'

Ella nodded and followed her out of the house. She was still wearing the leotard and hadn't even removed her stage makeup.

They arrived at Dax's house thirty minutes later.

'You want me to come in with you?' Lucy asked, looking over at her.

Ella stared up at the townhouse. 'No, I'll be fine. But do you mind waiting in the car in case he's not home?'

Lucy reached across the console and squeezed her

hand. 'Do you honestly think I would just drive off? Of course I'll wait.'

Ella took a deep breath as she stepped through the gate and followed the narrow path to the front step. Her hand hovered a few inches from the door as she thought through all the possible outcomes. Maybe he wasn't there or didn't want to see her. What reason would he give for not returning to the house?

She withdrew her hand, suddenly doubting her decision.

As she stood there debating what to do, the front door swung open and Miller appeared, his eyebrows lowered and jaw tight.

'Oh. Hi,' Ella said, taking a small step back.

Miller leaned his shoulder on the door frame and crossed his arms in front of him. Ella knew the next words out of his mouth were going to destroy her. She could see it in his expression, his body language, his inability to maintain eye contact.

'Where is he?' she asked.

'I'm so sorry. We tried to talk him out of it, but he went anyway.'

Ella stared at him. 'Went where?'

'That's the thing. We don't really know. It's kind of the point.'

'What does that mean? The point of what?'

Miller struggled to form words. 'We're ondines. Sometimes we just need to go home for a while.'

She stood very still. 'You mean home to the sea?'

A nod was his only reply.

'Oh. Okay. When will he be back?'

Miller was looking at the doormat again. It was crusted with sand and lifting at the corners. 'When things get a bit much on land, we take a long swim. I did it myself a while back, needed to clear my head.'

'How long were you gone?'

Miller hesitated. 'A few years.'

Ella's heart pounded and she put her hand over it, pressing hard to prevent it from bursting through her chest. She took a moment to gather herself. 'He wouldn't just leave without telling me where he was going. I'm his *mate*. He wouldn't leave me behind.'

As soon as she said it, she knew she was wrong. Of course he could leave her if he thought it was for her own good. He could leave, and he could lie. He'd done them both before.

Stepping back from the door, she pulled her phone from her pocket and dialled Dax's number. Her heart sank when it went straight to voicemail. She was shut out again.

'He won't answer,' Miller said, his face twisting. 'He didn't take his phone with him. He doesn't want to be contacted—by anyone.'

Ella opened her mouth to speak but swallowed instead. She tried again. 'So he just walked out the front door, into the sea, and swam away?' She laughed even though it wasn't funny.

He nodded. 'He'll come home eventually. His family's here, his pod.'

He didn't say mate.

Ella bit down on her lip as she turned away from the door.

'Do you want to come in for a bit?' Miller called to her.

She shook her head and kept walking, refusing to come apart in front of him. She made it all the way to the car before the tears began falling. Tearing the door open, she collapsed into the seat and covered her face.

Lucy rested her hand on Ella's back. 'Oh my God, what the hell did he say?'

Ella reached for the door, pulling it closed. 'Let's go.'

'Ella—'

'He's gone.' She turned to Lucy, eyes pleading. 'Please, just drive. I need to get out of here.'

CHAPTER 43

The only plan Dax had was to swim north. He was hoping the distance would strengthen his resolve to stay away. There was no way he could remain in the same city as Ella and not be with her. He would look for her in every crowd, in every coffee shop, on every street in Melbourne. And she would likely do the same. With him gone, she had a real chance to succeed at her simple human life.

The one she'd told him she wanted soon after they'd met.

The one she deserved.

Ella had already proven she could build a life without him. She'd done it in a matter of weeks. It was clear now that the burden of finding his mate was his alone to carry. She was human, which meant her feelings could be neatly contained if necessary. He just needed to stay out of her way.

He could do that.

Stay busy, distracted, and on the other side of the country. The pay-off for his own misery was her happiness. It might not come straight away, but it would come eventually.

So he swam the Indian Ocean, only returning to land to eat and sleep. Then it was back into the water, swimming through the Great Australian Bight until he reached Western Australia. He stopped at coastal towns along the way, explored caves, and encountered great white sharks that circled him curiously. The perks of moving water meant he never became a snack for one of them.

After spending a few days at the Leeuwin-Naturaliste National Park, he hitch-hiked to Dunsborough. From there he swam Geographe Bay, Warnbro Sound, and Cockburn Sound, then spent a few days exploring Fremantle. He gave the waters of Marmion Marine Park a wide berth because he knew it was a tourist hotspot.

It took him a few weeks to make his way up the coast. He spent time in West End, Drummond Cove, Gregory, Kalbarri, Shark Bay, Dirk Hartog Island, Ningaloo Conservation Reserve, and Cape Range National Park. The waters grew warmer and his heart heavier the further he was from Ella. That was normal, and it helped knowing that.

When he reached Sunday Island in the Timor Sea, he gave himself five days to wallow. But because his savings wouldn't last forever, he pushed on. He would need to find work eventually.

Dax explored King Sound, Mary Island North, Hidden Island, and many others. When he finally emerged from the water at Nightcliff in Darwin, he was met with the unrelenting humidity he remembered from his last trip north.

A man in his late fifties approached, concern etched in his leathery face. 'You can't swim in there. It's stinger season. And if the jellyfish don't get you, the bloody crocs will.'

Dax had actually swum through a smack of jellyfish

while making his way to the shore. Their venom could kill a human in under five minutes, but an ondine's skin was tough, repelling the tentacles, meaning stings were rare and not nearly as dangerous.

'I didn't realise,' he said, clapping the man on the shoulder. 'Thanks for the heads-up.'

The man looked him up and down, eyes narrowing on the waterproof pack slung over his shoulder. It contained a change of clothes, a pair of sunglasses, and his wallet. That was all he needed for his new life.

Dax wandered up to the takeaway shop overlooking the beach and ordered a hamburger, which came with enough chips to sink a boat. He sat with an icy beer, watching the water change colour beneath the setting sun. Within minutes, the beer was warm and his thirst unquenched. Grabbing a bottle of water from the drink fridge next to the counter, he paid and wandered down to the beach, dropping onto the sand to wait. He didn't have any phone numbers or addresses with him, only a memory that the Beagle Gulf boys swam at that particular beach after dark.

The sand was warm and his body tired, but he forced himself to stay awake. It was a little before nine when he finally spotted a group heading for the water. He searched for a familiar face among them, relieved when he saw Gordy trailing behind. Standing, he brushed sand off himself and wandered towards them. Gordy stopped when he spotted him, eyes widening in surprise.

'What the hell are you doing here?' he said, shaking Dax's hand and clapping him on the back. 'You didn't tell me you were coming up.'

Dax returned the smile. 'Last-minute trip.'

'When did you fly in?'

Dax looked around. 'I swam.'

Gordy's eyes fell to the waterproof backpack. 'Uh-oh. Please tell me you're not on the run from the cops.'

'Not the cops.'

'Ah.' Gordy appeared to understand then. 'This have something to do with that mate of yours?'

Dax glanced down at his sand-covered feet. 'I'm looking for work, and I was hoping you could help me.' His fatigue was catching up to him.

Gordy looked him over, then nodded. 'Yeah, man. I can help you.'

CHAPTER 44

$\mathcal{E}$lla called Dax every day for forty days. She continued phoning until the day she got an automated message saying his mailbox was full. An optimistic part of her was hoping he'd check his messages remotely from another device, and the realisation that he'd cut himself off from her was like a fresh wound. If she'd had any idea where to look for him, she might've gone searching. While his family and pod were content to let him roam the sea and do whatever it was that ondines did, Ella couldn't shake her human reaction of logic and grief.

For the remainder of the summer, Ella went down to the water every night. She would paddle in the sea until the sun disappeared and the air turned cold. Then she would wander up onto the sand, wrap herself in a large towel, and watch the water. Eventually she'd return home, always hopeful that her phone would ring at some point during the night, or maybe there would be a knock on the door.

But the phone never rang, and the door stood silent.

When autumn arrived, Ella took walks in the shallows because it was too cold to go all the way in.

Winter was shoes-on weather, but she missed the feel

of the water. So off came the shoes, and she gritted her teeth against her throbbing feet.

Had it really been two seasons without laying eyes on him?

Away from the water, she threw herself into teaching, dance, and the relationships she had left. It was Lucy who drew attention to Ella's improved strength and muscle definition, something she had struggled with in her younger years. She wondered if it had anything to do with spending more time in the water—but she never wondered it aloud.

Winter was always the longest season, stretching past the three months assigned to it. September bought no reprieve from the cold, but it did bring sun, the kind that lied to you through the window, then laughed at you when you stepped outside.

It held no real warmth.

Occasionally, Ella would Google Dax's name or search for him on social media, even though she knew the pod didn't use those platforms. She did it because she didn't know what else to do.

For a while, she'd caught up with Greta, until Lucy had pointed out that her mood was always flat on the days following those catch-ups. It was true. They brought Dax to the forefront of her mind, and then she would spend the next few days pushing him back into a place where she could function properly, smile, and be present for all the people who deserved it.

Ella didn't see Greta again until October, when she showed up at the house with Ariel. Lucy was there with Caleb, and she took Greta's daughter out back so the two of them could talk. Ella chewed her lip as she sat at the table waiting for Greta to speak. She could tell by the serious expression that she had news of Dax.

'Everything okay?' Ella asked.

Greta's car keys jingled as she placed them on the table. 'We found Dax.'

It was strange how just a few words could make Ella feel like she was drowning. It felt like he was leaving her all over again. 'Oh.'

'He's working as a marine engineer in a town just outside of Darwin. Adrian heard it from a friend who lives up there.'

'Darwin?' She tried to picture him in the humidity, fighting off the saltwater crocs that dominated the north. 'Great place to spend a winter.'

'Apparently he's living in a share house.'

Ella didn't know how to feel about that. On one hand, she was angry that he'd built this entire other life without so much as a text message from a borrowed phone to let her know he was okay, but on the other hand, she felt this strange pride at him getting a job in the field he'd studied in.

She swung between the two emotions for a moment. 'Has anyone spoken to him?'

'Miller's going to fly up and check in on him.' She hesitated. 'I thought you might want to pass a letter along or something.'

A letter.

Or something.

Ella thought about that, wondering if she could condense all her thoughts and feelings into a few words on a page. She'd already said things to him, said them the day he'd left.

'Stay.'

'Fix us.'

Still, he'd chosen to leave, to shatter the remaining pieces of her heart into a fine powder that could be carried off with the slightest breeze.

'I'm not sure I have anything to say,' Ella said. 'I thought

315

I wanted to know where he was, but now I can't remember why.'

It had been ten months since he left, and he'd known exactly where she was for every one of those months.

Greta looked down at the table. 'I understand. Our kind do things a little bit differently, and Dax does things a little bit differently again.' She attempted a smile. 'I will say this though. I know he left because he believed it was the best thing for you. He didn't want to mess up your life and get in the way of your happiness.'

Ella pressed her hands on the table. 'I'm not sure I can hear that again. He destroyed my happiness when he left. It didn't have to be a choice between this life and him. I could've had this life *and* loved him.'

Greta tilted her head. 'Sure, but that's not an easy life. How many times could you have lied to the cops before it started to eat away at you, do you think?'

'Maybe Dax could've stopped breaking the law so I didn't have to lie to anyone.'

'You mean your laws?' Greta asked. '*Human* laws? And how many times did Bass Fuel break those laws, anyway?'

Ella remained silent.

'We have our own laws and values to uphold,' Greta continued. 'We have responsibilities too.' She shook her head. 'Do you know how lucky Adrian and I are to have Ariel? We were trying for *years*. It's because of the water.'

Ella swallowed. 'I didn't realise. Sorry.'

'The difference between you two is that you want him to change to fit your world. Dax left so you wouldn't have to change a thing.' She picked up her keys and rose from the table. 'Ariel, we're leaving.'

Ella rose slowly.

'Bye!' the little girl shouted as she ran past. She was dressed in stretchy jeans with a tutu over the top.

Ella followed her to the door. 'I hadn't noticed how beautifully you're dressed.'

'I'm going to be a ballet teacher like you when I'm big,' Ariel replied.

Ella smiled. 'You'll be an amazing teacher, because you're an amazing dancer.' She looked up at Greta. 'I really appreciate you driving all the way here.'

Greta waved away the gratitude before taking her daughter's hand. 'Your feelings are valid'—she met Ella's eyes a final time—'but so are his.'

CHAPTER 45

When Dax stepped off the boat at the end of his shift, he froze when he saw Miller standing at the end of the wharf, dressed in cut-off jeans and a singlet. Dax could see the sheen of sweat on his forehead even at that distance. It was a brave move for a Melburnian to visit Darwin during the build-up. Even locals were suffocating as they waited for the rain to arrive.

Recovering from the surprise, Dax headed over to his brother. He knew it would only be a matter of time before word got back to his family of his whereabouts. He certainly hadn't sworn anyone to secrecy.

'There he is,' Miller said, watching him approach. 'I've only been waiting here for two hours.'

Dax took hold of the hand extended to him and pulled Miller into a hug, eyes closing briefly. He wasn't ashamed to admit he'd missed his brother. He clapped him on the back before letting go. 'Let's find you some air conditioning and a beer before you combust into flames.'

What Dax had always appreciated about Miller was that he skipped the dramatics, lectures, and guilt speeches.

318

He wasn't there to deliver a sermon, he was checking in on his little brother. Now it was up to Dax to ensure he left feeling good about what he'd found.

They walked up to the nearby licensed cafe and ordered two stubbies before taking a seat at the table by the window. Miller frowned at the collection of beer cans in the fridge behind the counter—or rather looked down his pretentious Melbourne nose at them.

'Please tell me you don't drink from cans now.'

Dax chuckled and swigged his beer. 'This life is not without sacrifices.'

Miller studied him across the table. 'You look good. I expected to find you drunk on a beach somewhere at half the weight you left.'

'Sorry to disappoint.'

'It's a relief, trust me.'

Dax twisted his beer on the table. 'You going to fill me in on everything or what?'

Miller got comfortable and caught him up on ten months of Bass Strait pod news. He spoke of everyone and everything except Ella. While Dax was desperate to ask about her, he didn't know what that information would do to him. He'd coped well enough. Well, he'd stayed away, at least.

'Tell me about the job,' Miller said. 'I nearly fell off my chair when Gordy told me you're working in the fuel industry. You taking down another rig or what?'

The corners of Dax's mouth lifted. 'These big corps are going to drill for oil whether we like it or not. The company I work for carries out inspections of the machinery. I can't swim around the world sinking every rig, but I can ensure shit works properly when stuff goes wrong.' He paused to drink. 'How's things at the construction company?'

Miller filled him in on their upcoming projects and

broke the news that Frankie had left shortly after his departure.

'Left the company?' Dax asked.

'The company and Melbourne. She's living in Sydney right now.'

Dax took that as a positive sign. She was moving on.

Still no mention of Ella.

They were on beer number three when Miller pulled something from his pocket, placed it on the table, and slid it towards Dax. He recognised his old phone.

'You need to either answer this one or give me another number,' Miller said. 'We've given you space. Now it's time to pick up the fucking phone and say hello once in a while.'

Dax reached for the phone and pushed it into his pocket. He had a mobile for work but hadn't bothered replacing his personal one. The local pod had the number if they needed to contact him.

'So you're really not going to ask about her?' Miller said, eyes on the table.

Dax's body temperature rose. Picking up his beer, he took a long drink, then another before setting it back down on the table. 'I don't know if that's a good idea.'

'You're not curious how she's doing?'

Dax wore a guarded expression. 'What do you think?'

Miller looked out the window.

'I know her dance school's taken off,' Dax said.

Miller's eyes returned to him. 'And how do you know that?'

'There might've been a night I drank too much and looked her up online.'

'Just one? I'm not sure her website's a very accurate representation of her life.'

Dax closed his eyes. 'There's some photos of her on the Happy Toes Facebook page. She looks good.'

'You think she's going to post photos of herself crying into her Weet-Bix?'

'If Ella's eating Weet-Bix for breakfast, then she's really gone off the rails.'

Miller laughed, and Dax looked out of the window. He knew she'd added more classes to cater for demand, so that had to be a good sign. He also knew she still had Lucy and dance in her life. One particularly drunken night, he'd studied every photograph of her closely, trying to figure out how deep the smiles ran.

'Have you seen her?' Dax finally asked.

Miller's expression turned serious as he picked at the corner of his beer label. 'She came to the house the day you left. I haven't seen her since. Greta kept in contact for a while.'

Dax reminded himself to breathe as he unpacked those three pieces of information. 'What do you mean "for a while"?'

'They were catching up, but then Ella pulled the plug.'

He told himself that was a good thing. Greta would've been a constant reminder of him, and he didn't want Ella anchored to the past. 'Good. Better she's not associated with the pod at all.'

Miller frowned. 'You picking her friends too?'

'She already had friends before I came along.'

Miller leaned his elbows on the table. 'You left. You don't get to play godfather from the other side of the country.' He picked up his beer. 'I wish you could've seen her broken expression the day she showed up looking for you.'

'Don't.'

'Come on. What did you expect to hear? That she was grateful for your grand sacrifice?'

'She will be one day.'

'Maybe, but right now she's still pissed at you. Greta offered to pass on a message, and Ella declined.'

'She knows where I am?'

'Relax. She's not following you up here anytime soon. You disappeared. You went and built another life without her.' He set his beer down again. 'The funny thing is, you went and built a life you knew she'd approve of. You could've done that in Melbourne.'

Every word landed like a punch.

'You broke her heart and your own in the process. You've got family who miss you. And for what?' Miller drew a breath. 'You're supposed to be her mate, not her guardian.'

'You finished throwing grenades at me?'

Miller relaxed back in his chair. 'Yeah. I'm done.'

Dax stared down at the table between them. 'I just kept messing up. It would've been the same thing over and over until she hated me.'

'What do you think she would've preferred? Your mistakes or this?' Miller exhaled. 'You're my brother, and I love you, but this trip feels a lot like you running scared. Or maybe you wanted to go away and find out if you could grow into the man she needed you to be. I don't know. What I do know is the longer you stay away, the harder it'll be to win your mate back when you finally realise what a dick you've been.'

Dax's fingers sat loose around the neck of an empty bottle.

'Another round of the same?' the waitress asked, stopping next to their table and looking between them.

Dax nodded. 'Yep—and keep them coming.'

When Dax arrived back at the share house that night, drunk, he popped his head into Gordy's room to say hello, then made his way to his own room. Pulling the mobile phone his brother had given him from his pocket, he plugged it into his work charger and waited for it to turn on. He wasn't too surprised to see a notification that his voicemail was full. He'd basically fallen off the planet for ten months. His thumb hovered over the 101 number, wondering if it was a good time to do that to himself. Deciding the alcohol would cushion the blow, he tapped his phone and brought it to his ear.

He stilled when Ella's voice came through the phone. It had been far too long since he'd heard that sweet voice of hers. He listened to the soul-crushing message, then waited to see who the next one was from. It was Ella again. Then again. Most of them were from her. She'd called him every day until there was no more space on his phone for her. It killed him to think of her leaving those messages, knowing she wouldn't get a reply from him. They read like a journal of her pain, always finishing the same way.

'*Come home.*'

Maybe it was the voicemails, or maybe it was his brother unleashing on him earlier, or the large quantity of beer swirling in his stomach, but his resolve crumbled and he rose off the bed, returning to Gordy's room.

His housemate looked up.

'I need to borrow your laptop,' Dax said, holding onto the door frame.

Gordy leaned back in his chair, regarding him. 'Am I allowed to ask why?'

Dax rested his forehead on his hand. 'I need to book a flight.'

Unplugging the power cord on his laptop, Gordy handed it over. 'For work?'

'No, not for work. I need to go to Melbourne.'

CHAPTER 46

*D*ax arrived in Melbourne Friday morning. Miller had flown home a day earlier. He'd offered to pick Dax up from the airport, but he'd declined, instead catching a taxi straight to Ella's house. After paying the driver, he stepped out onto the gravel between the road and the footpath, eyes landing on the unfamiliar car parked in the driveway. He hesitated, wondering if he should call ahead first, then decided it was better to do it in person so he could gauge exactly how much damage he'd done.

As he walked up to the front door, he could hear classical music blaring from the house. He wondered if perhaps she was teaching a class. Just as he was pulling his phone from his pocket, the door swung open and Caleb appeared.

'Hi,' Dax said, glancing past him to the empty hallway. 'Look at you. You're huge.'

The boy made himself as tall as possible. 'Soon I'll be bigger than Mummy.'

'I don't doubt it. Did someone tell you to open the door?'

He shook his head. 'I saw you through the window. Mum's really busy.'

'She teaching?'

Another shake of the head. 'They're getting ready for the concert. Ella and Peter are doing a *Nutcracker* song.'

Dax hadn't considered the possibility that it was Peter's car out front. 'Right. Can you let Ella know I'm here?'

Caleb stepped aside. 'I'm not allowed to interrupt or I won't get Tiny Teddies at the end. Do you want to watch them?'

'I don't think your mum would like you letting me into the house.'

Caleb looked up at him with a curious expression. 'Why does she call you arse-hat?'

Dax couldn't stop the smile. 'You should ask her.' He stepped into the house, quietly pulling the door closed behind him. 'How about I wait here until they're done, and then you can tell Ella I'm here?'

'Okay.'

The door to the studio sat wide open, and Dax found himself with his usual view of the mirror. He didn't feel he had a right to look, but it had been ten months since he'd laid eyes on her, so looking away wasn't really an option.

His heart faltered when she swept into view, wearing leopard print leggings and ballet shoes. Her hair was up in a high bun, strands poking out in all directions. Somehow she was more beautiful than he remembered.

His eyes shifted to Peter, who wore a tight T-shirt with tracksuit pants and bare feet. He was holding Ella's hand, then her waist. All the small hairs on Dax's neck stood on end, even though Peter appeared to be more focused on what Lucy was saying than Ella. Lucy was pacing the wall, arms crossed and nodding as she assessed them.

'Good,' she called out. 'Here comes the lift. Maybe try

staying on his shoulder this time, Miss Ella.' Her tone was teasing.

'I can stay anywhere I'm put,' Ella shot back, breathless, 'so you can direct your feedback at Peter.'

He'd really missed that voice.

Peter turned her a few times. 'Let's remember I'm not getting paid for this gig, okay? You're supposed to be stroking my ego and making me feel like the star attraction.'

Ella stretched a leg out behind her. 'To be clear, the *kids* are the star attraction.'

'Absolutely,' Lucy agreed. 'That's why we've been staying up until all hours of the night sewing costumes for them. You'll have to steal your costume from work.'

'Ready?' Peter said to Ella, placing one foot behind him.

'Ready,' Ella replied, rising onto her toes and bending backwards at an impossible angle. When she straightened, Peter hoisted her up in the air, lifting her over his head. Ella extended one leg, the other bent as he turned. He placed her back on the ground, keeping hold of her hand as he pulled her this way and that, like an elastic band.

Dax watched with irritation, wondering how long a piece of music could last, all the while knowing he had no right to be agitated. They were just friends. Or maybe he was having her in the studio every night after rehearsals. They could be Facebook official for all he knew.

Humans loved their relationship status updates.

Dax looked down and was surprised to find Caleb staring up at him with a thoughtful expression.

'Do you love Ella?' Caleb asked.

Another hard-hitting question from the kid.

'It's complicated.' Oh, that was perfect for Facebook.

Just then, Lucy walked out of the studio, gasping and swearing when she spotted him.

'Mummy said the F-word,' Caleb said, giggling into his hand.

Dax glanced at him. 'My fault. I surprised her.'

'That's an understatement,' Lucy said, walking over and crouching in front of Caleb. 'What did I tell you about opening the front door to strangers—'

'Dax isn't a stranger.'

She put a finger to his mouth. 'I'm not finished. Strangers *and* Ella's ex-boyfriends—'

'But when Peter knocked, you told me to open the door.'

'Still not finished. Strangers and ex-boyfriends who use Ella's heart for fish food.' She rose, glaring at Dax, but before she had a chance to resume her assault on him, Ella wandered out, freezing when she saw him.

Neither of them moved.

'What the hell is he doing here?' Peter said as he stepped through the door behind her. He looked between them. 'You want me to get rid of him?'

Dax would've liked to see him try, but instead of breaking the guy's nose, he waited for Ella to speak. If she wanted him gone, he would go.

Her gaze fell to the ground as she stepped past him and headed for the door. 'Outside,' she said quietly.

The heat of Lucy's stare followed him out.

Dax noted Ella's body language as he closed the door: arms crossed, chin raised, and blue eyes blazing.

'What are you doing here?'

He knew from her tone that he didn't have much time to present his case. 'I got your voice messages.'

Her nostrils flared. '*What?*'

'Miller came up north. He brought my phone with him. It was the first time I'd heard them.'

She was looking at him like she had no idea who he

was. 'So what? You didn't know how I felt until you heard them?'

His hands were clammy. 'You said "come home". You said it in every message.'

She looked away while she composed herself. 'I also stood in this very spot back in January and asked you to *stay*.'

He'd prepared a whole speech on the plane, but suddenly it didn't seem to fit the conversation. 'I honestly thought I was doing the right thing.'

He watched as her eyes turned an angrier shade of blue.

'What do you actually want?' she asked, throwing her hands up. 'Why are you here? Don't tell me it's because of a few voice messages. *What do you want?*' Her tone was firmer this time.

What he wanted was to not have three feet of space between them, to erase all his mistakes and have her look at him with love in her eyes, like last summer. But he didn't deserve those things.

'I'm not good at this,' he said.

'At what? I don't even know what you're doing. Is this some sort of apology? Because I'll save you the time and energy. I don't forgive you.'

He searched for better words. 'I'm not expecting forgiveness. I just wanted to tell you that I know I messed up—big time. I see that now. Like I said, I really thought I was doing the right thing.'

'Which time?'

He shifted his weight. She really wasn't going to make it easy on him. 'All the times.'

She shook her head and looked away. 'Right. All the times.'

'I fucked up.'

'You did.'

'I know there's no point in saying sorry. I know it's meaningless.'

Her eyes returned to him. 'What *are* you here to say, then? Because I need to get back inside.'

His time was up. Clearing his throat, he said, 'I shouldn't have decided our future by myself. I should've come back at two o'clock, like you asked me to.'

Her expression didn't change. 'This is sounding a lot like an apology.'

'I should've stayed. I should've fixed us. It's a miracle you gave me the chance after all the rig shit, and the stuff with your mum, and I blew it.'

Her stoic expression faltered. 'You really did. You chose to run scared, and now we both have to live with your choice.' Her voice cracked for the first time, and she looked away, getting her emotions under control again. 'You said you'd always be there if I needed you. You told me that's what it means to be a mate. You said those things, and I believed you.'

'And I told you mates always find their way back to each other.'

She exhaled sharply through her nose. 'You make it sound like we were lost. I was never lost. I was right here, loving you, and waiting for you to come home'—her hand went to her chest—'and dying a little each day you didn't show up.'

He raked a hand through his hair, gripping tightly before letting go. 'I wanted better for you.'

Her eyes moved between his. 'Better? Who's better? Tell me. Who ticks all the boxes of your checklist? Who'll love me better than you? I'm dying to meet him. I'm literally fucking dying.' She drew a breath and stepped back from him.

'No one. It's not possible for anyone else to love you more than I do.'

She stepped up to him then, making herself taller. 'Then why did you leave?' She screamed the words in his face. 'Did you ever ask me what *I* wanted? I would've forgiven everything, all your mistakes, all the lies. I just needed a little time to get there.' She pointed at her chest. 'I knew, right from the start, that the kind of love we had would never come again, and you just threw it away like it meant nothing.' She pressed her palms against her eyes. 'I mean, not even a text message to tell me you're okay. Can you imagine if that had been reversed? Imagine for just a second if I'd disappeared without a word.' She pulled her hands away. 'I know you. I know your heart. I know you love me, that you still love me. I don't doubt it, even now. What I don't know is why you choose to keep hurting me over and over.' Tears fell. 'What the hell am I supposed to do when you just show up and expect too much from me?'

His chest was heavy as he watched all her pain spill out, months of pent-up hurt. The wounds were still raw. What else had he expected? He'd been slowly bleeding out for months himself.

'I'm sorry.' And now he was apologising, sounding like a pathetic, abusive spouse.

'Don't.' She raised a hand in warning. 'Don't you dare.'

They both fell silent. She continued to watch him cautiously, like she was waiting for him to pull a weapon on her.

He selected his next words carefully. 'The life you're living right now is the one I wanted for you. I thought by leaving I was somehow gifting that to you. I didn't think through the cost of that decision.'

She shook her head. 'You didn't gift me this life. I built it myself. All you did was rob me of a mate.'

Stepping past him, she slowly headed back to the house. 'Go back to Darwin,' she called over her shoulder. 'You can't fix us now.'

CHAPTER 47

*E*lla sat opposite her father at the enormous oak dining table. She had no idea why he'd purchased one designed for a large family. The thought of him eating alone at it every night made her feel bad for him. It was why she tried to have dinner with him at least once a week.

It was November, Melbourne Cup Day. They'd watched the race together at a local pub before returning to his house for tacos. She marvelled at her father's ability to eat them without dropping one shred of lettuce or cheese. It was an art form.

'Do you remember when you were sixteen and you failed to mention you'd gone gluten-free?' Michael asked. 'You'd heard it caused inflammation, and you were worried it was affecting your joints.'

She smiled as she loaded avocado into her taco. 'It *does* cause inflammation, and I didn't tell you because you always tried so hard with the cooking, and I just kept changing the rules on you. Sixteen was probably the age I realised how lucky I was to have a father who cooked for me at the end of a long workday.'

'I figured it out when I made pasta and realised you

were only eating the sauce.' He reached for his glass of red. 'I still buy gluten-free products to this day. It's a habit now.'

'You'll thank me for it when you're old.'

He chuckled into his glass. 'I'm already old.'

'Not *that* old.' She took a bite of her taco and saw his eyes slide to her plate as all the fillings fell to it. Covering her mouth, she chewed, then said, 'I think you should start dating.'

He lowered his glass to the table. 'Why's that?'

'Because you deserve someone to eat with besides me.'

'I happen to like you.'

'You could tell me your type. I could help you find someone.'

He cast a disapproving glance at her. 'Kind of you, but I'm quite capable of finding my own dates.' He picked up the wine bottle and refilled his glass. 'Speaking of which'— he set the bottle down—'Dax called me today.'

Ella's taco snapped at the curve and the entire thing fell onto her plate. She picked up her fork. 'What did he want?'

'He's looking for work, thought I might know of something.'

Her fork stilled mid-air. 'In Melbourne?'

'Yes.' He pushed his plate away and regarded her. 'You didn't tell me he was back.'

'I didn't know he was *moving* here. I thought he came for a visit.' She was annoyed at the small thrill that ran through her at hearing that piece of news.

'Seems he gave notice back in October. He had to work out his notice period, but he's back in Port Melbourne now.'

Ella pushed her own plate away, her appetite completely gone. 'Why doesn't he just return to his family's business?'

'He's been working as a marine engineer. He doesn't want to go back to construction.' Michael leaned his elbows on the table. 'He's changed, grown up a bit. I'm guessing you had something to do with that.'

She shook her head. 'Nope. I got the messy Dax, all destruction and no ambition. He grew up *after* he bailed.' She rose from her chair. 'Dessert?'

'You don't eat dessert.'

'I eat dessert when it's someone's birthday, and yours is coming up.'

His eyes shone with amusement. 'My birthday's next month.'

'At the beginning of the month.'

He watched her a moment. 'Are you running from the conversation?'

'No.' Busted, she sank back down into her chair.

'You're not fooling anyone with your indifferent face and smiles that never quite reach the eyes,' Michael said. 'I know you've missed him.'

She regarded him with suspicion. 'Where are you going with this? I thought you hated him. I'm actually surprised you didn't tell him to go back to Darwin.'

'Great opportunities to help others seldom come, but small ones surround us every day.'

'Sally Kock?'

Michael nodded. 'Dax did what he thought was best for you, at a great cost to himself. I know you don't want to hear this, but he did the right thing leaving you alone through that mess in January. You were starting a new business, and you had the police breathing down your neck. He protected you the only way he knew how.'

'Then he abandoned me after he was in the clear.'

'I never said he was perfect.'

'He didn't even say goodbye.'

Michael raised his hands. 'He definitely could've handled things better. I'm sure he'd do it differently now.'

She picked a piece of cheese off her plate, eating it

while she thought. 'I can't trust him. He loves, he lies, and he leaves. The three Ls.'

'You forgave me for the lies—eventually.'

'I didn't have a choice. You just kept showing up.' Her tone was teasing.

He laughed, then fell quiet. 'Dax was always going to tell you about your mother, you know. Right from the moment he found out, he wanted to tell you. He came to me and gave me the opportunity to do it. In hindsight, I saw glimpses of a good man, but I resented him for dragging up the past and forcing me to face it.' He paused. 'He came to me a few times. He said I had to tell you, that he wasn't going to keep a secret like that from you. Then you found out.' Another pause. 'I think if I'm honest, I couldn't stand the thought of you hating only me. It was easier to have you hate both of us.'

There was remorse in his voice.

'He could've put the whole thing on me,' Michael continued, putting his glass down. 'But he didn't.'

Ella sat there, head swimming. The last thing she'd expected was for her father to come in batting for Dax.

'Of course, if you do decide to give him another chance, I'll be keeping a close eye on him. One wrong move and I'll call the cops on him myself.'

Ella rose slowly. 'Would you mind if I left you with the dishes?'

He leaned back in his chair. 'Take the car.'

No one was home at Dax's house. She assumed it was still his house. Greta had never mentioned anyone moving.

It was dark as she crossed the road and wandered down to the beach. The tide was coming in, so she chose a spot back from the water and sat. She didn't really have a plan beyond that, hadn't thought to call ahead and make a time to talk. She didn't even know if he was in the water. It was an act now, think later moment.

The beach was abandoned. Ella glanced at her phone to check the time; it was a little before eight. She sat there for an hour, but no one emerged from the water. Disappointed, she rose and brushed sand off the back of her jeans, glancing a final time at the sea. She froze when she saw Dax standing fifteen feet away, knee deep in the water, watching her. Her stomach had that feeling like she was falling. She hadn't thought to prepare a speech.

He walked towards her, his movements slow as though approaching a nervous rabbit. He stopped a metre or so from her as the water rolled over his feet, not quite reaching her.

'Hey,' he said.

She studied his face in the weak light that reached him from the street. Water dripped from his fingers.

'Hey,' she replied.

'Were you looking for me?'

'No. Is Hurley about?'

Dax exhaled a laugh and looked down at the water.

'I heard you moved back,' she began. 'I heard it from Dad, which was slightly weird.'

He pushed wet hair back from his face. 'Hope you don't mind me calling him. I thought he might know of something. I'd rather not go back to construction if I can help it.'

She nodded. 'Congratulations on the new job, by the way. I don't think I said that last time you were here.'

'You mean the job I just left?'

'That's the one.'

His teeth flashed with a smile. 'Thanks.'

A long silence stretched out between them, Ella growing more nervous with each passing second.

'What are you doing here, Ella?'

She pulled her hands from her pockets. 'Why did you move back?'

He looked back at the glistening water. 'I was born here, raised here. My family and friends live here. Plus it's bloody hot up there in the wet season.'

'Of course.' She was thankful he couldn't see her turning red in the dark.

'And you're here,' he added. 'I know you don't want anything to do with me, but I'd like to be close by just in case.'

'In case of what?'

He shrugged. 'In case some piece-of-shit boyfriend breaks your heart and you want me to beat him to a pulp.'

Her first instinct was to laugh, but she hated him talking about her with someone else, as if it were inevitable. It sounded like he'd grown used to the idea. The thought of dating someone else was ridiculous. Who could possibly follow him? Sometimes she even forgot there was anyone before him.

'Actually.' Ella cleared her throat. 'I was wondering if you'd like to come to our end-of-year showcase.'

He watched her carefully. 'Is that like a concert?'

'Yeah.'

'When is it?'

She bit her lower lip, wondering why on earth she'd suggested a meet-up a month away. 'December.'

His eyebrows rose. 'Oh, okay. Sure. I mean, if you want me there.'

'I'm doing a dance.'

'The one with Peter?'

She nodded.

'It looked good at the rehearsal.'

'Thanks.'

'You two back together?' He shook his head and

336

pinched the bridge of his nose. 'Sorry. That's none of my business.'

'Peter volunteered to partner with me because he knows no one else will perform with toddlers.' She laughed, then fell quiet. 'He's been a good friend of late.'

'Great.' He crossed his arms over his chest. 'Good. Well, just text me the details, and I'll be there. How much are tickets?'

'Expensive. It's a very prestigious production, as you're probably aware.'

'What are we talking? Double digits?'

'High teens.'

He winced. 'Ouch.'

She scrunched up her nose. 'Since you're unemployed right now, I'm happy to let you work for it. We've hired the hall at the local primary school, and I have a few props I need painted.'

He watched her a moment. 'If it means I get to see you before December, then I'll do it.'

She nodded and glanced back at her father's car, not wanting to leave but having no reason to linger.

'It's pretty cold out,' Dax said. 'Did you want to come inside for a bit? I could make you some tea.' His eyes moved over her. 'You're freezing.'

'How can you tell?'

'By the way your shoulders are lifted slightly.'

The familiarity warmed her. 'I still love you, you know.' The words came out on a breath she could no longer hold in. She looked down at the sand. 'I never stopped, even when I hated you.'

The water rolled in again, almost touching her feet.

'I tried really hard to push everything down,' she continued, 'to bury it deep enough that I could pretend I was fine. But Dad just informed me my act wasn't very convincing.' She smiled when she looked up. 'And now I have this naive idea that we might be able to go back to the way things were before, before it grew into something ugly.'

She waited for him to say something, but he was silent for the longest time.

'I don't want to go back to how things were before,' he finally said.

Now she felt the cold. 'Oh.'

'I want it to be better. *I* want to be better.' He linked his hands atop his head. 'I didn't think I'd get another chance.'

She nodded, understanding. 'The thing is, there's ondine blood in these veins.' She held her wrists out to him, as though it were visible. 'And our kind take our mating *very* seriously.'

'We do.'

She lowered her hands again. 'A wise creature of the sea once told me that mates always find their way back to each other.'

'That sea creature does sound very wise.'

She drew a nervous breath and clapped her hands together. 'Would you like to go swimming?'

'What? Now?'

She walked into the sea, her sneakers filling with water. 'Yes, now.'

He caught her face as soon as she was within reach, bringing his warm lips to hers. She took what she needed from him in that kiss.

All the love and tenderness that poured from him.

All the heat his body offered.

All the air she needed—straight from his lungs.

And just like that, a tiny piece of her was restored.

Dax picked her up, and she gasped when her body pressed against his wet torso.

'You sure about this swimming idea of yours?' he asked, grinning mischievously.

She nodded.

He turned and carried her in. 'We'll make an ondine of you yet.'

Her breaths came faster as he lowered her into the water up to her waist. The weightlessness was bliss. She kissed him, soaking up his warmth, then pulled away to read his expression. It was pure mischief.

'Don't you dare—'

Down into the freezing water she went, cocooned in strong arms, her body screaming in protest and heart singing. It was a baptism of sorts, a washing away of past mistakes, of all the resentment she'd held onto.

Pushing off the bottom, Ella came up gasping, laughing and shivering. 'Oh my God! That's so much colder than I was expecting.'

He rubbed his beard on her neck, then pressed his lips to her goosebump-covered skin. 'I'll warm you.'

'And you'll stay?' The laughter was gone from her voice. 'You won't leave me behind again?'

'I'm not going anywhere, Miss Lewis of legal age.' He brought his lips to her neck again. 'I love you. So I'll stay, and I'll fix us.'

Her fingers went into his hair just as his knees bent, plunging them into the black water once more.

EPILOGUE

*D*ax leaned against the back wall of Ella's house, watching her move around the yard with a plate of mini quiches she had made during an anxiety-induced baking blitz. She had spent the week leading up to the barbecue cooking, cleaning, and gardening. It was like she was preparing for a royal visit instead of lunch with her grandparents. They were coming from Queensland for the reunion, now a part of the Coral Sea pod.

'There's a lot of food coming out of that kitchen,' Miller said beside him, a smile on his lips.

Dax took a sip of beer. 'Oh, she definitely over-catered. She also over-cleaned. Even caught her washing her make-up off this morning because she'd over-applied. I asked Lucy about it. Apparently it's a nervous thing, and I'm not allowed to mention it.'

Miller laughed and swigged his drink.

It was early March, the beginning of autumn, yet the summer heat lingered. Trestle tables covered the lawn, dressed in white linen and holding vases of native flowers. The casual barbecue Dax had suggested was now a rather fancy affair.

Michael stood talking to Irvin and June. Their encounters were becoming less and less awkward as the months ticked by. Lucy and Greta sat with flutes of bubbles, halfway to drunk at noon. Caleb and Ariel were dancing next to the speaker. Adrian and Hurley were chatting with Frankie and her "good friend", an ondine she'd brought with her from Sydney.

Dax wasn't going to touch that. She could call him whatever she wanted.

Somehow, it all worked. A mess of ondines, humans, and hybrids. They looked normal enough to an unsuspecting outsider.

'I'll go wait out front,' Miller said, emptying his beer and tossing it into the tub by the door. 'They'll be here in a minute.'

The noise made Ella look in their direction. A smile spread across her face when her eyes met Dax's. She looked stunning in a floral singlet and rolled-up jeans, her hair out and lightened from sea and sun. She couldn't have looked more beautiful as she made her way over to him.

'Hey, you,' she said, arms winding around his neck.

He gathered her close. 'Nervous?'

'I think the containers of food stacked on the kitchen bench and bursting from the fridge suggest I am.' She released a breath. 'It's possible I'm overcompensating for my lack of ondineness by trying to be extraordinarily human.'

He laughed quietly. 'They don't care what you are, because they're your family. They already love you. They only stayed away out of respect for your father.' He looked in Michael's direction. 'He's certainly changed his tune.'

'I nearly fell over when he suggested it.'

Dax kissed her face. 'You wouldn't have fallen. I would've caught you.'

She rubbed her nose on the soft part of his neck. 'Did

341

you ever think we would get to this point? Have all the people we love in the same space, not fighting?'

He looked around. 'I was quietly optimistic.'

She laughed. 'Oh, sure. So optimistic you ran away to the other side of the country.'

He traced his fingers along the bare skin between her singlet and jeans. 'And then came crawling back to you.' His mouth found hers, kissing her deeply. She tasted of blueberries.

The sound of the side gate opening made them break apart. Ella took a step back from Dax, her fingers entwining with his.

'They're going to love you,' he whispered, squeezing her hand.

She attempted a smile as she turned away, holding her breath. A moment later, Miller stepped into sight, eyes landing on Ella. He winked some encouragement at her before moving aside, revealing a couple in their late sixties, hand in hand. They stood like a mirrored image: familiar faces from Dax's youth, just older.

Diana Abbott let go of her husband's hand, covering her mouth. Then, opening her arms, she rushed forwards. Dax squeezed Ella's hand before letting go and stepping back. He heard the air leave her lungs as loving arms wrapped around her.

Tears ensued.

'Oh, darling girl,' her grandmother cooed. 'You look just like your mother.'

Dax brushed a finger down his nose and looked at the ground. If there was one wish he had for Ella, it was more love. More love, more family, more people seeing her as he did.

Caleb chose that moment to come running over. He tugged on Ella's singlet, forcing her to withdraw from her grandmother.

'What is it, sweetheart?' she asked.

He scratched his arm as he looked up at her. 'What's lightning crotch?'

Lucy was across the lawn in two strides, dragging him away by the arm. 'So sorry. We were talking about pregnancy.' She waved a hand. 'Such a lovely moment between you two. Please, carry on.' She gestured to Muirin Abbott, Ella's grandfather. 'Don't be shy.'

Ella glanced over her shoulder at Dax.

'Love you,' he mouthed.

A smile lit up her face, and her blue eyes shone.

Muirin had shuffled over to join them, wiping his face as he grinned down at his granddaughter. Feeling like he was intruding, Dax wandered over to where Michael now stood alone beneath a blue gum, glass of wine in hand, watching his daughter.

'You must feel pretty good being the brains behind this,' Dax said, standing shoulder to shoulder with him.

Michael kept his eyes forwards. 'Actually, I feel like an arsehole for keeping them apart as long as I did.'

Dax smiled into his beer as he drank. 'Don't worry, you won't get any lectures from me about past mistakes.'

'It's cute you think I would stick around and listen.'

Dax laughed quietly. 'If I'd raised that girl over there, I'd be feeling pretty smug right now.'

'She's something.' Michael glanced sideways at him. 'And she's head over heels for you. You better make sure you're worthy of that level of devotion, make her happy.'

'How am I doing so far?'

Michael took a drink. 'Her business is thriving. *She's* thriving. She's the healthiest and happiest I've ever seen her.' He cleared his throat. 'Can I ask you something?'

'Sure.'

'Do you think it's the water?' His throat bobbed. 'I know she swims with you. There's always a wetsuit drying out back when I visit. Maybe all those years she struggled to dance, all those times she was injured...' He was silent a moment. 'Maybe she just needed the sea like her mother.'

Dax never looked away from Ella. The thought had occurred to him long ago, but he'd never said anything. He didn't want Ella to look back with regret. It was clear she could survive without the sea—she just couldn't thrive without it. 'They told you she was human, so you raised her as one. Give yourself a break.'

Michael stared into his glass. 'Wouldn't be the first time I've been wrong about something.'

'Join the club.'

'I was wrong about you.' Michael took a drink. 'I couldn't ask for a better mate for her.'

Dax stared ahead, throat tightening. 'I think the soppy scene playing out in front of us is making you soft. Or should I blame old age?'

'Watch it, kid.'

Ella looked in their direction and waved them over.

Michael emptied his glass. 'Time to catch up with the in-laws.'

ELLA STOOD inside the back door, a salad bowl in one hand and the other resting on the flyscreen. She wanted to mentally capture the scene outside. Everyone she and Dax loved most in the world, with the exception of Lucy's parents, were all seated together, eating, talking, and laughing.

Her entire life, Ella had strived for more. She was always working towards bigger and better things. She didn't know if that came from being a dancer, her own high expectations, or if it was just human nature. Probably a toxic mix of all three. It was an unsettling moment to look out across her backyard, with its patchy lawn, thirsty trees, and odd assortments of friends and family, and realise it was enough.

What she had was more than enough.

That was her lawn to feed, her trees to water, her friends and family to treasure.

The glass bowl grew heavy in her hand, so she brought her other one up to take the weight. Dax's gaze drifted in her direction at that moment.

He was so much more than enough.

Breaking off his conversation with Hurley, he rose from his seat and headed over. She watched him approach, absolute perfection in his faded cut-off jeans, black T-shirt, and bare feet. His hair hung in a mess to one side, those silver eyes never leaving her.

She stepped back from the door as he tugged it open, making room for him.

'You okay?' he asked, tucking her hair behind her ear and taking the bowl.

He read her with astonishing ease. An inkling that she needed something, and he was at her side a moment later trying to fill the void.

It was love in its purest form.

It was mateship.

'Everything's perfect,' she said, finding a smile for him.

He searched her eyes for a moment, then relaxed when he saw she was telling the truth. 'Okay. Good.' He kissed her forehead, then stepped back to hold the door open for her.

She stepped past him out into the warm sun and felt him behind her as she raised her face to the sky.

After everyone had finished eating, they headed to the beach for a swim. Her father said he would build sandcastles with the kids and watch their belongings. Ella didn't push him to go in the water; it was enough that he had joined them instead of going home.

Everything was enough that day.

The ondines headed out into the deep, diving below the surface. Ella insisted Dax go with them while she and Lucy waded in the shallows and exchanged their thoughts on the day.

'I don't think I've ever seen old people in such good shape,' Lucy said as she watched Ella's grandparents swim in the distance.

'I think they like me.'

Lucy splashed her. 'Of course they like you, you weirdo. They're your grandparents, and you're bloody adorable.'

Ella wiped water off her face. 'I tried to call you last night.'

'Why? Did you have a polenta crisis?'

'No, it was a meatball thing. Where were you?'

Lucy looked out to sea. 'I just had a friend over. We grabbed Indian takeaway.'

Ella was immediately suspicious. 'Which friend?'

'You don't know him.'

Scooping up some water, Ella threw it at her. '*Him?* Why are you being cagey? Who's him? Was it a date?'

'No, it was a casual… hang.'

Ella suppressed a smile. 'Well, well, well. Look who had a curry date.'

'His kid was in the next room with Caleb. It was all very PG.'

'But you like him. You *like* him, like him. That's why your face is going red.'

Lucy splashed her twice. 'Stop it.'

'Where did you meet him?'

'Around.'

'Around *where*?'

Lucy covered her face with her hands. 'This is why I didn't want to tell you. You're going to be all judgey.'

Ella laughed. 'I'm not going to be judgey. Tell me.'

Lucy drew a breath. 'You know Max from my junior hip-hop class?'

Ella's eyes widened as she realised where the story was going. 'Oh. My. God. You're sleeping with that hot single dad from your class? The one who all the mums watch instead of their own kids?'

Lucy smoothed back her hair. 'Not yet, but I'm one curry and a babysitter away from it.'

Ella covered her mouth with both hands.

'I'm not going to be in some sort of legal trouble if it happens, am I?'

Ella burst out laughing. 'Of course not. He's not a student. It's perfect.' She reached for Lucy's hands. 'Friday. I'll babysit for you on Friday. Caleb can stay the night.'

Lucy pulled her hands free. 'Stop.'

'Does he call you Miss Lucy?'

The splashing resumed. '*Stop*. This is why I didn't want to tell you.'

'Oh, Miss Lucy, can I have a word about Max's progress?' Ella said in a deep voice, splashing her back.

'Stop!'

Ella squealed as water pounded her. 'Oh, Miss Lucy, can we discuss it over a korma?'

Lucy burst out laughing, then cupped her hands together, scooped up as much water as she could hold, and hurled it at Ella.

Ella turned her face away and closed her eyes, waiting for the water to hit—but it never came.

'Well, that's hardly fair,' Lucy said, crossing her arms.

When Ella opened her eyes and looked, she saw the water remained in the air like a clear wall between them— a vertical splash. Dax shot up behind Ella, causing both girls to jump and squeal. The water between them fell to the sea as Ella turned to face a smirking Dax.

'You think you're so clever with your tricks,' she said, head shaking.

He pulled her to him, and she sucked in a breath as her sun-soaked skin pressed against his cold body.

'Muuuuuuuuuum!' Caleb called from the edge of the water. 'I peed on the sand!'

Lucy winced. 'Well, that's one way to clear a beach. I better go help. Your dad's working with a very small spade right now.' She waded towards the shore.

Ella gave her a sympathetic look before turning back to Dax, wrapping her arms around his neck. 'Did you swim all the way in to protect me from Lucy's vicious splashing?'

'Actually, I heard you talking about some hot single dad and thought I better intervene.' He was grinning when he said it.

'You hear far too well underwater.'

'I'm always listening out for you, Miss Lewis. You should know that by now.'

And she couldn't have been more thrilled about the fact.

'Come out deep with me,' he said.

'You're forgetting I can't breathe underwater.'

Warm lips brushed her ear.

'And you're forgetting my promise to breathe for you.'

'On land, in the water,' she said, quoting him. She stepped back, hands sliding from his body. 'I forget nothing, Mr Coburn.'

Drawing a large breath, Ella dove into the sea.

ACKNOWLEDGMENTS

I would like to express my gratitude to the many people who contributed to this book. My biggest thanks goes to my readers. Without you guys, I wouldn't get to do what I love. Next, a huge thank you to my rock star husband who supports and encourages me even though my writing takes time away from him. I love you to bits. A big thank you to Joanna Walsh for your ongoing support and to David Kelly for answering all my questions about oil rig leaks and emergency procedures. Thanks to Rachel Brookes for teaching me to dance and letting me be the oldest person in the room each week ;) A big shout-out to my beta readers, who each brought a unique perspective. Thank you to Kristin and the team at Hot Tree Editing for polishing the manuscript into something beautiful, and to my proofreader, Rebecca Fletcher, for catching everything I missed. A round of applause for my cover designer, Domi, from Inspired Cover Designs, for another gorgeous cover. And finally, a huge thank you to my Launch Team for your encouragement, honest reviews, and being the final set of eyes on my work. You guys are amazing.

ALSO BY TANYA BIRD

The Companion series

Roman Hearts series

Standalones

Printed in Great Britain
by Amazon

49126347R00213